"Do you think," she said harshly, "that I can't grieve as you do? Do you think you're the only one in the universe who knows what it's like to be alone?" She battled the urge to release the tumult of her emotions, clenching her fists and welcoming the pain as her nails bit into her palms. "I do understand. I understand better than you'll ever know."

Rook stood with his body half turned away from her, his profile stark in the common room's dim light. "I almost believe you do," he said softly.

Aching grief filled Ariane then—a thousand sorrows layered one upon another. Two small steps would carry her to Rook—two endless, impossible steps to touch his rigid back and stroke the broad sweep of his shoulders, feel the warmth of his body against hers.

He saved her from her own folly. Abruptly he pivoted to face her again. "I almost forgot to thank you, Lady Ariane. You handled the ship very well. My compliments." His eyes swept from her halfboots to the crown of her head. "Without you, I couldn't have made it."

His expression turned praise into a taunt. The familiar shield of Ariane's anger snapped into place. "Don't read too much into it," she snapped. "I won't be making a habit of accommodating you."

A dangerous light flared in Rook's copper eyes. He reached out to touch a strand of her hair, and her heart nearly stopped. "A pity. You could accommodate me so well. . . ."

BANTAM BOOKS BY SUSAN KRINARD

PRINCE OF WOLVES
PRINCE OF DREAMS
STAR-CROSSED

STAR CROSSED

Susan Krinard

Bantam Books
New York   Toronto   London
Sydney   Auckland

STAR-CROSSED

A Bantam Book / August 1995

ISBN 0-553-56917-1

Published simultaneously in the United States and Canada

Bantam Books are published by Bantam Books, a division of Bantam Doubleday
Dell Publishing Group, Inc. Its trademark, consisting of the words "Bantam
Books" and the portrayal of a rooster, is Registered in U.S. Patent and Trademark
Office and in other countries. Marca Registrada. Bantam Books, 1540 Broadway,
New York, New York 10036.

PRINTED IN THE UNITED STATES OF AMERICA

RAD   0 9 8 7 6 5 4 3 2 1

This book is dedicated to Marilyn Prather and Ruth West-man, who always believed in me—
and to all those marvelous writers of Science Fiction, Fantasy and Romance who keep my sense of wonder alive.

Thank you.

✳

PROLOGUE

*R*ook Galloway watched in mute horror as his world crashed down around his ears.

For all but the past six years it had been his only world—the Warren in the Low Town of Lumière on the planet Espérance, where the Kalian refugees lived and died and waited for a future beyond grim survival. And after six years on the university world of Tolstoy, earning his degrees, Rook had almost forgotten.

But he was still Kalian. And the miasma of violence and hatred and fear he had sensed in the night, drawing him from his dormitory at the Marchand mansion, pulled him inevitably back to the place of his birth.

The Warren was filled with smoke—somewhere a gas main had blown, or an arsonist had set fire to the contents of a warehouse on the edge of the slum. The prefab shacks and market stands wouldn't burn, but there was plenty here that would.

Kalians wouldn't burn their own scanty possessions. It made no sense, no sense at all. A shriek rent the thick air, and Rook pressed back into the wall of a crumbling building as three Lumière gendarmes ran past, disruptors in hand.

Why? Rook asked. *By the Shapers, why?*

Gendarmes attacking Kalians, Kalians fighting back—a nightmare.

Another shriek, this time of anger, and a Kalian plunged out of the smoke. He skidded to a halt before Rook, his eyes wild, all pupil. The disruptor clenched in his hand swung to aim at Rook's head.

Rook went still, searching the man's face. Heron Matthews, who didn't know what violence was. Even as a boy Heron had avoided the roughest play of the other children in the Warren.

But now Heron threatened Rook and bared his teeth in a snarl of mindless hatred.

"Heron," Rook said urgently. "It's me, Rook. I'm back."

A flicker of confusion came and went in Heron's eyes, a touch of sanity. He began to tremble, long legs bent under him like a bird about to take flight.

"Heron—" Rook murmured, extending his hand. The 'ruptor quivered, and Heron lifted it sharply to aim at the invisible sky.

"Rook. Rook?"

His voice was almost a whimper, the cry of a cornered animal. Sweat-drenched black hair clung to his temples. But Heron's eyes came into focus again, fixing on Rook's face.

Rook took a single step forward, and Heron's gangly arms lifted like wings. "Heron, what's happening? By the Shapers, what's happened to you?"

Heron pressed the back of his hand across his mouth. "Too late," he whispered. "It's all over. Nothing to lose . . ."

"What's too late? Heron—" Rook slid forward in one swift motion, grasped Heron's arm, and felt the muscles bunch under his fingers. There was no Sharing in this contact, but Rook sensed what lay under the surface. Fear. Desperation. Madness.

"They came," Heron said slowly. "In the night. Took them. Too late. We fought." His wide mouth grew tight with emotion. "The Marchand."

There was loathing in the word. The Marchand—one of the most powerful families on Espérance—had sponsored the Kalians for two generations. They had sent Rook to Tolstoy. . . .

Rook caught Heron's other shoulder in his hand. "What about the Marchand?"

"Betrayed," Heron said hoarsely. "They came—"

The flash of a disruptor beam burned a path through the smoke and darkness. Heron howled in pain, his own 'ruptor tracing a flashing arc as his hand shattered. Rook felt the splatter of blood on his face.

There was no time for shock. Rook grabbed Heron and dived for the shadows, but he might have been holding a Kalian treedevil. Heron wrenched free and stumbled back into the open street. With his one good hand he found his 'ruptor where it lay on the broken pavement and fired into the night.

Somewhere a harsh voice shouted in Franglais; the drum of boot heels echoed from the alley walls. Rook watched it happen, frozen in place: Heron crouched with the 'ruptor in one hand and blood dripping slowly from what remained of the other; the gendarmes suddenly there, shouting, aiming, firing. Heron fell with a strange grace, long arms and legs folding as he crumpled.

Rook felt a hoarse protest lock in his throat. The gendarmes were slow, slow and clumsy when they turned; he was beside Heron before they realized he was there. Rook set his hand on Heron's forehead and chanted the death chant silently, the words strangled by grief and horror.

"Halt! Stay where you are!"

He almost obeyed then, schooled to peace and shocked by what seemed beyond understanding. But he said a silent farewell to Heron and sprang out and away, a low-level 'ruptor beam singeing the close-shorn hair at his temple.

"Stop him! There he goes—don't let him get over that wall!" The guttural Franglais of the gendarmes was unreal, words melting into meaningless sound, like the baying of hellhounds. Rook let his instincts carry him to freedom, ignoring a rational mind that demanded he stop, go back, talk to the gendarmes like a reasonable, civilized Espérancian. . . .

He ran. He leaped the high wall as if it were nothing. Debris crunched under his feet as he found another alley, deserted and silent. The harsh chemical smell of something on fire scoured his lungs. For a brief moment Rook opened his senses fully and reeled under the assault of so much insanity.

Heron was dead. A man who had never lifted a hand in violence was dead, victim of Espérancian gendarmes and his own madness.

There had to be some explanation, something that would make sense. The sun was rising; through the haze of smoke Rook could feel the touch of light.

He started out into the street, running hard for the center of the Warren. The Elders—the Elders would know, voices of calm wisdom that even chaos could not silence. Disembodied cries and struggling figures emerged from smoke and mist only to vanish again. Flames arced up from a makeshift wooden shack as Rook passed, and the Kalian woman who had set the fire laughed and danced in a parody of the hunting rituals.

Rook stopped, his heart in his throat. He knew her—Willow MacNeal, a woman whose husband had disappeared from the Warren seven years ago, just before Rook had left for Tolstoy. There was no recognition in her face as she brandished her makeshift torch and saluted Rook with a shriek of triumph.

Like Heron. Like Heron, she had gone mad.

Rook hesitated only an instant before he moved in her direction. She was oblivious, standing in full view of any gendarme that might pass. Rook shuddered with the realization that they might hurt her.

As they had hurt and killed Heron.

A hand fell on his shoulder, and with the swiftness of instinct he whirled to face the one who held him.

"Leave her alone," the woman said, her voice harsh. "She has a right to her revenge."

Rook stared into her eyes, copper-colored like his, her hair a deeper darkness in the dim light. She recognized him, unlike the others; her mouth twisted into a bitter smile.

"Sable," Rook grated. He caught at her wrist but made no move to dislodge it. The same hatred was there behind Sable's eyes; the same wildness, but not quite lost to reason.

As if she read his thoughts, Sable Reece laughed.

"So you do remember me. I would have thought mere Kalians would be beneath your notice now."

Her words might have been spoken in some alien tongue. Rook lowered his heartbeat with deliberation and willed his muscles to loosen. "Sable," he said, staring into her eyes, "What has happened here?"

Sable's smile faded. "You wouldn't know, would you—living the soft life on some alien world, learning to be a Marchand slave."

His fingers tightened on her wrist, and she wrenched her hand away. "You should know, Rook Galloway—you should know what your precious Elite friends have done to our people."

The Marchand. Rook remembered the loathing in Heron's voice. "What the hell are you talking about?" he breathed. "Sable—"

She tossed back her hair, and for the first time Rook saw the distinct mark of the Hawk insurgents smeared across her forehead like blood. "You could have helped us, Galloway. You could have helped your people, if you'd listened to Tiercel when he came to you. But you had already given your loyalty—to Espérancians who think we're no better than dirt." She turned her head and spat; a siren wailed overhead.

Rook's denial locked in his throat. Several weeks ago Tiercel, one of the Hawks, had accosted him just beyond the gates of the Marchand mansion; a dangerous thing, for a Kalian to be outside the Warren after curfew. But Tiercel had come, defiant and unafraid. *"An educated Kalian"*—Tiercel had made the words almost a mockery—*"one with connections to the Marchand, could help us."* When Tiercel had made his intentions clear, Rook had understood what the Kalian underground wanted of him.

And he'd refused.

The Marchand Family had brought his people here, kept them alive after the destruction of their homeworld, the planet Kali. And they had educated the brightest among the Kalian children, had given them a chance at a better life. A life outside the slums and the prejudice and hopelessness of the Warren.

Rook had been one of those children. And from the day he'd been sent to Tolstoy at the age of seventeen, Rook had known he'd find a way to help his people. If it meant serving the Marchand, so be it.

He would never betray his people's benefactors. . . .

"They came in the night," Sable whispered, as if they were alone in the world and in a place of peace. "No uniforms, all in assassin's black. Breaking into our homes, taking people without cause. They said nothing, except that we were conspirators who threatened the peace of Espérance. And they took our people, even children."

Rook wanted to deny her words, but he knew she spoke the truth. Sable had always been hard, almost un-Kalian in her devotion to equality by any means. And when the Hawk movement had been driven underground, she had never lost her hatred of the Marchand Elite.

But he had never known her to lie.

"Children, Rook," she continued hoarsely. "Do you understand? We fought back. And they killed several of our people. We had no choice but to defend ourselves. Do you know what we found when we searched one of the bodies?"

The brilliant headlights of a gendarme transport caught them in its beam. Sable moved with the flow of shadows that fled before the light, and Rook followed her into the scanty cover of a pile of discarded crates. The beam swept over the place they had been and passed on.

Sable looked after the transport, her voice muffled. "We found a small knife hidden under the Espérancian's clothes. A Marchand stiletto, the kind only the Marchand Guard carry."

Rook stilled in the act of touching her shoulder. "Impossible. The Marchand wouldn't—"

"No?" She whirled on him with bared teeth. "How long have we been a burden to them? They bought themselves an expense they hadn't bargained for when they brought us from Kali—"

"Kali was a dead world! Without them—"

"We would have died. And saved the Marchand the trouble of getting rid of us now that we've become—inconvenient."

He caught both her shoulders in his hands. "No, Sable. Not the Marchand. Those men who came in the night—"

"Are you so blind?" With a sharp motion she threw his hands off. "But how can I forget you haven't been here to see it all—the harassment, the attacks, the disappearances over the past years? Worse and worse. No recourse for the barbarians, Galloway. Not for the unprivileged. Not for us."

She looked him up and down, scorn in her eyes. They caught the rising light of dawn, dancing like flames. "No justice for those of us not chosen. Who would listen to us? The Elite *magistrats*? They couldn't concern themselves with casteless savages."

Staring at her contorted face, Rook shook his head. His chest felt tight, as if he'd been trying to breathe vacuum. "But this—" Several sharp reports shattered the air, and he licked his lips. "Violence. It isn't our way."

"Would you let them kill us, Galloway? Have you become so much a Marchand possession? They drove us too far with this. Too far. Too late."

Heron's words echoed in his head. *Too late.* "There must be some terrible mistake. If we find the Elders—if I go back and talk to the Marchand, to the Patriarch—"

Sable's laugh was savage. "No more talk. I've always known there would be no other way in the end. If we die now, we'll die free."

A wave of black pain swept out from her, a Sharing he didn't want. It beat him back. It denied his pleas for peace and silenced all his arguments for sanity.

This could not be happening. Not now. Not when there had been so much hope.

He gathered that hope and everything he had learned on Tolstoy, his deep belief in rationality and the brotherhood of all people who had once, long ago, come from a place called Earth.

"You can't win, Sable," he said softly. "If you fight them, if you kill, there'll be nothing left. All of Lumière—all of Espérance will turn on our people. They've always feared us, and now—you have to stop this, Sable. I know you have the influence. Talk to the people." He reached for her arm again. "I'll go with you. I'll talk to the Marchand. This is all some tragic misunderstanding—"

"Coward." The word was low-voiced and deadly. "Marchand slave. Go back to them with your tail between your legs, and maybe they'll let you live. We haven't forgotten what we are." She smiled again, slowly. "And perhaps the Marchand will remember as well, before they see one of their own suffer as our people have suffered."

Something in the way she spoke, the harsh satisfaction that twisted her smile, betrayed her meaning. Before Sable could prevent it, Rook took her by the collar of her ragged shirt. "Sable," he hissed, "what have you done?"

But her eyes flickered beyond his, widened and narrowed again. He pulled her into a crouch beside him and followed her gaze.

There was just enough light to see her by, the girl hunkered down in the rapidly diminishing shadow of a prefab wall. The expensive tailored suit she wore was torn and dirty, but it was unmistakably the clothing of an aristocrat. Her skin was pale and smooth; her hands, clenched on a broken piece of molding, were beautifully manicured. Soft brown hair fell over her face, as if she could find shelter behind it. And she was watching them like a trapped animal.

Rook swallowed as he recognized her. *By the Shapers,* he swore silently. Sable gave a low growl of triumph.

"The other one," she breathed. "When we have both of them, the Patriarch won't dare lift a hand against us." She leaped up, and Rook caught her and held her while she fought him like the sleek Earth beast after which she was named.

The girl in the shadows made no attempt to run. Rook silently begged her to stay quiet as he trapped Sable's hands. "You have Jacques Marchand," he said.

"We have him. The Marchand heir." She laughed. "He was stupid enough to think he could help us, but he should have stayed away."

Panic turned Rook's knees to water, and he altered the flow of blood and adrenaline until he could stand solidly again. If any harm came to the Patriarch's great-grandson and heir . . .

"And now the other one," Sable repeated. She broke free, and Rook used the inhuman speed he had so seldom needed on Tolstoy to overtake her, setting himself between Sable and the girl like a living wall.

"Stop this, Sable. Stop now. If she gets back safely, if you let the Marchand heir go, there may still be a chance of ending this. You're committing suicide, condemning all of us—"

She surged forward, and he blocked her again. Suddenly a disruptor was in her hand.

"Get out of the way," she said harshly.

"No. I can't let you have her. Listen to me, Sable—"

The beam passed only a centimeter above his shoulder. "I'll kill you if I must, Galloway," she rasped. Her hand trembled on the gun.

"Will you, Sable? Will you become like the people you hate?"

Sable's cry of rage mingled with the pulse of sirens, and she fired again, into the lightening sky. "Damn you to hell, Galloway," she snarled. And then he was alone.

Rook turned slowly to face the girl frozen against the wall and looked into her terrified brown eyes.

"Lady Ariane," he said.

•   •   •

As the Kalian woman turned to her, Ariane Burke-Marchand knew that her uncertain luck had run its course.

Finch had warned her not to venture out that night. She'd seen the veiled emotion in her old Kalian nanny's eyes—a reflection of the strange unease that had troubled Ariane for the past year. Something having to do with the Kalians. Something that Jacques felt, too, that drove him again and again to the Warren in defiance of their great-grandfather's orders.

A few hours—a lifetime—ago, Ariane had seen Jacques leave the mansion in the night, when her own restless dreams of chaos had kept her roaming the wide halls like a phantom. And she had followed him. Slipping by the guards, she had passed the Kalian dormitories outside the mansion's gates just in time to see Rook Galloway melt into the shadows behind her brother.

The temptation had been too great. She had always wanted to know what Jacques did down in that forbidden part of the city, among the savages.

And there had been another reason, enough to overcome the last vestiges of common sense. She would see *him,* possibly meet him at last—the handsome Kalian just returned from Tolstoy, a man separated from her by birth and caste and mansion walls. A man she had seen only from a distance, and loved with an unrequited and impossible passion.

Until now. Now he stood there and looked at her, alien and terrifying.

Grand-père will be furious, she told herself absurdly, as if a dressing-down from the Patriarch would outweigh the disaster she faced now. *And Wynn will call me a foolish child.* Alone in the Warren, in the middle of a riot. And discovered.

This close the Kalian was almost frighteningly tall, imposing in the lithe, clean body that seemed so natural to his kind. He had moved like something not quite human.

Not human, Ariane thought, staring up at him. His copper eyes were alien, his dark hair cropped short from his years at the university on the world of Tolstoy. And he was beautiful and strange and drew her in ways past all reason.

"Lady Ariane," he said again. He took a step forward—flowed forward, she thought—and put out his hand. "Come with me."

He knew her, though he'd never been privileged to meet her. The Patriarch's great-granddaughter moved in a sphere to which no casteless Kalian could ever aspire. But he knew her.

He didn't ask her why she was there, where she had no business being, in the middle of a riot. His steady gaze was not in the least bit humble. He was like the calm eye of a storm. She shifted indecisively, her knees almost giving way under the strain of movement after so long in hiding.

He had driven the Kalian woman away. Ariane had seen the mark on the woman's forehead and knew it for what it was. Jacques had told her of the Hawks. They were the only Kalians, he said, who were truly dangerous.

And the Hawk woman had been coming for her. Rook Galloway had stood between. But he had known the woman well—that much was clear. And all around them in the smoky light of dawn, the Kalians were rioting. Stronger and faster than normal humans. Alien.

Rook Galloway was Kalian.

Ariane was very much afraid.

He moved forward another gliding step, and she found herself retreating. His eyes were expressionless. "I will protect you, Lady Ariane," he said softly. "Come with me."

She might have trusted him. He was an educated Kalian, sworn to repay his debts in service to his Marchand benefactors. He was to be among the first Kalians to crew a Marchand starship.

But Ariane, who had always prided herself on her courage, fled.

Perhaps she surprised him; it took him several seconds to catch up with her. When his strong fingers closed on her wrist, she felt a shock that coursed through her body with such force that she staggered. Anger, despair, fear—emotion that threatened to blind her with searing, unendurable brilliance.

And then the unnatural sensation ended, like the sudden death of a star. Rook Galloway swung her around to face him almost violently, his face taut with strain. "Do you know what's happening here, Lady Ariane?" he demanded, his fingers digging into her arms to the point of pain.

She shook her head before she found the words. Her mind spun and her entire body quivered. He, Kalian that he was, could ask her such a question with his own people running mad on every side? He stared at her, searching her eyes for answers she couldn't give, and closed his own. "I can't take you back," he whispered. "No time."

Muscles worked in his strong jaw, betraying an inner struggle that held Ariane unwillingly fascinated. When he opened his eyes, they fixed on hers again, grim and desperate and red as an animal's. "You'll come with me, Lady Ariane. You'll stay close to me at all times. Do you understand?"

She wanted to demand explanations, call up some outrage at his handling of her, at his ordering her about as if she were a common laborer. She wanted frantically to run. But she remembered Jacques, and the way Rook Galloway had followed him from the mansion.

Jacques had disappeared.

"Where is Jacques?" she demanded at last, chagrined at the high, childish pitch of her voice.

He flinched, and she could almost read the succession of emotions that passed over the handsome lines of his face. He looked away. "I don't know, Lady Ariane."

Dueling techniques she had honed to perfection since childhood allowed her to take advantage of his momentary inattention. She wrenched herself free of him again. "I saw you follow him," she hissed. "From the mansion, when he passed the dormitories. I saw *you.*"

A thrum of engines overhead nearly drowned her accusation. An armored police floater passed above them, and Rook pulled her into the scant shelter of abandoned crates scattered along the alley wall.

Ariane watched the floater pass and disappear. She could have tried to hail it, get it to take her back home. But there was still Jacques.

Rook's hand touched her face and turned it. "I didn't follow Jacques," he said softly.

She almost berated him for his insolence in using her brother's name as if he were an equal, until she recognized her own absurdity. Pride was a luxury she could ill afford. Shoving her tangled hair back from her face, she set her jaw and stared him down.

"Then let me go. I have to find him." She tensed to break away, but he held her still as easily as if she'd been a kitten. He was so close—exotic, frightening, a beautiful creature made of hard muscle, leashed power, and masculine mystery.

With all the strange and terrible yearning of her sixteen years, she had longed to be touched by him. But not like this. Not here, not now when his nearness shamed her into fear.

He hardly seemed to notice her. "No time," he muttered. He lifted his head as if to scent the wind. It was said that Kalians had the senses of beasts. Or savages. Ariane shivered, and Rook's attention snapped back to her. "If the Maker is with us, we'll find Sieur Jacques before it's too late." Without another word he hauled her to her feet. And he ran.

She had no choice but to stumble after him, out of the alley and into the smoke, away from the Haute-Ville and home. Ariane concentrated on keeping up, knowing instinctively that he held back for her sake, feeling the restrained energy that seemed to beat from his body in waves.

He'd said they might find Jacques. For now that was all that mattered, even if it got her deeper into trouble. Her brother was an idealist, a gentle soul who believed that all rational beings were equals. If he was caught in the middle of this . . .

A mob of Kalians, wielding broken pieces of wood and prefab, clashed furiously with gendarmes in the early-morning shadows. Rook dragged Ariane down, blocking her view; she heard screams and bit her lip savagely. She had never seen this kind of violence; pain and fear had never been allowed to touch her life among the Elite of Lumière. Grand-père had seen to that. In the old days there had been bloody feuds among the Patriarchs, before the coming of the League and the new ways. But even then there had been rules that no Espérancian would break. Rules and honor.

Here there was only mindless frenzy.

Grand-père had always told her that the Kalians were barbarians. "Marchand honor requires us to pay our debts," he'd said. "But the Kalians must always be controlled. Perhaps, if they are educated, they may serve Espérance one day. . . ."

Rook pulled her up again, ignoring the shouts of the gendarmes. Ariane looked back and recognized the livery of her great-grandfather's Guard. Marchand people—men she knew, safe and loyal. "Where are you taking me?" she gasped, setting her slight weight against Rook's momentum. He hardly glanced at her as he swept her up in his arms.

Panic erased the last of her resolve. She beat at him with her fists, designing each blow to hurt. "Let me go, you—*sauvage! Canaille,* dog—"

The flash of a disruptor beam narrowly missed her head. Rook flung her down and covered her with his body. She could feel his heat, his weight, a strange flare of excitement that eclipsed even the fear.

But he was Kalian. She lunged upward, thrusting her knee into the soft flesh of his groin. He stiffened and lifted off her, only an instant's surprise revealed in his expression. With grim deliberation he pinned her arms to her sides with his hands.

"Listen to me," he hissed. "You were foolish enough to come here to the Warren, to a place you don't belong. I don't know why, and I don't care. But if anything happens to you, Lady Ariane, it will be my people who suffer."

"Your people have gone mad," she gasped, unable to do more than twist futilely under him. "After all my family has done for you—fed you, educated you—"

Confusion passed over his face, so close to hers, and suddenly he seemed young and very human. He wet his lips.

"All I know is that I have to keep you safe, Lady Ariane. You and your brother. Your lives are worth more to the Patriarch than all of my people combined." He hauled her up, and they were running again, until the old buildings pressed inward and the smoke grew thicker, the weak sunlight veiled like a Nirvanan temple dancer. This was the center of the Warren, the Vieux-Quartier of Lumière, long since abandoned to the Kalians by the poorest of the Laborer caste.

It seemed almost deserted. Rook made for an ancient building of cerulean brick, half crumbled, and stopped at what looked like a blank wall.

"Here," he murmured. "Let them be here—" He ran his hand along a row of bricks and pressed. The hidden door swung open a mere centimeter, and he forced the crack wider with the weight of his body.

Ariane tried resistance one last time, as pride demanded, but he pulled her through the gap easily and shut it behind them. She found herself up against the cold brick, his body along the length of hers, his heart beating with steady regularity against the rapid flutter of her own. She thought she heard distant voices; Rook stiffened and cocked his head. The warmth of his breath bathed her face.

"Listen to me, Lady Ariane. Stay with me. No matter what happens, stay with me."

"What are you—"

"Do you want to see your brother again, Lady?" he snapped.

Ariane pressed her lips together and met his stare. The voices grew louder as he led her deeper into the building, along debris-cluttered corridors and past doorless, empty rooms. They came at last to a barricaded entrance, and Rook, shoving her behind him, gave a sharp, eerie cry that echoed in the sudden silence.

A scrape of movement sounded from behind the barricade, and an invisible panel in a plasteel sheet just above Ariane's head slid aside. Copper eyes appeared in the gap, looked from Rook to Ariane; abruptly another opening appeared at the side of the barricade, and Rook pulled Ariane through and into a dimly lit room.

"So you came to your senses."

Ariane recognized the Kalian woman who confronted them and, for a shameful instant, almost cringed behind the shield of Rook's body.

The woman smiled coldly. Her eyes raked Ariane, spitting hatred. "With both of them, they won't dare touch us."

Pride made Ariane meet the contemptuous stare of the Kalian, but she had no time to make sense of the woman's words. She heard the sound of her name, looked beyond Rook and the woman to the pack of Kalians who stood at the far end of the room.

"Jacques!" As she moved, Rook caught her and held her back. He hissed something in her ear, but she was aware only of her brother, slumped between his captors, dirty and bruised. Jacques smiled at her a little crookedly.

"I should have known you'd show up sooner or later, *petite soeur*," he said. One of the clustered Kalians moved threateningly to silence him; Ariane counted them quickly. Every one of them bore the mark of the Hawk rebels.

"Don't move," Rook's voice said behind her, harsh with strain. "Be silent."

Resistance was futile. Jacques was bound, and the Kalians were clearly desperate. Ariane met Jacques's eyes and returned his smile, her heart in her throat.

"Your lives are worth more than all my people combined," Rook had said. And now she understood. Grand-père would do anything to keep his heir and his great-granddaughter safe. Ariane closed her eyes. The dishonor was unbearable, to be held hostage at the whim of Kalian traitors. . . .

Rook was speaking again, in Kalian patois so rapid that Ariane had no hope of following it. The woman who led the Hawks grew grim, slashed at Rook with words as sharp as a duelist's blade. She reached for Ariane, and Rook knocked her hand away; the two bristled like Kalian hellhounds in a battle for dominance.

Ariane felt the vivid fear of her helplessness. These were not Espérancians, accustomed to behaving with honor. They were little better than animals. The lure of that wildness had drawn her to Rook Galloway, but now it repelled her. She *felt* what they were, as she had sensed the impending chaos in the Warren the night before. The taint of that unwanted sense made her shudder.

If I had my disruptor, she swore silently, *or even my saber, they would understand Marchand honor.* As it was, she could only stand there, utterly helpless, while two Kalians debated her fate, and Jacques's, as if they were no better than outcastes. . . .

The barricaded doorway exploded behind them. Rook whirled, holding Ariane against him; two city gendarmes in heavy armor burst into the room, others crowding behind.

The Kalian woman's voice rose in a harsh command. Rook tensed, releasing Ariane, and in the same instant blinding smoke burst upward from the place where the woman had been.

And then Rook was gone. The gendarmes swarmed around Ariane, past her, to the place where Jacques had stood. Disruptor beams sliced through the smoke. Hands grabbed her, held her when she would have run to the rear of the room; the face looking down at her was blessedly familiar.

"Wynn," she gasped, clutching at his sleeve. He gathered her close, barking orders to the gendarmes over her head.

"You're safe now, Ariane," he murmured into her hair, rocking her like a child. "They can't hurt you now. You're—"

She broke free. "Jacques! They had him—"

Wynn looked up and snapped a sharp command. The city gendarmes and Marchand Guard, along with other guardsmen in Slayton colors, scattered to the walls of the room as one of the trapped Kalians returned fire. The smoke cleared like a veil drawn away, revealing Rook Galloway with Jacques trapped in his grip.

A cry of alarm died in Ariane's throat as one of the Marchand guardsmen charged from the side. She saw it happen, though it seemed unreal, the stuff of nightmares: Rook swinging Jacques away, the guard slamming against him; a flash of violent movement as Rook struck at the guard's wrist, the two struggling for possession of the guard's disruptor; Jacques in the middle, his face gone blank with astonishment as the deadly beam seared a hole in his back; falling, falling to the ground.

Ariane screamed. And Rook stood there, the disruptor in his hand, staring down at her brother's body. The gun clattered to the floor, bitterly loud in the shocked stillness.

Wynn's voice thrummed in Ariane's ear. She hardly saw the guardsmen swarm over Rook like stripflies on a carcass. Jacques's gentle face seemed untouched above his ruined body, lips relaxed and parted, as if he were inviting her to play a game for which she didn't know the rules.

She looked up once when they seized Rook and fettered him with bonds even a Kalian couldn't break. And she rejected the plea in his copper eyes, cursed him in her heart and then aloud, faster and faster until they dragged him away and Wynn took her in his arms again.

The words he spoke to her were meaningless, but she clung to him because he was the only familiar thing left in the world. *Commissaire* of the Gendarmerie, her great-grandfather's most trusted ally. Heir to the wealthiest family in Lumière. The man whose sister Jacques was to marry.

Now there would be no grand alliance between the Marchand and the Slaytons. The bridegroom was dead.

She didn't cry. Wynn spoke of justice and punishment and courage, but such fragile concepts shattered against the hard core of stone her heart had become.

When the guardsmen lifted Jacques's body gently between them to take him home, she kissed his still lips and turned away. Her brother was no longer there.

It was Rook's face that burned in her memory.

Wynn Slayton smiled.

No one saw his satisfaction. Ariane leaned against his chest, her head buried in his uniform jacket. The gendarmes and guardsmen had taken the rebel Kalians away; the ambulance was already leaving with Jacques's body.

He had planned well over the past few years, but fate had played into his hands. The Marchand heir was dead, and he was rid of a threat and an inconvenience at the same time. The Kalian who had been caught holding the disruptor would never be believed if he dared to claim innocence.

Ariane shuddered in his arms. Her thick brown hair was limp and dirty; he turned his face away from the top of her head. Little Ariane Burke-Marchand, the Patriarch's great-granddaughter, was a child; the thin body he rocked so gently moved him not at all. She was no exotic beauty to arouse and please him as Sable did.

He smiled again, thinking of the Kalian woman who had escaped. Sable would return to his estates, as he'd conditioned her to do; she would evade the retribution that would come down on her people. And she would remain ignorant of the role he had played in today's events, his true plans for the Kalians and the Marchand. She was far too useful a tool to waste.

Soon enough the other Kalians, those not condemned for their part in the riots, would become his tools as well. And Ariane—he whispered words of encouragement to her as he led her from the abandoned building. Ariane would be added insurance. The Patriarch of the Marchand would never dare abandon the marriage contract between their families. He'd never risk the old bitterness again.

Ariane would become Wynn's bride. In time he would hold the Marchand name and power in his own hands. And until then . . .

Until then he would weave the web of revenge thread by

thread, with exquisite care. When the Marchand fell and Lumière was his, the Patriarch would know what it was to be dishonored and helpless.

He pulled Ariane to him and kissed the top of her head. "Don't worry," he whispered. "I'll take care of everything."

CHAPTER ONE

"*I*'d advise against it, Lady Ariane," the warden said, his hands clasped behind his back. "The workstations have minimal security. Out there we don't need it. But it's not set up for visitors. The men out there—"

Ariane smiled patiently as he shook his head, but her thoughts were far from this small, cluttered office so removed from the harshness of the Tantalan wilderness. *Out there,* he said. Out there where prisoners from all the worlds of the League labored to fill their sentences, and died if they were lucky.

Out there, where Rook Galloway was condemned to a life of endless misery. She'd read about the prison world before she'd come to drop off the shipment of drugs and electronic equipment from Espérance; Tantalus was a convenient place to dispose of criminals who were judged to be beyond rehabilitation.

Like the murderer of her brother.

Eight years ago. Ariane turned to look out the tinted window at the jungle. Eight years ago she had seen the Kalian condemned to death, only to have his sentence commuted to life imprisonment on Tantalus. The League had been responsible for that. Grand-père had wanted him dead. But the League did not approve of such barbaric practices, and the Patriarch had bowed to the pressure.

Ten Kalians had been sent to Tantalus. Only one was still alive, according to the records the *d'Artagnan*'s computer had accessed.

Rook Galloway.

In eight years Ariane had come to terms with her grief. She thought the bitterness and hatred were finally behind her.

It should have been possible to forget Galloway and let him rot on Tantalus.

In two Espérancian weeks she would be meeting Wynn on the League space station Agora. In two weeks she would be giving up her freedom, putting behind her the three glorious years in space piloting a swift courier ship between Espérance and her family's business interests throughout the League. And she would go home to become Wynn's bride, confined to a sedate life in Lumière, no longer a rebellious girl but a woman of the Elite, bred to bear heirs and keep her husband's honor as she'd once kept her own.

There would be no room for dreams or regrets.

Once she had dreamed of exploring the stars. Finding new worlds, free to do as she chose. If Jacques hadn't died . . .

Ariane shook her head. She had come to terms with the loss of freedom, of everything she had become. But she had not been able to forget the Kalian who had made her understand the meaning of sorrow.

She could still remember his face. Remember the way he had looked at her, pleading, begging her for something she couldn't give. And during the trial, when he'd testified—because Grand-père favored the League ways now—when he'd had a chance to defend himself. And had claimed innocence.

Innocence. Ariane closed her eyes. He could not be innocent. And yet when she had been sent with a shipment to Tantalus, she had found herself unable to leave.

Not until she'd seen him. One last time.

She turned to face the warden. "I understand the dangers, but I must speak to this man. It's of grave importance." Fixing him with her most commanding gaze, she played her family's rank and reputation for all it was worth. Even here the Marchand name was known, and long ago she'd learned how to use the beauty and poise and unconscious authority bestowed by her breeding to get what she wanted.

The warden blinked. "Uh, Lady Ariane, we—"

"Just Ariane, please, Warden Rostov." She leaned forward, placing her manicured hands flat on his battered clairewood desk. "Family business, you understand. I promise I won't be any trouble."

Rostov masked a frown without complete success and picked up a comp pad from the desk.

"You know he's the last one left here. The last Kalian. You'd think they'd have had a better survival rate than"—he coughed behind his free hand—"ordinary humans."

Ariane suppressed a shudder. *The last one.* Perhaps the last Kalian in existence. The warden's voice was casual. How many non-Espérancians had ever seen a Kalian outside of news broadcasts or old litdisks? How many cared that those not condemned in the Warren riots had been lost on their way to Agora in a Marchand cargo ship?

"I know," Ariane answered softly. "It's because of this that it's—even more vital I speak to him."

Pursing his lips, the warden regarded her for a moment longer before slapping the pad back on the desk. "Very well, Lady Marchand. I'll provide you with a list of rules and regulations that will make your journey as safe as possible. And I'll have to ask you to sign a release—" He shrugged apologetically.

"Whatever is required," she put in.

"I'll have Hudson here escort you," he said, nodding at the tall young guard who stood silently just inside the doorway. He checked his watch. "Early afternoon now. It may take me a few hours to arrange transport—"

"I have my own—a Dragonfly. Very fast and safe," she added quickly when he seemed about to object.

But the warden was well aware of the capabilities of Espérance's Dragonfly helijets, far more reliable than anything Tantalus could provide. And he must know her capabilities as a pilot; no novice could handle a starship like the *d'Artagnan.* After a moment he nodded.

"If you'll return to the lounge, Lady Ariane, I'll see that instructions and the release are brought to you there within the next hour. Good luck."

His attention was already elsewhere when she left the office. Ariane smiled wryly. If the male warden of an isolated prison world could dismiss her so quickly, she must be losing her touch.

Such idle thoughts of flirtation were all she had. She would go to Wynn a virgin bride, according to all the ancient customs of the Elite.

Her smile faded. She couldn't go to Wynn at all, couldn't lay the past to rest, until one last question was answered. Until she could erase the haunting memory of Rook Galloway's face.

And then, for her family's sacred honor and in Jacques's memory, she would give up her freedom forever.

The young guard pointed down at the jungle through the Dragonfly's canopy. "There, Lady Ariane."

She eased the helijet into a turn as she examined the smudge of lighter green where a clearing had been hacked out of the jungle. Beyond a jumble of low buildings there were open fields, and the tiny shapes of men laboring in them.

Hudson whistled through his teeth. "First time I've been out here, Lady Ariane," he said. "First six months of duty they've kept me back at Base. They only send the veterans out here, they said." He gave an uneasy chuckle. "I had my doubts about getting into space by contracting to Tantalus—but back on Liberty it takes a lot of credits to get the training." He sighed wistfully. "I sure miss home, though. Here I can earn the money to . . ."

Ariane hardly heard the voluble guard's words. Her attention was fixed on landing the helijet on the small circular landing platform, empty except for one primitive Hummingbird skimmer and a transport that looked due for major servicing. She set the Dragonfly down light as a feather, earning an almost worshipful glance from the young guard.

Galloway was here. Somewhere. Ariane shut off the engines, locked the helijet down, and stared around her.

The heat was sweltering. She could feel her borrowed coverall beginning to stick to her skin, though the warden had assured her it was top of the line for tropical environments.

Raucous noise came from the jungle that pushed in at the rows of barracks and offices, cries and screams that made Ariane shudder.

The records said that the mortality rate here was higher than on any other world in the League. Being sent to Tantalus was as good as a death sentence.

Ariane left the helijet and began to walk across the landing pad toward the buildings, Hudson in tow, not surprised that there was no one to meet her. No amenities here, no unnecessary ritual. This was a place of punishment—for the guards, she thought, as much as for the prisoners. Except that the guards got double hazard pay.

Rook Galloway was a Kalian. The Kalian prisoners here had had an advantage over their ordinary human peers: they'd come from a world even harsher than this one. Kali.

But now only one Kalian remained.

Stripping already-wet hair from her forehead and gathering it into a twist at the base of her neck, Ariane let the young guard take the lead as they arrived at the unadorned building designated for prison personnel. Hudson pressed his badge against the IDlock, and the triple doors slid open one by one to admit them.

The deputy warden for the workstation rose to greet her, his expression harried and almost hostile. The sporadic hum of an overworked cooler stuttered somewhere behind his desk.

"Lady Ariane?" he said sharply. "We didn't expect you so soon."

She smiled at him. "I'm sorry for the inconvenience. I assume the warden explained the reason I'm here. . . ."

"Yes. Yes, he did. But if I had my way, I'd—" He shut his mouth with a snap and took a deep breath. "The man you want to see is being brought in from the fields." He looked her up and down; Ariane could see the way he cataloged her and considered her origins. "If you're willing to wait, we can have him cleaned up first, arrange the proper security. We don't often have—visitors—here. And for this prisoner, in particular—" He frowned. "We'll set up a force shield for the interview. You'll be perfectly safe. I'll assign guards to—"

"That won't be necessary." *Fool,* Ariane told herself. *Take all the security he's willing to give.* But she only shook her head. "I haven't much time. I'll see him as soon as he arrives." Her smile took the edge off her words, but the deputy warden couldn't mistake the command. He scowled and shrugged.

"You signed the release, Lady Ariane. He'll be secured with manacles, in any case." He turned away to make a quick call, spat out a series of orders, and confronted her again, briefly eyeing Hudson over her shoulder. "Come this way."

The place was bleak enough. Cold gray walls, featureless corridors. *As a prison should be,* she thought. But she imagined herself trapped there, committed to some tiny cell at the end of each day's hard labor, knowing she would go mad. She had always been terrified of confinement.

She shuddered. Here there could be no future, no escape. No hope.

The deputy warden took her into a bare room with a single table and several hard-backed chairs. There were no windows looking out into the jungle. The room stank of fear; Ariane could feel it. As she'd once felt fear and pain and chaos on a night eight long years ago on a world light-years away.

Hudson and three other guards ranged behind her as she sat stiffly in the chair at one end of the table. The far door hissed open.

She saw him almost immediately, half a head taller than his guards—dark hair matted and damp, the black slash of eyebrows above eyes fixed on the ground.

And then his guards moved aside and he looked up. The guards, the room, the world outside vanished. Ariane opened her mouth and found herself gone mute.

He was changed. Horribly changed.

The handsome young man she had been infatuated with eight years ago might never have existed. There were scars marking his face, some light and faded, others new. The high cheekbones and strong jaw were sculpted in harsh relief, as if every last ounce of softness had been burned away. His mouth was set in a grim and bitter line. His black hair flowed down to his shoulders, drawn back loosely with a scrap of rag. He looked like a savage.

But his eyes . . . Ariane could not look away from his eyes. They were like burning coals, red-hot metal, utterly inhuman.

She saw the change in those eyes as recognition came, reflecting eight years' metamorphosis from the girl she had been.

She saw him remember, relive it all as she had done so many times since the day of Jacques's death. And a face that had been hard grew implacable.

"Marchand," he said, his voice a hoarse rumble. Sleek, powerful muscle bunched under the sweat-soaked work clothes that clung like a second skin. He stopped where he was, resisting the guards who pushed him toward the empty chair at the end of the table.

One of the guards behind him removed a black rod from his belt and lightly touched Rook's shoulder. Ariane flinched from the pain she could not truly feel, watched the shock course through Rook's body, a faint tightening of his muscles, a tic set to jumping in his cheek.

Rook's face revealed nothing as they shoved him forward again and pushed him down in the chair, fixing adamantium cables from his manacled wrists to bolts in the floor. His eyes never left Ariane's. Runnels of perspiration dripped from his jaw to the table in a slow, maddening rhythm.

"Lady Ariane," the deputy warden said behind her, clearing his throat, "I suggest you—"

"Leave us alone," she said.

The guards looked at each other. The one with the black rod fingered it as if he hoped for another opportunity to use it.

"Impossible," the warden snapped. "We can't leave you with this—"

"I signed your damned release." Ariane got to her feet,

turned, and stared at the warden coldly. "Now, please—go. I'll call you when I'm finished."

Perhaps if the warden had had any idea of how the Patriarch of the Marchand on Espérance would react to knowing his great-granddaughter was alone with a murderous Kalian, he would never have agreed. But as it was, he merely favored her with another shrug and motioned for the guards to leave. They filed out reluctantly, Hudson the last to go, his open young face deeply concerned.

Ariane sucked in a deep, ragged breath and turned slowly from the door. Turned to face her nemesis.

"You know who I am," she said, bracing her hands on the tabletop.

For a moment she thought he wouldn't speak at all. "I have reason to remember," he said at last, his voice unnervingly even. "When they told me I had a visitor, I never expected such an honor."

In the very flatness of the words she heard a subtle mockery. The man condemned for killing her brother looked at her without remorse.

Ariane felt as though she were the one being judged.

"What did Kalians ever know of honor?" she said under her breath.

For the first time his expression changed, a slight lift at the corner of his grim-set mouth. "Eight years ago," he countered, "we learned the meaning of Marchand honor."

She clenched her fists on the table, grasping at emotions that threatened to slip out of control. It was harder, much harder to confront him than she had thought it would be. Harder to see him so changed. Harder to be certain of his guilt, when she *must* be certain. . . .

"Why did you come here, Lady Ariane?"

He moved suddenly, shifting in his chair, and Ariane flinched. Cables hissed, pulled taut, and released again. Copper eyes followed her like a predator's.

"You see the last Kalian on Tantalus," he said softly. "The last of those your family sent to rot here."

Both sickened and fascinated, Ariane let her eyes wander

over his body: the lean muscle honed by heavy labor, the scarred face, the red welts of bites and scratches on every centimeter of tanned skin. His words, his eyes, condemned her and what she was, and yet *he* was the condemned. *He* was the criminal.

His eyes had narrowed to slits when she met them again. "Your Espérancian punishment was very thorough, Lady Ariane." He leaned closer, almost whispering. "Did your family send you to see the last of us dead?"

Ariane found herself lost in his stare, in the bitterness of his words, in the memory of the man he'd been. A man she'd thought she'd loved. A young man whose face had shown only grief and shock and bewilderment when they'd taken him away. No hatred. Not then. Not yet.

Now he hated. Hated her. Hated what she was.

As she looked at him now—chained like a wild beast, his copper eyes unblinking and fixed on hers—Ariane fought desperately for distance. She'd come here for only one reason, to ask one question. To try to understand.

She hadn't come here to feel her heart pound and her breath come short. What she felt was not what she had prepared herself to feel.

Fear, yes. Pain at old memories.

But there should have been hatred instead of pity, contempt instead of fascination.

The things a sixteen-year-old girl had felt for a forbidden love should have been long dead, buried with her innocent brother.

Ariane swallowed and met his stare. This was a duel, no more—a duel of wills, of minds. So he hated her. What he felt mattered not at all.

Deliberately she moved away from the table, stopped a bare meter away from him, nothing between them but his bonds.

"My family didn't send me here," she said quietly. "I came to ask only one question." She swallowed again. "Why?"

Rook leaned back as far as his shackles would allow, and

Ariane's eyes were drawn to the dark vee of his broad chest where the stained and ragged work shirt was open nearly to the waist. "Why?" he echoed.

"Why did you kill my brother?"

His closed expression shifted, revealing a flicker of uncertainty, as if her question had truly startled him. "What does it matter, Lady Ariane?" he grated. "Eight years ago it didn't matter."

Closing her eyes, Ariane felt her heart stop and start again with painful slowness.

He didn't deny it.

"I thought—" she began, and caught herself. "It matters." She opened her eyes again. "He wanted to *help* your people. He believed you were worth helping. Even if you hated—the rest of us—you had nothing to gain by killing him. Nothing."

Eight years dissolved in a wave of vivid memory. *"All I know is that I have to keep you safe, Lady Ariane. You and your brother. Your lives are worth more to the Patriarch than all of my people combined."*

His words. Words she had never quite forgotten. A contradiction of everything that had come after.

Suddenly she was sixteen years old again, betrayed and grief stricken and lost. She struggled with her weakness, met his gaze and held it as she had done on that terrible day.

He looked away. Deep, unutterable weariness crossed his face, harsh lines relaxing into despair. "I had nothing to gain," he repeated softly. "Nothing."

Ariane balled her hands into fists, welcoming the sharp pain as her nails cut the skin of her palms.

"Tell me," she demanded, drawn closer to him almost against her will. She could smell his sweat and some other scent too subtle to name. "Do you still deny that you killed him?"

Astonishment registered on his face, there and gone in an instant. He looked up at her again and his eyes searched hers, swept over her as if seeing her for the first time. The bronzed skin of his bare arms shuddered, a trapped animal's shivering.

"You were there," he said, his voice almost inaudible. "You testified against me."

Ariane fought a sudden wave of nausea, remembering. "Do you deny it?" she repeated.

The silence between them became oppressive. Rook's face changed again, hardening, mocking her vain and childish hopes. *He is not innocent,* she told herself bitterly. *The evidence was too strong. Wynn was right. I was only a child. . . .*

Rook's hands worked, clenching and unclenching below the manacles. "Would it change anything if I did?" he said harshly.

She wanted to hit him, wipe that bitter contempt from his face. "Was it an accident?" she persisted, driven by something in herself she didn't understand. *"Pour l'amour de Dieu,* if you were innocent—"

"Innocent?" He made a sound deep in his throat, a strangled laugh. "No, Lady Ariane. Not anymore." Hard calculation moved behind his eyes. "Are you?"

Control snapped. Her hand came up, intending to strike, but she caught herself in midswing. Her palm slapped the warm, damp skin of his shoulder.

She staggered as white light flared behind her eyes, clutched at his arm to keep from falling. Violent colors, images, sounds stripped sanity from the world.

Like that terrible night eight years ago, when she had felt and seen and heard too many things she did not understand.

He could not touch her, and yet he did—as if invisible bonds like those that confined him had coiled up at his command to snare her hands and feet. Bonds that tightened in a stranglehold, severing her connection to all she knew. And in a chaos of sensation and emotion not her own, Rook's eyes drew her in to the center of the storm.

"It was no accident," she heard him say. And she saw Jacques's death again, watched it happen, knowing she could do nothing to stop it. *No accident, no accident, no accident . . .*

Violently she pushed herself away, breaking contact, and the floor rose up to meet her. She fought to draw air back into her lungs; a scarred face hovered somewhere above her, drained of color. *Go away,* she told it, and it vanished, along with the memories she could not bear.

"Lady Ariane!" Gentle hands touched her, helped her up. "Are you all right?" Other voices followed, barking commands; she let Hudson guide her from the stifling room.

She leaned against the corridor wall until the sickness receded. Hudson put a glass in her hands. She gulped down the lukewarm water and drew a shaking hand across her mouth.

"Lady Ariane—are you sure you're all right? They took him away. If he hurt you—" Hudson's anxious words spun out into a meaningless drone. When the deputy warden came to question her, they told her she had fainted. The last thing she could remember was Rook's scarred, bitter face and his mocking denial of innocence.

It was no accident.

She wanted to run, to escape this place that held him, but they would not let her leave. "Morning," they told her. "Too dangerous at night." And so she lay in the narrow bunk in the small gray room they appropriated for her use, and listened to the wild night cries that the thick barracks walls could not completely banish, and let go of the last forbidden hope.

Rook paced his cell, three strides up and three back, using the mindless, familiar rhythm to bring his thoughts back under control.

He had never expected to see her again. He had never believed that it could all come back with such staggering force to reawaken emotions only the old Rook Galloway might have recognized.

One by one his companions had died, until only he remained. And he'd survived—survived because it was the nature of his kind, and because Elder Fox had asked it of him.

Even Fox was gone now. Rook had learned the old, almost forgotten secrets from Fox and concealed the knowledge he'd been given, believing then that he might use it one day. To escape.

Like a captive shadowcat he'd struggled, clung to the fragments of hope, driven by anger. Anger had kept him alive, fighting fate, refusing to surrender. But after eight years despair had entered his soul at last and eaten at his resolve like some alien, insidious disease for which there was no cure. He had learned to accept, to cast off emotion. There had been a kind of peace in the acknowledgment of despair. Peace in his utter aloneness.

Until *she* had come to Tantalus and shattered that peace.

The guards had taken him to the interrogation room and he'd seen her face. High walls had crumbled in an instant, and the man hidden within them had lain exposed. Weak, cringing, thrust again into a holocaust of bitter memory.

He'd wanted to run, but it was too late. He had learned to feel again.

Rage. Sorrow. Yearning.

Hope.

And hatred. Hatred for the woman who had come to torment him, and for all she was. He tasted that hatred, turned it over in his mind, greeted it like an old friend. Hatred was an anchor in the maelstrom of emotion. He could find strength in it, a new means for survival. A new purpose.

Ariane Burke-Marchand. She had given him that purpose.

Rook closed his eyes and let the images play out in darkness. He thought of the woman, and of the child she had been—the one person who symbolized the tragedy that had befallen his people and condemned him to hell.

He remembered the smudged, anxious face of a girl just old enough to believe herself a woman; a tangle of dirty hair, wide dark eyes. He remembered her angry curses, her loyalty to a brother she loved. He remembered the way she had looked at him in the end: accusation and horror, a gaze stripped of innocence.

He remembered her at the trial, when she had spoken softly of what she had seen when her brother died. She'd been only a tiny part of it, of the deliberate web of lies spun to trap his people. Conspiracy, they'd called it—a conspiracy of the educated Kalians to turn on their patrons, careful plans of revolt and blackmail and violence exposed just in time.

But he had never hated *her*, even when her carefully

guided words had helped condemn him. He could not hate a child.

But she was no longer a child. She was Marchand. And she had come to Tantalus with her doubts and her questions eight years too late.

Rook worked his hands, still feeling the shackles. He had wanted to touch her. He had wanted it desperately, without comprehension, even as he'd hated her and everything she was.

And when she'd touched him— He shuddered, remembering light and sensation and denial. Something had happened between them, something inexplicable. In a single moment he'd relived the tragedy that linked them, Marchand and Kalian, and he'd wanted to make her feel it, force her to understand, to know the truth. He had wanted *her*. . . .

The clear shielding of his cell rang with a sudden blow, and Rook pivoted to face the guards who stood on the other side.

"Hey, Galloway!" the older one said, rapping his stinger against the shield a second time. "Missing your girlfriend? Hear she came all the way from Espérance just to see you!" He snickered. "Who'd have thought you were worth it, eh? Such a nice little armful she is. Too bad your hands were tied, eh?" Both guards laughed, and the younger one made suggestive movements with his hands.

Black rage shivered through Rook, more familiar this time, almost sweet. A day ago he would have been indifferent to their jibes. Now he held himself in control, silent and still, staring—until they dropped their eyes with scowls and curses.

"The warden wants to see you, Galloway," the younger guard said at last. He fingered his stinger. "You gonna give us any trouble?"

Rook looked away to conceal his sudden, fierce joy. *Trouble*. Let them believe he was still the broken savage, a dull creature good only for backbreaking labor, lost in his own world. Let them believe until it was too late.

The guards raised the shielding, and he let them push him into the corridor while he listened to the Tantalan night.

He could almost feel *her,* somewhere near, just out of reach. He went quietly with the guards and thought of Ariane Burke-Marchand.

She had resurrected him. She had made him feel again. Unwittingly, she had restored his purpose and given him the means to act.

She was his link to the past, and his key to the future.

Today Rook Galloway had been reborn.

The flight back to the main prison grounds and the world's single spaceport was accomplished in silence. Morning light, heavy with mist, pressed like something solid against the helijet canopy.

Hudson, in the seat beside her, seemed sobered by what he had seen. Ariane hardly noticed his uncharacteristic quiet; she concentrated on piloting the helijet and keeping her mind a perfect blank.

She couldn't seem to dislodge the hard knot in her throat.

The sleek, familiar shape of the *d'Artagnan,* poised for flight on the spaceport landing field, was a sight that Ariane could focus on with relief. The starship was still hers—at least for a few more days. Ariane refused to think beyond those remaining days of freedom as she flicked the switch that opened the docking bay in the *d'Artagnan's* stern. She guided the Dragonfly smoothly into place, and Hudson turned to look at her, his young face grim.

"There's a routine security check I'll have to run on your ship, Lady Ariane," he told her. His voice was low and gruff with strain.

Ariane closed her eyes. "I need to be on my way as quickly as possible," she said, securing the helijet. Lights came on in the bay as the outer doors sealed behind them. Hudson followed her as she hopped down onto the deck and paused to consult her wrist remote, initiating preflight procedures on the main computer.

"It won't take long, Lady Ariane," he said. "By the time you get clearance, I'll be finished." He gave her a strange, apologetic smile.

Sighing, Ariane started for the air lock that connected the docking bay to the small cargo hold. "What do you need?"

He ducked his head. "Permission to examine your hold and cabins, Lady Ariane. A formality."

A breath of wry laughter escaped her. "I'm not likely to be harboring fugitives on my ship, but I'll clear you."

She led him into the cargo hold and left him there, making her way through the final air lock and into the *d'Artagnan*'s living quarters. There was something almost oppressive in the empty silence of the common room; even the cockpit seemed less a sanctuary than a cell.

Ariane shuddered and dropped into the padded pilot's seat. *Don't think about it,* she commanded herself. *At least this ship is something you can count on. Something certain.*

One by one she ran through the preflight routines: checking the stardrive's balance for sublight flight, priming the ship's life-support system, carrying out all the necessary tests. Again and again she forgot sequences that she knew by heart, remembering Rook's face.

Remembering how he had made her feel . . .

No. Her fingers trembled on the keypad as she made the final entries. *You won't have to think about it much longer. It's over. It's out of your hands.*

But the memories remained while the ready lights came up on the control panel. She leaned back in the pilot's seat and passed her hand over her face.

Honor. All her life she'd been raised by the codes of the Espérancian Elite. Like the *d'Artagnan*, honor was solid and real. It had been insanity to doubt, to question. Duty and honor would send her back to Espérance. Honor would give her the courage to face a life of confinement. To accept.

To forget Rook Galloway.

Letting out a shuddering breath, she rose and began to pace the tiny space of the cockpit restlessly. Hudson should have been done with his "routine" check by now. She flipped on the ship's intercom.

"Mr. Hudson? I'm ready for takeoff." She waited, tapping her fingers against the smooth console. "Mr. Hudson—"

"Here, Lady Ariane."

She spun around. Hudson stood just inside the cockpit, a disruptor in his hand.

Aimed at her.

Her first impulse was to laugh. Hudson looked so deadly serious, his mouth set in a grim line that seemed so much at odds with his boyishly untouched face. But she clamped her lips together and balanced lightly on the balls of her feet, waiting.

"Did you find some—irregularity, Mr. Hudson?"

He moved another step closer. And another, until he was within touching distance. "Call for clearance to take off," he said, gesturing with the 'ruptor.

Ariane revised her first assumption. It wasn't anything she'd done; Hudson had simply gone crazy.

"I know—how it must be, Mr. Hudson. Alone here, far from home—you want to go back home, is that it? To Liberty?"

He stared at her, light-blue eyes shadowed beneath his uniform cap. "Liberty," he repeated.

Considering the best way to move, Ariane tensed her muscles for action. "You must feel trapped here, so far from home. After what we saw . . . I understand. But—"

His smile vanished. "Trapped," he said softly. "What do you know about being trapped, Lady Ariane?" His voice had gone very deep and strange. "Call the tower for clearance. Now."

For the briefest instant Hudson's eyes flickered to the console behind her, and Ariane moved. She darted at Hudson, whirling like a dancer in the ancient way her family's old Weapons Master had taught her as a girl. She might as well have attacked a plasteel bulkhead. Powerful arms caught and held her; the 'ruptor's muzzle came up against her head.

Shock held her utterly still for one blinding instant. Hudson's hand burned on her arm like the bitter cold of space.

"I don't have much to lose, Lady Ariane," Hudson said softly. "You'll call for clearance. Everything is perfectly—normal."

She considered fighting again; to put the *d'Artagnan* in a starjacker's hands was unthinkable.

But there was far more at stake. Marchand honor and Marchand interest demanded her safe return, to wed Wynn Slayton by inviolable contract that would bind their families forever. Her death now would gain nothing at all.

Clenching her teeth, Ariane hailed the prison port and made the final in-person request for clearance. The bored officer's voice on the other end of the commlink never altered; her own was perfectly steady as she acknowledged her clearance to lift.

Abruptly Hudson let her go. "Very good," he murmured. "Take her up."

Ariane thought quickly as she dropped into the pilot's seat, Hudson breathing harshly over her shoulder. *He's only a boy. He can't know much about Caravel-class starships.* . . .

Her hand hovered just above the control stick. It shouldn't be too difficult to fool the young guard, make it seem as if they were leaving the system. And then—

Warm fingers feathered along her shoulder and slid under the thick hair at the base of her neck. "Oh, no, Lady Ariane. It won't be so easy this time."

Her throat went dry as her hand fell from the console. Abruptly he let her go, stepping away. She turned in the seat to look up at the man who stood over her.

And he *changed.* As if he were made of something other than mere human flesh, he began to change: slowly, so slowly that at first she didn't realize what she was seeing.

The young man's softness vanished, cheekbones and hollows and sharp angles drawn forth from Hudson's unremarkable face. Sandy hair darkened in a slow wave under the uniform cap. An old scar snaked over skin tanned by relentless heat.

The eyes were the last to change. Blue faded, warmed, melted into copper.

Rook's eyes.

They held hers as he swept off his cap, freed the dark hair that fell to his shoulders.

The man who stood before her wore the tailored uniform of a Tantalan guard as a hellhound might wear a collar. A wild beast crouched on the deck of the *d'Artagnan*.

A Kalian.

Reaction coursed through her, numbing her hands and stopping her breath.

"Mon Dieu," she whispered. "You."

No table separated them now, no adamantium cables confined him. His hard gaze swept over her with contemptuous insolence.

"Yes," he said softly. One straight dark brow arched, stretching the scar that slashed down across his cheekbone. "No words of welcome, Lady Ariane?"

She knew the voice now, deeper than Hudson's—a difference never questioned, as she had never questioned the young guard's grim silence on the return from camp.

Rook was here, and Hudson was gone. Hudson had never been here at all.

"How—" she began, but he spoke over her whispered question.

"Another gift of the Shapers, Lady Ariane," he said, "one your kind never knew about. The ability to reach into our bodies and alter our very cells as you would put on a mask. Uncommon even among my people." He held up his hand, and it blurred before her eyes. Strong, scarred fingers narrowed to Elite elegance. "I've waited a long time to use it."

By sheer force of will she stilled the clamor in her mind. "Where is Hudson? What did you do—"

"He's safe enough," Rook said. For a moment his attention wavered, metallic eyes moving over her head to the control boards.

Ariane thought of his hand holding the disruptor. He was too fast, too strong. Disarming him would be next to impossible. Fear rose like bile, alien and unwelcome.

No, she thought, beating the emotion back fiercely. *You have to think. Your mind has to be clear. . . .*

The heat of his palm came to rest again on her shoulder, moved toward her neck to slip under the open collar of her shipsuit. His thumb made slow, intimate circles on the delicate skin over her collarbone. She focused on the steady motion of his breathing, the stolen uniform stretched taut across his chest.

"How—" She swallowed, counting her heartbeats until she could speak with the appearance of perfect calm. "How did you take his place?"

His harsh croak of laughter drew her eyes back to his face. "More questions, Lady Ariane?" He said her name the same way he had in the prison camp, as if it were a curse. "Haven't you learned the danger of asking questions?"

Pride forced her to meet his gaze unflinchingly. Her skin shuddered and jumped under his touch.

"A pity there's no time to satisfy your curiosity, Lady Ariane," he said at last. "But as I said, I'm desperate. I have nothing to lose."

His hand closed lightly about her neck, turning her inexorably back to the console. He could have snapped her neck with no effort at all. He ordered her to lift—a casteless criminal, a murderer, commanding a woman of the Espérancian Elite.

And she found herself obeying him, taking the *d'Artagnan* up as if she had no will of her own, clearing atmosphere with Rook's hand always there, like a lover's.

The blackness of space closed around them at last. Ariane clenched her fingers on the arms of the pilot's seat and stared at the ready lights until they blurred in her sight.

With almost painful slowness his hand slid down her shoulder.

"You should never have come to Tantalus, Lady Ariane," he said in a tone devoid of emotion.

Ariane jerked. "You won't get away with this," she said calmly.

Rough fingers lifted her hair away from her neck, let it fall slowly back to her shoulders.

"No, Lady Ariane?" he whispered. The cold muzzle of the 'ruptor caressed her cheek. "You'd better hope that I do."

CHAPTER TWO

*H*e was free.

Rook savored the slow and powerful upwelling of triumph. He was free. Free, with a ship to carry him back to Espérance.

Beyond the cockpit canopy the void of space stretched into infinity. No walls, no chains, no limits.

Somewhere among those innumerable stars lay sanctuary. For himself, and for his people. Rook held hope firmly in check, knowing it for the danger it was.

When his people were free again, he would hope. When he was no longer alone. . . .

Rook let his eyes wander over Ariane's lithe form as she stood tensely against the far bulkhead of the cockpit. Her dark eyes never left him. There was no emotion on that aristocratic face.

He met her gaze and concealed the reaction that coursed through him. Hunger, triumph, hatred, lust—they washed over him in waves when he looked at her, drowning him in confusion.

No, he was not quite alone.

Rook expelled his breath harshly and turned his back on her, swinging about in the pilot's seat to double-check his work. The *d'Artagnan*'s computer system was under his control, keyed to respond only to his voice and code. An irony, that his wasted Marchand education had finally served a purpose. *His* purpose.

"What do you want?"

Her low voice cut into his thoughts, and he locked the control board down before swiveling to face her again. He ignored the disruptor on the passenger seat beside him. Her eyes flickered to the weapon and back to his face; she knew she'd never reach it in time.

Rook leaned back in the seat and regarded her with cold appraisal.

Ariane. Ariane Burke-Marchand, great-granddaughter of Bernard Marchand, the Patriarch of one of the oldest and most powerful families on Espérance. The prize with which he'd buy his people a new life.

And she was a prize. Thick, straight brown hair framed a face too stubborn for conventional Espérancian beauty. She didn't need beauty; such delicacy as the Elite favored in their women would have been wasted on her. The lines of her face were clean and strong, stubborn, willful. Arrogant. Her brown eyes, flashing defiance, were set at a slight tilt over high cheekbones. Delicate skin—unblemished, perfect skin—was smooth as Nuevo Tokyo silk. Her body was sweetly curved, tautly muscled under the concealing material of her shipsuit.

She was only a woman under her aristocratic mask. A woman grown from the child he'd met in the Warren. Rook worked to slow his heartbeat, ignore his irrational response. Only a human woman—his captive, no more than that. She had no power over him at all.

With an act of will Rook kept himself locked in the pilot's seat. Even now she drew him. It was as if he looked into those eyes and saw more than an enemy. As if he saw the ghost of what he had been and the shadow of what he would be. His destiny.

Curling his mouth into a snarl of self-contempt, Rook leaned back in the chair and forced his thoughts into easier channels. He let his eyes wander over her body again. A flicker of emotion crossed her face, betraying her.

Ariane Burke-Marchand was no longer a child. His physical reaction was easy to understand. The hunger to touch her was no more than simple lust. For eight years he'd hardly seen a woman. She had awakened more than his emotions, and his Kalian body had the same needs as any ordinary man.

Needs. Rook smiled bitterly. Needs were weaknesses that

could be controlled, as he'd learned long ago to control the pain and despair.

He acknowledged his desire for power over her because of what she was. He wanted her, but he could control the wanting. She was a symbol. A tool.

His enemy.

Her eyes looked down at him as if he were some loathsome beast escaped from its cage. "What do you intend to do?" she repeated, the trace of an edge to her voice. All Marchand, all arrogance, certain of her place in the universe. Of her own inborn superiority.

Abruptly he got to his feet; her muscles tensed, her hands spread flat against the plasteel bulkhead. He picked up the disruptor and holstered it casually. With one hand he opened the shirt of the snug guard's uniform, watching her eyes follow the movement.

"What would you do, Lady Ariane?" he asked softly. The cultured accents of Espérancian Franglais came strangely to his tongue after so many years; nothing so civilized existed on Tantalus. Like the sweet coolness of the ship's air and Ariane herself, it was part of a world he had almost forgotten.

Two strides carried him to her. Her breath quickened; her tongue darted out to touch her lips. She was tall, but he stood very close, forcing her to look up at him. To feel her helplessness. He set one hand flat on the bulkhead to either side of her shoulders.

"What would you do, Ariane Burke-Marchand, if your enemy fell into your hands?" She hardly flinched when he spread his fingers and combed them through her hair.

Need. The need to touch her was overwhelming. *My enemy,* he repeated to himself. *To use to my best advantage.* Her hair was a drifting mass in his hands. Soft, like nothing he had known on Tantalus.

She set her full lips in a hard line. "If I were Kalian," she said, "I would by definition be a savage."

He almost reacted, as if her contempt could touch him. *Her* contempt. He let her hair fall.

She called him savage. She had come to Tantalus to question him for reasons he could not begin to understand. Questioning his guilt, as if the truth could matter to her. As if she almost believed her people could have been wrong.

But to her and all her kind he would always be a savage. After the betrayal, after so many years on Tantalus, perhaps it was what he had become.

He brought his hand up under her chin. Her pulse beat very fast against his palm. "A savage. Very well, Lady Ariane. What would a savage do?" Abruptly he let her go. "What would a savage do after eight years of slavery, after watching his companions die one by one? What would he do when he found himself free, holding a ship and a woman of those who discarded and betrayed his people?"

All the color drained from her face. "Betrayed," she said in a choked voice. "It wasn't we who betrayed—"

He silenced her with a finger on her lips. Soft lips, that remained stubbornly closed against his pressure. "I wondered why you came to Tantalus, Lady Ariane. I considered for a few brief moments if it might be possible for a Marchand to be interested in justice."

With a sharp jerk she turned her face aside, her expression set. "Justice was served when you were sent to Tantalus," she said under her breath. She looked back at him, her brown eyes implacable, her fists clenched against the bulkhead. "No. True justice would have demanded your death, for my brother's—"

"Marchand justice," Rook snarled. With supreme effort he turned inward, suppressed the anger and wild urge to violence that she aroused in him.

Her shaking voice trampled his self-control. "I was a child," she said, "a child who believed a Kalian could be something more than an animal. I was wrong." Her aristocratic face grew suddenly wild. "You'll never escape. They'll hunt you down, Kalian. Murderer—"

Rook moved with blinding speed, hardly aware of what he did, grasping her arms and lifting her against the bulkhead. He felt like everything she had accused him of being, lost to reason. He remembered Sable's expression in the Warren,

Heron's, the alien rage he had seen in their faces then. Hating, wanting.

As he hated and wanted now.

Make her fear you, some lost thread of intellect insisted. *Use her belief in your guilt. Use her.*

He pushed his face close to hers until he could feel the soft, urgent puffs of her breath against his skin. Fear would control her. Fear would cripple her. He would enjoy seeing her fear, remembering the terror of his people when they had been rounded up like cattle for the slaughter. . . .

"I didn't kill your brother."

The words escaped him, driven from his lips by the look in Ariane Burke-Marchand's accusing eyes.

He became conscious of the feel of her supple body through her shipsuit, heat and warmth, a blinding physical awareness that no discipline could banish. His body tightened in response. With some distant part of himself he watched her catch her breath, go utterly still in his grasp.

"I didn't kill your brother," he repeated. He stared into her eyes because he could look nowhere else, held prisoner by needs he didn't understand. The need to make her believe. To force this one Marchand to acknowledge his innocence.

She shuddered. "You said it was no accident," she whispered.

Rook remembered his words, and the bitter humor of the situation broke his strange and terrible weakness. He let her drop back to the deck.

"Your brother's death wasn't an accident," he said. "But it was no Kalian who killed him."

She blinked rapidly in shock, the dark sweep of her lashes brushing high, strong cheekbones. "No—"

His hand moved of its own volition to touch her face. "I didn't think it mattered why you came to Tantalus, Lady Ariane," he said slowly. "You gave me the means to escape. But now"—he watched his fingers stroke her skin with fascination—"now I wonder why you asked the questions you did."

Her breath grew shallow. "Take your hands off me," she hissed, reaching up to clasp his wrist.

"What put the doubts in your mind, Lady Ariane? What did you learn in eight years that compelled you to cross nineteen star systems to question a convicted savage?"

For the first time her eyes left his, focusing somewhere beyond his shoulder. "I owe you no answers, Kalian," she said.

Rook caught her jaw and forced her head back up. Brown eyes flashed with outrage, but he could see the doubt. He could sense it, as if it came through the very pores of his fingers. "I could almost admire your stubborn Elite pride," he said, "as I once admired your family. I can almost believe you're innocent."

"Innocent," she echoed, her face a mask of disbelief.

"You were a child," he repeated, staring at the smooth plasteel above her head. "A child to be manipulated as my people were manipulated."

Sharp pain at his wrist drew his eyes back down. Four parallel scratches crossed the back of his hand where her nails had scored the skin. He released her chin and let his hand fall.

"You asked me if I was innocent, Lady Ariane," he said softly. "Once, long ago, I *was* innocent. Innocent enough to believe that the Marchand would treat my people with compassion, that we would have a future beyond the Warren. I even believed in the vaunted Marchand honor."

Ariane jerked her head in denial, but he gave her no chance to speak. "I believed in Marchand justice when they took me away, knowing I was innocent. I believed there was some terrible mistake that would be resolved when Kalians and Espérancians spoke as equals. I believed it until the moment they condemned me and turned their backs on my people."

A slow sweep of vivid color rose to flush the shocked white of Ariane's face. Moving with unexpected swiftness, she darted to the side along the bulkhead. He heard her behind him, spinning to face him in the center of the cockpit. "You dare," she gasped, "you dare to impugn Marchand honor? You dare to claim innocence for Kalian treachery, rebellion, the taking of Espérancian lives?"

Rook turned slowly, observed her wild eyes with odd detachment. *She is Marchand,* he told himself. But the muscles in his belly were knotted with tension, as if in some distant corner of his mind he'd expected her to listen.

Because once he had tried to protect her. Because she had come to Tantalus. And because something in her drew him like a moth to a flame. . . .

Fool.

"A savage may dare anything," he said. "A savage who holds the Patriarch's great-granddaughter in his hands—" He advanced on her, coming so close that she was forced back one step and then another. "You wanted to know my intentions, Lady Ariane. I intend to find answers."

She stopped, bracing her feet on the deck. Her proud, lovely face was drained of emotion.

"You and your ship will find me those answers," he continued. "Your beliefs and your honor mean nothing to me. Your Marchand blood is worth only what it can buy me."

He expected her to spit defiance, but she was silent and still. She gazed at him as she had done in the interrogation room, as if she could look deep into his soul.

"It will buy you nothing."

She spoke so softly that an ordinary human would never have heard her. No challenge in the words—no hatred or threat. Only a kind of weary acceptance.

She was intelligent enough to realize that open rebellion would gain her nothing at all. And she must know her own worth. The Patriarch would never leave her to the mercy of a Kalian fugitive. He moved closer, resisting the desire to touch her yet again, capturing her eyes.

"You're wrong, Lady Ariane. Eight years ago your brother's death condemned my people. Your Patriarch valued his great-grandson's life above justice. Now your life will buy back their freedom." He felt a sudden fierce joy, still painfully unfamiliar. "My people are survivors. They survived on Kali, and in your Warren. Eight or eight hundred years in an Espérancian internment camp wouldn't break them. Whatever you've done to them—"

Ariane turned away so sharply that he almost didn't see the expression of horror in her eyes. He stared at her back, the rich brown hair falling past her shoulders, her folded arms pulling the shipsuit tight to her body.

Now, now at last she realized what she faced, and her arrogance was utterly gone. He should have taken pleasure at her fear, at his triumph over the faithless Marchand.

But he felt oddly empty, as if emotion had burned him out like a dying star.

Leaving her where she stood, Rook moved to the control board and dropped into the pilot's seat. The course to Espérance was already plotted: five jumps, with eight hours' recalibration at each jump point. Each star system he'd chosen was lightly populated or empty; the archaic vessels that passed for starships on Tantalus would never find them until it was too late.

But the *d'Artagnan*—Rook looked around him, newly amazed at what had come so easily into his hands. A Caravel-class starship, even one of the smaller courier models, was faster than almost any other ship in existence. Eight years ago the ships had just come onto the market, and Rook had only read about them during his shipboard training on Tolstoy.

The Marchand could afford such a wonder for the idle pleasure of the Patriarch's great-granddaughter. Now the ship was his, as *she* was his.

He turned back to the board, fingers moving lightly over the controls, readying the ship for the jump into hyperspace.

Her footsteps on the deck were almost silent, but he heard them. The fine hairs rose at the back of his neck. He could feel her breath and smell the scent of her as she came up close behind him.

"No. *You're* wrong," she said.

He ignored her, completing the final sequences. The ready lights went to a steady green.

"You're wrong, Rook Galloway." His name on her lips

was strange and compelling. He heard her swallow. "There are no Kalians left on Espérance to free."

Ariane was almost prepared when he swiveled to face her. She knew she was mad to tell him. She hardly understood what had driven her to reveal a truth that might see her dead.

Honor, she thought. *Honor demands truth.* And inwardly she laughed at herself. He spat on her honor. And he hated her.

She'd come to Tantalus to learn the truth, and the truth had trapped her. Just as *he'd* trapped her on her own ship. As his copper eyes held her captive and reached deep into her soul.

Of all the incredible things he'd claimed, she was certain of only one: he hadn't killed Jacques. Perhaps she was mad to trust the painful conviction that had come to her slowly over the last eight years. Perhaps she was doubly mad to trust a Kalian's word. Rook Galloway had been convicted of more than murder.

But she *knew.* She had known from the moment he'd said the words and his body had pressed against hers as he'd lifted her from the deck. He had not murdered Jacques, though she would not examine the implications of his innocence.

Ariane closed her eyes and refused to think. He was still a kidnapper, a traitor to the Marchand who had lifted him out of the Warren. . . .

"What did you say?"

She opened her eyes and met his hot alien stare. It was harder, far harder than she'd expected to face him without flinching.

"Your people—seven years ago your people were offered sanctuary by the League, after they had been interned on Espérance for nearly a year." Her breath caught, and she forced the words out one by one. "They arranged to resettle the Kalians if we—my family—would transport them to Agora."

In one swift move he was out of the chair, nearly lifting her off her feet. "My people left Espérance? Where did they go?" He shook her, not gently. "Tell me!"

Ariane had heard of Kalian predators, extinct now along with their world, that were known to rend their living prey into bloody fragments. The man who held her could have torn her limb from limb with hardly any effort at all.

"They were sent out in a Marchand cargo ship, bound for Agora, as soon as it could be arranged," she whispered. His powerful fingers tightened dangerously on her upper arms, but she refused to let him see her pain. "Halfway to the League station the *Bonaventure,* and all its crew—"

The pupils of his eyes shrank to pinpoints, as if he knew what was coming. He was no longer looking at her.

"—was lost. When they'd been overdue for a standard month, a search was conducted system by system. They found the wreckage in the Krentz system. No survivors, Marchand or Kalian."

Ariane was sickened by the dry recital of the death of Rook's people, but she continued grimly. "They thought that the stardrive had overloaded. It was an accident that no one anticipated. Most of the bodies had been—lost when the hull was breached by the explosion."

Rook was ominously silent. His grasp loosened on her arms, and her feet touched the deck again, but she was unable to move away.

She searched his scarred face framed by a wild tangle of black hair, trapped by the blank shock in his eyes. Lifting her hand, she found her own lashes wet with tears. It was almost as if she felt his pain, felt what it was to lose one's people forever.

No, she protested silently. It was easy, far too easy to imagine herself bereft, as Rook was bereft of everything that defined his place in the universe. She had lost her mother and father, her grandparents, her brother. But she still knew who she was.

Ariane shivered. The barriers of contempt and hatred and fear were not there when she looked for them within herself. The threats and accusations Rook had made faded to insignificance.

Without thinking, she reached for him, her fingers touching the sleeve of his stolen uniform, and agony swept over her; despair so terrible that it threatened to carry her into oblivion. And yet her hand tightened on him, and he responded, powerful arms pulling her against his body. He buried his face in her shoulder as his hands spread at her back, the hard muscle of his chest and thighs an unyielding pressure.

Unnatural hunger rose in her, chaotic and primitive; her body responded in defiance of her will, pulse beating wildly as she breathed in the scent of his skin, his hair, heavy dark strands mingling with her own. Resistance melted and flowed beyond her grasp, leaving her weak with yearning.

There was nothing beyond Rook Galloway, nothing outside of his pain and the echo of it that hummed through her body. Nothing but need, his need and hers. . . .

He began to shiver violently, shaking her free of him, pushing her away. The animal sound that came from his throat paralyzed her until his eyes locked on hers again. She stumbled back.

His hand came up slowly, callused fingers brushing her eyelids. He stared at the moisture glistening on his fingertips.

"Tears?" he whispered. "Can a Marchand feel sorrow for the extinction of savages?"

His contempt released her, pushed her away from the brink of madness. She stared at his hard, emotionless face, trembling with shock.

"There is still one Kalian left alive," he said.

And he turned his back on her to lean over the console of her captive ship, his rejection more terrible than his hatred.

CHAPTER THREE

Think.

In the silent darkness of the *d'Artagnan*'s common room, Ariane listened for the sounds of his presence.

She might as well have been alone, on her way to the last stop on her itinerary. Before Agora. Before going to Wynn, who would be leaving Espérance soon to meet her at the League station.

Wynn and Espérance seemed a lifetime away. Ariane got up from the padded chair against the bulkhead and paced the length of the deck. A mug of *café* lay untouched and rapidly cooling on the sideboard.

Steady red warning lights glowed on the forward air lock hatch as Ariane reached the end of the cabin. Outside, visible through the porthole, a barren world of the Mailloux system spun in blackness. Eight hours they'd be here until they jumped again; eight more hours of desperate planning. Of waiting.

Eight hours to face and overcome her frightening weakness.

He was in the guest cabin, hatch sealed. He had never spoken to her again after those last contemptuous words beyond a terse command to web herself in before the jump; immediately afterward he had left her, free to go where she would.

Think, she told herself for the thousandth time.

The ship's small weapons locker was barred against her, and he had control of every part of the ship that mattered. He believed she could do nothing, that she was helpless to resist him.

Staring blindly out the air-lock porthole, Ariane wrapped her arms around herself. It was *his* arms she felt, holding her close, his hard, masculine body; his sudden vulnerability, his pain.

She could feel him even now.

Ariane turned on her heel and paced back in the opposite direction, clenching her fists behind her. Perhaps Rook Galloway was right. She had never felt such contempt for herself.

Weakness. Cowardice. Grand-père would be ashamed.

She stopped to stare at the light dueling sabers hung on the wall. Three years ago she had negotiated with her great-grandfather for a few years of adventure before a lifetime of duty. Once she'd dreamed of the stars, worlds beyond Espérance, freedom a woman of the Elite could never know.

Two days ago she'd believed the adventures were almost at an end.

Now you have more than you can handle, she thought grimly. There had to be a way to stop Rook Galloway from carrying out his plans to use her as a hostage against her family. If those plans held, now that he knew about his people.

But the *d'Artagnan* was still headed for Espérance. She imagined Grand-père's reaction when he learned what had happened to her. He was no longer young. If it weren't for the precious longevity drugs manufactured by Wynn's family . . .

Wynn. Ariane bit her lip. She'd known Wynn all her life. Now, for the first time, Ariane doubted her knowledge of the man to whom she was promised. She was to come to Wynn untouched, her honor unstained. She would bring to the alliance a name that went back to the first colonists on Espérance, as he would bring his family's fortune and the business acumen that had won the Slaytons' Elite status and had helped build the Marchand empire. Their children would inherit the influence and wealth to carry out Grand-père's dreams for the future—as Jacques's children would have done had he survived.

The Marchand name was above reproach. That she, Ariane Burke-Marchand, should be held for ransom was unthinkable, a gross dishonor to her family. That it should be a Kalian criminal who held her . . .

She closed her eyes as she remembered what Rook had said about her family. How he had looked when she'd told him the fate of his people.

And she remembered his arms going around her, holding her with the desperation of a man who has lost everything, reaching for the only comfort he can.

Even the comfort of a hated enemy.

Abruptly she strode over to the wall and released one of the sabers from the rack. She gripped the hilt until her knuckles whitened. She slashed recklessly at the air, falling automatically into the warm-up patterns she knew as well as her own heartbeat.

"Coward," she said under her breath as she executed a practice lunge. "Are you so lost to honor? Have you forgotten who you are?" She spun and stabbed viciously at an unseen opponent. "He's a Kalian traitor, a savage. You are Marchand. You have no choice but to stop him by any means necessary—"

"Then kill me, Lady Ariane."

She pivoted as Rook came out of the darkness, drifting as silently as a shadowcat.

"Kill me," he repeated softly. Copper eyes glittered as they caught the dim light. His gaze dropped to the saber held loosely in her hand, and he smiled.

Ariane regarded him warily, every muscle taut and ready for battle. His challenge was a taunt; the hard planes of his face might have been carved of diamarble. His eyes held no expression at all.

He moved closer with natural grace. The stolen guard's uniform shirt had been abandoned; the trousers molded the long, lean muscles of his legs. Her gaze moved down to his bare feet and up again to the ridged muscles of his abdomen, his chest with its dusting of dark hair, his powerful shoulders.

He was beautiful, beautiful as a dangerous animal is beautiful. Ariane swallowed, struggling to control the wild beating of her heart.

There were scars on his body—scars that made him look almost human. The Kalians had always been known for their almost miraculous powers of self-healing, for bodies that resisted damage that would kill an ordinary man or woman.

He bore the scars, but he didn't fear the saber in her hand. Her fingers tightened on the hilt.

Another gliding step carried him forward, and he spread his hands. "You have the weapon, Lady Ariane. I am unarmed."

He still mocked her, though the smile was gone. *Enemy,* she cried to herself. "Unarmed?" she said between gritted teeth. "The Kalians in the Warren were unarmed, against trained gendarmes." She lifted her chin. "If you wish to kill me, I would die with honor. The other saber is there—"

His eyes changed, and she shivered at the hostility in them. "Kill *you,* Lady Ariane? No. You and your ship are far too valuable."

There was no emotion in his voice. None at all. Ariane took a single step back, widening the space between them.

"You have nothing to buy," she said softly. "Nothing to gain. My family's honor will never permit—"

"Honor is irrelevant," he said in that same dead voice, "as your Patriarch will learn soon enough."

In spite of his stillness she felt the leashed violence in his body, jumping like a current across the small space that separated them. Her attention riveted on Rook's alien copper eyes.

For the first time she noticed the splash of red streaked across his forehead above the black brows. The mark of the Hawks, those who had led the Warren rebellion.

The saber trembled in her hand. "Whatever you plan can't succeed, Kalian." Her face set into an arrogant mask; it seemed that some other woman spoke, a woman too desperate for compassion. Or doubt. "We knew of your strength and cunning. We knew you were no longer human when we took you from your dying world. But in the end, you could never adapt to civilization. You were brought down by your own savagery."

Rook's hands clenched at his sides. Only his eyes were alive. Alive and burning like banked flames.

"You believe the lies of your own people," he said. Abruptly he set his back to her, walked to the bulkhead, and took down the second saber. He grasped the hilt in one hand and the bare blade in the other.

"This savage," he continued softly, "had the great privilege of learning civilized ways. He learned how to serve those who called themselves his benefactors. And he discovered that even the refined Elite of Espérance understand revenge."

"Revenge," she echoed. Rook turned to face her again. With studied deliberation, his eyes on hers, he drew the cutting edge of the saber across the bare palm of his hand. Bright blood welled in the deep cut. Ariane watched it drip slowly to the deck.

"There was a time when Espérancians made war on each other, on their own kind—like savages. And then they adopted their codes of honor so that dealing death became a thing of art. Civilized." Rook planted the tip of the saber on the deck and drew it through the pooled blood. "The Elite made a life's work of carrying on their vendettas under the guise of honor. And honor became a flexible thing to be discarded at whim."

Held mute by the power of his deep voice and the hard knot in her throat, Ariane watched him trace a pattern in red.

"Revenge is not merely the province of savages," he said. "But a savage has no need to claim false standards of honor. What price for the death of a people, Lady Ariane?"

The clatter of the saber was loud in the silence as he dropped it.

Ariane closed her eyes. *Revenge.* Oh, yes, she understood revenge. Her marriage to Wynn was intended to seal the fifty-year truce of two families who had fought bitterly for generations. No Elite ever forgot a wrong, or dishonor. Until the League had come a century before, more Elite lives had been lost in duels than from any other cause.

She understood revenge. She knew the rules by which her own people carried it out.

But Rook was a Kalian. For him there would be no rules.

For him there would be only the taste of bitter loss and carefully nurtured hatred.

Sucking in a deep breath, she let her own saber drop to the deck.

"It won't bring them back," she whispered. Her eyes dropped to the pulse beating in the hollow of his neck. "You'll spend your own life for no purpose—"

"No purpose?" he grated. "For a thousand years your kind has found purpose enough in revenge. You care nothing for how I spend my life. But you fear for yourself, Lady Ariane. For yourself and your family and your so-called honor."

Ariane's gaze snapped back to his, and Rook closed his eyes to shut her out. The sight of her repelled and drew him, tore him apart. In Ariane Burke-Marchand he saw his lost people and his hated enemies as if they were one, a mingling of Kalian and Marchand, oppressed and oppressor.

But his people were gone. Unless she lied—and he knew beyond understanding that in this one thing she had not—he was the last Kalian in existence.

The last. The last, the only one left to see that the Marchand paid in full.

His foot caught the saber where it lay and sent it skidding across the common-room deck. He opened his eyes and followed the flash of metal as it spun in the faint red glow of the air-lock lights.

The blade came to rest against the bulkhead, as impotent as his resolve. He could have kept to his cabin or confined her to the other, held her away until the time came to make use of her. A few days of solitude, of waiting, secure in his triumph. He could have ignored her if he hadn't learned the truth. If she hadn't told him about his people, weakened him with her unexpected compassion. If he hadn't held her in his arms for one brief moment . . .

His hand ached, and he closed his fingers over the wound. In his cabin he'd felt her presence, haunting his memory, drawing him out to confront her again. Why had she told him of the fate of his people? Why had she risked herself against his bleak and bitter rage?

For he raged. At himself, for surviving when his people were dead; at the boy he had been, for trusting the Marchand—and at her, because she was everything he should hate.

But he could not hate her.

He raised his eyes to hers. Her chin was lifted, her dark eyes vivid with defiance, but her chest rose and fell rapidly under her loose-fitting shipsuit. The shape of her body was imprinted on his: thigh and hip, the curve of waist and breast. The smell of her was still in his nostrils—the heady scent of her hair and skin when he'd held her. Held his enemy because there was no one else, and he was alone.

Even now he could want her.

He grasped the weakness in his soul as if it were a rotworm coiled in his gut, crushing it until he could look at her and feel nothing at all.

"You have reason to fear, Lady Ariane," he said deliberately. "In your Code of Vendetta there are no rules to limit the vengeance earned by genocide."

Her eyes widened in horror, nothing feigned or false or arrogant in the look she gave him.

"Genocide?" she gasped. "No! No, you're wrong." She took a step toward him. "We never hurt your people. We did everything we could to help them. Everything, even after the riots. Your people were—"

"What did you know of my people, Marchand?" Inevitably he touched her, lifting his hand to catch her jaw. Cool skin soothed the slash on his palm. "What did you know of Kali in the days before your Elite ship landed on our world?"

For a moment he drifted back, into the last time of Sharing, when his people had still remembered the art. When he had been a boy in the Warren. The Elders had Shared with those who had never seen Kali: the hunt, the harvest, the harsh shift of the seasons, the oneness with the flesh of the earth, the acceptance of life and death. The legacy the mysterious Shapers had bequeathed to dying colonists from a long-lost world called Earth.

The eldest of the Elders could still recall the original Changing. Kali had never been intended as a colony world, fit to hold human life. When the lost colonists had crashed on Kali, they had faced certain death—until the Shapers had come. The benevolent aliens had molded the colonists to fit a world never meant for humankind. Made them stronger, to survive; faster, to hunt and flee; quick to heal, to adapt, to learn. And gave them the Sharing, so that they might always know who they were. A new people free on their own world.

Until that world had been lost forever.

"What did you know of us?" he murmured. And Ariane made some sound that brought him out of the past, an answer he silenced with his thumb on her lips.

"We were never welcome on your world," he continued grimly, "even though we'd brought an end to your war with the Fahar. Did we become an inconvenience to you, so many years after the end of the Conflict? A blight on your family name in the eyes of all Espérance and the Elite? An expense too great to bear? Or was it simply what we were that you feared? *Changed*—no longer human. Superior." He smiled. "Superior but uneducated. Simple. Easily led into a trap."

Ariane jerked her chin free of his grasp. "Trap?" she repeated incredulously. "There was no trap. Your people turned on us—rioted without cause, burned and destroyed their own homes, and then carried the violence out of the Warren." Her voice shook. "People were killed. My brother—he was trying to help you. Why? After all we did to help your people, why did they destroy themselves? What possible reason—"

"Reason?" Rook clenched his fists, struggling with violent emotion. "Is it reason enough to rebel when your people disappear, are harassed and beaten, taken from their homes—even children—in the dead of night by Marchand guardsmen? Is it reason enough to refuse to go quietly into the grave?"

"Marchand guardsmen—" she echoed. "You're insane.

No one was taken away. You were under Marchand protection—"

Rook spun away before she could see his face. "Marchand protection, like Marchand honor. Do you remember that day, little Ariane? A woman—" He swallowed, thinking of Sable. Dead, like the others. "A woman tried to tell me what was happening. She tried to warn me, and I refused to believe. Until I saw your gendarmes attacking my people. Until I saw the travesty of justice after the trial. Until I was sent to Tantalus."

In the silence that followed he could almost hear the beat of her heart.

"It never happened," she said at last, hardly above a whisper. "My—the Patriarch wanted to give your people a chance—to get out of the Warren, earn a new place, perhaps a new world. He trusted you. He believed you could be productive, that your abilities could serve Espérance—" She broke off, and her words gained strength. "You're wrong. Terribly wrong. There was no trap. Even in the end the Patriarch tried to help you, sending your people to the League, releasing them from the internment camp. They were to be free."

With legs that felt leaden Rook walked across the cabin, passing Ariane without a glance, until he stood at the air-lock porthole. The unnamed world below was as cold and empty as his heart.

"Free to die. Your family's burden lifted at last."

Her protest was sharp and immediate. Rook twisted his hands behind his back.

She believed her denials, of that he was certain. It would have been far easier to consign her to that dark prison of hatred that he reserved for the Marchand if she had been a part of the treachery against his people. If she were as guilty as her grandfather.

But she was not entirely innocent. *Not innocent,* he reminded himself. No Marchand, no Elite, no Espérancian could ever be that.

She, too, would suffer.

"I never told you who killed your brother, Ariane," he said quietly. "The gendarme who aimed his disruptor at Jacques was like any other, and I never knew who gave the order. The *magistrats* weren't interested in anything an accused Kalian had to say."

His fingers clenched against each other until they threatened to snap. "I never understood why one of your people would want the Marchand heir dead. But your Patriarch was never interested in the truth. Perhaps that was all part of the plan to cover your brother's murder."

Ariane had thought she was beyond shock, beyond outrage. She stared at Rook's tense back, struggling to find a response, any response, to this last and most odious charge. *He didn't kill Jacques,* she reminded herself as she caught her breath. But what he suggested was beyond comprehension.

"You're insane," she gasped. "So filled with hatred that you'd believe—" She broke off, remembering their conversation on Tantalus. *No accident,* he'd said. Of course he believed, as he believed all those other things he'd said about her family. He had convinced himself that he and his people had been the victims of some bizarre plot.

He would never listen to reason. She knew that, as she knew his certainty of Marchand guilt would make him even more deadly. But she fought her pulse down from its wild tempo and forced herself to try one last time.

"No," she said, matching the implacability of his tone. "No. My great-grandfather—no member of my family would have hurt Jacques for any reason."

Rook turned to face her again. He searched her eyes, looking for signs of weakness. Of doubt.

"Someone wanted your brother dead," he said, "or wanted to see that a Kalian took the blame. Does it surprise you that your Elite would turn to the old ways to eliminate an obstacle?"

Ariane flinched. The hiring of assassins had been outlawed fifty years before the coming of the League; most Elite looked back on it with public contempt.

"I was there," she said hoarsely. "I saw what happened—"

Twisting his mouth into a smile, Rook touched the scar that ran from eyebrow to jaw. "Did you, Lady Ariane? Keep your belief in my guilt if it pleases you. Perhaps it will give you comfort in the days to come."

He was the first to look away, brushing by her again before she could summon a reply. Ariane stood and stared at the saber near her feet and wondered if she could reach it in time.

At that moment she hated him. She could have taken the blade and run him through, ridding her family of a deadly threat and herself of doubt and confusion and fear.

"Are you ready to beg, Marchand?" Rook asked.

Her head snapped up. He was mocking, mocking, watching her with those alien eyes from across the cabin.

"Will you beg me to have mercy, Ariane?" he repeated, her name sliding from his tongue with a strange and terrible intimacy. "What would you do to spare your family my vengeance?"

Rage blinded Ariane; her muscles bunched to hurl herself at him, to claw at his eyes, to do whatever damage she could before he took her down.

She dropped her eyes as she struggled to bring herself under control. *Think.*

Kalian that he was, he must have a weakness. A weakness she could exploit. Attempting to reason with him had failed, as it must always fail with a savage. She knew the limits of her own strength against a Kalian.

Her ship was in his hands. With the computer programmed to accept only his commands, she couldn't hope to take it back. Unless . . .

Her heart skipped a beat and began to hammer. *Of course.*

Slowly she raised her eyes to his. The trembling she'd worked so hard to conceal claimed her body, and she let him see it—urged him to see it.

"Please . . . ," she whispered.

Rook stared at her as if he could see through her subterfuge. *Even Kalians can't read minds,* she thought grimly. She imagined what he would do if she failed to stop him, filling her mind with visions of ruin and death.

"Please," she repeated, walking toward him. Her legs quivered and threatened to give way. It was altogether too easy to let her eyes fill with tears. "I'll do anything. Don't hurt me—don't hurt my family." Slowly, painfully she dropped to her knees. "I'll beg—" She reached for his legs in a gesture of supplication.

He stepped back before she could touch him. Ariane looked up until she could see his face, the growing contempt in his eyes. His hard mouth curved into a bitter half smile. The deep, unexpected pain she felt in seeing it made her catch her breath.

But she needed his scorn, his twisted and misguided desire for revenge. Dropping her gaze, she let her muscles loosen, her body assume a stance of capitulation and despair.

Rook had to be stopped at any price. For the sake of honor, the marriage that must take place, her family's very existence . . .

He moved again, almost violently, powerful bare feet crossing her line of vision. She heard him pause behind her and return to stand over her. Metal flashed.

"Get up," he snarled. Hard hands bit into her shoulders; his touch was hotter than starfire. Ariane stared at the tendons that bunched and strained under the weathered skin of his neck and shoulders.

Cool metal grazed her fingers as Rook pushed the hilt of the abandoned saber into her loose hand. Instinctively she grasped it, and Rook's grunt of satisfaction forced her eyes back to his. He held her at arm's length.

"One last chance, Lady Ariane," he said, guiding her hand up until the tip of the saber rested against his bare chest. "One last chance to carry out Marchand justice."

Frozen, Ariane fixed her gaze on the dimple in the bronzed skin where the blade touched him. He released her hand, and the saber remained poised where he had placed it. Over his heart. Even a Kalian could not survive such a blow at close range.

"Strike," he urged. "Strike. I'll have no mercy, Lady Ariane. No more than your family had on my people."

No mercy. Ariane tightened her grip on the hilt, and the saber's tip scratched the surface of his skin. The beat of his heart throbbed against her hand, conducted through the metal. And he waited—still, mute, mocking her. Testing. Judging. Condemning.

With a gasp she stepped back and tossed the saber aside. He left her as silently as he had come.

CHAPTER FOUR

In his dreams she was naked, kneeling before him, her lush hair veiling too little of her body.

"Please," she said. "I'll do anything, anything at all." There was no sound, only the dead silence of space, but he watched the seductive movement of her lips, felt the feather-stroke of her hands on his thighs. He, too, was naked, and his arousal defied his control, challenging her, a duelist's implacable weapon.

And she smiled. "I'm not a child anymore," she said. Her hair drifted back from her face to reveal her firm, full breasts. "Don't you want me, Kalian?" The smile became mockery. "We're two of a kind."

No. He tried to move away, but her hands, with their beautiful aristocrat's fingers, closed around him.

"Yes," she said. "We're made for each other, you and I." She bared fine white teeth. "There is no one else, Kalian. Only me. . . ."

The emergency siren brought Rook up out of sleep and to his feet in one motion. For a moment he stood in the center of the cabin, the alarm ringing painfully in his ears, until he remembered where he was.

Ariane, he thought savagely, his arousal still straining against his trousers. He pivoted to scan the flashing red letters on the cabin's terminal screen.

He was moving again before the screen began to scroll out its catalog of disasters. The cabin door was sealed shut, and it took three attempts before the ship's computer would accept his manual override. He sucked in a deep breath and stepped out into the common room.

The bitter cold of space sank icy teeth into his bare skin as the cabin's air rushed past him in a cloud of frost. His body reacted instantly to vacuum, hoarding the supply of oxygen still in his lungs. His ears sang with pain as his body tried to adjust to the violent change in air pressure. Needles of ice stabbed at his eyes. Every part of him turned to the purpose for which the Shapers had molded his ancestors: survival.

Rook had no thought to spare for the changes in his body. Five minutes ago they'd been crossing the starless void of hyperspace, en route to the Hideyoshi system jump point. Now they were in real space, far too soon, and somewhere air-lock doors had opened into vacuum.

Vacuum that he could tolerate for a few brief minutes because of what he was. Vacuum that no ordinary human could withstand. . . .

Ariane. He ran across the common room, images of her lifeless body seared into his mind. Red emergency lights winked in the darkness like the eyes of scavengers.

His heart almost stopped when he found her, unmoving, sprawled on the carpeted deck. The closing cockpit hatch had caught her legs, pinning her down where she had fallen. Her hand was stretched for the oxygen masks just out of reach on the nearest bulkhead, grasping for her last hope of life.

She was only human.

Rook wrenched one of the masks from its holder. He dropped to the deck beside her, lifted her shoulders, and pressed the mask to her pale face, searching frantically for the beat of her heart.

She breathed—in a deep, shuddering breath.

Instantly he was on his feet again. The hatch that held Ariane trapped between cabins was jammed, unresponsive to manual override. Rook used his own strength to force it open the rest of the way, dropping quickly to catch her up in his arms. Her lips parted in a soundless moan.

He ran for his cabin, settled her on the recessed bunk, and tossed a blanket over her. He located the oxygen feed valve above the bunk and opened it all the way. A moment later he was in the common room again, the cabin door safely sealed behind him.

The dead silence of vacuum shattered with the return of the siren's wail. Air pressure increased as the ship's life-support systems began to work again, releasing precious oxygen. Rook double-checked the common room air lock and found it sealed; the two in the cargo hold in the stern of the ship were secure. The hull was unbreached, but something was very wrong.

Cursing softly, he ran for the cockpit and found the control board a chaotic display of glaring red and yellow lights. Within seconds he had assessed the most critical aspect of the emergency.

The *d'Artagnan* was heading right into a star.

Rook dropped into the pilot's seat and absorbed the image framed in the forward canopy. He could almost feel the blistering heat of the sun as the ship hurtled toward it, bent on self-immolation.

He sucked fresh oxygen into his lungs and grabbed the control stick. It was frozen in his grip. The *d'Artagnan*'s main computer had gone off-line, struggling to reboot after the catastrophic drop from hyperspace; the drive was out, and the sheer force of momentum propelled the ship inexorably forward. The navcomp displayed a frantic jumble of colors and symbols. Rook didn't need it to determine where the *d'Artagnan* was going.

Fiery hands of flame reached out from the star, big enough to swallow a world. "I haven't come this far to let you have me," Rook snarled. With one hand he found the lever that switched the attitude controls to manual mode and snapped it down, pulling harder on the control stick with the other.

Compressed gas jetted from the attitude rockets at the bow of the ship. Still the *d'Artagnan* hurtled for the star; Rook bore down on the stick with all his strength. At last the rockets responded with full thrust and the ship began to turn —slowly, by tiny, harrowing increments. Not enough.

Brilliant light engulfed the cockpit just as the canopy shields blocked the fatal vision from Rook's sight. The ship's sensors had already gone dead. Flying blind, Rook cursed and yanked on the stick one last time. The low rumble of the attitude rockets died as the last of the fuel was consumed.

It was over. Rook stared at the opaque canopy and waited

for the inferno. The temperature rose steadily, but he made no effort to wipe the sweat from his face. With luck Ariane would never regain full consciousness; she would never see the adamantium hull of the ship split open like a sailpod in Kalian summer, or feel the agony of searing death.

He tried to remember the Warren, all the people he had known there—his parents, long dead, Sable and Heron and the others; his years on Tolstoy; all the aspirations and hopes that had been buried on Tantalus. But it was Ariane's face that came back to him, brown eyes soft with pity, lips parted.

Ariane.

He closed his eyes, but oblivion slid out of his grasp. The ship shuddered; Rook felt the heat begin to recede a moment before he realized they were going to survive.

The canopy slid open to reveal the light of distant stars, gentle in velvet blackness.

His hands were shaking as he unclenched his fingers from the control stick. On the console a row of red lights faded to steady amber, and computer screens announced that the *d'Artagnan*'s main functions were back on-line. Rook shut off the emergency siren with a blow of his palm. Silence settled over the ship again, so profound that he could almost hear the song of the stars.

He initiated a damage-control survey, taking just enough time to note that the *d'Artagnan* was no longer in immediate danger. He let the ship drift and closed his eyes, the after-image of disaster burned into his eyelids.

One by one his muscles relaxed, his heartbeat steadied, all the finely tuned responses dropped into their normal pattern.

On Kali—or on Tantalus—"normal" meant that you'd survived another day.

His moment of peace was short-lived. The woman's face that had filled his thoughts in the duel with death was still before him.

Ariane. She might have died. A few more seconds exposed to vacuum would have done irreparable damage.

She might have died. . . .

"Is it over?"

Rook lunged up to face her where she stood with her hands braced against the back of the copilot's seat.

His first reaction was to take her, hold her, shake her until her teeth rattled. But he held himself back and locked his muscles, raking her with his gaze as he searched for any sign of hurt.

The oxygen mask was gone and her face was flushed, chin tilted up, jaw set under his inspection. Her body trembled— faint, almost undetectable shivers—and her eyes were very bright. Her hair was tangled, and there was a spreading bruise on one high cheekbone, but she might have suffered nothing worse than a bad night's sleep.

A sharp tremor worked its way from Rook's feet to the tips of his fingers. He let reaction take him, and fed it with anger. It was easy to let the rage come; the fearful joy he felt at seeing her safe was deadly.

Ariane moistened her lips and leaned forward over the chair back. "Is she badly damaged?" she asked softly, her eyes flickering past him to the control board.

The corner of Rook's mouth lifted, and he stared at her in silence until her eyes were drawn back to his.

Defeated. He'd thought her defeated, and she'd played the part so well that he'd badly underestimated her. He'd left her free—free to try a desperate ploy when his back was turned.

"If your objective was to kill yourself and take me down with you," he said harshly, "you nearly succeeded."

She licked her lips, the first betrayal of unease. "I didn't expect—"

"What did you expect? You pulled the ship out of hyperspace in midjump—a bold plan, if your intention was to seal yourself in the cockpit and open all the air locks." He took a step toward her, and she stiffened. "Even a Kalian can't breathe vacuum. It might have worked if the hatch hadn't jammed."

Her eyes widened, and an answering spark of anger made them catch fire. "You believe I'd go so far just to kill you?" Her expression changed slowly, until the bitterness in it mirrored his. "Of course you believe it. You believe my family's

driving purpose was to destroy your people! You think I—"
She broke off, blinking rapidly.

They stared at each other. A readout on the console
changed, indicating that life support had returned to full normal.

Clenching his teeth, Rook turned back to the console,
touching a red-banded lever set off from the other controls.
The hyperspace shunt had been designed as a last resort for a
starship trapped in hyperspace; only a few ships had been
known to use it and survive. He'd barred Ariane from the
ship's computer, but access to the computer wasn't necessary
to activate the hyperspace shunt—only a powerful measure of
suicidal desperation.

"You flushed the system," he said, "in midjump. Did you
think you'd have time to reboot the computer and take control, even if you survived the drop out of hyperspace?"

She swallowed. "You left me no choice. It was a calculated
risk—"

"Calculated risk? You planned so well that you weren't
even prepared when the air-lock and cockpit doors malfunctioned." Rook forced the image of her limp body from his
mind. "You little fool—"

"This is my ship." Both her fists were clenched on the
chair back, and her eyes were lambent. "Did you think I'd
simply crawl into a hole and let you have her, destroy my
honor and threaten my family?"

The harsh sounds of their breathing dueled in the silence.
"No," he said slowly, aware of a strange exultation within
himself, eclipsing the anger.

He had felt no triumph when he'd thought her defeated,
even when she had refused to turn her saber against him. Was
he mad enough to encourage her defiance, admire her resistance?

Mad enough to want her . . .

Abruptly he turned back to the controls, driving the dangerous ambiguity from his mind with hard calculations. "You
almost had me convinced," he said tonelessly. "Too bad your

ruse failed, Lady Ariane. The ship is still in my hands, and the delay you've won changes nothing."

He heard and felt her move closer. Too close. "Why did you save my life when you could have let me die? You could have had your vengeance. My great-grand—the Patriarch would have—" Her breath shuddered. "I'm his only direct heir. You could have destroyed us both with one blow—"

He rounded on her. "Are you so ready to die for your precious honor?"

She held her ground. "No one wants to die," she whispered. "But I'll do what I must to save my family."

Rook was the first to look away. The haunting visions of his dream came back in a rush; Ariane at his feet, offering herself. His body tightened painfully. "There's nothing you can do," he said between his teeth. "I won't make the same mistake again."

Her breath caught, and he thought she would retreat at last. But she stood very still, as calm and composed as an Elder.

"You didn't answer my question," she said. "You could have let me die, and instead you saved my life."

His skin shivered at her nearness. "Don't deceive yourself, Lady Ariane." He moved suddenly to catch her wrist in his hand. "You're worth much more to me alive. You and your ship."

"Of course," she murmured. Some trick of the cockpit lighting misted her eyes. He expected her to struggle, but she only flexed her fingers in his grip and gave him the full measure of her Marchand pride. "But your motives are irrelevant. I owe you my life."

"As your family owed my people their lives fifty years ago, on Kali?" he said, mocking her as he propelled her away from the console and across the cabin. "As your world owed my people for the end to war with the Fahar?" She stumbled as they reached the cockpit hatch, and he caught her against him.

By the Shapers. Rook spent several seconds imposing control on the chaos her nearness created in his body. Ariane stiffened and then went pliant in his arms, her face averted.

"I'd almost forgotten Marchand cunning, Lady Ariane," he said, jerking away and pulling her toward the cabins adjacent to the common room. "You won't have another chance to use it."

It wasn't until they reached the door to her cabin that she resisted, stiffening her legs so that he dragged her the last few steps. "No!" she said sharply. "No."

Her surprising strength and the alarm in her voice stopped him. Fear, real fear she couldn't hide; he felt it so clearly that he wondered how he could have been persuaded by her false display in the common room the night before. He let go of her wrist and she snapped it back, folding her arms across her chest.

"No," she repeated, her eyes locked on his. "I won't try to take the ship again. I know my word means nothing to you. But I owe you my life, and I will repay that debt."

Rook wanted to laugh in her proud Marchand face, but the sound locked in his throat. As if the ship's gravs had malfunctioned, he felt disoriented, no longer anchored to the certainties that had driven him for eight years.

And then she unfolded her arms and touched him, grounding him again. "I never intended to kill you. And if it means anything, anything at all—I know you didn't kill my brother," she said, her voice catching.

The calm admission checked him as her defiance had never done. He understood the barriers that must stand between them, the barriers he desperately needed. With one quiet statement—with one touch—she had breached those barriers, twisted the rules and shattered his assumptions.

He looked at her, bereft of answers. The dream returned, but this time Ariane held no mockery in her eyes. No enemy met his gaze now—no lying, treacherous Marchand, but a woman. A woman impossible to resist.

Instinct guided his hands to return her touch, and control vanished. His arms moved like separate entities to pull her against him. Ariane swayed and flowed into him, into an emptiness he recognized only as she filled it. He lost himself in sensation: the scent of a woman's body; the feel of his own unshackled and whole and alive; warmth; the sweet ache that began at the root of his belly and spread with every beat of his heart.

On Tantalus there had been only pain, endless days of heat and nights that were never long enough. Here was the absence of pain, a completion, the echo of something he remembered feeling as a child among his own people in the Warren.

Rook let himself forget who she was, let himself imagine for a moment that he shared the ship with a Kalian woman.

Thoughts rose unbidden in his mind, images he had no will to suppress. His fingers spread across her back, caressed the warm skin of her neck and the thick cascade of rich brown hair that fell loose over her shoulders. He closed his eyes, let himself do nothing but feel, granting himself the luxury of desire.

Her lips were parted and ready when he lowered his mouth to claim her.

Surrender was such an easy thing. Ariane gave herself up to Rook's kiss, and her body came alive in his arms.

It was more than mere defiance of the void that had almost taken her, more than gratitude or guilt or the need for simple human comfort.

She was not a complete innocent. She knew how to meet Rook's lips with her own. But that was the sum of her experience, and it was not nearly enough.

Power enveloped her—masculine, alien hunger that called a response from deep within herself. Something forbidden stirred in her own soul. Rook's hands burned a path along her back through the soft fabric of her shipsuit, tangled in her hair, cupped her jaw, held her still as he deepened the kiss.

Her own hands moved to hold him, feeling the rough and smooth textures of his bare skin. Her fingers traced scars on his back and shoulders and curled over hard muscle; he moaned softly against her mouth.

For the barest instant her hands stilled. The memory of Wynn's last kiss, three years ago, swept into her mind. She had not held her betrothed then as she held Rook now. Wynn had kissed her, and she had submitted to him as she must to her future husband. She knew her duty, and there had been nothing unpleasant in Wynn's restrained caresses.

But this was submission of a different kind. She had never known passion, this blind emotion that overwhelmed her body and submerged her will. She had never felt this melting weakness in Wynn's familiar arms.

The love she'd believed she felt for Rook Galloway eight years ago had been a child's innocent delusion.

There was no innocence in this. And she didn't care, didn't fight the heady freedom of newly awakened hunger. No part of her will remained to stand against Rook's sensual assault.

Rook urged her lips apart with his own; her fingernails dug into the skin of his upper arms as his tongue slipped inside her. Sensation like a spear of light stabbed downward from his penetration to a place of gathering heat between her thighs. She knew what it was, what her body yearned for with all the drive of instinct, but that knowledge could not slow the force that overwhelmed her.

Pulling her harder against him, Rook explored her mouth and conquered it, giving no quarter. The ache low in her body grew almost unbearable.

Yes. Ariane felt her hips move, thrust against his unyielding strength, wanting. Wanting, demanding as he demanded, accepting his invasion.

Darkness enveloped her, darkness that seethed with the heat of a thousand suns waiting to be born. Liquid heat that gathered where her hips and thighs touched him, and where his mouth moved on hers. Desire, unfamiliar and potent and uncontrollable.

His thumbs rested under her cheekbones and his callused fingers worked into the hair at the base of her neck, forming a cage from which she could not escape. The heavy coarseness of his black mane brushed her brows, her eyelids. She met his tongue with her own, and the shock of that touch drew a moan from her throat.

The moan of a creature of sheer sensation, devoid of intellect. The cry of an animal in heat. The abandon of a savage.

Ariane Burke-Marchand remembered who she was.

A woman of the Espérancian Elite held in the arms of a Kalian. The great-granddaughter of the Marchand Patriarch yielding to a deadly enemy. The betrothed of the heir of the Slaytons lost to all honor and reason.

"No," she gasped. Rook grunted in protest as she clamped her lips together and wrenched her face aside. His mouth was hot on her cheek, her chin, her neck; his hands dropped to lock about her waist. "No!"

Panic engulfed the last of her desire. Ariane set her strength against his and knew herself trapped. She clawed at his shoulders, tensed every muscle in her body and pushed, yet he held her with no effort at all. She wedged her hands between them, palms flat against his chest. His heart beat like a drum, sounding the rhythm to some wild Kalian dance of power and lust and need.

"Let me go!" she cried hoarsely, and when his mouth brushed hers again, she caught his lower lip between her teeth.

His grunt of startled pain gave her all the encouragement she needed. She threw her weight behind her arms and thrust him away, using the bulkhead for leverage. Confusion flashed in his copper eyes, the dazed expression of a man waking from a dream. Fragile vulnerability shattered as her open palm cracked against his cheek.

Shock sliced through her, mirrored in his face. Ariane tensed to run, but his hands caught her again, adamantium bands about her wrists. His breath came harsh as the bitter twist returned to his mouth.

"So," he said, with dangerous softness. "There are limits to your willingness to pay your debts."

Ariane gasped and closed her eyes. Comprehension—bone deep, soul deep—had come to her with that kiss, knowledge she hadn't sought burned into her body.

She felt the shadow of the girl she had been, infatuated with the alien and the forbidden; the woman she was, bound by honor and duty; the woman she might become.

She felt the echo of his desire, his aloneness, his need to seek the renewal of life in the face of death. And she was afraid beyond any fear she had ever known.

I am Marchand, she cried silently, and clung to that unalterable fact. *He is—he must be—my enemy.*

He saved my life. . . .

She'd nearly got them both killed, and he'd saved her life. And when he'd rounded on her in the cockpit, his angry words had held more than condemnation.

He'd been afraid. For her. *"Are you so ready to die for your precious honor?"*

Impossible, and yet she knew it was true. His rage had been as much for himself as for her. She remembered his quiet answer when she'd demanded if he expected her to tamely submit to his plans of vengeance.

"No."

Mon Dieu. Ariane fought desperately to keep her confusion from her face.

He was Kalian, a man who wanted to destroy her family. But she owed him a debt, and his bitter words, his unthinkable accusations of betrayal, were whips that drove her to repay that debt.

As his touch drove her to madness. . . .

When she opened her eyes, his own were focused on something beyond her sight. Empty. She flexed her hands, and his grip loosened just enough to relieve the pressure.

"What would you have of me, Kalian?" she asked calmly. "I am your hostage. Will you accept my word?"

His eyes came back to hers. There was nothing human in them at all. "What word? That you'll give up all thoughts of resistance? Let me take my vengeance?"

Ariane pushed her anger and fear deep where it could not touch her. "My word that I won't try to take the ship again." Something in his gaze loosened her tongue. "I'll promise nothing else."

Rook smiled that familiar half-mocking smile. "Honesty from a Marchand?" he asked. "I'm almost tempted to believe you."

Before she could protest, he lifted her arms high against the bulkhead and held her there while his mouth covered hers again. He used it as a weapon, without gentleness, sharp and hard and blessedly brief.

"Partial payment of your debt," he said. Abruptly he let her go. "As for the rest—perhaps I'll test your honor, Lady Ariane. You won't have another chance at the ship, in any case."

Beyond any response, Ariane clenched her fists and half raised them, feeling the heat rush to her face when his gaze took in her futile gesture of defiance.

"I have work to do, Lady Ariane," he said. "With any luck I'll be able to find out where we are. One way or another, we're going home." He turned his back on her then, leaving her free at the door to her cabin.

Home.

She stood there against the bulkhead and trembled, tasting the bitterness of defeat.

It isn't over, she told him silently, watching the powerful muscles of his back and arms flow with his long stride. Her hand lifted to reach out to him, and she snapped it back. *The duel is just beginning. And I have no choice but to win.*

As if he heard her thoughts, he turned again at the cockpit hatch. "Remember one thing, Ariane," he said softly. "You are mine."

Ariane groped blindly for the cabin's IDlock and let herself through, shutting out the sight of him. She leaned against the hatch, her eyes taking in the cramped, familiar sanctuary of her cabin.

This was the only part of her ship he hadn't claimed. Ariane smiled grimly to herself, doubtful that he'd deliberately respect her privacy—he could come in any time he chose. She had no defenses against him.

You are mine.

She unclenched her fists slowly. The cabin looked bare

without the holopics she'd always kept on the desk next to the computer terminal, though the Anubian tapestry above her bunk and the intricate ghostwood sculptures from Nirvana had been left in their accustomed places.

Instinct had led her to hide the holopics the moment she'd been free to do so. The 'pic of Jacques was harmless, and she doubted that Grand-père's image would provoke Rook any further. But Wynn— Ariane glanced uneasily over her shoulder and knelt to open the locker at the foot of her bunk. She shifted the old-style books and litdisks, lifting the holopic of her affianced husband.

Wynn was smiling in the picture—handsome, only a trace of gray at his temples. The longevity drugs that had made his family's fortune gave him the appearance of a man much younger than his fifty-three years.

Ariane brushed her fingers across the holopic. She'd known Wynn all her life, trusted him and admired him. Love was not necessary; Grand-père had assured her of that.

Wynn cared for her. He'd bounced her on his knee when she'd been a babe, brought her sweets as a child. When Jacques had died, he'd begun to treat her with gallant courtesy as befit a high-bred young woman. He had given her a respectful, affectionate courtship, even after the betrothal vows had been made.

And he wanted her. She shivered, remembering his last good-bye. He had kissed her, gently but with the certainty of possession. For the first time she recognized the promise that had lain behind Wynn's kiss. Rook had taught her in one blinding instant.

Wynn wanted her, and he would never doubt that she was his—would be his in every way. But his kiss had not stirred her; even then her innocence had remained unsullied.

Until the moment she had nearly betrayed him in Rook's arms.

Ariane replaced the holopic carefully, covering it again. Something primitive had stirred to life in her with Rook's kiss, refusing to be banished. Something primitive that recognized that she was a prize to be won, to be fought over by two dominant males who would stop at nothing to have her.

Rook and Wynn. Savage and gentleman, enemy and trusted friend, captor and husband-to-be.

There could be no question about her loyalties. She had been Wynn's from the moment the contract was signed.

No question at all.

She bit her lip and got up, longing to feel a saber in her hand. A hard duel with a skilled opponent—that was what she craved, what she needed. A conflict in which the rules were clear and simple.

I won't give up, Wynn, she promised silently. *I'll come to you in all honor, and be the wife I swore to be.* She closed her eyes. *I'll learn to love you. . . .*

But the promises rang empty.

When she lay down on her bunk and tried to sleep, it was the vivid memory of Rook's kiss and his final words that carried her into the escape of dreams.

Release came with satisfying intensity. Wynn rolled away from the woman beneath him and stretched sensually.

Her fingers feathered a caress along his thigh and came to rest on his belly. "Satisfied?" she purred.

Wynn trapped her roving hand under his. "More than satisfied, *minette.*" It amused him to call her "kitten"—tame enough to be eating out of his hand, a jungle cat broken to the collar.

Sable stretched in a gesture that mirrored his, her black cloud of hair fanning out over the pillows. "I wouldn't like to believe you were thinking of *her,*" she said lightly. Her copper eyes fixed on his face.

Wynn smiled. Sable seldom admitted her jealousy of his promised bride. Now, so close to the time when he would meet Ariane to bring her home, when his plans were so close to fruition, she had begun to worry.

"I've told you before, *minette,*" he said lazily. "I care nothing for the child."

Sharp-nailed fingers moved with the speed of a striking

lamia to trap his manhood. The pressure she exerted was almost pleasurable. "You wouldn't lie to me, Wynn. . . ."

He went very still and turned slowly to face her. "Don't forget who and what you are, Sable," he said softly. "Don't presume to threaten me."

Her eyes widened, never leaving his. Her touch on him loosened and withdrew. With a soundless whimper she drew into herself, folding her arms across her breasts.

Wynn relaxed. She could still test him like this; her will was never entirely lost, that inner fire that had first drawn him to her. A little freedom made her an exciting bed partner, an amusing distraction. But he could never let her escape his control.

He rested his weight on one elbow and stroked her soft skin from hip to shoulder, again and again, soothing her until she began to unfold. Her eyes grew hooded, dark lashes sweeping down in contentment.

"Don't worry, lovely Sable," he said. "You'll have your part, just as I promised. And we'll both have our revenge."

All but purring, Sable drifted into untroubled sleep. For a moment Wynn watched her, his hand still on her hip.

Lovely Sable. She'd been the key from the very beginning. He still remembered vividly that day twelve years ago when he'd caught her picking his pocket in the old Lumière marketplace. She'd known well enough the penalties that faced a Kalian thief, especially one who chose the Elite as her prey. And he'd been *commissaire* of the Gendarmerie.

Even so, she'd resisted his bargain at first. He'd meant it as a simple diversion, because she was pretty in a savage way, and he had come to find his string of Elite and upper-caste mistresses tedious. He smiled at the memory of her fierce hellcat's face. She'd very nearly spit in his.

But she'd gone with him in the end, back to his mansion on the Rue d'Or, deep in the bastion of the Elite. Her strange eyes had gone wide at the luxury and splendor, and he'd felt a tenderness that he'd long since ceased to question.

He'd intended only to calm her down with the dose of Euphorie. The drug was technically illegal, but the *magistrats* closed their eyes to the trade; a few bribes, a few threats were enough. And Euphorie was one of thousands of drugs, legal and illegal, that had made the Slayton fortune and bought their way into the Elite caste.

Euphorie acted on ordinary humans as a powerful hallucinogen; when he'd slipped Sable a dose in the drink he'd given her, her reaction had been astounding.

The hellcat had become a kitten in his arms, pliant, responding with abandon to every whispered suggestion. It hadn't taken long for him to understand the connection.

And so had begun the experimentation—casual at first, until he was certain that Sable was under his complete control with regular dosages of the drug. It was a small step from there to "acquiring" other Kalians and having them brought to his personal laboratory; the jails of Lumière provided a steady supply at first. Later he'd found other methods.

No one bothered to question the disappearance of a few savages. Not even their supposed benefactor, Bernard Marchand.

And he learned that what worked for Sable worked for all Kalians. The inmates of the Warren, so feared and despised by the populace of Espérance, could be tamed. The very changes that made them more than human made them vulnerable to Euphorie in a way no human could ever be.

They were the perfect puppets. And more. Some of them—a rare few—were human chameleons. They could take on the appearance of anyone they chose. They were ideal agents to be programmed and planted wherever he wanted eyes and ears among the Elite—or, if need be, a swift blade to remove an inconvenience. Obedient, discreet, and undetectable as no human operative—or assassin—could ever be.

The day his Kalian mistress had told him of her hatred of the Marchand was the day he had begun to form his plans.

Wynn rolled across the bed and got to his feet, padding to his desk terminal. A quick scan of the new data assured him that all was proceeding more smoothly than even he could have hoped.

Once or twice he had wondered what Sable would do if she ever learned the truth. Not that she could; she was ignorant of his part in the riots, in Jacques's death and the condemnation of her people, and would remain so forever. She would continue to believe that his only goal had been to help her people—and to win the revenge they both sought.

Slipping into a clean suit, Wynn smiled. What would Bernard do if he knew that Ariane's father, the late husband of his late and beloved granddaughter Chantal, had raped a Kalian woman and sired a half-Kalian child? Pierre Burke-Marchand's marriage to Chantal Marchand had never been a love match, though Ariane and Jacques had proved that Chantal had done her duty.

Pierre might have had by-blows aplenty. But one of his bastards hated all the Marchand for the sins of one. Sable would never forgive the family of the man who had ruined her mother and left her to rot in the Warren. And so it all worked out admirably; Sable would have her revenge, though she would never know the extent of her part in the downfall of the Marchand.

Or what the cost had been to her people.

Any price, Wynn thought grimly. *Any price is worth it.* He moved back to the terminal and put in a call to the compound on the polar continent. When the time came, he'd have to be rid of most of the Kalians; their usefulness would be at an end once he had Ariane in his hands and was legal heir to Bernard Marchand—after he had made his final strike.

He looked back at Sable, and she stretched luxuriously under his gaze. *But I'll keep you, lovely Sable,* he promised silently.

Before his eyes she *Changed:* her hair lightened to lush brown, and her body altered subtly to that of another woman.

She opened her eyes—brown Marchand eyes—and smiled.

Ariane's smile.

Oh yes, he thought. *I'll keep you.*

Chapter Five

The distress beacon flashed on the main screen, a single set of characters and numbers repeating in a steady rhythm.

Ariane sat up in the copilot's seat and bit her lip. Instinctively she listened for Rook; he was asleep, or so she assumed, holed up in the guest cabin with the hatch sealed. The white-hot intensity of their last confrontation had evaporated like New London fog. Rook had avoided her scrupulously: no threats, no promises, little contact; leaving her free to roam at will. Accepting her word.

But his kiss still burned her lips. And she never believed for an instant that he'd abandoned his hunger for revenge.

The message scrolled across the screen for the hundredth time, and Ariane rose stiffly. Rook had left the cockpit shortly after they'd come out of jump; the coordinates he'd brought them to were only vaguely familiar to Ariane. The repairs he'd effected on the ship had made it necessary to make more stops, and this one wasn't on the regular route back to Espérance.

They were in little-known space here. Neutral space, near the border of Fahar territory.

The distress signal was not of human origin.

Setting her jaw, Ariane opened the commlink and buzzed the guest cabin. Her heart began to pound. For two days she'd hardly seen him. For two days she'd had the ship to herself, and Rook had been no more than an ominous shadow. . . .

"What do you want?" Rook stood in the hatchway, his hands curled around the edges, copper eyes fixed on her. There was nothing but unremitting hostility in his gaze.

He was bare-chested again, thick black hair pulled back loosely from his face. A fine sheen of sweat slicked the supple lines of his body. The red mark of the Hawks had faded from his forehead, but his stance proclaimed him a warrior far more than any symbol.

A warrior bent on destruction.

Ariane answered him with perfect calm. "We've picked up a distress beacon," she began, but he had already moved into the cockpit and past her, leaning over the console. His fingers flicked lightly over the controls.

"Fahar," he breathed. The computer screen flashed the data he had called up. "An escape pod, orbiting the fourth planet."

She thought he had forgotten her presence entirely as he settled into the pilot's seat and set a course for the origin of the signal. He handled the ship as if he'd been born to it; of course, Ariane remembered bitterly, he'd been trained at Marchand expense. If Jacques had lived, if there had been no Kalian betrayal, Rook might have been serving aboard a Marchand ship at this very moment. . . .

"There," Rook muttered. As the ship began to cross the small system, he turned suddenly in the seat and studied Ariane with guarded eyes.

"You surprise me, Lady Ariane," he said. He stretched; muscles rippled under bronzed skin. "I thought your kind would avoid giving aid to the Fahar under any circumstances."

Ariane stiffened. *Your kind.* "We are not at war with the Fahar," she said, enunciating each word. "The Conflict ended over fifty years ago."

"But your kind never forget an offense—even though Espérance itself started the Conflict. But then again, you've always believed what suited you—"

"We didn't start the war," Ariane snapped. The urge to strike at his mocking face was overwhelming, but she contented herself by meeting his gaze with open scorn. "The Fahar attacked us without warning—"

"They tell a different story," Rook interrupted softly. "We were there, remember?"

In spite of herself she almost flinched at his oddly gentle

rebuke. *We,* he said. His people, the Kalians, who had known of the Fahar long before the first Espérancian ship had battled over disputed space with the alien race. If it hadn't been for Kalian intervention, the Conflict might have continued for years, costing innumerable lives.

Espérance would never have surrendered. The deadly misunderstandings that had provoked the Conflict would have continued if the Kalians had not provided the means for reconciliation.

And that had been part of the debt the Marchand had owed Rook's people. A debt they had tried to repay by saving Kalian lives when Kali had become uninhabitable.

A debt that had brought only treachery and sorrow.

"You weren't there," she retorted. "You were born in the Warren. You know only what you've been told—"

"As you do," he finished. He gave her a strange, oddly wistful smile. His hostility was gone. "But my parents were there. My father's father was part of the negotiations." His smile faded. "He died on Kali."

For an instant there was pain in his eyes—pain, not hatred. A fragile peace trembled between them. Ariane took a slow step toward him, raising her hand and letting it drop again to her side.

"My grandmother was there," she said. "Anne-Marie. She—her husband died on Kali, and my mother—" She stopped abruptly, cursing whatever had driven her to reveal anything of her past. She could not afford vulnerability. Not after what had happened when Rook had held her in his arms.

Anne-Marie had returned to Espérance after the negotiations with a child in her womb—Chantal, Ariane's mother. And then she had died in childbirth; they'd said she'd had no will to live after losing her husband. Chantal had grown up alone, raised by her grandfather, who had also been on Kali. Bernard, Patriarch of the Marchand.

Now Chantal was gone, and Pierre, Ariane's father. And Jacques. *Only the two of us left,* Ariane thought, and clenched her teeth. *You won't destroy us. . . .*

Rook's subtle movement snapped her attention back to him. The corner of his mouth turned up, and he gestured to the terminal beside his seat. "I've been studying the recent history of the League and your relations with the Fahar over the past eight years—it seems the peace was not as certain as you believed," he said. "Over seven years ago the Fahar delegation withdrew from Espérance, and afterward from the League consulate on Agora."

She understood his implication and felt the heat rise in her face. She had never learned the whole of it, but she knew that Bernard had been deeply troubled when the Fahar delegation, so painstakingly established, had withdrawn. There could be no doubt that it had been directly related to the aftermath of the Kalian riots—and the disappearance of the Kalians on their way to Agora.

"The Fahar," Rook murmured, "were our brothers. Does that surprise you, Lady Ariane? They're little more than beasts—but then again, we are savages." He swung around in his seat and took the controls to guide the d'Artagnan into orbit alongside the alien vessel.

A cloud of debris closed around them as they took up a position parallel to the escape pod. Moving up behind Rook, Ariane watched him maneuver the d'Artagnan carefully amid the remains of a demolished Fahar ship. Large chunks of wreckage scraped against the hull. Her fingers itched to be at the controls. "If you read the reports," she said between her teeth, "then you know that the Fahar returned to Agora over a year ago."

"But not to Espérance," Rook said almost absently, matching their speed to that of the pod. Ariane turned to look at the small, almost featureless sphere visible through the starboard porthole. She forgot whatever retort she'd been about to make as Rook hailed the pod in the sibilant cadence of an alien language. Only silence answered.

Rook got to his feet, his expression grim, and brushed past Ariane. She caught up with him at the suit locker just outside the cockpit.

"There are two space suits," she told him as he palmed the locker door open. "They were custom-made to fit me."

He hesitated for only an instant before lifting one of the suits from the locker. The hard lines of his face tightened.

"You can change your appearance," she said evenly. "Can you condense your mass to fit into the suit?" His expression was answer enough. "No, that wouldn't make sense, would it? Your mass would have to stay the same, no matter what face you put on. You can't shrink down to my size."

Rook's fists clenched on the heavy suit.

"You won't be able to go out there unless you can survive hard vacuum for the time it'll take to stop the pod's spinning and attach the tube—"

Rook replaced the suit carefully, his copper gaze icy. "I won't abandon them," he grated. "You knew this all along. Did it amuse you to—"

"I'll go."

His expression was so startled that she almost laughed. But there was nothing remotely amusing in the situation. Nothing at all. Her mouth felt as dry as the Anubian desert. "I'll go," she repeated softly.

The muscles in his jaw tightened. "Would you take such a risk to save the life of a Fahar, Lady Ariane?"

There was no mockery in the question. He stood bare centimeters away from her and looked down with searching eyes.

"I know what has to be done," she evaded. Leaving the ship in a suit was nothing fearful—she'd done it several times, to perform small repairs on the *d'Artagnan* or to keep herself in practice.

But this wouldn't be strictly routine. The wreckage would make it tricky, and to leave the safety of her ship and put herself in close contact with unpredictable, possibly hostile aliens . . .

Ariane dismissed her fear with a wry inner laugh. She was already in the hands of an unpredictable, hostile alien; another would make little difference. She'd made her choice when she'd called Rook to the cockpit.

She met his gaze. "I'll suit up," she said. As she reached toward the locker, Rook caught her arm and pulled her close.

"Understand this, Lady Ariane," he said very softly. "If you still have intentions of sabotaging the ship or committing honorable suicide, forget them."

Ariane's anger was drowned in the overwhelming sense of his nearness. He held her lightly, and yet she could not move away. Caught by the intensity of his eyes, she had no desire to do so.

She wet her lips. "Is that a threat, Kalian?"

The mockery returned in his smile. "A warning."

But there was no warning in his eyes before he grasped her other arm and pulled her closer still, until their lips almost touched. "I saved your life once. Don't put it in danger again."

Ariane's eyes fell to his mouth, to the slightly curved, sensual lips so close to her own. "I—"

"Your word, Lady Ariane," he said. His warm breath caressed her oversensitive skin.

"My word," she echoed. Just as the sense of helplessness became unbearable, he released her. She stepped away from him quickly, but even after he withdrew, she could feel his stare consuming her body.

The rescue ended successfully two hours later. Rook had been waiting for her just inside the air lock, and Ariane had seen the naked relief on his face before he'd concealed it under an expressionless mask.

When he'd taken the Fahar from her, his eyes had locked on hers with an intensity that seemed to strip her to the soul. It wasn't until she removed the suit and stowed it away in the locker that he turned from her without a word and carried the Fahar to the guest cabin.

Ariane stood in the corner and watched Rook run a medical diagnostic on the unconscious alien. Rook's hands, which had held her with such ferocity, were oddly gentle as they touched the Fahar.

Rook straightened up from the bunk, flicking off the

ship's portable med-scanner. "He'll be all right," he said, resting his hand on the Fahar's broad forehead. The gesture was almost tender, as all of Rook's actions in caring for the Fahar had been. Ariane clenched her hands tightly behind her and kept her face carefully blank.

"It's only a matter of time," Rook continued, as if she'd answered with a polite inquiry instead of silence. "We won't need the automed after all. His metabolism is already readjusting to the new conditions—in a few hours we should be able to give him solid food." He moved away from the bunk to check the diagnostic readings on the computer screen.

Ariane stared after him, mesmerized by the play of muscle and sinew in his back and shoulders, and then deliberately turned her attention to the alien who lay in Rook's bunk.

The Fahar was most definitely male. That had been obvious from the moment Ariane had found him, curled up in the lifepod webbing like a sleeping cat. Even unconscious, the Fahar was impressive. And very much an alien.

Holopics and distant glimpses didn't do the Fahar justice. Sleek muscle rippled under a velvet pelt of soft tan. A body that was too supple to be human sprawled with unconscious grace on the bunk, long fingers tipped by elegant claws resting on his broad chest. And the face—the face was almost indescribable: sensual and feline, beautiful and strange.

This was the creature Rook called "brother," the bestial enemy that had destroyed Espérancian ships and taken Espérancian lives. . . .

Ariane looked away and found Rook's eyes on hers.

"Do you regret saving his life, Ariane?" Rook asked softly, setting the med-scanner on the desk. "The Fahar have their own way of repaying debts."

"I'm not the heartless monster you think me, Kalian," she answered, lifting her chin. "I have no interest in a Fahar's gratitude for an act that any civilized being would perform."

"No?" Rook walked slowly across the cabin. "Then the debt is mine to repay." The unfamiliar gentleness in his face made Ariane catch her breath. The same gentleness that he had shown the alien.

Not meant for her at all.

She swallowed. "I want only one thing of you," she whispered. "Leave my family alone. Never return to Espérance."

The softness in his expression vanished. "You saved one life," he answered. "Your family took thousands."

Ariane closed her eyes, driving back the pain of his words. *At least you understand his hatred. His hatred is something you can deal with. . . .*

"Humans hate what they don't understand," Rook said, startling her out of her thoughts. "My people were feared by yours because they were different. *Changed.* But the Fahar accepted us for what we were from the very beginning. They knew us for brothers."

Brothers. Ariane looked from Rook to the Fahar and suppressed a shiver. "The Shapers," she said.

Rook's sharp glance raked her. "Yes. The Shapers. They came to the Fahar world long before they reached Kali, thousands of years ago. Even the Fahar don't know where the Shapers traveled when they left Harr. Until a few hundred years ago the Shapers were the Fahar's gods."

It was absurdly easy—safe—to slip into the dry recital of history that Bernard had taught her as a child. "The Shapers —whoever they were—found intelligent animals on Harr and changed them," she said, "altered them genetically to speed up a natural process that would have taken aeons."

Rook seemed to look right through her. "But the Shapers were not gods. The Fahar weren't given perfection. They had to struggle their way to civilization just as humans did." He moved to the bedside and cocked his head as if he were listening to something beyond the reach of ordinary ears. "In time the Fahar realized that the Shapers were mortal creatures like themselves. But they never lost their fascination with the beings who had changed their ancestors so irrevocably."

As they changed you, Ariane thought grimly. "And then the Shapers came to Kali," she said. She felt herself being drawn closer to Rook and the Fahar, step by step. "Just in time to save the dying colonists who came from Old Earth."

With a long, harsh expulsion of breath, Rook folded his arms across his chest and turned his copper gaze back to her. "You know the truth of it, Lady Ariane," he said, "and yet you're as quick to judge as all your kind."

"You speak of judging—" she snapped, realizing with a start how close she had come to the Kalian. Yes, she knew the truth—from records of the first Espérancian ship's contact with Kali, and from the stories Finch had told her as a child. Tales of how the survivors among the Kalian colonists, facing inevitable death on a world far too harsh for ordinary human life, had gone into a deep sleep one night and had woken to find themselves changed.

Changed to survive on a world of extremes, savage predators and poisonous flora. Changed to compete and co-exist with the native life-forms as part of an alien ecology.

For a moment Ariane lost herself, drifted back to the sound of her Kalian nanny's singsong voice: *". . . and the People found the marker left by the Shapers, and came to understand the gift they had been given. They took the names of the Earth creatures they had left behind, in memory of the old world, and learned to live as the creatures of Kali lived, at one with the New Earth. And so they survived. . . ."*

Until Kali itself had been destroyed by an act of nature even the Shapers could not have controlled.

"Ironic, Lady Ariane," Rook said, the very softness of his voice compelling her attention. "Your kind hardly recognized us as human, but to the Fahar we were fellow children of the Shapers. The Fahar made peace with Espérance and the League because the Elders of Kali asked them to recognize you as our people. *Our people.*"

Ariane closed her eyes, feeling the impact of his words with the shock of almost physical pain. "We paid that debt," she whispered. "When the asteroids hit and Kali was destroyed—"

"You gave us the sanctuary of the Warren." She heard him

breathe a laugh. "And so we've come full circle, Lady Ariane. I have no interest in hearing your protestations again."

Air redolent of Rook's masculine, subtly exotic scent swirled about her as he moved away. Ariane almost followed him, envisioning herself closing her fingers on his hard-muscled arm, pulling him around, cursing into his contemptuous face.

But he was right. They were enemies, on opposite sides of a chasm that could not be bridged by mere words. Not even by a kiss. And to touch him again—that was a risk greater than she was willing to take in the name of pride. Or honor.

She turned sharply back to the Fahar, studying the beautiful, alien face. It was almost easier to believe she had more in common with this elegant, soft-furred Fahar than with Rook Galloway. At least the League and Harr were at peace. . . .

"*S'haya.*" Ariane started at the sound of the slightly rough voice as two brilliant emerald eyes fixed on hers. "*S'haya,* Sister. I rejoice to know that the Wise were wrong when they reported that the people of Kali were no more." The Fahar bared impressive teeth in an imitation of a smile. "I am Kamur."

Wolfing down another three portions of the ship's dwindling store of rations, Kamur paused to aim the equivalent of a Fahar's smile at his human rescuers. Rook watched with bemused satisfaction. Kamur had recovered from self-imposed hibernation as if he'd just awakened from a long night's sleep, and was rapidly making up for his body's weeks-long deprivation.

Rook begrudged the Fahar nothing, but the *d'Artagnan*'s supplies would have to be replenished before they reached Espérance. He glanced at Ariane, who leaned against the galley bulkhead, her narrowed eyes following the Fahar's movements with half-concealed speculation.

"Sister," Kamur had called her. Rook frowned, cradling the scalding mug of *café* in his hands. Kamur's joy at finding two supposed Kalians still alive had been no less sincere for his mistake. And Rook hadn't had the heart to tell Kamur the truth: that the human female was Rook's enemy, and no Kalian at all.

Even though she had put herself in danger to save Kamur's life.

Rook drove the doubts from his mind. The Fahar was very young. He had no part in Rook's fate. He had to be kept in ignorance, just as the Fahar people had been kept free of human entanglements on Espérance. It shouldn't be overly difficult to provide the cub with a story plausible enough to satisfy him. By the time Kamur returned to Harr to report that Kalians had survived, it would be too late for intervention.

Rook sipped the *café*, welcoming the searing heat on his tongue. Kamur's presence was a problem, but Rook found himself strangely unconcerned. To hear himself called "Brother," to be certain of friendship, to know a brief time of peace—after eight years he could still savor such small pleasures.

As he had savored the feel of Ariane's mouth under his, her surrender in his arms. . . .

Resisting the urge to seek Ariane's eyes again, Rook turned his thoughts to calculations of how long their food supplies would last. Ariane's sleek, toned body had never known real hunger; Rook had already discarded the possibility of forcing her to experience it now. The thought of her discomfort brought him oddly little satisfaction.

He shook his head impatiently. There were a few places he might take the ship where the chances of being identified were small. And there was still the question of what was to be done with their unexpected passenger. . . .

"I must get to Agora."

Carefully setting down his mug, Rook looked at Kamur. The Fahar had finished his last mouthful and regarded Rook expectantly with slanted green eyes; tufted triangular ears twitched several times. Fahar spoke as much with their ears as with their tongues, but even the Kalians had never learned all the finer nuances of the aliens' nonverbal speech.

"I was on my way to Agora when my ship encountered

difficulties," Kamur said, his Standard nearly impeccable. He rose and left the galley's small table, gliding across the deck on bare, noiseless feet. "My lifemate is there. We have been separated for five *ila.*" Kamur stopped at a precise distance from Rook and lowered his ears in a gesture of conciliation. "Brother, you know what this is to my people. I must have your help."

Rook closed his eyes. *By the Shapers.* He'd been prepared for the complications Kamur's presence would create in his half-formed plans, but this. . . . He looked over the Fahar's broad shoulder at Ariane. She could not quite hide the flare of hope in her eyes.

And he knew Ariane would not hesitate to use whatever means for escape he unwillingly put in her hands.

"Kamur," she said. She stepped away from the bulkhead and stopped just behind the galley table. "You said you were —separated from your lifemate?"

The Fahar turned to her almost eagerly. "We had been mated less than an *ila* before they sent her away. But her Clan did not know that we had bonded, and—"

"Brother," Rook interrupted. He stared at Ariane, considering. Every instinct had warned him to lock Ariane in her cabin the moment Kamur regained consciousness—but she had saved the Fahar's life.

Kamur glanced from Ariane to Rook with a hopeful twitch of his ears. "I knew you would understand. The Children of the Shapers are the same. You are mates, yes?"

His question seemed to hang in the silence that followed. Ariane's eyes widened in comprehension, and Rook stared fixedly at a patterned whorl of tan fur on Kamur's shoulder.

"No," Ariane said at last, her voice strained. "No, we aren't—"

Rook was at her side before she could finish the sentence, taking her elbow and pushing her into the nearest seat. His heart drummed against his ribs. She threw him a rebellious look and subsided, lips tightening.

"My Brother," Rook said, "tell us how this came about— from the beginning."

Kamur's ears came fully erect. "Surra," he said, pronouncing the name like a prayer. "She is the daughter of a Lawmaker, who came to the Sanctuary to view the ancient Shaper obelisks while I was in my second level of training for the Priesthood. I had been one of those chosen by the head of my Clan to aspire to the Wise; I knew my duty." Abruptly his ears flattened against his skull. "I did not mean to *seal* Surra. Our meeting was never intended. But once we tasted each other's scents . . ." Kamur closed his eyes rapturously.

Ariane shifted in the seat, and Rook clamped down on her shoulder with such force that he could feel her wince. "The Fahar," he whispered harshly in Franglais, "mate for life. They form an unbreakable bond with their chosen mates. They train as children to control what they call 'sealing'—the instinctive process by which a Fahar selects a mate —so that appropriate, planned matings can be arranged. But even the Fahar don't entirely understand what draws one Fahar to another. It's something mystical to them—a legacy of the Shapers."

"But if they don't consider the Shapers gods—"

"They don't. But the Wise—their Priesthood—devote themselves to studying and analyzing the obelisks that the Shapers left behind. The Wise are among the highest-ranked Fahar, and they are celibate." Ariane's skin seemed to burn his palm through the thin material of her shipsuit; Rook snatched his hand away. "For Kamur to break his vows—"

"It was too late," Kamur continued, turning to glide across the length of the galley with haunting grace. "We could not fight it. Surra's parents came to take her away, and the Wise set me to punishment. But they did not know." He stopped and regarded Rook and Ariane anxiously. "We had already mated. Surra promised to make them understand, but they sent her from Harr with her sire—to Agora, with the Peacemakers. And my Clan would not listen to my pleas. They feared disgrace and forced me to resume my studies."

Rook stepped away from Ariane's seat and clasped his hands behind his back. Her shallow breathing nearly matched his own, breath for breath. "So you went after her," he said.

"Yes." Kamur turned to stalk in the other direction, his claw-tipped fingers flexing as if he would climb the walls. "I had no choice. Surra sent me a message at great risk to tell me where she was. I acquired a small ship to carry me to Agora, but—" In an almost human gesture, Kamur grimaced. "I was not an able pilot. My ship was destroyed when I failed to allow sufficient time for the hyperdrive to complete recalibration after I entered this system. I slept in the lifepod for nearly two *ila*. So you found me, my Brother and Sister."

He said the final words with such trust and hope. Rook clenched his jaw until the muscles tightened to the point of pain. Trust and hope were things this young Fahar could still believe in.

Kamur's mate was on Agora, the hub of the League. Rook's escape from Tantalus would be posted there soon if it hadn't been already; it would be suicide to dock there for any reason.

But it was suicide to return to Espérance. Rook was already living on borrowed time.

Deliberately ignoring Ariane, he moved around the table to collect the empty ration containers and toss them into the recycler. "Return to the cabin and rest," he told Kamur quietly. "I'll lay in a course for Agora."

He endured the young Fahar's thanks and turned to stare out the galley porthole. Long after Kamur had left, he was aware of Ariane's presence behind him, her unspoken questions suspended in the silence.

"I don't understand you, Kalian." The fine hairs at the back of his neck bristled at the sound of her voice, the tease of her soft-scented breath against his skin. "You'll go to Agora and risk capture, give up your revenge for the sake of a lovelorn Fahar."

He maintained his control even when she drew nearer, her warmth radiating at his back. "You almost had me convinced that you're as ruthless as you pretend," she whispered.

Rook turned on her so quickly that he caught a glimpse of the unguarded bewilderment on her face. "What more will it take to convince you?" he said with deadly softness. He drove her back step by step, forcing her to retreat. "I'll give up nothing, Lady Ariane—not revenge, and not you."

Her back came up against the table, bending her body in a supple curve. "If you go anywhere near Agora, they'll catch you," she said, her eyes snapping with familiar anger. "They'll know you've escaped. There are people who'll be looking for me."

Rook smiled crookedly. "Do you enjoy my company so much?" he asked, cupping her chin in his hand. Sensation and desire pierced his body. "I'm flattered that you're reluctant to risk being parted from me, *chérie,* though I wonder at your change of heart."

"Let go of me—"

Almost against his will he brought his face closer to hers. "Don't worry, Ariane. I won't let you out of my sight. If the League authorities on Agora know about my escape and our —relationship—they won't be in a hurry to risk your life by threatening me. You're still mine. I won't let you suffer any temptation to infidelity."

Her mouth opened, lips parted and moist. Her tongue darted out to touch them, and he followed the movement with dark fascination.

Sheer force of will kept him from seizing her mouth with his own. "Kamur believes that we are mates, *chérie.* It wouldn't be difficult to play the part." His thumb caressed her cheek. Rich color flooded her face, and her gaze dropped to settle at some point on his chin.

By the Shapers, it would be all too easy to play the part.

Rook shook himself. "Once mated," he continued softly, "the Fahar undergo a biological change. In the first year after bonding, they suffer such a powerful physical need for their mates that any separation results in Kai-horo—pain of the soul—so intense that it can lead to madness or death."

"Madness," Ariane repeated. Rook felt her tremble. Her shudders moved through her and into his restraining hands.

"If Kamur's Elders had believed the truth, they wouldn't have separated him from his mate," Rook said. "But as it is—"

He released her so sharply that she would have fallen without the support of the table. "As it is, I wouldn't condemn any being to that kind of suffering. And so I must disappoint you, Lady Ariane. We go to Agora."

He strode from the galley, trying and failing to shut her from his thoughts. The expression on her face when he'd let her go—confusion melting slowly into comprehension—haunted him. She had seen his weakness. If she understood it, she could use it against him.

She might find the power to defeat him. . . .

Cursing himself soundly, he stopped at the hatch to the guest cabin. *"You are mates, yes?"* The echo of Kamur's naive question raced along his hypersensitive nerves.

The young Fahar, poised in the midst of a graceful gesture, looked up as Rook entered the cabin. Kamur completed the move with only a slight hesitation and slipped smoothly into another stance. Rook recognized the ancient Fahar martial art and waited until Kamur ended the exercise with a ritual flourish.

"Is all well with you, Brother?" Rook asked.

"All is well." Kamur approximated a human grin. "Thanks to you and your woman, my Brother. When I find Surra—" With a blissful growl he leaped up onto the bunk and performed an extravagant stretch that set his tan fur to rippling.

Rook looked away. Kamur's innocent joy cut like a blade and twisted in his heart. There was still a course to be set; the cockpit was a sanctuary of privacy where he could remember his purpose. Remember what Ariane Burke-Marchand was. And what she could never be.

As he turned to go, a strong, elegant hand fell on his shoulder. "But you, my Brother," Kamur said softly. "All is not well with you."

Rook stiffened. The gentlest pressure of claws pricked his skin. He looked over his shoulder at Kamur's lowered ears.

It would take only a few well-chosen words to put Kamur off the scent. As perceptive as the Fahar were known to be, their understanding of humans—even Kalians—was imperfect. "Kamur—" he began.

"She is not your mate," the Fahar said suddenly. His hand dropped from Rook's shoulder. "But it is the woman who gives you Kai-horo. I feel it."

Rook flinched at Kamur's gentle words. "No, Brother, it—"

Kamur moved to face Rook like a shadow. "I don't perfectly understand the ways of humans, my Brother. But we are Children of the Shapers. It is obvious that you want her, and she wants you. You have sealed each other. Why, then, have you not mated?"

Rook never remembered afterward what answer he gave to satisfy Kamur. He made his escape from the cabin and locked himself into the cockpit, holding his seething emotions at bay while he set a course for Agora.

But the damage was done. Kamur had spoken aloud what Rook had known from the moment Ariane had appeared in the interrogation room on Tantalus. What he'd fought each and every hour aboard the *d'Artagnan*. What her simplest touch had seared into his blood.

He wanted Ariane. He wanted her with a fierce, primitive violence. The savagery of which she'd accused him was there, just under the surface, waiting to be unleashed.

It had been the savage who'd claimed Ariane as his own, who had branded her with a kiss—wanting far more, barely restrained. And when she had responded with her own unwilling passion . . .

Rook let out a deep, shuddering breath, bracing his hands on the armrests of the pilot's seat. He had dreamed of her. He had imagined her naked under him—lips parted, skin flushed with excitement, her woman's heat enveloping him. He imagined it now, so vividly that his arousal was heavy and aching with need.

"Why have you not mated?" For Kamur it was a simple thing.

Rook clenched his teeth. It could be simple. Ariane was his prisoner; he could take her whenever he chose, and she could do nothing to stop him. He had the superior strength and speed; she had nothing but her proud defiance.

To lose himself in her supple body, to forget pain in pleasure, grief in lust, loneliness in physical union . . .

Take her, the savage urged. What sweet revenge it would be to take her and know that she would suffer the shame and dishonor of a Kalian criminal's possession—that her Family would share that shame. And she was surely a virgin.

Groaning, Rook leaped up from the chair and slammed his fists against the canopy's thick glasteel. The thought that she might be untouched was a temptation almost beyond bearing.

Take her. They'll buy her back in the end, and you'll have everything you want.

But he remembered Ariane's compassion when she'd told him of his people's fate, her quiet courage when she had offered to go after the Fahar, a being she had no reason to love. He remembered the thick, unfamiliar fear that had knotted in his belly when Ariane had left the ship.

And he remembered Kamur's serious young eyes, his earnest concern. A Fahar's bond to his mate was more than mere lust. It went almost beyond human understanding, though the Elders had said that in the old days—on Kali, before the Sharing had been all but forgotten—even humans could know such perfect wholeness.

Never again. Rook drove the savage from his heart and clutched at that temporary victory. *Weak,* the savage cried. *Coward.* But Rook silenced the mocking voice, schooled his body to tranquillity with every shattered fragment of self-discipline he possessed.

You're alone, he told himself. No soft woman's body, no frantic grasp at physical pleasure, would change that fact. He settled back into the pilot's seat and stared blindly at the indifferent stars.

You'll always be alone.

CHAPTER SIX

*T*he vast concentric wheels of Agora space station hung in the orbit of Bujold's Star like a glittering torque, heart of the League and hub of commerce in all of known human space.

Ships of all sizes from League and non-League worlds—Espérance, Liberty, Nirvana, Tolstoy, Midgard, Anubis, and many others—sailed into the system and docked at one of Agora's countless berths, or departed with empty holds or new cargos. Ariane had seen Agora many times in the past three years of conducting Marchand business, but never had it held the importance it did for her now.

She stood a safe distance behind Rook as he piloted the ship toward the berth that Station Control had assigned to the *d'Artagnan*. A station of Agora's size could easily accommodate unexpected arrivals, and the Control official had hardly raised an eyebrow when Ariane had requested permission to dock. The simple explanation Rook had concocted for the *d'Artagnan*'s brief and unscheduled stop at Agora would not be likely to arouse suspicion.

It had been all too clear from the official's reaction that no one on Agora suspected that anything was amiss with Ariane Burke-Marchand and the *d'Artagnan*.

Not yet.

But soon. Soon they'd discover that Ariane's ship had been Rook's ticket off Tantalus. News traveled across the galaxy as fast as starships could carry it, and the *d'Artagnan* had not taken the most direct route to Agora. Yet Rook had not even hesitated when he'd ordered her to hail the station. . . .

Ariane folded her arms across her chest and stared grimly at the back of Rook's head. For the past few days Rook had utterly ignored her. After that moment in the galley, when she'd been sure he would kiss her again—when she'd almost grasped some deeper, profound understanding of her enemy, and of herself—he had dismissed her as if she didn't exist.

As if she'd imagined everything.

She laughed softly to herself. He had made it easy for her. Easy to plan her escape on Agora. Easy to dismiss the aberrant feelings she'd held for a savage.

But the thought brought little comfort. She glanced at Kamur, crouched beside her with his wide eyes fixed on the station. He, at least, had acknowledged her presence. More than once Ariane had felt those emerald eyes on her, watching.

She might have learned more about the Fahar if Rook hadn't always come between them, spiriting Kamur away without a word whenever she got too close.

Ariane had never felt quite so alone, not even on her longest solo runs. But she liked what little she knew of Kamur. There was nothing threatening or bestial about him at all. He was no more than a man longing for his mate with all the intensity of a bond beyond human understanding—an alien love that drove him across the galaxy at the risk of his life.

Love. Longing.

No. Ariane quelled emotion and deliberately recalled all the stories she'd been told of Fahar savagery during the Conflict. It troubled her more than she cared to admit that something she'd always believed could be so wrong.

How much else is wrong? she asked herself. But she pushed the crippling doubts aside, focusing all her thoughts on the station that filled the cockpit canopy.

Wynn might already be there. He wasn't due for another week Standard, but Wynn could be unpredictable; he had been waiting a long time for this marriage.

I am promised to him. And he wants me. Ariane swallowed and took a step forward to brace herself against the copilot's chair as Rook maneuvered closer to the station's outer wheel.

Rook glanced aside at her, copper eyes remote. Callused

fingers brushed the controls lightly in a subtle adjustment; the *d'Artagnan* slipped into sync with Agora's rotation.

"I've called up Agora's docking roster," he said quietly in Franglais.

Ariane started at the sound of his voice. She composed her features and turned to look at him.

"No ships from Tantalus have put in for well over two months Standard," he continued. "The last Espérancian vessel left three days ago, bound for Tolstoy. No stationwide alerts have been called." He stretched, muscles sliding under bronzed skin. "Tantalus's fleet is made up of cast-off ships from twelve systems. Notoriously unreliable. News of my escape hasn't reached Agora."

Ariane glanced back at Kamur. It was clear that the Fahar didn't understand Franglais. *There are things you don't want Kamur to know.*

"How fortunate for you," she said tightly in the same language.

"It seems there won't be any welcoming committee for either one of us, Lady Ariane—unless someone is expecting you?" One dark eyebrow lifted, but his eyes were suddenly intense.

For a moment Ariane was certain he could read her mind. *He doesn't know,* she reminded herself. *He doesn't know I was bound for Agora. . . .*

"Not even Marchand can afford to keep employees idle, waiting for unscheduled arrivals at every port of call," she said, matching his detachment. She spoke only the truth—there was always a window of uncertainty for any ship's estimated time of arrival—and she was a week ahead of schedule. But the Marchand representative on Agora would be expecting her to make her final report and drop off the ship's records before returning to Espérance to become Wynn's bride. . . .

A prickle of awareness drew her attention back to Rook.

"Scheming, Lady Ariane?" he asked. "I won't make the mistake of underestimating you again."

They stared at each other. Ariane read something in his

eyes that made it difficult to keep her gaze steady. Contradictory emotions stung her nerves and tensed her muscles. "Are you admitting that you find me a worthy opponent, Kalian?"

Rook blinked slowly, like a Midgardian fay-tiger shamming disinterest in its intended prey. "Are you admitting," he countered, "that I have reason to call you my enemy?"

A sharp buzz from the commlink snapped the tension between them. Rook turned to the console.

"Something to keep in mind, Lady Ariane," he said as his hands moved nimbly over the controls. "I know the temptation to bolt on Agora will be considerable. I've rigged the *d'Artagnan* reactor to overload at my signal. There'll be a large hole in the station docking bay if you go to the authorities or try to escape." He lifted his hand to display the remote clasped about his broad wrist. "The decision is yours."

Ariane tensed in shock. "No," she said. "You're bluffing—"

"Am I?" Rook leaned back in the seat and regarded her coldly. He had never looked less human. "Am I, Lady Ariane? After all my people supposedly did to yours, you have no reason to be shocked at the extremes I'd go to for my revenge." His fingers tightened around the chair's arms. "I warned you."

She shook her head in disbelief. *"What will it take to convince you?"* he'd asked when she'd doubted his ruthlessness. The casual tone in which he threatened unthinkable destruction numbed her soul.

For a time—for a few brief hours of madness—she had let herself be drawn to him, had almost questioned her Family's honor. And her own.

He glanced at her now with the corner of his mouth quirked up, as if he found her horror amusing. Ariane swallowed the bile in her throat and met Rook's gaze, hating him.

"How could I ever have doubted that you were a savage?" she whispered.

He said nothing, only searched her eyes until his own grew as hard and reflective as the metal they resembled. And then he returned to the task of docking the ship, while Ariane fled to the rear of the cockpit.

Kamur followed her with slanted emerald eyes, his ears flickering erratically. "I do not perfectly understand humans," the Fahar muttered in Standard.

Ariane clenched her fists. "Neither do I, Kamur," she said. "Neither do I."

"You need have no fear for me, my Brother," Kamur said. Behind and above him the dock Concourse bustled with activity and sound: crates and containers being loaded and unloaded, officials checking lists, the continual buzz of Standard and several other languages competing for dominance.

Kamur's ears swiveled back to take in the din and flattened in a Fahar wince. "I will find Surra—she will be expecting me. We have it all arranged. We must only find an appropriate ship leaving Agora, and then we will make our way to M'nauri." He grinned. "You have not heard of M'nauri, my Brother? It is a free colony where humans and Fahar live in peace. Yes, it is true, Sister." He pricked his ears at Ariane. "Few know of it, but there we will make our home."

Rook sighed, and Ariane looked at him warily. He shifted under her glance, his bare feet flexing on the ship's boarding ramp. "We'll be here," Rook said to Kamur, "for a few hours to pick up supplies. If you run into any trouble—"

Kamur performed a graceful bow that no human could have imitated. "All will be well, my Brother." He looked at Ariane. Abruptly he glided forward; a soft-palmed hand touched Ariane's. His ears danced. "Shaper's Fortune to you, Sister. Do not fear what must be."

With an effort Ariane held her hand still until Kamur let go. His gentle words echoed in her ears. *"What must be . . ."*

"And you, my Brother—" The Fahar closed his eyes, and a slow shudder worked its way from his clawed toes to the tips of his ears. "You will find what you seek, but do not let it destroy you."

Rook's face was impassive, but Ariane saw a muscle jump

in his cheek. Before the moment could stretch beyond bearing, Kamur opened his eyes and beamed at both of them with oblivious delight.

"And now I must go. We will meet again." The Fahar turned from the threshold of the ramp and bounded away, drawing stares from idlers along the Concourse.

Ariane released her pent breath slowly. She stared after Kamur until he disappeared from view behind a milling crowd of tourists from Liberty.

When she looked around, Rook was gone. She gnawed her lip, watching people move back and forth from the row of ships that followed the curve of the station to disappear upward into the horizon. There were a thousand possibilities for escape here, if she dared use them. But Rook held her prisoner as surely as if he'd locked her within her own ship.

Ariane swallowed the hard lump in her throat just as the hollow drum of footfalls drew her eyes back to the ramp.

Rook had *changed*.

Concealing her unwilling fascination, Ariane relaxed her body and watched him approach. The man who joined her at the top of the ramp was no longer a bare-chested, long-haired Kalian; he'd become a thoroughly ordinary human who wore Marchand coloring and features as if he'd been born with them. His height and weight remained much the same, but his new appearance somehow lacked the impressive magnetism of Rook's natural body. He'd found a spare shipsuit—one intended for a male passenger's use—and had donned a pair of half boots. There was little to mark him out from the countless men and women who worked and played along the vast sweep of the Concourse.

But she would have known him. She would have known him anywhere, with any face, and the thought made her shiver.

Rook smiled with a Marchand's well-bred mouth, his own cynical twist behind it. He executed a mocking bow. "Your cousin," he told her, "if anyone should ask. Surely you have enough of them to spare."

Ariane clenched her teeth and refused to acknowledge his

gibe. Her eyes dropped to the remote on Rook's wrist, half-hidden by the sleeve of his shipsuit. If she could distract him just enough to take the remote, he'd be unable to carry out his threat to blow up the ship. And then she'd be free to escape. . . .

"We have work to do, Lady Ariane." Rook touched her arm almost gently. The fingers that rested on her elbow were unscarred. An aristocrat's fingers. She wanted to jerk free of his light hold, but she could not seem to move at all.

Rook tucked her arm in the crook of his elbow and smiled an aristocrat's smile as he led her onto the Concourse.

Ariane retrieved her credit chip from the IDplate as Rook shifted the packages in the carryall to accommodate the case of ship's rations. Behind the counter the shopkeeper beamed at them. "If I can be of any further service, Lady Marchand . . ."

"Thank you," Ariane murmured, oppressed by the claustrophobic drabness of the place. With hardly a glance at Rook she fled out into the Concourse, looking instinctively to the right and left like a hunted animal.

There was a woman staring at her from across the Concourse—an elderly, nondescript woman with steel-gray hair and faded eyes, half-hidden behind a collapsible peddler's cart. Something in that intense regard drew Ariane's attention; the old woman seemed to raise one gnarled hand in greeting. Unthinkingly Ariane started across the lane between the shops, but before she'd gone more than a step, the woman had vanished.

"Someone you know?"

Ariane kept her back to Rook until she could hear the deep cadence of his breathing. She gathered her defenses and turned to him slowly. "No. No one at all."

Rook's mocking smile took shape on a stranger's face. "It would be unfortunate if any of your—acquaintances—became involved in our affairs, Lady Ariane."

She raised her chin. "Your threats were clear the first time."

Moving toward her, he herded her into the flow of tourists and browsers strolling the Concourse. "Not clear enough," he retorted. Grim amusement tinged his voice. "You asked me if I thought you were a worthy opponent. The answer is yes." She felt the warmth of his breath brushing the crown of her head and walked faster, pushing by a pair of oblivious Nirvanans in brilliant blue robes.

Rook was right on her heels. "And if I were an honorable man rather than a savage, I might admire your courage enough to release you."

Ariane stubbornly refused to rise to the bait. As they approached the berth where the *d'Artagnan* was moored, she stared through the docking-bay porthole at the sleek lines of her ship and stopped at the top of the boarding ramp, letting Rook enter the ship alone. He brushed by her without another word.

Ariane closed her eyes and struggled to remember her purpose. *Time,* she thought. *I need time.* Even if no one had reason to check the docking rosters a week before she was due to arrive, the moment Rook had used her credit chip the transaction would have shown up in Marchand financial records on Agora. Once the family's agent on Agora was aware she'd used her credit chip and hadn't contacted the station's Marchand offices, he'd send someone to locate her. It could be a matter of minutes, or hours.

But if they came looking for her, she would still be Rook's hostage. She opened her eyes and curled her fingers into fists. Rook would force her to play along with his false identity as one of her numerous Marchand cousins, and her people wouldn't know that anything was wrong. Not until it was too late. She might simply have given an unscheduled lift to a member of her family from one of the several worlds with developing Marchand interests. She'd done it many times before in her role as courier.

And even if they realized something was wrong, Rook would still have her. As long as she was in his hands, he could hold the Marchand and the League authorities at bay. And he could use *her* to revenge himself on her Family.

For the hundredth time she tried to imagine Rook taking action that might snuff out innocent lives along with the *d'Artagnan*. The image refused to form in her mind.

The riots, she reminded herself. *The Warren, the people who died, the conspiracy, Jacques* . . . But all she could remember was how Rook had cared for Kamur and spoken of the Fahar, how he had saved her life and warned her not to risk herself again—the pain in his eyes when he'd talked of his lost people—the searing intensity of his kiss.

The man who had kissed her was not a ruthless killer.

No. He was a savage. A threat to her world and everything she was. . . .

"You said no one was expecting you."

She whirled to face Rook. His brown Marchand eyes were expressionless. "Someone left a message for you, Lady Ariane. Someone who knows I'm here."

Ariane read the message on the computer screen once again, hardly aware of Rook at her shoulder.

Ariane Burke-Marchand: Come to Wheel One, Section Gamma, Block 349, #G-30. Urgent. The truth must be known. Bring hidden Shaper's Child. All will be explained.

There was no name, nothing to indicate who had sent the message—except that the sender knew Ariane had a Kalian with her. *Shaper's Child.* And the sender knew that Rook was "hidden"; did that refer to his fugitive status, or his wearing of another face?

The truth must be known. What truth? Ariane's definition of the word had been eroded steadily and painfully since she had met Rook Galloway on Tantalus.

I won't let go of all my certainties, she thought, setting her jaw. *I can't.* . . .

She glanced up at Rook. Even under the refined Marchand mask he looked forbidding.

"Who is it?" he asked.

Ariane rose and slipped by him carefully. "I don't know any more than you do."

In the silence that followed she could feel his disbelief. "The address means nothing to you?" he said at last.

"Only that it's a residential section, and not one of the better ones. I don't know anyone who lives there. I don't know anyone on Agora except my family's employees. And this can't be one of them."

He moved up behind her. "Who could know I'm with you, Lady Ariane?"

Deliberately she held her ground. "I've told you I don't know. If you want answers, you'll have to go find them."

His half boots whispered restlessly on the deck. "And taking time to find them will provide you with more convenient delays. If you hadn't been with me every moment—"

"But I was." She turned to face him. "No, I didn't send the message myself. You'll have to take my word, Kalian."

His brown eyes narrowed and the cynical smile appeared.

"I have a savage's curiosity, Lady Ariane. And I want to know my enemies—or allies. We'll answer this message, you and I." He touched the remote on his wrist. "But if this is a trap—"

"It isn't of my making," she said urgently. "I won't try to escape again."

"You relieve my mind, *chérie.*"

Resisting the urge to strike the smile from his face, she accompanied him in silence while he locked up the ship.

The location to which they'd been directed was near the hub of the station, in the oldest section that long ago had housed the first inhabitants of Agora. Now it was the cheapest and most run-down residential district, dimly lit and vaguely oppressive.

Ariane and Rook exited the levitrain that had carried them up from the outer wheel and paused at the terminal doors. This far up the gravity was one fifth that of the Concourse level; Ariane took a few moments to adjust as she got her bearings. From there the address they'd been given was within walking distance along one of the many featureless corridors branching out from the levitrain terminal.

An overhead light sputtered erratically as they reached the end of Block 349. They stopped at a graffiti-marked door, like all the others in the corridor, its painted numbers faded almost to invisibility.

Ariane glanced at Rook and tapped the buzzer. For a long moment nothing happened; Rook shifted and looked up and down the corridor as if he expected ambush. His lips parted to speak, and the door slid open with a hiss.

The woman who faced them blinked and smiled slowly, leaning heavily against the door frame. Ariane recognized her with a shock—the elderly woman who'd gestured to her in the Concourse. A woman she'd never seen before.

"You have come," the old woman said. "Thank the Maker, you have come."

A thousand questions jostled in Ariane's mind, but before she could give voice to any of them, Rook pushed by her to stand over the tiny woman.

"Who are you?" he croaked.

"Ah," the old woman sighed. "I knew it could be made right—" And her face began to shift, blur, the colorless eyes darkening, warming to copper. The bones changed subtly under deeply lined skin. "I prayed I would not die before it was too late. . . ."

"Finch." Ariane forced the word out past the knot in her throat.

"Yes, little Ariane. Finch." The old Kalian woman smiled her gentle, ageless smile. "It has been so many years—you were no more than a child when I left."

"But I thought—I thought you were dead—" Ariane braced her hands against the door frame. "You disappeared the night after the riots. . . ."

Finch nodded slowly, and her eyes moved to Rook. He was staring at Finch as if she were a phantom. "There is much to explain, children. I have little time." She stepped back, and like an automaton Ariane followed her into the cramped, spare quarters.

Rook moved to Finch's side, gently guiding her to a battered chair.

"Little mother," he said, settling her into the chair with infinite tenderness. Finch reached up to touch his jaw.

"I know what you are, but not who, child."

Rook turned away. A moment later it was Rook's copper eyes that looked down at Finch, his own familiar features stripped of all bitterness.

"Rook Galloway," Finch whispered. "I knew your grandmother on Kali. I saw you often at the mansion when you returned from Tolstoy." Suddenly she looked at Ariane. "I do not know why he is with you, child—I only recognized what he was when I saw you both in the Concourse. And I knew he was free—" She stopped, bent her head, and shivered.

"Free?" Ariane echoed. "I don't understand what—"

"I am dying, child," Finch interrupted quietly. "When I saw you, I knew the time had come."

Dying. Ariane swallowed. Until Finch had disappeared after the riots, the Kalian woman had been as much a part of Ariane's life as her great-grandfather or Wynn or her faith in Marchand honor.

Finch had not been young when she'd met Anne-Marie Marchand, Bernard's daughter, on Kali during the peace negotiations with the Fahar. When Anne-Marie had returned to Espérance to bear her child—Chantal, Ariane's mother—Finch had come with her. The Kalian woman had become a part of the Marchand household, quietly assuming the duties of nanny to Chantal Marchand. In time Chantal had grown to womanhood and married Pierre Burke-Marchand; Finch cared in turn for the child of that union after Chantal had died in childbirth.

Ariane had been that child. Ariane Burke-Marchand, who had taken Finch for granted, forgetting she was Kalian, regarding her almost as the mother she'd never known. Finch would always be there, as certain as Marchand honor.

Until the day Jacques had died, and Finch vanished.

Among all the other losses, that had seemed a small one. Finch was Kalian; Ariane had hated all Kalians then. But there had been no one to rock Ariane when she had cried in the night, her childish illusions shattered. Ariane had driven

Finch from her heart, mourning only in the deepest part of herself.

But Finch was here. Here, inexplicably, on Agora, eight years after the riots. Dying.

"I cannot wait, children," Finch murmured, lines of pain deepening in her face. Rook knelt beside her, and she shook her head. "This is beyond Healing, child. I have fought it long enough. My time has come."

Ariane stared numbly at Rook. The hardness was gone from his expression; it was a boy's vulnerability she saw there, a sorrow beyond despair. *He was not the last Kalian, after all,* Ariane thought. *But soon he will be. . . .*

"I know," Finch said softly, "what happened after the riots, and during the trials." She drew in a shuddering breath. "I was there, Ariane, though you did not know it. I thought I could help you, help my people, if I—disappeared. Took on another form, such as the one I wear now—an Espérancian servant. I stayed with you as long as I could, and escaped to Agora after our people were taken away." She raised a shaking hand to forestall Ariane's questions. "I will explain all, children. Tell me"—her gaze swept from Ariane to Rook, encompassing them both—"how is it that you are here, together? Did they release you from your prison, Rook Galloway?"

"You know I was condemned, little mother—"

"Yes. I know, as I know of all that came after."

Rook was silent, staring blindly into space. "He—" Ariane began, turning to Finch. "I—"

"I escaped," Rook said softly. His big hand dwarfed Finch's as he touched the old woman's trembling fingers. "Lady Ariane helped me. She came to Tantalus because she had learned to doubt her family's justice."

Words jammed in Ariane's throat, denials she could not speak. Not now, not before a dying woman she had loved.

"Praise the Maker," Finch murmured. "I was right. I knew. I should have told her long ago. . . ."

She drifted off, muscles loosening. Rook started up in alarm, and Ariane reached for Finch as if by instinct. The moment her hand touched Finch's arm, she felt the blackness that waited to claim Finch, held at bay by an old woman's fading strength. Ariane flinched away almost at once, but Finch's eyes were open again, fixed on hers and bright with joy.

"You—" Finch whispered. "It is within you. You have such strength—by the Maker, I have so little time. . . ."

"Rest," Rook said, his voice hoarse. "Rest, little mother."

"No." Finch straightened, clenching blue-veined hands on the arms of the chair. "Not yet. Leave us, my son."

Copper eyes met copper, and Rook shook his head. "You need—"

"Leave us for a moment, Rook Galloway. There are things I must say to Ariane alone." She wheezed, and Rook rose slowly, backing away, his fists clenched. He glanced at Ariane once, utterly blank, and hesitated only an instant before vanishing through the outer door and closing it behind him.

"Come close, child," Finch urged. "There is something you must know—something I promised to keep hidden from the day of your birth. I swore it to your mother, and your mother's mother, and your Patriarch as well. Because I loved Anne-Marie and Chantal, as I love you."

Only Finch's last words made sense to Ariane. They were enough. She drew closer, careful not to touch the Kalian woman, and listened.

"I can keep it hidden no longer," Finch sighed. "Perhaps you and Rook are the only hope." She leaned forward, her ancient eyes intense. "Pierre Burke-Marchand was not your father, child. Chantal Marchand found a mate among the Kalians in the Warren the year after Jacques was born."

The air rushed from Ariane's lungs as if she'd been struck. "What—"

"It is true, child. Pierre did not treat her well, and Chantal sought comfort among her own kind.

"You—my child, my daughter—are Kalian."

CHAPTER SEVEN

"No," Ariane gasped. "My father—"

"Was Kestrel Tremayne—one of the first generation of Kalians to be born on Espérance. Pierre never knew of the affair. You were raised as if you were Pierre's daughter, and none but a few of us knew of your true parentage. That was my greatest charge, Ariane—to hide what you were."

The station seemed to spin under Ariane's feet. "No. . . ."

"It is true, child." A cool, fragile hand reached across the space between them to touch Ariane's face. "Feel it. Know it is true."

And Ariane knew. She knew as if she could feel the truth flowing from Finch's fingers into her skin, her bones, her very soul.

Kalian.

"Do not blame your mother, child," Finch continued quietly. "She was drawn by her blood, for she herself was half-Kalian. Anne-Marie secretly took a Kalian man as mate during the negotiations with the Fahar—Sedge Allen. Her father, Bernard, could do nothing to stop it until it was too late and Anne-Marie was with child. Sedge died on Kali, but when your grandmother left for Espérance, I went with her. Even then Bernard knew that the child Anne-Marie bore would not be accepted on Espérance, would not be heir to the Marchand name. So it was given out that she had married one of her own kind on Kali, and that her Espérancian husband had died in an accident."

Finch's fingers stroked Ariane's face one last time and drew away. Ariane shuddered, spasms that left her blind and deaf to everything but Finch's damning revelation.

"You see, my child—I came back with Anne-Marie to

care for Chantal, to help hide what she was. I had some skill as a Healer on Kali, and I knew the way of Changing. As Rook knows." She smiled sadly. "That gift, at least, is not lost, as so many were when we came to Espérance. But you—"

"Hide—what she was—" Ariane lifted trembling hands to her own face, traced the familiar curves of cheek and jaw.

"Yes, my child. You as well. I touched your mind and taught your body before it could understand how to control the changes. But I did no more than hide what would mark you for one of ours. Eyes"—her fingers hovered just over Ariane's fluttering lashes—"and hair."

Ariane squeezed her eyes shut as if she could block the images from her mind: Finch's face blurring, becoming suddenly familiar before her eyes. Rook changing, taking on the features of Hudson and a Marchand cousin as easily as he might change his shipsuit.

Rook. Kalian. As she was Kalian. . . .

"You can learn to Change, Ariane. You have the ability, as you have so much else. . . ."

"No. I won't—I don't want it. I am Ariane Burke-Marchand." The name sounded false on her own tongue.

"In time, my child. In time you will accept."

Never. Never. Wrenching away, Ariane lurched up and strode blindly to the nearest wall. She stared at the dull gray surface, filled with such fury and grief that she would have welcomed the pain of slamming her fists into it. She leaned against it instead, letting it hold the weight her legs would no longer support.

My grandfather was Kalian. My mother was half-Kalian, and my father—Ariane struggled for breath. *Bernard knew. He knew.*

Terror engulfed her. *I am not myself.*

From some great distance she seemed to hear a voice calling, faint and urgent. *I am alone,* she thought desperately. *Alone.*

Heart racing, she swung away from the wall in search of

escape. The voice calling her grew louder, stronger, drawing her toward it in spite of her resistance.

"Ariane," the voice said. "Don't be afraid, child. Be at peace."

And suddenly Ariane's vision cleared: Finch was there, on her feet, reaching out for her, swaying, tottering, falling. Within a heartbeat Ariane had the old woman in her arms.

Finch seemed to weigh nothing at all as Ariane lowered her gently to the threadbare carpet. A fierce, alien protectiveness surged through Ariane, shattering her fear.

Death. The blackness was closing in.

"No," Finch gasped. Her translucent eyelids fluttered. "No time." With one fumbling hand she reached within her patched blouse and withdrew a wide gold band set with a plain black stone. "Take this, my child. It is all I have time to give you now. When I—" She gasped, her breath coming sharp and harsh. "My strength is gone." Glazed copper eyes fixed on Ariane with deep tenderness. "You were like a daughter to me, Ariane. But you were always of my blood. Sedge Allen was my son."

Ariane could do nothing but hold the old woman, feeling life drain away with every heartbeat, the long battle coming to an end.

She could do nothing. Nothing.

"Take it," Finch gasped, and Ariane took the ring and shoved it on her finger without thinking. It hung loose, and she clenched her fist around it. "And now you must send Rook to me." Ariane stammered a protest, but Finch only smiled, her face radiant. "Do not fear to trust Rook Galloway —or your own heart." The old woman's eyes closed. "The Maker be with you, child."

Before Ariane could move, Rook was there beside her, taking Finch from her arms. Ariane rose jerkily and staggered away; she found the door to the small lavatory and stepped into it, staring at her face in the mirror.

Brown eyes stared back at her accusingly. *Great-grandmother,* she thought. The features in the mirror blurred. *Grand-maman. . . .*

"She's gone."

Rook's eyes met hers in reflection, dry and clear. His face was an expressionless mask. No sorrow, no rage.

No accusation. No recognition of what she was.

He did not know. And now Finch was gone.

"No," Ariane whispered. The tears spilled over when she shut her eyes.

"The words have been said, Lady Ariane," he murmured tonelessly. His fingers moved swiftly on his wrist remote. "There is no more time."

Ariane looked at him in the mirror and brushed her tears away with the back of her hand. Her grief was genuine; in his own sorrow Rook was certain of that kindred emotion.

He wanted to ask what Finch had told her—what had brought the shock to Ariane's face before Finch had called him to her side. He wanted to touch her, hold her, give comfort and receive it.

He had thought he'd known what it was to be truly alone.

Turning to face him, Ariane swallowed and dropped her eyes from his. "We have to do something for her—"

"No." With impersonal coldness he reached for her, and she let him pull her from the tiny lav and into the main room. Finch's body lay stretched out on the small bunk in the corner where Rook had chanted the final words of Passing.

Ariane's breath caught on a sob, and she wrenched her arm free of his loose grasp. She knelt at the side of the bunk, brushing a kiss on Finch's still, soft cheek.

Rook granted her that silent farewell. There was still something left in him of the forgotten, innocent young man of eight long years ago. Finch had reawakened that man with a few gentle words, but he could not long survive Finch's passing, and Rook wanted him gone. Gone forever.

In Finch's face there was only peace—peace, and acceptance.

"There was no pain in the end," Rook said. He moved behind Ariane and stood looking down at her bent head. "She'd been fighting a long time. She had only to let go."

Let go.

Icy rage welled up in Rook, so cold that he could grasp it like a solid thing and mold it to his will. "Come," he commanded, grasping Ariane's shoulder. She leaped to her feet and spun to face him.

"*Dieu,*" she gasped, her brown eyes feverishly bright. "*Mon Dieu.*"

Rook glanced at his remote and the flashing alarm that reminded him brutally how little time remained. The ship from Tantalus—the one he'd been expecting—was approaching dock at that very moment. He initiated the sequence that would begin powering up the *d'Artagnan* for immediate departure.

"Now," he breathed, propelling Ariane to the door of the cubicle. He looked back once at Finch's quiet face and left the old woman to her rest.

The corridor was as dark and empty as when they'd arrived, but with every footfall Rook felt the trap closing in around them. The wait for the levitrain seemed endless. Rook studied Ariane with cold-blooded detachment. The shock he read in her sightless gaze was something far more than grief. She obeyed his terse commands without protest, the unconscious pride she wore like a shield utterly gone.

It had been Ariane whom Finch had kept at her side. Not Rook. Not one of her own people.

Not until the very end.

The soft command of Finch's final words echoed in Rook's brain. "*Take care of her, Rook Galloway. Take care of my Ariane.*"

Rook jerked his gaze away from Ariane's as if that single act could banish her from his sight and from his heart.

"*Take care of her.*" Finch had been an Elder—a woman of great power and wisdom, who had chosen to serve the Marchand of her own will.

"*Take care of my Ariane.*"

Clenching his hand into a careful fist, Rook felt each muscle and tendon shift under the Marchand skin he wore.

The levitrain settled to a stop with a gentle hiss. Doors slid open to reveal the Concourse terminal on the outer wheel. Rook steered Ariane into the crowd and glanced again at his remote.

The Tantalan ship had docked. Within minutes all Agora station would know Rook Galloway, Kalian, had escaped from the prison world. Only a matter of time before they'd send League police to question the crew of the *d'Artagnan*.

Rook kept his pace just short of a run, half carrying Ariane along the vast tiered boulevard of restaurants, shops, and offices and into the docking bay that ran along the outer rim of Agora's main wheel. Ariane came to a halt and held fast just as they reached the barrier that marked the restricted portion of the dock.

"They'll know," Ariane murmured, the first words she'd said since they'd left Finch's cubicle. "They'll know you're here."

Rook followed her gaze to the vast screen that listed arrivals and departures. The name of the Tantalan ship, *Daedalus,* flashed rhythmically at the bottom of the roster.

He dug in the breast pocket of his shipsuit and pulled out Ariane's IDchip. "Yes. And I have no intention of being caught." Pushing the chip into her hand, he turned to look casually up and down the length of the bay. When the docking-bay IDlock granted them access, he offered Ariane his arm and walked slowly toward the *d'Artagnan*'s berth, several ships down the ring.

"No alarms," he breathed. "Not yet."

Ariane looked up at him, her expression tense and unreadable. The fingers resting lightly on his arm clenched into the fabric of his sleeve. "What will you do if they're already waiting?"

Rook understood the source of her fear, but he could no longer summon up a bitter smile. "I'll deal with that when I must. I don't intend to—"

Ariane's soft intake of breath caught his attention before he could finish the reassurance.

Two figures were visible across the last short distance to

the *d'Artagnan,* waiting at the top of the ramp. Rook slowed and nearly stopped, and it was Ariane who kept him moving.

"Kamur," she said. "And another Fahar."

Relief washed over Rook and ebbed instantly. "His mate," he said harshly under his breath. He swore fluently in old Kalian Anglic. "I should have known that—"

"Something went wrong," Ariane broke in. She startled him by taking the lead, long strides carrying her to the Fahar.

Rook reached them just as Kamur, in a burst of agitated Standard, began to explain what had happened. The female Fahar at his side—silent, her ears flickering uneasily—gazed unblinkingly at her mate.

Kamur hardly twitched an ear at Rook's changed appearance, recognizing Rook with one of the Fahar's inhuman senses. His monologue continued unbroken as his emerald eyes moved from Ariane to Rook and back again.

Under other circumstances it might have been amusing. The young lovers had been outflanked by their parents, and a member of the Fahar Priesthood had been waiting for Kamur on Agora. In a burst of youthful impetuosity, Kamur and his mate—whom he introduced with a worshipful glance as Surra—had slipped away from their elders before the couple could arrange transport from Agora or be coerced into surrender.

"For, you see, Surra's sire was in a rage because she was to have been sealed within her own Clan, and though we had mated, we feared—"

"It is a simple thing," the female Fahar cut in softly. She blinked orange-gold eyes at Rook. "Kamur has told me of your great help to him, Brother of Kali. Now we would ask this help again."

Rook took in Surra's quiet request with only a fraction of his attention. He could feel Ariane's eyes on him, her gaze like a tangible thing.

Trapped. He knew well enough when he was trapped.

The Fahar didn't know the truth of how he'd come to be on the *d'Artagnan,* but they'd undoubtedly learn soon enough. He couldn't keep them in complete ignorance of the risks he faced.

"There is danger for us," he said to the lovers, turning his head to watch the passersby on the Concourse beyond the docks. "There's no time to explain—but if you come with us, you'll be facing the same danger."

Kamur and Surra glanced at each other, their ears dancing in wordless communication. "We understand," Surra said. "We have chosen."

Rook stared at them, forgetting his vigilance, lost in the intensity of the Fahar's unmistakable bond. The fine hairs rose on the back of his neck in unconscious response to Ariane's presence beside him: to her scent, the warmth of her body, her utter femaleness.

Kamur's words reverberated in memory: *"You have sealed each other. . . ."*

A flash of motion caught out of the corner of his eye snatched Rook from dangerous reverie. A woman in a gray tech's shipsuit walked swiftly away from a cluster of crates at the adjoining berth that had appeared deserted only moments before.

All thoughts of anything but escape fled Rook's mind. With a soft curse he turned Ariane toward the ramp. "We leave now," he said. Kamur and Surra bounded down the ramp, but Ariane remained.

"Danger," she said with the breath of a laugh, a reckless light in her deep-brown eyes. "It's you who's putting us in danger. Are you going to tell them the truth? Or did you plan to use them to make sure you get away? The League isn't likely to fire on Fahar now—"

"And they won't fire on you either, Lady Ariane," Rook said between his teeth, sealing the ramp's dockside air lock with a slap of his hand. He lifted Ariane bodily and carried her down the ramp. Her accusation that he might intend to use the Fahar stung him deeply. "I need only one hostage."

The strange remoteness that Ariane had shown since Finch's death had vanished. "They won't let you simply undock, Kalian," she snapped. Her voice shook on the final word.

"Perhaps not," he conceded grimly. "But even savages occasionally prefer to avoid a fight. Come on." At the foot of the ramp he followed her through the accordion tube that linked the ramp with the *d'Artagnan* and closed that air lock as well, flicking the switch that pulled the tube back within the hatch. "You're going to ask for permission to cast off as if nothing is wrong. We gave them a window of departure, and we're well within that time frame."

She set her mouth in a rebellious line but obeyed his sharp gesture, preceding him into the cockpit and dropping into the copilot's seat. Rook glanced at Kamur and Surra, who were waiting for them. "Go to the guest cabin and web in," he told them. "We may have a rough departure."

Kamur looked as though he would have commented, but Surra drew him away with a light touch, and they retreated through the hatch into the common room.

Rook turned his attention back to the control board. "No tricks," he warned Ariane softly, running a final check on the ship's systems.

"If it were only me," Ariane said as she flicked on the commlink, "I might take a few risks." Her voice was bitter. "But since you have the *d'Artagnan* rigged to blow. . . ."

Irrational anger, almost like pain, twisted in Rook's gut. She had believed he'd do it all along, as he'd intended she should, but it brought him no satisfaction. She truly thought him a savage. He gripped the back of her chair and spun her around. "It was a useful fiction, Lady Ariane, since it kept you in line. But the station was never in any danger. You could have run anytime, *chérie*. Anytime at all."

Ariane stared at him in silent fury.

"Don't read too much into it, Ariane. Savages are notoriously unpredictable." He pushed the commlink headset into her hand.

Ariane looped it over her head and swung back to the console. "Control, this is *d'Artagnan*, Reg. ES-C-959D, requesting permission to depart." She hesitated only an instant, glancing at Rook with troubled eyes, and transmitted the coordinates of the fabricated destination he'd given her on their arrival at Agora.

There was a long moment of quiet as the ship's computer exchanged data with Agora Control's vast communications network. A woman's voice addressed them expressionlessly. *"D'Artagnan,* this is Control. Please stand by. I repeat, stand by. We're processing your request."

Ariane's breath hissed out slowly. "They know. . . ."

Rook slammed into the pilot's seat and took the controls.

"D'Artagnan, this is Control. Negative on departure; request delay until seventeen thirty. Mining convoy entering local space on your flight path. Repeat, we cannot clear a corridor for departure until seventeen thirty. Acknowledge."

This time Rook's curse was in flawlessly profane Franglais, but Ariane only stared at his hand on the control stick and touched the mouthpiece of her headset. "Acknowledged," she murmured.

Rook cut communications with the station and turned to Ariane. "Web yourself in," he commanded. "We're taking the hard way out."

There was no surprise in her face. "Do you know what you're doing?" she asked simply.

He looked at her, long and hard. No protests, no warnings of dire consequences. "In theory," he answered grimly. He punched a button and examined the resulting readout. "They've already jammed the docking clamps."

Ariane's long, slender fingers hovered above the instrument panel. Agora Control would not release the docking clamps that held the *d'Artagnan* in its berth, and she knew as well as he did what must happen. "You'll tear her apart," she said.

He sensed the genuine distress hidden under the evenness of her voice. There were still a hundred things he didn't know about Ariane Burke-Marchand, things he hadn't thought he wanted or needed to know. Why she was in space with her own ship, far from the safety of the Marchand mansion on Lumière. Why she could be hated enemy one moment and ally the next, arrogant aristocrat and all soft, desirable woman . . .

He didn't know her at all.

"If my ship's going to be ripped apart at the seams, I'd rather be the one to do it," she said. She had never looked more beautiful: challenging him, daring him to trust her with the controls. She tossed her head, and her hair floated over her shoulders in a cloud; her eyes were dark as space.

An alien joy rose up in Rook then, as ungovernable as it was unfamiliar. He rose from the pilot's seat. "When I was a student on Tolstoy," he said softly, "I always wanted to see what a Caravel-class starship could do."

Her answer was a grin—fleeting, as if she'd caught herself before it could take full possession of her face. But she slipped into the pilot's seat, accepting the controls as he ceded the ship back to its owner.

Ariane threw the *d'Artagnan* into full reverse. A shriek of metal resounded through the cockpit. Ariane's face became set, wincing with the ship's protest. Rook watched her intently, braced and webbed into his own seat as she began to wrench the *d'Artagnan* free of the docking clamps.

An alarm sounded over the din; Rook shut it off while a row of indicators on the console went red. Another light flashed urgently, Agora Control attempting to reopen communications. Ariane ignored both. The ship lurched forward sharply and back again at full thrust. Outside the canopy the docking clamps began to bend and buckle. With a groan of agony the ship broke free.

And then they were speeding backward, clearing the berth platform. Ariane spun the ship about in a deft, expert move, and for the first time they got a clear glimpse of the League Patrol ship waiting to intercept them.

Rook almost unwebbed then to take the controls, but Ariane was one step ahead. As if she'd evaded pursuit all her life, she dodged the swift Patrol ship easily and made for free space.

"They can't outrun *d'Artagnan*," Ariane said under her breath, piloting the ship in an arc that passed between two freighters making for the station. There was something like satisfaction in her voice.

Flipping the switch that opened the communication band, Rook refused to allow himself the luxury of hope. "They'll have pulse torpedoes that can immobilize the ship before we can jump out of the system," he said. "The d'Artagnan has a disruptor cannon—"

"You won't use it!" Ariane said sharply.

He gripped the armrest of his seat. "Not unless I have no other choice. I'll have to buy time."

Ariane bit her lip and executed another complex maneuver through system traffic as Rook hailed the Patrol ship. "This is Rook Galloway. I have control of the Marchand ship d'Artagnan out of Espérance. Call off your pursuit. I have hostages. Repeat—call off your pursuit, or the hostages will suffer."

For the first time since she'd taken the controls, Ariane looked at him—a bewildered look as if she had only then remembered who she was. *Hostage.* The excitement faded from her eyes.

Rook took in the Patrol ship's clipped reply from a distance, lost in Ariane's stricken gaze. With a curse he forced his attention back to the thrust and parry of his verbal duel with their pursuers. He felt strangely detached from the harsh, coarse voice that threatened violence to the woman at his side.

But Ariane heard. Her face was white as she guided the d'Artagnan to the outer edge of the system. The Patrol ship hung back, persuaded by Rook's warnings. Rook broadcast a systemwide alert of his intention to jump and turned to Ariane again.

He knew he should reclaim the ship at such a critical moment; the stark desperation in Ariane's face was reason enough. But he punched in the final coordinates and leaned back into his seat as the all clear sounded.

"Take her out," he said softly.

She never hesitated at all. A second later they were in hyperspace, Agora station far behind.

• • •

In the elegant stateroom of the Slayton yacht *Perséphone*, Wynn downed his last swallow of expensive Midgardian brandy and gazed at Agora station through the wide porthole.

He lifted his empty glass in salute. *To my bride,* he thought with a smile.

She was waiting for him there. He had no doubt that she would be ready for him; she was Marchand to the last drop of her blood. As proud and stubborn as her great-grandfather. Fatally proud.

He wondered if she'd outgrown her yearning for adventure, that rebellious streak of defiance that so few Elite women possessed or dared display. Bernard had allowed her a surprising amount of freedom; he'd held firm in his request to allow Ariane these three years in space before her marriage. Wynn had been more than happy for the additional time to strengthen his plans.

Would she still cling to impossible dreams of leading a Marchand expedition into uncharted space? Wynn moved from the porthole and idly considered pouring himself another measure of brandy. The Marchand were dreamers; they'd counted such dreams the privilege of being one of the oldest families on Espérance. Leave the practical, mercenary matters to world-bound upstarts such as the Slaytons.

He smiled humorlessly. Slayton talent, Slayton ambition, Slayton money had fueled Bernard's grandiose dreams—and now the Nouveau Elite were accepted as equals in the highest circles.

But that wasn't enough. No, not nearly enough to make up for past humiliation. Even upstarts of bought caste could bind themselves to an honorable cause.

Or revenge.

Setting down his glass, Wynn moved to the wall to study the old-style painting of his parents. Fifty-eight years—fifty-eight years ago Bernard Marchand had rejected Ria Santini-Slayton on the day of their betrothal. Fifty-eight years ago Tyler Slayton, Wynn's father, had dueled to defend Ria's impugned honor, only to be defeated by Bernard and humiliated with charges of rank dishonor and cowardice.

The Slaytons had been newly made Elite then, their standing among the great families uncertain. They'd been years in recovering from the events set in motion by Bernard Marchand and his arrogance, but Wynn's father had never outlived his shame. He had died in the first Fahar Conflict, when Wynn had been only a small, bewildered boy.

Wynn gazed at his mother's beautiful, tragic face. He had heard the story so many times he felt he had been there himself, a witness to Ria's disgrace. None but the Slaytons had questioned Bernard's word when he'd claimed that his would-be betrothed had been born out of wedlock, sired by a man of the lowly Laborer caste. None of the Elite had blamed the heir to the Marchand for refusing to mingle his pure blood with that of a half-caste illegitimate.

Now, so many years later, with the Slayton name and fortune restored, with wealth and power tied irrevocably to that of the family that had once come so close to destroying them, few Slaytons dwelt on the past.

Few except Wynn Slayton. And his hatred was more than sufficient.

He turned from the portrait slowly. Ariane Burke-Marchand came from a long line of righteously pure-blooded, honorable dreamers. Perhaps she would cling to her dreams, believing he would be the avuncular friend he'd seemed when she was growing up. In that she'd be doomed to far more than mere disappointment.

Not that it mattered. She'd be his obedient wife because she was sworn to it by vows of betrothal unbreakable save by death. She had become a woman at last; he would enjoy her willing body while he could. And when she learned his true purpose . . . Wynn smiled. Then—then it would be far too late.

Wynn returned to his study of the vast space station as his pilot guided the *Perséphone* to its berth. He could not feel easy contempt for the Marchand; they had been the first to embrace offworld trade and in so doing had made their name known throughout the League above any other family of Espérance.

The Marchand had been the first to treat with the League ships that had appeared in the Espérancian system nearly one hundred years ago. The newly formed League had one goal: to bring the scattered colonies of ancient Earth together again after centuries of isolation. There had been many on Espérance who'd wanted no part of other worlds, but the Marchand influence had prevailed in the end.

And so the Marchand sphere of power had spread outward, establishing virgin trade with the other worlds of the League, building ships, claiming new resources. On Espérance the Slaytons had consolidated their fortune in pharmaceuticals and research. The discovery of the drug Longévité, derived from a native Espérancian plant, had bought the Slaytons into the Elite; soon they were the wealthiest family on Espérance save for the Marchand themselves.

The Marchand name had gained respect beyond Espérance, their honor unquestioned on fifteen worlds. Their position on Espérance was paramount; few chose to oppose them. They were the virtual rulers of Lumière, and Lumière was the greatest city of Espérance.

Two families at odds: one ancient and drunk on dreams of other worlds, the other vigorous and ambitious and pragmatically earthbound. It had seemed natural that these families should make a formal alliance to mutual benefit. And it would have been so if not for Bernard Marchand, fifty-eight years ago.

Now everything had come full circle.

"Sieur Slayton, we're preparing to dock. Please web in."

Tilting his head at the sound of his pilot's voice, Wynn moved to the padded chair set in a private alcove just off the stateroom. He picked up the report on the Louve-system operation that he'd put down an hour before and scanned the figures with satisfaction. Marchand contacts and influence had enabled him to become established in illicit offplanet drug manufacturing; from small-time operation the Louve project had become a major business and a significant part of

Wynn's personal wealth. Bernard Marchand would be horrified to know his offworld connections had unwittingly allowed Wynn to expand his drug-running far beyond the limits of Espérance.

Wynn set the report down again and, closing his eyes, settled into the chair as the *Perséphone* began to maneuver into dock. The Louve operation was only one of the ways the Marchand were contributing to their own downfall. The Kalians were yet another. And Ariane—Ariane would be the consummation of it all.

For the Marchand had one great weakness. In his lust to push the boundaries, Bernard Marchand had taken great risks. He had thrown the Marchand fortune into expensive projects that would take time to pay off, amassing debts that would stagger any other family, creating a deceptively powerful empire backed by the virtue of the Marchand name.

Wynn had made himself an essential part of that empire, the trusted adviser, the partner who knew almost everything there was to know about Marchand operations on Espérance and within the League.

Bernard trusted him. The Marchand Patriarch trusted him because it eased his old guilt about the feud nearly everyone else had forgotten, and because Wynn Slayton had the wealth to help make Bernard's dreams come true.

The shell of the Marchand empire held a dragon waiting to be hatched. A Slayton dragon to swallow the Marchand whole.

Wynn felt the *Perséphone* slip gracefully into her berth with a deceptively gentle click.

It was the first crack in the egg.

CHAPTER EIGHT

*O*ne day out from Agora, at the first layover on the way to
M'nauri, Ariane retreated to her cabin and struggled to keep
her sanity.

She knew there was nowhere to hide. The *d'Artagnan* had
been large for one person, adequate for two. But it was far
too small for two human adversaries and a pair of mated
Fahar.

Ariane lay on her bunk and tried to shut out the vivid
images that crowded her mind.

There were no true humans on the *d'Artagnan* at all.

Kamur and Surra were locked in the guest cabin as they'd
been almost from the moment the ship had left Agora, and
even soundproofed walls could not hold Ariane's hyper-
awareness at bay. The Fahar had made no secret of their frank
lust for each other, and after such a long separation it was
clear they had no time to waste.

Pushing a damp strand of hair away from her forehead,
Ariane shifted again on the bunk.

Desire. She could feel it—smell it in the air like an elusive
scent. Desire that made her heart labor, her mouth dry, her
body ache in ways beyond her control.

Her rational mind told her what it must be. *Kalian,* she
thought, twisting on the mattress. *Kalian senses.*

She hated it, this knowledge she didn't want. Now that
she knew what she was, a thousand proofs of her heritage
seemed to leap out at her like hellhounds to rend her body
and soul.

Like the night of the riots, when she had been drawn to
the Warren. Drawn there as her mother had been drawn. To
her own kind.

And like her first meeting with Rook after eight long

years, when she had touched him and felt what she couldn't understand. Until now she had pushed it from her mind, denied it, forgotten. She was only beginning to realize how much she'd forgotten.

You are Kalian.

Kamur had known from the beginning, and she'd been too blind to see. *"Sister,"* he'd called her. *"Child of the Shapers."*

The blindness had been lifted by an old woman's dying words and her own raw, undeniable certainty.

You are Kalian.

Almost every time she touched Rook, it happened: her body's recognition of what she was. Deeper senses of emotion and need and compulsion than anything merely human.

Now it all made terrible sense.

No. Ariane covered her eyes with the back of her hand. There was no sense to it at all.

No sense to the way she felt when the man who was her enemy touched her, when he held her in his arms, when he kissed her.

Eight years ago she had felt it. She had lived the intervening years with a sense of something incomplete, a nameless yearning, an inability to let go. And so she had gone to see Rook Galloway.

Like calling to like, blood to blood, a primitive mating dance of savages . . .

Ariane bolted upright and plunged from the bunk. *I am Marchand.* She repeated the words to herself like a litany, clinging to the one thing that hadn't changed. She was still Bernard Marchand's great-granddaughter. And Bernard had known what she was.

"Oh, Grand-père," she whispered. Moving blindly to the lav cubicle in the corner of the cabin, Ariane thought of the mother and father she'd never known, the distant man she had always believed was her father. Pierre Burke-Marchand had meant little to her. Bernard had raised her—Bernard and Finch, hiding her secret from the world.

But Jacques— She swallowed painfully, bracing herself on

the tiny sink without meeting her gaze in the mirror. Finch had said nothing of him. Had he, too, been drawn by his Kalian blood to the Warren, only to die?

Forcing herself to look into the mirror at last, Ariane stared at her unremarkable reflection. Her face had always been too strong for traditional Elite beauty; now she wondered how much of it was real. Somehow Finch had changed her—against her will, without her knowledge, to hide what she was.

Ariane lifted a heavy lock of brown hair and let it sift through her fingers. Had her hair been raven-black at birth? And her eyes—had they been copper, like hot metal? If she stared long enough, could she make them change to what they should be, back to the true template of her kind?

"You have the ability. . . ."

Adrenaline surged through her body, potent as Midgardian brandy, strength unfolding like the petals of a brilliant flower. Warm light flickered in her eyes. With a gasp she pushed away from the mirror and strode across the cabin. Her booted foot caught the corner of the open storage locker, and she stared down into it, at the ring Finch had given her, tossed in among her other things.

There was no escape—not from the ship or from herself. But she fled, driven to any action that would hold her desperate thoughts at bay. Her sabers hung in the common room; she would run through the exercises and do battle with phantoms until her body—her *Kalian* body—was exhausted beyond reason. The risk of confronting Rook seemed less terrifying than being alone with this woman she no longer knew.

She was almost running when she struck a warm, solid wall of muscle and bone. Rook caught at her and held her when she would have fallen; unbearable awareness coursed through Ariane, wrenching a gasp from her throat.

Desire. Desire, physical longing, dark passion stirred like a deadly serpent coiled to strike.

Terror gave her the strength to break free. Rook looked down at her with a frown, more perplexed than threatening.

Ariane waited with sickened dread for him to say the words marking her for what she was.

Savage.

His lips parted. Her eyes were drawn to them, inevitably, and lower to the open vee of the loose shirt he wore. Taut muscle rippled as he drew in a sharp breath. She felt her own lungs drain of air.

And he stepped back, a single long stride that put him beyond touching distance.

"What did she tell you?" Rook asked suddenly.

Ariane started, shaking the confusion from her mind. Finch. He meant Finch.

"She was—my nanny when I was a child," Ariane said slowly, buying time. "She disappeared from Espérance after the riots—" With an act of will she blocked the old images from memory.

Rook's eyes narrowed. "Your nanny." He shook his head. "She was an Elder—one of those who still remembered the old ways. An Elder serving the Marchand." He raised his hand and let it fall again, clenched into a fist. "She was Kalian. What did she say to you, Ariane Burke-Marchand, that she could not tell one of her own?"

There was pain in his words—hidden, disguised in the deep roughness of his voice. She had heard that pain when he'd spoken gently to Finch in the moments before her death, and again when he'd told Ariane that his threat against the station was a bluff to keep her with him.

One of her own. Ariane stared up into his shuttered eyes. He didn't know. Finch had not told him. He could touch Ariane and not—*know*—what she was.

"She said good-bye," Ariane said calmly. The partial truth felt bitter on her tongue, almost like a betrayal. *"Do not fear to trust Rook Galloway,"* Finch had said. But she had not known about Rook's plans for vengeance.

"Good-bye?" Rook echoed. He took a half step forward. "Did it affect you so deeply to lose a servant you hadn't seen in eight years?"

Ariane jerked her head. "I loved her," she whispered fiercely.

He took the bait. "Did you, Lady Ariane?" His stare burned like a white-hot star. After a long moment he looked away. "She saw something in you," he said under his breath. "Something important. . . ."

Desperate to distract him, Ariane reached out and brushed his rigid arm with the tips of her fingers. The contact was too brief to disturb her deeply, but it caught Rook's attention. "She could change, like you," Ariane said slowly. "I didn't know. She never told me."

Rook pulled his arm behind him. "If your kind had known that some among my people could Change . . ." His expression finished the thought clearly.

Ariane swallowed, forced to drop her eyes. "Finch used it to stay on Espérance, to be with me. If she'd only told me—"

"She would have been condemned along with the rest," Rook said bitterly. "She was Kalian."

Confusion and anger and fear broke free of Ariane's tenuous control. *I am Kalian,* she screamed silently, but she locked gazes with Rook and answered him with deceptive calm.

"I would have protected her. She did nothing wrong. Nothing."

She thought it would begin again—the accusations and counteraccusations, a battle that could have no resolution, that would drive her to madness. But Rook looked away, and his eyes closed. In that single small gesture lay a wealth of despair, a fragile instant of vulnerability Ariane could not withstand.

"She was fortunate to have earned your loyalty, Lady Ariane," he said tonelessly. "But it doesn't matter anymore." He turned to go, but she moved quickly to block his path.

"Do you think," she said, "that I can't grieve as you do? Do you think you're the only one in the universe who knows what it's like to be alone?" She battled the urge to release the tumult of her emotions, clenching her fists and welcoming the pain as her nails bit into her palms. "I do understand. I understand better than you'll ever know."

Rook stood with his body half turned away from her, his profile stark in the common room's dim light. "I almost believe you do," he said softly.

Aching grief filled Ariane then—for Finch, for Jacques, for herself, for Rook—a thousand sorrows layered one upon another. Two small steps would carry her to Rook—two endless, impossible steps to touch his rigid back and stroke the broad sweep of his shoulders, feel the warmth of his body against hers, comfort him and herself.

He saved her from her own folly. Abruptly he pivoted to face her again, the corner of his mouth lifting. "I almost forgot to thank you, Lady Ariane. You handled the ship very well. My compliments." His eyes swept from her half boots to the crown of her head. "Without you I couldn't have made it."

His expression turned praise into a taunt. The familiar shield of Ariane's anger locked into place. "Don't read too much into it," she snapped, throwing his own words back in his face. "I won't be making a habit of accommodating you."

A dangerous light flared in Rook's copper eyes. Once again he examined every centimeter of her body, his gaze lingering in ways she could not misinterpret. Heat flooded her cheeks. Tossing back her hair, she set her hands on her hips and returned his regard with the same thorough insolence.

"And I'd foolishly hoped for a change of heart," Rook murmured. He reached out to touch a strand of her hair, and her heart nearly stopped. "A pity. You could accommodate me so well—"

"Your pardon."

Rook nearly leaped backward, snapping his hand from Ariane's face. Kamur blinked at them from the doorway of the guest cabin, ears flickering.

"I did not mean to disturb you, Brother. Sister." The Fahar took several gliding steps toward them. "My mate and I have need of sustenance. The past day has been a most exhausting one."

Ariane stared at Kamur, the heat in her cheeks redoubling.

The Fahar's green eyes were brilliant, the soft velvet skin of his nose flushed. If an alien could display a foolish grin, Kamur did so as he looked from one human to the other.

"Kamur . . ." Surra appeared in the doorway behind him, her voice a rich purr. "Return to me quickly. I cannot wait."

The expression on Kamur's face grew even more blissful. "You will pardon me," the Fahar murmured, and he padded away in the direction of the galley, his walk noticeably unsteady.

Rook's almost inaudible curse caught Ariane's attention. His high cheekbones were stained dull red under the tan, and his eyes were focused on some particularly fascinating portion of the nearest bulkhead. It wasn't until Kamur returned, laden with a tray of heated rations, and disappeared into the guest cabin again that Rook regained his composure.

"Two more days," he said hoarsely. "Two more days to M'nauri. And then—"

Ariane could almost hear the threat he didn't speak aloud. *Then home,* she thought. *Espérance, and your revenge. . . .*

Unable to bear his presence, she turned on her heel and fled to her cabin, Rook's hot stare burning into her back.

Rook locked himself in the cockpit after the first day out.

In the endless hours between jumps, when he was alone with his thoughts, he felt her. Painfully, overwhelmingly, suffusing his body in a dull and constant ache of need.

For all he knew of their ways, he hadn't been prepared for the effect of mating Fahar on his senses. Their desire hung like musk in the recycled air. It was a kind of madness, and it had contaminated Rook to the point of agony.

He could no longer trust himself. The savage lay very close to the surface. The savage that would take Ariane and damn the consequences—or what remained of his conscience.

Rook leaned back in the pilot's seat and returned to the ancient technique of meditation that Fox had taught him on Tantalus years ago. One by one he relaxed his muscles, willed his heart to slow. He felt each cell, each drop of blood singing in his veins. He took control of his arousal and adjusted the flow of blood until his body was almost relaxed.

And then he let his mind follow, spiraling down into a place of peace.

But she was there, waiting.

In a burst of violent motion Rook leaped from the chair and flung himself at the cockpit hatch. His clumsy fingers required three attempts to override the locking sequence he'd put on it. Striding out into the common room, he looked for her, footsteps as silent as a predator on the hunt.

The common room was empty.

He stalked the length of the room and checked the galley. Faint sounds came to him through the guest-cabin doors; he shut them out savagely.

The hatch to Ariane's cabin was sealed. Rook set himself before it, laid both hands flat on the cool metal surface. He tried to speak her name, but his throat could no longer form words.

He clawed at the IDlock, and the hatch slid open.

Ariane's scent flooded from the cabin, rich and seductive. His eyes swept the room intently, lingering on the rumpled bed.

She was not there. There was only one other place she could be—the cargo hold—and nowhere else she could run.

Sanity returned, leaving Rook almost weak. With deliberation he stepped fully into Ariane's cabin and locked the hatch behind him.

This was the one place on her ship he had not claimed. He knew it was a violation to linger there, but he had gone past anything as fragile as guilt. And it was a far lesser violation than the one the savage in him had intended.

Cursing under his breath, Rook searched the cabin hungrily. His eyes returned to the bunk and settled on the cloud of pale, sheer fabric that trailed across the tousled blankets.

Ariane's. A sleeping gown, delicate as spun starlight. Something fit for one of the Elite.

Rook grasped a handful of soft fabric in his fist and lifted it to his face.

Her scent almost overwhelmed him. The firesilk of the sleeping gown drifted across his face, caught on the roughness of his scar. He held it to his mouth and tasted it, the taste of her body and forbidden desire.

He had never seen her in anything but a loose-fitting ship-suit, covering her from neck to ankle. But he could envision her in this, her body revealed to his eyes and his touch. . . .

Groaning softly, he let the gown fall and forced his eyes from the bed on which she had lain. For the first time he noticed the open storage locker at the foot of the bunk.

An impulse he didn't question drove him to crouch, sift through the litdisks and mementos piled haphazardly in the locker. These, too, were hers—old-style printed books, an engraved medallion on a frayed ribbon, a plain gold ring set with a black stone—bits and pieces of her life. The life of an Elite, a Marchand, a woman he didn't understand.

And he wanted to understand. He paused with a holopic in his hand, frozen by the revelation. He wanted to understand her.

Because she is your enemy. But the thought was a lie, a coward's evasion.

Rook stared down at the holopic in his hand as if it might provide all the answers. Ariane's face gazed back at him, smiling, younger by several years. And the older man who held her looked at her with the pride of a father.

Or the possessiveness of a lover.

The holopic seemed to burn his fingers as he pushed aside the remaining litdisks and found the 'pics hidden at the bottom of the locker. He recognized the one of Jacques, and another of the Patriarch, Bernard Marchand. And then he found two or three clipped together, pushed far to the back.

The man was dark, arrogant, unmistakably Elite. There was another 'pic with Ariane, in formal dress, her face serious as she stood beside him.

Rook almost missed the scrap of paper that fell from between the last two 'pics.

He scanned the elegant handwritten lines, composed in lyrical Franglais. The signature at the bottom engraved itself into his mind.

At the last moment he stopped himself from crushing the letter in his fist and slipped it back between the holopics, replacing Ariane's things with utmost care.

He rose and stood very still, listening. After a long moment he moved to the cabin's computer terminal and settled into the seat, shoving his hair back from his face.

Ariane's private code was remarkably easy to break. And Rook felt no guilt at all.

"May I enter?"

Ariane completed her practice parry and turned smoothly to face the Fahar who stood in the open hatch of the cargo hold.

Pulling free the band that held her hair away from her face, Ariane lowered the saber and drew in a deep breath. "Surra."

The Fahar was all sinuous, sensual grace as she glided into the hold. "My Sister— May I call you Sister?"

Ariane shut her eyes briefly. There'd been no escape from the battle within herself. She had hardly seen Surra since Agora, but it was impossible not to like the Fahar female. Even when her gentle words struck like the searing beam of a disruptor set to kill.

"Yes," Ariane whispered. Surra studied the hold with cocked ears while Ariane took a long swallow of recycled water, struggling to ignore the deep, hollow ache in her body.

"Sister, why is it that you have not yet mated with Rook Galloway?"

Ariane choked and almost dropped the glass. Heat rose to her face and curled in her belly like a fever.

"Are matters of mating so difficult among humans?" Surra continued, her ears flickering. "Kamur and I do not perfectly understand human ways, but we have long been brothers and sisters to your people. Have you not sealed each other?"

Leaning against the nearest bulkhead, Ariane grasped at

sanity. Wild laughter bubbled up in her throat. "Humans—" she began. "Humans don't—it isn't—"

Surra slid closer. "Perhaps it is not so with all humans, but Kalians are Shaper's Children. Kamur has told me that your people are much like us in the choosing of mates. Is it not so?"

The sibilant melody of Surra's voice faded into meaningless sound. A deeper, rougher voice took its place, mocking and heavy with desire.

"You could accommodate me so well. . . ."

With fierce resolve Ariane shut the voice out, and the memories and the vision of Rook Galloway's touch. "It's—not so, with humans," she said with remarkable calm. "Rook Galloway is not my mate."

She realized she was staring blindly at the bulkhead when Surra came up beside her. "Then it is most strange, my Sister. Kamur and I can smell it. Even the most scent-blind would know." Delicate claws plucked at Ariane's sleeve. "Forgive, Sister—but can it be that you deny the sealing?"

"I deny nothing!" Spinning on her heel, Ariane broke away and nearly ran to the opposite bulkhead of the hold. The words threatened to spill out then—the truth about Rook Galloway and his plans for revenge, about her own captivity and the terrible duality of her heritage.

She caught her breath on a sob and met Surra's brilliant orange-gold eyes. No. The Fahar had no part in this. They, too, had been enemies once, but that time was long past.

And the truth was no longer something she could grasp.

"Ah, my Sister," Surra sighed. Her ears were lowered in sympathy. "I smell your distress. You must not fight what must be. There is no fear in the sealing. It is only in this way that you can be whole." The Fahar smiled a human smile. "You will not regret the mating. Ah, the pleasure of it. . . ."

A sound drifted through the open hatch, melodic and rich with yearning. Surra's ears swiveled sharply. The fine hairs rose on the back of Ariane's neck, her entire body responding to the call.

"Ah, the pleasure," Surra sighed.

After the Fahar had gone, Ariane unclenched her fists and stared at the neat red crescents her nails had cut into her palms.

"Heal," she whispered. "Heal, curse you." And the tiny cuts began to fade before her eyes.

Ariane's cry echoed in the empty hold.

The unspoken truce held for three days.

On the morning of the third day, the last before they reached M'nauri, Ariane hurried from her cabin to the sanctuary of the cargo hold. It had become a ritual with her: restless, dream-haunted sleep, followed by a hasty meal in the galley and a daylong session in the hold, dueling her own shadow.

There was nowhere else to go. Two nights before, Ariane had returned to her cabin and felt such a powerful sense of Rook's presence that she'd known she was no longer safe there.

Ariane scanned the common room and stared at the sealed cockpit hatch. Rook spent his time locked away with the ship's controls, but Ariane's heart beat heavily in her chest in the expectation of seeing him, dread and yearning intermingled.

Safe. She almost smiled at the bitter humor of it. Safe from him, or from herself?

Palming the IDlock of the cargo hold's hatch, Ariane stepped into darkness. The lights came up one by one.

Rook was there, a saber in his hand. Ariane froze in midstep.

He didn't turn. Bare-chested, his powerful body supremely graceful, Rook executed a near-perfect *flèche,* gliding forward noiselessly. Ariane forgot to breathe as she watched him, lost in the beauty of his movements. No Kalian was privileged to learn the ancient way of dueling, yet instinct guided him in a dance of elegance and restrained power.

Never did he look at Ariane where she stood in the hatchway, but he called to her—called with his body and his scent and the flow of his black hair, the whisper of his bare feet and the flash of his blade. He called to the savage within her, and the savage struggled to break free. To go to him, to surrender, to be one with him. With one of her own kind.

Ariane closed her eyes and fought. As Rook battled shadows, she battled herself. Ariane Burke-Marchand, woman of the Elite, great-granddaughter of the most powerful Patriarch of Espérance, promised on her sacred honor to a man of her own people. And Ariane the Kalian, half-breed savage, bound to nothing but primitive need and hot, dark desire.

"I was waiting for you."

Rook stood before her in a fighter's stance. His eyes burned through the thick strands of dark hair that shadowed his face.

The victor of Ariane's inward battle gazed back at him, her body straight and her face cold with contempt.

"You handle a blade well, Kalian," she said, looking him up and down.

He bared his teeth. "For a savage," he finished. He returned her look measure for measure, lingering on her set mouth.

Ariane let her eyes drop to the saber in his hand. "Yes. There is something to be said for instinct. You might have been a formidable opponent with the proper training."

His hand tightened on the hilt. "I'm a very fast learner," he said softly. He took a single step closer. "You could teach me, Lady Ariane."

Her eyes snapped back to his face. He was deadly serious. Ariane's heart lodged in her throat.

"Teach you?" she said scornfully. "To master the art of dueling requires honor, Kalian. And that is something you can never learn."

Her blow struck home. The muscles in Rook's jaw bunched. "Honor again. Marchand honor." He turned away and strode across the hold to the rack that Ariane had moved from the common room. He grasped the second saber in his free hand and stalked back to confront her again.

"You prize your honor highly, Lady Ariane. Now I'll give

you a chance to keep it." When he thrust the second saber at her hilt first, Ariane took it without thinking, tightening her fingers on the corded leather of the grip.

"I challenge you, Ariane Burke-Marchand," Rook said.

For a moment she could only stare at him. His simple words, the way he held his weapon, bore no resemblance to the careful ritual of a true Elite challenge. And yet the adrenaline beat through her body, her muscles clenched in anticipation, her very blood betrayed her.

She laughed. She flung back her head and laughed because she could do nothing else. And Rook seized her with his free hand and wrenched her against him, silencing her laugh with his demanding lips.

It was enough to awaken the savage. Ariane pushed against him desperately, the saber trapped at her side, drowning in liquid heat. He released her mouth to speak, his lips brushing hers with each word.

"I want you, Ariane."

She tried to shake her head, but he laced his fingers in the hair at the nape of her neck and held her easily. "I want you, and I think you want me."

"You're insane—"

"A savage, perhaps, but not insane." Rook drew her lower lip between his teeth and released it slowly. She could not control the shudder that racked her, that betrayed her so easily. "I feel it, Ariane. Kalian senses. You're no innocent. You want me to take you—"

"No," she moaned.

"Is it because you wonder what it would be like to let yourself go—give in to what your body desires? Or is it some twisted fascination with the last male Kalian your family left alive?"

Rage and fear sang along Ariane's nerves. "*Canaille*—I'll never let you have me—"

Rook let her go abruptly and stepped back, his eyes lambent. Trembling, Ariane gasped for breath, swaying in the overheated air.

"You can't stop me, Ariane." He smiled, a cruel uptilt of

one corner of his mouth. "I have a Kalian's strength, and no fine concept of honor to restrain me. And you are my captive. *Mine.*"

Across the space that separated them Ariane could feel the bonds with which he held her, invisible and unbreakable.

"If you touch me—if you touch me, the Patriarch will see you dead," she whispered. Bluff, all bluff. She was powerless, against him and against the savage within herself.

Rook shook his head, his mane sweeping across the breadth of his shoulders. "I can lose no more than I already have." His chest rose with his indrawn breath. "You have a simple choice, Ariane. Accept my challenge, or pay the penalty."

A wild recklessness surged through Ariane. She swept the forgotten saber up before her as if it could hold him at bay. "And if I do accept your challenge, Kalian? What do I stand to gain? What will you give me if I win?"

His voice was almost too low for her to hear.

"Your freedom."

The words held her still; even her heart seemed to stop.

Freedom. Freedom from this unbearable trap, from the constant reminder of what she truly was. Freedom from the conflict tearing her apart. Freedom to keep her pledge to Wynn, preserve the honor of her Family. . . .

She pulled herself back from the edge of hope.

"And how do I know I can trust an honorless Kalian's word?"

His face had gone utterly expressionless. "Can I give you an oath that you'll believe? No. I've deceived you before. But if you win, Lady Ariane, I *will* let you go."

He spoke the truth. As she had known when he'd claimed innocence in Jacques's death, she knew he would keep his word.

She could win her freedom. Her skill with a saber was almost unmatched in Lumière, and she had won several exhibition matches held each year among the Elite devotees of the art. But she had never fought a duel in earnest. Such adventures were not permitted the great-granddaughter of the Patriarch of Marchand.

This would be in earnest. In deadly earnest.

The breath she had held shuddered out. "Very well, Kalian. I accept your challenge."

CHAPTER NINE

There were no proper forms to follow, no solemn chants of honorable ancestry thrown up like a shield in the face of the enemy.

Ariane was the first to attack, testing him swiftly with a brutal thrust. Rook parried, his blade meeting hers and pushing it aside. His riposte was slow, as if he feared to hurt her. Anger and pride and desperation caught fire in Ariane, but she doused them with cool reason.

This was a duel she meant to win.

Rook was naturally gifted with the blade, but she had years of training. He was taller and heavier than she, but her smaller frame gave her a lightness he couldn't match. At first he held back; she ruthlessly took advantage of his hesitation, feinting and riposting while hoarding the greater part of her strength.

This was the escape she had sought, this balancing on the brink of disaster with only a saber to hold her from the edge. An abyss of madness waited to swallow her, but for the moment she was alive, fighting, acting to shape her own fate.

She set aside tactics, any attempt to deceive Rook into believing her weak and uncertain. When he refused to engage, she came at him again and again with controlled ferocity.

Gradually he began to fight with greater purpose, and Ariane gave herself to the dance. Her body seemed to move of its own accord to meet his thrusts, to match him strength for strength and speed for speed. Rook's eyes betrayed him; they narrowed and widened again, revealing his surprise at her ability to hold him at bay.

Cool reason surrendered to something far more primitive. The part of Ariane that fought was Kalian, faced with one of her own kind. Wild, unvoiced laughter caught in her throat, a feral joy in the midst of desperation. *Don't you know me, Rook Galloway?* she cried silently. *Are you so blind that you don't recognize your own?* And she drove at him savagely, forcing him to retreat.

He faltered for the barest instant. His blade dropped, and he stood staring at her, breath coming harsh and fast.

"You are beautiful, Ariane," he said. She stopped in mid-thrust, the tip of her saber skidding wildly to the side just before it would have scored his flesh. His eyes were like metal warmed by fire, blazing across the distance between them. She had another second to curse him before he took up his blade again and the dance resumed.

Now he fought as much with his eyes as with his saber, shattering her concentration. She recognized the unbridled lust in his gaze, the fierce wanting that echoed in her own soul. This was the male of the species bent on claiming his consort. A mating dance with the finale preordained.

And the end came swiftly, between one heartbeat and the next. With a reckless lunge Ariane left herself open to Rook's riposte and brought her blade up in a parry that he beat aside with a single powerful blow.

Rook's blade came to rest gently at the base of her throat, in the delicate hollow where her pulse drummed against her skin. A fine sheen of perspiration slicked the flesh below, the collar of her shipsuit open just enough to hint at the upper swell of her breasts.

Ariane was very still, her dark eyes fixed on Rook's hand. Shock flickered across her face and was vanquished as her gaze lifted to his.

"I don't know the words, Ariane," Rook said softly. With all the force of his will he kept his grip on the blade absolutely steady, so that he would not so much as scratch her pale skin. "Do you yield?"

He thought she would defy him yet again. Her deep-brown eyes seemed to glow in the cargo hold's harsh light, sheened with brighter shades, the trapped look in them fading rapidly. Her cold superiority was gone; what lay in her face now was more powerful, stronger than the pride of privilege.

He might almost have been looking at himself.

His hand began to shake, and he withdrew the tip of the saber a hair's breadth from her skin. "Do you yield," he repeated hoarsely, "or will another Marchand break her word?"

Ariane flung back her head, offering the elegant curve of her throat. "No," she whispered, the denial hardly audible, not meant for Rook at all. Her fists clenched, every muscle in her body rigid.

And then she lowered her head again and looked at him. "I yield, Rook Galloway."

It was the first time she had spoken his name since Agora. Her voice trembled, but her eyes held steady. Unafraid. Resigned.

Rook jerked back the saber and let it clatter to the deck.

He had thought it would be enough to defeat her, throw her honor back in her face and take the two things he wanted most in the universe: revenge and Ariane Burke-Marchand. Two days ago, in her cabin, he'd learned enough of her carefully planned future to realize how easy it would be to fulfill both needs with a single act of possession.

But this was not what he had wanted after all. Not this emotionless surrender, this blank indifference. With an animal growl Rook closed the small space between them and pulled her pliant body to his.

"Ariane," he murmured, burying his face in the sweet-smelling hollow of her neck. "Ariane." He heard the shallow pull of her breath, felt the rapid beat of her heart under his chest. His hands shaped the curves of her hips, drew warmth through the soft material of her shipsuit.

He didn't want her unwilling. He wanted her helpless with desire, at his mercy of her own need. He wanted to love her until she forgot everything she was. He wanted her to gasp his name and beg him to take her prized virginity.

The virginity she saved for another.

Fierce, hot possessiveness pulsed through his blood. His

arousal was taut against his trousers, pressed to Ariane's firm abdomen. Her muscles contracted and shuddered at the contact.

"Don't fight it, Ariane," he whispered, his mouth at her cheek, her ear, the nape of her neck. "You want me. Your pride won't let you admit it, but you want me as much as I want you."

"No," she said hoarsely. Suddenly she was all sharp edges and resistance. "You will have my body, Kalian, but you'll never have my honor."

Rook thrust her back, lacing his hands in her hair so that she could not look away. "I will, *chérie*. In the end I will. Because your own body is already betraying you."

Her eyes darkened, an acknowledgment that would not reach her lips. He kissed her, lightly at first, moving his lips on hers with all the persuasive power of his own hunger.

Yes. This was right, more than mere vengeance. "Were your Elite lovers so indifferent, Ariane?" He slid his tongue over hers. "They never aroused you. They were too weak to match the fire in your blood. All your fine principles can't hold against this"—he reached down to cup her buttocks and pressed his arousal against her—"or this." He wedged his hand between their bodies and stroked the sleek material that lay between his touch and her intimate heat.

She gasped again, a wild, tormented sound. Suddenly the tension in her body changed; the muscle and bone and sinew that had subtly resisted him shifted like water to flow around him. And her hands, which had been still at her sides, moved to touch him.

Light, the brilliance of a supernova, exploded behind his eyes. For an instant he was back on Tantalus, chained, and she was touching him, forcing him to relive the tragedy eight years past that had bound them. But now it was different. Now the light beat with life, unfamiliar joy, luminescence that could cross a billion kilometers and never falter.

Like some irresistible, impossible Sharing. . . .

His mouth refused to form her name. He fit it to her lips instead, locking his arms around her. Her mouth matched his perfectly. The taste of her was sweet almost beyond bearing, overwhelming his Kalian senses. He moved his mouth to part her lips, and she closed her eyes and admitted him.

Deep shudders racked her as his tongue traced the warm, wet curves, plunged deep and withdrew again. Her eyes widened at the first penetration, and her fingers clenched on his upper arms. When he felt her uncertainty and began to withdraw, her tongue chased his and curled around it. With a groan Rook took her mouth roughly, muffling the soft cries that rose from her throat.

She was a virgin. In spite of his taunting, he knew she had never had another lover. She had been protected all her life.

But she was not ignorant. She responded instinctively, knowingly, with a savage's abandon. Rook released her lips and lowered his mouth to the soft angle of her jaw, trailing kisses.

Ariane let her head fall back, her delicate eyelids fluttering closed. Her fingers spread across his back and held him as if she would fall without his support, nails biting his sweat-slicked skin. Rook felt his tenuous control slipping at the sweet revelation of her arousal. He paused on the edge of a precipice and stared into the swirling void.

When he let himself go, there would be no turning back.

He was a Kalian without honor. She had told him as much, and he knew in this moment that she had been right. Losing himself in the veil of her hair, Rook drove the last doubt from his mind.

Ariane felt Rook's hands slide down her back as his lips and tongue stroked her arched neck, leaving a trail as hot as starfire. She felt the hardness of his arousal against her belly, straining for release; she felt her wild longing to throw off the shipsuit and everything that lay between her skin and his.

She *felt*, and sensation was all. It had become the universe from the moment she'd surrendered, from the instant she had abandoned her Marchand honor.

She had accepted his challenge. Honor demanded she pay the penalty, no matter how terrible, for her defeat—even when her Marchand blood screamed that the price was far too high.

And when Rook had taken her in his arms, she had determined to face what must be with courage and dignity. The sacrifice would be made without shrinking, but she would give no more of herself than he would demand. He would have no more than her body.

Her fine resolve had lasted for all of five minutes.

She had let the savage win.

Now she was beyond regret, or shame. With his first possessive touch she had been lost. And when his hot words had broken her resistance, when she had willingly touched him— then she had felt the luminescence, the unspoken communication between one Kalian and another, scouring her soul clean of fear and doubt.

Desire had come with the light—her own or Rook's she could never tell—desire beyond anything she had known or guessed could exist. *"You want me,"* Rook said, and she did. She wanted his mouth on hers again, and more: she wanted the things she had only imagined, her body filled with Rook's potent masculine essence.

She was a virgin, promised to another. She was also Marchand, but neither word had meaning. Only once had she recoiled, when his tongue thrust deeply into her mouth. And then her innermost knowledge had answered, until she pulled him closer and met his passion with her own.

Rook's mouth came to rest lightly on her collarbone. His breath whispered over her damp skin. "Ariane," he said. "You are beautiful." Big hands released her, pushed her gently back. And his eyes—Kalian eyes—moved over her with eloquent hunger.

Ariane looked at his face. It was no longer hostile, no longer alien, though the intensity of his expression could have been that of an enemy.

Or a lover.

His thick mane was wild, tumbled about his bare shoulders and over his eyes. His lips were parted as his gaze came to rest on the swell of her breasts. Ariane closed her eyes and trembled when his fingers stroked down from the base of her neck to the edge of the shipsuit and began to undo the fastenings.

Cool air caressed Ariane's breasts. She could hear her own shallow gasps of anticipation in the moment before his hands cupped her.

Rook made a sound, a whispered Anglic curse, uttered in a voice of reverence. The weight of her breasts rested in his roughened palms. Her nipples tightened, and Rook caught his breath. He began to stroke her, slowly, feeling each curve.

"You are beautiful," he said again. Each place where he touched her seemed connected to distant parts of her body, liquid fire whirling in chaos and gathering at last between her thighs. His fingers found her nipples at last, and Ariane moaned.

Without conscious thought she pushed into his hands. Rook locked his arms around her waist and lifted her, drawing her breasts to his mouth. His tongue flicked out, circled her nipples hungrily, one and then the other. He caressed her with kisses as if he could never get enough of her.

Her hands clenched on Rook's powerful shoulders, Ariane tossed her head. Her legs came to lock around his hips. Rook jerked against her, thrusting as he pressed his face between her breasts.

"My sweet Marchand," he gasped. "I can't wait much longer." He tilted her in his embrace and pulled her legs free, gathering her up with his arms beneath her knees and shoulders. He carried her from the cargo hold, past the galley and guest cabin, and paused at the hatch of her cabin only long enough to slap the IDlock.

It was time. Ariane knew it, and knew there was no turning back. Kamur had recognized the inevitable from the moment he had woken on the ship; even Rook, who didn't know what she truly was, had sensed the truth. There was nothing, no one left within her to resist what must be. She closed her eyes again as Rook eased her down on the rumpled blankets, his weight coming down beside her.

She could not speak. To speak would destroy the fragile, tentative joy that had come when she had surrendered her honor, her pride, her very identity. Rook, too, was silent, but his touch spoke more surely than any words. And always there was the light—beyond grasping, but there. Between them and around them like a shield to keep out the universe.

Rook began to draw the shipsuit down her body, his knees to either side of her hips. His fingers were trembling as he pushed the fabric to her waist and lower, until she lay naked beneath him.

"By the Shapers," he breathed. Ariane turned her head on the pillow, waiting for his touch. His desire—her own—was a pulsing tide that swept down and down in the wake of his hands, bringing hot moisture to her hidden core.

His fingers brushed her breasts, her ribs, her belly. She jerked when he lowered his mouth to stroke the curve of her hip, but he put his hands to either side and pinned her to the bunk. His leashed strength, her own willing helplessness aroused her to a fever pitch of excitement. His long hair brushed her belly, the tops of her thighs. Surely there could be nothing more powerful than this. . . .

And then his mouth came to rest where all sensation gathered. Her cry was deep and low as he stroked her there, his tongue tasting, drinking, consuming her while the light exploded into a million fragments. His scarred hands separated her thighs and lifted her, cupping her buttocks.

"You want me, Lady Ariane Burke-Marchand," he said.

She opened her eyes to look at him. He crouched there between her thighs, a savage waiting to spring, and the sound of her name and title ripped her from mindless ecstasy.

Lady Ariane Burke-Marchand.

"You want me," he repeated, and he bent down again to taste her. This time she fought; she tried to pull her thighs together, but he held them apart and would not stop. While her own name echoed in her ears, the revelation came to her and left her stripped of her last illusions.

Lady Ariane wanted Rook Galloway. Not only the savage Kalian within herself that she had let take control. Bernard Marchand's great-granddaughter wanted what had always been forbidden.

"You want me," Rook whispered. He withdrew, leaving her bereft, and rose to remove his trousers. Ariane forced herself to watch him, knowing she should run and that she would stay where she was, waiting, longing for him to complete what he had begun. Her body ached and throbbed, crying out for release.

When he stood naked before her, she almost lost her courage. His manhood challenged her anew, a weapon that would pierce far more deeply and irrevocably than any blade.

No litdisk or lecture could prepare her for this.

He was beautiful as he glided toward her, leaning over the bunk. His eyes never left hers. Scarred, gentle hands stroked down from her shoulders to her hips and legs, closing above her knees. He lifted and settled her, touched her hot wetness with his fingers. Kneeling between her thighs, he stretched over her until the hard tips of her breasts brushed against his chest.

"Say it, Ariane," he commanded softly.

Mutely she watched him, struggling to find the simple words he wanted. With infinite care he slid his body down hers, skimming the slight roughness of his cheek along her breasts and belly.

"Say it." He kissed the moisture between her thighs and the inner curve of her legs. Ariane gasped, the aching hollow within her body eager to be filled.

"I want you," she breathed. Rook paused in his caresses, lifting his head. His copper eyes were ablaze.

He slid back up to cover her, and she could feel his heavy arousal pressing against her. She shifted to bring him closer, and he caught his breath.

"My name, Ariane. Say it."

Ariane arched her back. "I want you, Rook."

Triumph flared in his gaze. He lowered himself slowly, resting his weight on his powerful arms. The press of his manhood grew more urgent.

"Ariane," he sighed, and his hips moved downward. She felt the invasion of his body, hard and hot, by tiny increments. Her own body tightened in response, and she bit her lip.

His mouth caught hers. Her lips opened under his, and while he kissed her, he moved deeper, pushing at the fragile barrier that was her only shield.

Now, she cried silently. *Please, now.* But the words came out as a whimper, and he went utterly still; he lifted his head like an animal scenting the air. His muscles bunched and trembled, long shudders that rippled the length of him. Ariane reached up to lay her hands flat on his back, feeling the skin jump under her palms.

"Shapers," he grated. He dropped his head so that Ariane could see nothing of his face under the screen of his hair. He pushed again with his hips, and Ariane sucked in her breath.

Suddenly the pressure eased, his heavy arousal slipping free of her like a saber drawn from its sheath. Rook flung back his head, eyes wild, and stared at her; before she could protest, he leaped back and away, cursing bitterly.

"Rook—" she cried, protest and alarm and endearment, sitting up to reach for him where he stood at the foot of the bunk. But his eyes were an enemy's eyes—an enemy who deserted the arena before the duel was finished.

Ariane began to tremble as desire fled before harsh awareness. She caught up the nearest blanket and pulled it over herself, Rook's hostile gaze following each movement. She felt exposed as she'd never felt before, shamed at last, bared to a savage's inexplicable condemnation.

He had almost taken her.

"Damn you," she whispered, clenching her fists in the blanket.

A bitter, familiar smile twisted his mouth. "Consider yourself fortunate, Lady Ariane," he said harshly. "Your honor is safe after all."

And he turned on his heel and left her. Ariane stared at the hatch long after it had closed behind him, swallowing the hard knot in her throat.

Rook Galloway had already begun his revenge.

. . .

The *d'Artagnan* hung in the orbit of M'nauri, circling the green world below. Rook stared at the image framed in the canopy, remembering the Fahar's farewell.

"We will never forget what you have done, my Brother," Kamur had said, clasping his hand. "Please tell our sister Ariane that we will find some way to repay this great debt."

Rook hardened his mind against thoughts of Ariane. She had emerged from her cabin only long enough to mutter a strained, hasty "Au revoir" when the *d'Artagnan* had put in at M'nauri's primitive spaceport. Rook had seen the concern on Surra's face; he had almost flinched when the Fahar's wise eyes turned to him in silent question.

It was a question he could not answer. And so he had left the Fahar couple to begin their new life on M'nauri, driving away the strange ache that had settled somewhere in the vicinity of his heart.

With the Fahar gone there would be no more delays. The waiting was over.

Rook dropped his eyes from the view and turned back to his calculations, shifting the comp pad in his hands. The course for Espérance must be plotted carefully; the route he planned was little used.

But he would not take the risk that they might be found. Not now, so close to his goal.

And his goal had not changed. Rook gripped that fact like a saber in his fist. He had almost lost his purpose, as he had lost himself in Ariane's body; he had almost lost himself.

The revelation had come to him in the very crucible of passion, when Ariane's heat enveloped him and drew him to claim her for all time.

If he took her, he would lose—himself, all that he was, all that he must do. If he took her, she would be his: his to protect and defend, his to hold forever.

If he took her, there would be no revenge. In giving herself she would defeat him utterly. All the barriers would be broken, his loyalty, his very soul surrendered to the woman he should hate.

Irrevocably.

That was Kalian honor.

Rook tightened his grip on the comp pad, and the metal almost bent.

Silence had settled in the cockpit, broken only by Rook's harsh breathing. He listened for the Fahar, knowing they were gone; he tested the air for the scent of desire.

Ariane. Ariane. Ariane . . .

The very frame of the ship seemed to beat with the sound of her name.

Rook swung to face the console and punched in the numbers for their next jump. It was a long leap to the Louve system, and a somewhat risky one; the system was unmapped and uninhabited. Completing his final entries, Rook allowed himself a grim smile. His time on Tolstoy had been useful, after all—he'd been at the top of his class in astronavigation. If anyone could make it work, he could. . . .

He felt Ariane's presence long before he heard the sigh of her footsteps. Rising to meet her, he adjusted the immediate response of his body, nerve and breath and blood, back to normal parameters. Even so, he fought grimly to veil what he knew must show in his eyes.

She came to stand in the cockpit hatchway, regarding him silently. The distance between them was deliberate, a precaution neither one was willing to forgo.

"They're safe now," she said at last. Her gaze moved around the cockpit, cool and remote.

"Yes." His own voice sounded strained, uncontrolled.

"They deserve their happiness," she murmured. Taking a single step into the cabin, she looked out at M'nauri's green sphere.

"Yes." Rook let his eyes touch her as he could not, tracing the elegant lines of her body and the strong, sculpted beauty of her face.

"Have you laid in a course for Espérance?"

There was no challenge or concern in her words, nothing but remote indifference.

Rook set his jaw. "I have. Four days, if all goes well."

Dark eyes met his. "If all goes well," she repeated. She had brushed her thick hair into a severe style that matched the stranger's face she gave him. There were shadows under her eyes. "And then?"

Self-mocking laughter caught in Rook's throat. "Do you want to know my plans?" he asked, deliberately avoiding her name. "I have none."

"Except your revenge," she said. Suddenly her eyes grew hooded. "I wonder why you didn't start with me, Galloway. It would have been so easy."

Rook watched her approach, unable to answer. "You wanted me, Rook," she said flatly. "I'm still your captive. Your enemy. What are you afraid of, Kalian? Did you learn that wanting is a weakness you can't afford?"

She was too close. Too close to the truth. Rook barely stopped himself from going to her, holding her, betraying himself utterly.

Her chin lifted, but she could not quite hide the flare of pain in her eyes. "Listen to me, Galloway. You won't get another chance. I'll die before I let you touch me again."

And as she turned and strode from the cockpit, Rook knew she'd won their duel in the end.

✳

CHAPTER TEN

*A*riane had never visited the Louve system. It had been named by an explorer some decades before, but no one had bothered to exploit the few barren worlds so far off the established shipping lanes.

There were no bold colonists there to brave a new environment or miners tapping valuable ore in the asteroid belts. No one to see the *d'Artagnan* materialize out of hyperspace at the jump point, or send a courier drone to report that Ariane Burke-Marchand had been found. By rights the place should have been deserted.

The voice sputtered over the commlink again, joking in crude Franglais. Espérancian Franglais.

"Forget it, Alain. I'm not giving up my leave for any bonus, not with what I've got waiting for me back home."

Ariane bit her lip and glanced at Rook. He bent over the console with his hand to the headset, frowning darkly.

"Hey, but mon ami—the boss don't like it if his suggestions aren't taken. He would like this shipment gone by tomorrow, and we've got the only ships free. Seems Liberty can't get by without another few million hits of Euphorie. . . ."

Euphorie. Euphoria. A hallucinogenic drug so powerful and unpredictable that it had been outlawed on Espérance and throughout the League. Derived from an Espérancian plant, it was cultivated now only under the most stringent controls, for limited medical purposes only.

But someone was manufacturing Euphorie for illegal sale, and the runners were here.

Rook looked at Ariane, eyes narrowed. "Espérancian," he said, echoing her thoughts.

She nodded, clenching her fingers in her lap. When Rook had called her to the cockpit, she'd come—in her own time, but she'd come—to prove to him and to herself how little she feared what lay between them. Staring out at the slivers of light that marked the drug-runners' starships, Ariane turned her attention to the more pressing matter at hand.

"They haven't seen us," she said.

"Not yet." Rook adjusted a control and cocked his head. "What do you know about this, Lady Ariane?"

His renewed formality was a barrier that Ariane welcomed, but the words stung. "Nothing," she snapped. "Euphorie is illegal throughout the League. My great-grandfather was one of those who fought to have it proscribed. If there's trafficking going on—"

"The Marchand aren't behind it." Rook lifted one dark brow, but his mouth remained set. "That is what you planned to say, Lady Ariane? Even though your family has the interworld connections, and the influence, and the money . . ."

Ariane jumped from her seat. "Damn you, they have nothing to do with this. They don't control everything, not even on Espérance." Drawing in a sharp breath, she marshaled her thoughts. "There are other families, other Patriarchs with connections offworld. You—"

Rook raised his hand sharply. A crackle of static sputtered over the commlink.

"Yeah, I heard that. They're really stepping up production these days. The boss has this operation running smooth as a Nirvanan whore's backside. Pretty soon there won't be a planet without a nice, fat supply." The drug-runner snorted. *"You'd think M'sieur was on a holy mission."*

There was a long silence over the commlink. *"Maybe he is,"* the other runner said. *"Maybe he is. But you'd better not get in his way."*

Rook pulled off his headset and stared out the canopy. Abruptly he turned to Ariane, his face grim. "We'll have to risk an early jump," he said.

Ariane stopped her pacing. "The ship isn't ready," she protested. "We're only six hours into the recalibration cycle. If we try to leave now, the engines could fail in midjump."

"That's a chance we'll have to take." Rook tossed her the headset. "Listen for yourself."

She listened. "There are more of them," she breathed.

"Many more. Someone from your world has set up a very big operation here. They'll have sentinel probes scattered around the system, and it's only a matter of time before they spot us." Rook swung back to the controls and initiated the prejump checks. Without thinking Ariane dropped back into the copilot's seat and began to test the backup systems.

Whoever was running things in the Louve system might be Espérancian, but he was in the business of dealing death and sorrow. He was far more her enemy than Rook could ever be.

Euphoria. Ariane clenched her jaw as she adjusted a control. As soon as she was home, she'd tell Bernard what was going on here, and he'd put a stop to it. . . .

She froze for the briefest moment. She wasn't free to go home and tell the Patriarch anything. She still had no idea what Rook planned, and her options were growing very limited.

Rook held her captive more surely than ever before. His hand brushing hers on the console could make her tremble; his very nearness caused her pulse to race.

She had become his prisoner in every sense, and still she could not hate him, any more than she could come to terms with what *she* was. . . .

A violent blow struck the *d'Artagnan* like a giant's fist. Ariane grabbed at the console, felt Rook's hand closing painfully on her arm as the lights on the control board went from amber to flashing red.

"They've found us," he said, pushing her back down into the seat. "Web in."

Flinging off his restraining hand, Ariane did as he ordered and assessed the damage. She cursed softly, fury and outrage pumping adrenaline through her body.

"Give me the helm," she demanded, her eyes fixed on the readouts.

She could hear Rook's deep breathing, could almost sense

his thoughts running parallel to her own. "We won't make it out of the system now," he said grimly. "Their pulse torpedo took out one of the main hyperdrive modules. Our discannon—"

"Won't do a damned bit of good now." Another impact rocked the ship, and Ariane felt it in her bones. "Give me the helm," she repeated. "I'm taking her down."

He hesitated, turning to stare at her. Then a reckless smile transformed his hard features.

"Go," he said.

Ariane lost no time. She pushed the engines to full thrust and turned the ship in a tight arc, setting a course for the nearest planet. Distantly she was aware of Rook as he monitored their pursuers; the *d'Artagnan's* alarms shrieked as she swerved to avoid two more of the runners' torpedoes.

The planet she had chosen filled the forward canopy, a red ball laced with the patterns that marked turbulent dust storms on the surface. The landing would be dangerous, but at least there would be a chance of survival, of evading the runners until repairs could be made to the ship's hyperdrive.

The *d'Artagnan* plunged down through the murky atmosphere, and visibility dropped to zero. Ariane switched on the scanners, but they were nearly useless. She had no choice but to rely on her training and experience—and something less easily defined—to pilot the ship through swirling red dust and roaring winds. Beside her, Rook murmured encouragement and curses.

For a fraction of an instant the view cleared, revealing an open space among towering red crags. Ariane turned the ship into the wind and fought to keep it on the new course. She held her hands very steady on the controls as the *d'Artagnan* shuddered and skipped under the force of the gale.

It was Rook's voice that called her back when they were safe on the ground, his hands that eased hers from their grip on the control stick.

"You did it again, Lady Ariane," he said softly. "You saved us both."

He released her hands before she could snatch them away

and strode across the cockpit. For a long moment he stood with his back to her, his gaze fixed on the mindless fury outside the glasteel canopy. Ariane could feel the wildness in him, as if he and the untamed world beyond had become one dangerous entity.

"They can't locate us as long as this storm holds out," he said, "but I won't be able to begin repairs on the outer modules either. That wind could strip the skin from bones—" His voice held an unexpected trace of humor. "Even Kalian bones."

Ariane left her seat and went to stand behind him. "They —whoever they are—don't even know we survived the landing."

His hands clasped together behind his back. "They were firing with deadly intent, Lady Ariane. This system is uninhabited as far as the League is concerned. Whoever runs this operation will want to keep it that way. Men like these don't take any chances." He turned his head, showing her the chiseled lines of his profile. "I was on Tantalus a long time. Long enough to know what drives such men. I doubt they'd hesitate to kill even the daughter of a Patriarch."

"If the Patriarch knew about this—"

"But he doesn't know." Ariane could almost hear the words he didn't speak: *or so you claim.* "There won't be any rescue, Lady Ariane. They'll be looking for us, and when they find us, they'll do their best to make sure we never leave this world."

The way he looked at her, intent and grim, was a kind of challenge. "Then we'll have to work fast," she said. "And whether you like it or not, Galloway, we'll have to work together."

He frowned. "You're not going out there, even in a suit—"

"Gallantry, Rook?" she asked softly.

He snapped down a lever on the console with unnecessary force. "Self-interest, Lady Ariane. I may not be the expert you are, but at least I'll survive." He pretended to turn his full attention to the scanners that monitored the storm, but Ariane could see the muscles in his back tense, as if he could feel her steady gaze.

"All right," she said. "In that case, you're going to need me on the computers inside the ship." She glanced over his shoulder at the readouts. "If the main modules are disabled, you'll have no choice but to reroute the hyperdrive to the secondaries. Even the great Rook Galloway can't do that alone."

His hands paused in their movement. "If I give you access to the computer, you'll have control of the ship—"

"Damn you!" Ariane cried, her words echoing in the cockpit. "Do you think I'm going to lock you outside the moment the ship is repaired and leave you here to die?"

Something changed in Rook then, visible in the subtle shift of his body and the way he lifted his head, in the long, slow exhale of his breath.

"Then we'd better get to work," he said.

Rook had no doubts about the origin of the ship that broke into atmosphere just as the dull reddish sun began its descent below the horizon.

He pushed loose hair away from his forehead with the instrument in his hand and rocked back on his heels. Their pursuers had finally found them, and the *d'Artagnan* wasn't ready. It would take many more hours to get the hyperdrive working at all, and the discannon, the ship's sole armament, had been disabled by the runner's last shot.

Cursing, Rook set down the instrument and took a careful breath of the dust-laden air. Even now the wind was blowing, scouring the bare rock tumbled across the planet's surface. The layers of clothing he wore provided only minimal protection; he had set his body to the task of toughening and replacing the outer cells of his skin and healing the minor abrasions as he worked. His lungs had already adjusted to the thin, bitter air.

None of his Kalian adaptations could save Ariane or himself from the blast of a disruptor cannon. Rook touched his headset and signaled Ariane.

She took his news calmly. "They haven't fired on us yet," she said, her voice clear and unafraid through the commlink. "Maybe they want to find out who we are before they mingle our atoms with this infernal dust."

"It won't make any difference," he said. Once more he scanned the darkening sky, watching and listening. "They won't risk taking prisoners—or hostages."

There was a long silence. Rook closed his eyes, almost certain he could read her thoughts.

What does she have to lose? he asked himself. *She's already risked her life and honor to save her family from my revenge. And if she dies . . .*

No. Rook snatched up the instruments and stuffed them into his utility belt, ignoring the handholds as he clambered down the outer hull of the ship. "Open the weapons locker," he told Ariane. "Get out the biggest thing you have. I'm coming in."

She was standing just inside the air lock when he reentered the ship. In her arms was a top-model disrifle, sleek and deadly. Rook paused, struck by a thought that formed and disappeared before he could grasp it.

Ariane looked at him strangely, brown eyes alight. She shifted the rifle so that the muzzle swung in his direction. "Is this what you had in mind?"

Rook studied the competent way she handled the weapon, suddenly on his guard. Without breaking stride again he moved toward and past her, his skin prickling. "Are there others?"

Her footsteps were eerily silent, almost like a Kalian's. "No more like this. A few smaller hand weapons."

"Good." He walked quickly into the cockpit and checked the scanners. "I'll leave those with you." He began to strip off his extra layers of clothing, preparing his body for battle. Gritty sand spattered the deck. He could feel Ariane moving up behind him. "You were right," he said gruffly. "If they planned to hit us from above, they would have done it by now. We may still have a chance. I'll go out and—"

"You're not going anywhere."

The muzzle of the rifle stroked his shoulder, and he went very still. Ariane's voice was alien, vibrating with suppressed emotion. "How does it feel, Kalian, to be at the other end?"

He could have disarmed her in a single instant, but he only cocked his head with a bitter smile.

"Your timing is less than perfect, Lady Ariane. Taking me prisoner now won't do you a damned bit of good."

When Rook turned to face her, the dark eyes that met his were painfully vulnerable, as if she'd had no time to raise her defenses.

"You fool," she breathed. Suddenly she lowered the rifle and stepped back, the open hurt in her face disappearing beneath a mask of Marchand pride.

She thrust the rifle into his upraised hands. "You're not going anywhere without me," she said coldly.

"Do you think you'll be any use out there?" he snapped, deliberately cruel. "You'll stay here, where it's—where you won't get in my way." Ignoring her protest, he checked the charge on the rifle and adjusted the sight. "I won't abandon you, Lady Ariane. If I don't make it back, I'll be dead."

"Then we'll both be dead," she said, stepping forward until they stood mere centimeters apart. Her face was flushed and unbearably beautiful. "I can handle a 'ruptor as well as you can. Maybe better. And as for your vaunted Kalian superiority—"

"Will you give me your word to stay with the ship?" Rook interrupted softly.

Ariane dropped her eyes. *"Mon Dieu,"* she whispered. Her jaw worked as she looked up at him again. "I'll stay with the ship," she said. "Word of a Marchand."

Concealing the intensity of his relief, Rook slung the disrifle over his shoulder and started for the air lock. Ariane drifted at his back like a shadow, a part of himself he couldn't dismiss or ignore.

She slipped into the air lock with him, neatly preventing him from sealing the inner hatch against her. The scent of her was overwhelming in the small space.

He looped the headset around his neck. "Stay by the

commlink," he ordered. "I'll signal if I can't stop them before they get near the ship." Without further hesitation he punched the controls that opened the outer hatch; sand and dust and cold, bitter air swirled into the air lock.

"Rook." Her hand came to rest on his shoulder, unmoving. Even that slight touch almost undid him. "Don't—" Her voice caught. "Don't get yourself killed. Come back." Breath shuddered out, stirring his hair. "Come back."

Staring out into the darkness, Rook felt control slip from his grasp like a handful of sand. Ariane gasped when he turned and pulled her against him, the rifle slapping against his thigh. Her mouth opened to his, her arms laced around his neck as he lifted her off the deck.

He kissed her with a savage's ferocity, relentless and almost brutal. She met his assault fearlessly and dueled him with lips and tongue until the very air was driven from his lungs.

It was Rook who surrendered. Pushing her away, he set her on her feet again and strode out into the starless night, closing the outer hatch before she could follow.

And then he turned his thoughts and his senses to the simple matter of survival.

There were four of them, suited and heavily armed, picking their way among the wind-sculpted rock formations that dotted the barren landscape like broken teeth.

Rook crouched behind a jagged boulder and watched them approach. Sheer luck that they hadn't found a landing site closer to the *d'Artagnan;* as it was, they were at a disadvantage approaching on foot and in the dark.

And they didn't know they faced a Kalian.

Rook bared his teeth in a smile. His blood beat out a song of war in his veins. The lust and confusion Ariane aroused in him could be channeled now into battle; Rook flexed his muscles and prepared his body in the way of his kind.

The Kalians had never been a violent people, whatever Ariane Burke-Marchand believed.

Not unless they were driven into a corner.

The drug-runners paused in their advance, clumping together in consultation. Rook slipped from his concealment and drifted silently through the dust. His Kalian eyesight was almost as keen in darkness as in daylight—another survival mechanism given the colonists by the Shapers on a world where the smallest weakness could be fatal.

But Rook was in his element. He ducked behind another rock formation as the runners separated again, two and two. One pair split off in an arc that would bring them to either side of the *d'Artagnan*. The other two remained together, and Rook could see the reason almost immediately.

One of them carried over his shoulders a portable disruptor cannon, large enough to disable the ship permanently and kill anyone on board. The heavy weapon left its carrier exposed, but his companion covered him with a disrifle and numerous smaller weapons.

Constantly monitoring the progress of the two scouts, Rook began to retreat. He found a place where the rocks were clumped to form a narrow gully, one which the cannon carrier and his escort would likely pass through to reach the ship.

With inhuman agility Rook scrambled up the highest rock and flattened himself against it, waiting. The runners were no fools; they scanned the area around them systematically, relying on infrared goggles to do what Rook's eyes did naturally.

And they were not quite fools enough to enter the passage among the rocks without hesitation. They paused just long enough to let Rook get off the shot that took out the 'ruptor cannon and disabled the arm of the man who carried it; the other runner dropped into a crouch and returned fire instantly.

By then Rook was already gone. His feet hit the dusty ground and carried him swiftly to a position where he could fire again. But the second man had already abandoned his groaning colleague. Rook assured himself with one glance that the man with the cannon would be no further threat, and ran back toward the ship.

His time now was scant; the man who'd escaped would be alerting the others. But Rook had achieved his aim; the d'Artagnan—and Ariane—would no longer be at risk from the cannon, and the other three runners carried ordinary weapons.

He had to stop the others before they decided the odds were against them and called their ship.

A 'ruptor beam cut through the darkness, narrowly missing Rook's shoulder. He rolled and came up in one motion, firing in the direction of the shot. There was a heavy sound of something falling, and silence.

Rook beat back a primitive surge of triumph and moved swiftly toward his attacker. He rounded a boulder to find the runner coming unsteadily to his knees; Rook downed him easily and wrenched the man's 'ruptor from his hand. He stripped the runner's other weapons and commlink and tossed them into the brittle, spiny brush surrounding the rocks.

Two left. Rook's heart beat swift and strong, but he was beginning to feel the strain of his exertion in the thin, alien atmosphere. For a moment he paused, catching his breath and drawing every bit of precious oxygen out of the air. Then he started for the ship at a lope, Ariane's face hovering before him.

Perhaps it was that momentary distraction that betrayed Rook at last. A runner appeared suddenly in his path, disruptor raised in one flailing hand. The man seemed to be caught, his foot wedged among a jumble of low rocks.

With a feral grin Rook rushed him, darting to the side where the man's disruptor couldn't reach. Rook heard a whisper of warning sound an instant before the runner sprang his trap.

Hot agony seared through Rook's arm as the man waiting in ambush caught him from behind. His rifle seemed to explode in his hand. He fell hard, without a Kalian's grace; the commlink headset was knocked away by the impact. Shock vibrated through Rook's system, his body reacting almost immediately to the damage. But he was slowed by the wound and barely avoided a second, more lethal beam from the first runner's weapon.

Baring his teeth in pain, Rook staggered up into a crouch and charged the nearest enemy. As suddenly as they had attacked, both men vanished, retreating before him. The ground seemed to roll under his feet. He stopped, leaning heavily against the nearest rock.

Ariane. Again her face came to him, all pride and courage and eloquent beauty. He wasted no time searching for the headset but gathered himself and ran as if hellhounds bayed at his heels.

He didn't slow or allow himself to falter until the *d'Artagnan* came into view—until he saw Ariane, just outside the air lock hatch, balanced in a duelist's stance with a disruptor clenched in her fist.

He felt it when she saw him, a second shock atop the first.

Rook! Ariane shouted his name in her mind. She sucked in a painful breath of dust-laden air and started toward him.

Rook staggered, one arm useless at his side, lifting the other in an urgent gesture of warning. Just as he ran to meet Ariane, a suited man emerged from the concealment of nearby rocks and took careful aim. Ariane screamed a wordless alarm, turning to fire at Rook's attacker. The disruptor was knocked violently from her hand, and gloved fingers clenched on her arm, biting to the bone.

Something dark and primitive and powerful surged up in her, igniting her blood. With a cry of fury Ariane turned on the man who held her. The runner grimaced as Ariane struck at him, drove him back with blows no ordinary woman could have managed.

Ariane feinted under the man's guard and jerked the disruptor from his gloved hand. She turned away just long enough to see Rook locked in a deadly embrace with the other runner, and swung her arm around as her attacker pulled a second disruptor from his belt.

He never got a chance to use it. Ariane fired, and the man crumpled with a grunt.

She was running again an instant later, the shock of having killed a man barely held at bay by another kind of desperation. Rook and the last runner lay very still on the red earth, the runner sprawled across Rook's body.

Ariane could make no sound. She cried Rook's name again and again in her mind, pulling the runner's limp body free of Rook's and tossing it aside as if it weighed no more than dust.

The shirt was charred away from Rook's right shoulder and chest, his arm grotesquely twisted, the flesh seared almost to the bone. His eyes were closed, and his breathing was so slow and shallow that it was almost undetectable. Ariane sobbed silently and caught his still face between her hands. Her tears made runnels through the dust that coated his face and dulled his hair.

Through her mindless fear she remembered what she was. She remembered Finch and her cryptic words on Agora station: *"You have such strength. . . ."* And she remembered the time in the cargo hold when she had commanded her hand to heal.

And it had healed.

Rook, she cried mutely. *Don't leave me.* She turned inward, reaching for the strange and frightening strength that had come to her when she'd fought the runner—for the unearthly knowledge that had warned her that Rook was badly hurt, that had drawn her from the safety of the ship—that pulsed through her body each time she touched him.

She embraced what she had denied.

Like the nimbus of a star emerging from an eclipse, the light flared within her. It coiled outward, heat that seemed to boil in her blood and escape through her very pores. Her hands on Rook's cool flesh burned with it.

Live, she commanded him, the tears evaporating on her cheeks. *Heal, Rook Galloway.*

He stirred, the faintest of tremors vibrating under her palms. *Heal. Heal. . . .*

Something alien exploded into her mind. For an instant she felt Rook, and then she lost the fragile connection as his chest heaved for air. His eyelids fluttered open.

"Ariane," he croaked.

Dieu, she prayed silently, still unable to speak. *Thank God.* . . .

"Ariane—" Rook stirred with unexpected strength, pushing against her hands. Belated alarm flashed through her, and she scanned the darkness intently before gathering him into her arms.

"Quiet," she whispered. "Lie still. You've been badly hurt—"

He shook his head with one sharp jerk, drawing in several short, harsh breaths. "Listen. I didn't—kill—" His body lifted again and fell back into her arms. "Others. Escape. . . ."

As if those few words had consumed his remaining strength, he fell silent. Ariane could feel his struggle to remain conscious, the faint thrum of the warning he tried so desperately to convey.

She rocked him like a child. "You'll be all right, Rook. We'll both be all right."

And she closed her eyes to gather her strength again, lifted him with utmost tenderness, drew him up with her and took his weight without faltering. Somehow she made it to the hatch and got him through it and into her cabin. She eased him down onto her bunk and lowered the hood of the automed, her fingers trembling as she programmed the unit to administer medication and nourish Rook's damaged body.

She had just enough strength to set the ship's proximity alarms before exhaustion and shock claimed her.

Kneeling beside the bunk, Ariane lowered her head on her folded arms and let the light fade away.

✶

CHAPTER ELEVEN

*T*hirty-six hours later Ariane woke from deep sleep. Her half-open eyes automatically sought the watch on her wrist, and she blinked in confusion.

She wasn't lying on the bunk; soft carpet gave under her body as she rolled onto her side. She looked up and saw the transparent curve of the automed hood in place over the bunk, its lights glowing steady amber.

Rook. Rook, alive. . . . Ariane sprang up and stared through the hood at Rook's face, her fingers dancing over the controls.

He didn't stir as she ran the diagnostics. The automed had done all it could for him; his condition was stable. Ariane touched the controls that released the hood and tucked the automed back into its recess beside the bunk.

His chest rose and fell steadily under the soft webbing that covered the worst of his wounds. He was at peace, for these fragile hours; Ariane could sense it, an absence of the sorrow and rage that had driven him from the moment he'd taken her prisoner. Her throat tightened. He was at peace, the harsh lines bracketing his mouth less defined, his heavy brows relaxed. His black mane spread tangled and damp over the pillow, framing his starkly handsome face.

Ancient Earth tales flooded Ariane's mind, stories of gallant knights wounded in battle and ensorceled princes cast into endless slumber. She had no choice but to touch him; even in sleep he drew her inexorably. She laid her hand gently on his chest, feeling the beat of his heart beneath her palm. His eyelids fluttered, and she tensed, half-afraid he would wake to find her so vulnerable. But he only sighed once, deeply, and was still again.

With hesitant fingers she stroked his face, marveling in the texture and strength of it, at the sheer joy of life itself. She traced the scar that marked his face from brow to chin, as if her touch alone could make it disappear, erase the old pain behind it.

Why would he, a Kalian capable of self-healing and shape-shifting, have chosen to keep that reminder of terrible suffering? Had he deliberately preserved those brands to remind himself of his grim purpose? How much torment he had endured. . . .

Ariane closed her eyes. If she had had the ability, she would have taken his sorrow and bitterness and healed his soul, as she had tried to heal his body. The revenge he sought was part of that terrible legacy of pain.

Without thinking she cupped his jaw in her hands and reached for that profound awareness of him that had come so powerfully when he had hovered on the brink of death. She could feel herself slipping into a mist of pure sensation: warmth of skin on skin, the flow of rich oxygen into her lungs, flashes of pain that flared up and subsided. Deeper, and sensation gave way to drifting thoughts that were not her own, fading away before she could grasp them. Deeper still, and it was like wading into the ocean against the tide.

A wall rose up before her, as solid as if it existed in a physical realm. She probed it, pushed with all her inner strength, and the soul-deep knowledge slipped into her mind like starlight.

Before, she had acted on instinct, without comprehension, driven by desperation. Now she understood.

Beyond the wall she could sense the mending of Rook's cells, his body grasping for life in the Kalian way. She followed the path of his blood, felt the knitting of bone and tissue. And just beyond, just out of reach, she could feel the shadow of his mind.

She tried. She tried to breach the shadow, knowing that she had touched that place before, when there had been only the brilliance of light—when they had made love, and she had lost herself in feelings not entirely her own. But each time she approached, it tangled her in vague, dark emotions and thrust her back.

Even now he marked her as his enemy.

Ariane retreated slowly, drawing back through layers of awareness. She slipped into her own body again; it seemed almost unfamiliar. Alien. Her fingers flexed awkwardly on Rook's warm skin as if they belonged to someone else.

For a long moment she stared down at him, lost in the wonder of what she had done. She had been within Rook, felt him on the deepest level of his physical being. She had done what only a Kalian could do.

But being Kalian couldn't bridge the chasm between them. Ariane blinked and withdrew her hands. She stared at the bulkhead. *What do you want?* she asked herself. *You know it can never be. . . .*

Abruptly she got to her feet, shaking off her weakness. She had done what she could. Time was all Rook needed now.

Time. The harsh reality of their situation came back to her then, and she almost laughed. Time was the one thing they didn't have.

Ariane tilted her head and listened, as if she could hear the approach of their enemies. Thirty-six hours had passed, and there'd been no more attacks. She walked across the cabin to the desk and leaned over the computer terminal.

Nothing. No disturbances, no record of any human attempt to approach the *d'Artagnan* since the battle with the runners. The ship's close-range scanners showed only small, nonsentient life forms in the vicinity.

For some reason they were being left alone. Ariane bit her lip and looked back at Rook, remembering what he had told her.

Men like these don't take chances. And at least one of them had got away.

Rook stirred. His lips parted in a slow, deep breath; Ariane's other concerns evaporated like surface water in high Anubian summer. She took a single step toward him and stopped when his eyes opened, copper barely visible under the veil of black lashes.

"Ariane?" he whispered. His voice was hoarse with strain. "Ariane?" His uninjured arm moved, muscles tightening as it flailed upward.

"Here." She caught his hand, and the inner light flared between them and just as quickly vanished. "Here, Rook."

His fingers closed around hers. "The ship," he grated. "Fix—get away. . . ."

She knew he didn't see her; his eyes were blank and strange, turned inward. Amazed at his strength, she let herself be pulled down beside him, pressing him back with her free hand.

"We're safe, Rook. They haven't come back—"

The lines of his face tensed, forming the grim mask she knew so well. His breathing grew labored. "Fix the ship," he said. His body heaved under her; she spread herself across him to keep him still, taking care not to touch his wounds.

"Easy, Rook," she whispered urgently. "I'll fix the ship." It took all of her strength to hold him there; every one of his muscles strained against her. She tried to calm him with a flow of soft words, but he would not be appeased; at last she pushed inward with her mind, searching for the light she had felt moments before.

The shadowed wall within his mind crumbled. For an instant his emotions lay open to her, too brief a time for her to do more than set her determination against his. "Rest," she told him. "Rest and heal." Remarkably, he obeyed; his body went slack. His breath caught in his chest and released on the sound of her name.

With utmost care Ariane braced her weight on her arms and rose from the bunk, pausing to draw the blankets up over Rook's broad shoulders.

She would have lingered. If there had been no danger, she would have stayed at his side, smoothing back his hair and whispering words he would never hear. Words she could never hope to speak.

But the temptation was taken out of her hands. The ship had to be repaired if they were to have a chance at survival, any chance at all. Rook had gone far enough with the repairs that she could carry on by herself, though it would take several days to get the *d'Artagnan* hyperspace-capable again.

Ariane pushed her hair back from her face and, slipping out of the cabin silently, left Rook to his sleep.

If they survived—if they managed to escape the drug-runners and get out of the system—she and Rook would face each other again. The battle would be joined anew, and only one of them could win in the end.

If they survived.

Ariane smiled grimly. A Marchand never went down without a fight.

Neither did a Kalian.

A Kalian.

Wynn punched a button, and the terminal ejected the message chip with an almost inaudible click. He turned to the tech who had brought him the message capsule, frowning so darkly that the tech visibly trembled.

"Lay in a course for the Louve system. Sector M, GF 238905." Wynn stared at the tech until the younger man repeated the coordinates, and dismissed him with a wave of his hand.

The news had been all over Agora when Wynn had arrived; a prisoner—a Kalian, the last living convict from Espérance—had slipped his chains on Tantalus, confiscated a private starship, put in at Agora, and escaped again with hostages before the League authorities could stop him.

The private starship was the *d'Artagnan*. And the hostage —the hostage was Ariane Burke-Marchand.

Wynn slammed his fist down on the expensive ebonwood desk, knocking over a priceless crystal sculpture from Nirvana. It shattered with a delicate protest. He stood abruptly and strode to the porthole, looking out at the curve of the station and the stars beyond.

His bride had not been waiting for him. The one thing he had expected to go smoothly had thrown his careful plans awry.

The message chip bit into Wynn's fingers, and he dropped

it to the deck. The Kalian fugitive was none other than Rook Galloway. The irony was considerable. And by sheerest coincidence Galloway had chosen the Louve system for one of his layovers. Wherever he might be bound. Wynn's own runners had disabled the *d'Artagnan* and identified her. The message they had sent by courier drone was three days old, and all Wynn knew was that Ariane had still been alive.

But only Wynn knew where she was, he and his own people. By now the news of Ariane's capture on Tantalus would have reached Espérance, carried by swift courier ship from Agora. Wynn could almost feel satisfaction imagining Bernard Marchand's horror and shame, but even that was not enough.

Ariane must be in *his* power. He must hold the Marchand heiress in his grasp before he delivered the final blow. If she was dead, his victory would never be complete.

But if she was still alive— Wynn's mouth hooked up into a smile. He would come to her rescue as a husband should, gallantly restoring her to her great-grandfather. Bernard Marchand would be even more in his debt.

Wynn bent slowly to pick up the message chip, turning it in his fingers as he moved back to the desk. He pushed it into the slot in the terminal and scanned the message again.

Fools. Fools and incompetents. Galloway had managed to injure all four of the men who'd gone after him. And worse — Wynn's eyes narrowed to slits. The runners reported that Ariane had *cooperated* with the Kalian.

Cooperated. With a man of the breed she hated. Wynn gave a soundless laugh. Rook Galloway had been her brother's supposed murderer.

Wynn's smile vanished. So, and so. If he'd believed in fate or anything beyond his own will, he might have been amazed.

No. Whatever his runners' pathetic excuses for their failure, Ariane would never cooperate with her brother's murderer. In her eyes he would still be guilty. Rook Galloway had been no more than a tool convenient to Wynn's purpose, used and discarded without thought.

If the tool had unexpectedly turned in Wynn's hand, that was easily remedied. A Kalian was still a savage, inferior in every way that mattered. There would be no loose ends, and Ariane would be Wynn's within the week.

A muted whistle sounded in the stateroom, breaking into Wynn's dark thoughts. He rose and moved to the padded seat by the porthole. The *Perséphone* shuddered once and slid free of its berth as the station's docking clamps disengaged.

Wynn glanced at the holopic propped on the desk next to the terminal. Ariane's dark eyes, caught in a moment of intensity, gazed back at him. "Be brave, little one," he said softly. "You won't have to wait much longer."

When Rook woke, it was to a feeling of panic so intense that he was almost out of the bunk before he opened his eyes.

He expected alarms, the telltale signs of another disaster. But the ship was quiet, eerily so. A stab of pain, protesting his sudden movement, reminded him of everything that had gone before.

They were still planet-bound. And he was alive, his body functioning almost normally. The arm that had been burned nearly to the bone was stiff and sore, but he could feel the new skin under the bandage webbing. He could remember nothing of the healing, or of coming back to the ship.

But he remembered Ariane: standing defiantly before the ship, in terrible danger; bending over him, pleading, commanding. The blurred image of her tear-streaked face merged with another memory: caressing touches and warm flesh pressed to his.

The scent of her was still on his skin.

Rook took a step and the deck tilted under him. He braced himself against the bulkhead with his good arm and fought the dizziness until he could think clearly again.

Turning inward, he assessed the state of his body. The damage dealt by the drug-runner's disruptor should have been fatal, even to a Kalian; somehow he'd survived. More, he was on his feet, able to move, to walk—but he was already feeling the strain of pushing his body's limits.

He sucked in a deep breath and propelled himself away from the bulkhead. Urgency rose in him, more powerful than the instinct to rest and heal.

Ariane. The need to find her, see her, touch her, drove him step by step across the cabin, through the hatch, and into the common room. Fire seared his nerves and blood sang in his ears, but still he pushed on until he reached the cockpit hatch.

The air lock door hissed open. A shapeless suited form stepped into the common room, lifting gloved hands to a visored helmet.

Loose strands of rich brown hair tumbled about her shoulders as Ariane removed the helmet. Her dark eyes widened. "Rook!"

He drank in the sight of her. For a moment the pain vanished, defeated by a joy so intense that he was held mute by the wonder of it. She only looked at him, her hair coiled loosely atop her head, her face smudged and streaked, her lips parted on the silent repetition of his name.

And then his legs gave way. He fell awkwardly, catching himself at the last moment, his wounded arm slapping against the bulkhead. A wave of blackness clouded his vision.

Gentle hands touched him and eased him to the deck.

"You damned idiot," Ariane growled, her voice like music. "Why couldn't you stay safely unconscious?"

Light and heat surged through Rook, washing the pain away. He twisted his mouth into a smile.

"Still scheming, Lady Ariane?" he said hoarsely. "Forgive me for—not cooperating."

Ariane's eyes flashed. She swept a gloved hand across her forehead, leaving a streak of red dust. "Scheming to fix the ship. Scheming to keep us both alive—" She broke off with a soft exhalation. *"Grand fou. . . ."*

Rook wanted nothing more in that moment but to pull her down with what remained of his strength and kiss the scowl away from her mouth, but her words held him still. "How long?" he asked.

Her expression softened. "Since the attack? Nearly three

days." Ariane tugged her gloves off and tossed them onto the deck, working at the fastenings of the suit with impatient fingers.

Rook covered her hands with one of his. They felt icy cold. "No more attacks?"

She looked up, tossing hair out of her eyes. "None. Plenty of flyovers—they haven't forgotten about us." Under her even tone Rook could hear the suppressed panic, felt the almost imperceptible trembling of her hands. He laced his fingers through hers, willing her warmth.

"And the ship?"

"Another day, maybe two." Ariane laughed, a sound of sheer exhaustion. She refused to meet his eyes. "A humbling experience to find out how little I know about hyperdrive repair. Even a savage can do it better."

"A trained savage," Rook said softly. Her lashes fluttered down, brushing her cheekbones. She bit her lip.

"I'm—sorry." The apology was almost inaudible. She untangled her fingers from his and clasped them together so tightly that the whites of her knuckles strained against the chafed skin.

"For saving my life?"

Wide eyes snapped back to his. Her panic was a visible thing. "I—"

"You saved my life. You brought me back to the ship and treated my wounds. I would have died."

She shook her head, but the denial was not for him. "Maybe," Ariane said, a catch in her voice, "maybe it's because I knew I wouldn't make it out of here without your help."

There was no conviction in the words. None at all. Rook moved at last, easing himself up. She trembled.

"So you needed me alive," Rook said, moving closer with exquisite care. "Is that why you ordered me so eloquently not to get myself killed? Risked your own life to leave the ship?"

Ariane stared at him, hot color in her cheeks. "I wasn't going to let them trap me here like a cornered animal—"

Rook caught her chin in his good hand, discomfort forgotten. It was as if he held her very being in the palm of his hand: fear and courage, confusion and resolution, shame and pride. A thousand mingled emotions he read in one blinding instant.

"Ariane," he murmured, stroking his thumb across the delicate hollow below her cheekbone.

Her face lost all expression. "Trapped," she said in a hoarse whisper. She swallowed convulsively, and he felt the momentary resistance in her jaw give way under his caress. A soft groan of despair rose from deep in her chest, but when he pulled her gently toward him, she came willingly.

He held her. It was all he wanted then, to ease her into the crook of his good arm and feel her near him. Her warmth, her scent penetrated the bulky space suit as if nothing lay between her skin and his.

She gave a muffled gasp, turning her face into his shoulder, hands moving restlessly to find some part of him safe to touch. At last she folded them under her, curled against his bare chest like a kitten's. And then she began to sob—silently, holding back the tears with fierce resolve.

Deep and unfamiliar tenderness welled in Rook's soul. Like Ariane, he resisted—only for a moment, knowing himself already lost. This was no lust that he could channel with anger and mold to suit his plans for revenge. This was something more powerful, something that fed on life and hope and a thousand things Rook had forgotten.

Life. Life they might lose anytime, to killers from Ariane's own world. Life that seemed suddenly precious beyond reason.

He wanted to tell her to let go, to trust him, that he would never allow harm to come to her. He wanted to whisper sweet, comforting lies that denied everything but the moment.

But he could not speak. He only held her and stroked his palm up and down her back until her shuddering subsided. He felt the subtle change in her body as she became conscious of his touch; she stiffened, the muscles of her shoulders tensing as if to throw off his hand.

"Please. Let me go."

Unexpected pain seized Rook's body as he withdrew his hand; Ariane pulled back sharply and scrambled away, peeling out of the space suit and returning it to the locker. When her eyes came back to him, they were veiled and dry.

"You aren't healed yet, Kalian," she said gruffly. "I didn't save your life just to see you die now." She crouched down to offer support, impersonal and efficient, and he let her take a little of his weight as he got to his feet. Even now her touch seemed to soothe the bone-deep ache that beat through his overtaxed body. She led him to the cabin—her cabin—and eased him down on the bunk without a word.

He watched her move stiffly to the computer terminal. Catching her lip between her teeth, she tapped in a request and scrolled the answering lines of text and figures so fast that they blurred into a meaningless jumble.

"One more day," she whispered. "Just one more day."

Her face was perfectly expressionless when she turned to him again, but he could still see the desperation behind her eyes.

The *d'Artagnan*'s proximity alarms went off twice that night, jarring Ariane from nightmares of walls closing in to crush her.

She stared into the darkness and struggled with her irrational panic, listening to the deep, steady cadence of Rook's breathing.

Panic came all too easily when nothing was certain, when she had endless solitary hours to contemplate the unthinkable. Hours to remember, to replay her life and reach for meaning that eluded her.

It wasn't merely death she feared. It was the helplessness, the emptiness she felt when she looked for herself behind the facade she had always worn.

Marchand. Kalian. Both, and neither. Trapped, waiting—waiting for a resolution that would never come. If she died here, on this barren planet, there would be no purpose to her death. Or to her life. And the questions would never be answered.

Ariane shifted in the chair beside the bunk and gazed at Rook. Strange how she'd never thought anything of her ability to see so well in the dark.

Rook could see everything but what she truly was.

Since that one time he had left the cabin, he'd slept deeply; not even the alarms had pierced his shield of unconsciousness. It was safe now to gaze at him and let her fragile mask dissolve. When he'd held her in his arms, there on the deck by the cockpit hatch, she'd been terrified that he would guess the truth.

Which truth? Ariane asked herself bitterly, clenching her fingers on the chair arm. She clung to her final secrets with the desperation of one who has nothing else.

He had shown no contempt for her weakness when she'd cried into his shoulder, grasping at a moment's comfort. He had touched her without lust or the desire to possess. Tenderly, with wordless eloquence.

So easy, so easy to deceive herself with hope. He was capable of gentleness; she had seen that with the Fahar. Perhaps, so close to death, he allowed himself a brief respite from hatred.

But he had asked her why she had risked her life to save his, as if the answer mattered to him. . . .

No. She couldn't afford to snare herself in dreams and what-ifs and forget what she had struggled so hard to accept.

She needed him. In the waiting, empty silence he was all she had left. She had spent her nights in the chair beside the bunk, knowing she would truly go mad if she could not see him, hear him, touch him. He, her adversary, the man who had sworn vengeance on her family, had become her only anchor to sanity.

Laying her head back, Ariane closed her eyes. Fitful sleep came, and with it the nightmare. Obsidian walls closing in, sucking the light like a black hole, squeezing air from her lungs like vacuum. Wynn's face reflected on every side, distorted mirror images, stretching grotesquely; her great-grandfather's voice calling in agony from beyond the darkness.

She reached. She reached desperately toward the sliver of light that remained between the featureless walls. A hand appeared in the gap, slender and aristocratic. Her own. It beckoned her, and even as she stretched to grasp it, it changed, grew hard and heavy and masculine.

In the suffocating blackness she hesitated, regarding the hand with horror. Savage's hand, Kalian hand—salvation and destruction in bone and tendon and muscle. The closing walls pressed on the scarred wrist as if to sever it, but it did not withdraw—only hovered there, unmoving. And then from behind her came a beam of red light, tearing a ragged crack in the rear wall. She whirled, and Wynn stood there, triumphant, offering his arm.

She knew it for a dream then, but some part of her would not accept the release of waking. She turned back to the disembodied hand, watched it begin to wither before her eyes, knowing it would blacken and vanish in another instant.

With a wail of despair she flung herself forward to grasp the hand in hers.

"Rook!"

Ariane pressed her hand to her mouth, muffling the involuntary cry.

Her fingers shook as she pushed back her sweat-soaked hair. On the bunk Rook was moving in sharp, violent spasms, chest heaving, fingers clawing at the sheets. His mouth worked soundlessly.

Ariane gathered her legs under her and sprang to the bunk, reaching for his hands. It took all her strength to capture his wrists; the force of his thrashing threatened to tear her arms from their sockets. She called on her Kalian strength, and still it was not enough. Rook tossed his head; coarse black hair slapped at her face, nearly blinding her.

He heard nothing—not his name, nor the words she spoke to him with increasing urgency. She could find no way past the black turmoil that wrapped him like a shroud.

In desperation she pressed her full weight against him,

along his length, trapping his legs with hers. He bucked, but she pushed her face into the hollow of his shoulder and held on.

Stillness came suddenly, like the peace after a plasma storm. Ariane raised her head carefully. Rook's eyes were closed, no longer rolling under fluttering lids. His breath shuddered under her, lifting her and letting her down gently.

Without conscious thought she released his good hand and reached up to comb her fingers through the black hair that clung to his temples. Her lips followed, resting lightly on the damp, tanned skin above his brows. He tasted of perspiration and the essence of everything masculine; she breathed in deeply, savoring the sensation of being so close to him.

She kissed him, feather light, along the strong, straight line of his eyebrow and down to the hard curve of his cheekbone. His breath curled around her ear and bathed her already-warm skin in waves of heat. She touched the scar with her lips and then, carefully, with her tongue.

The rhythm of his breathing caught and held. Dark lashes trembled; his nostrils flared, and the firm, mobile lips, relaxed in sleep, parted. Memories of his kisses flooded her mind, turning her blood to liquid metal.

Ariane closed her eyes and rested her cheek against the slight roughness of Rook's jaw, letting herself feel every part of him. Her hands swept from his face to his shoulders, measuring the breadth of them. The hard muscle of his arms seemed to shiver under her touch as she moved down. With her breasts she felt the sculpted contours of his chest; her thighs were cradled on his. And lower, where sensation coalesced into need, she could feel the heavy firmness of his arousal.

With a soundless gasp she pressed into him, wanting more and afraid to seek it. This was safe; now, as he slept, she could be with him and still hold herself apart. The savage was tamed, the enemy vanquished. There was no greater struggle between them than the gentle dueling of their breaths. . . .

Big callused hands closed over Ariane, spreading flat against her back, locking her down.

"Ariane." Rook's voice was a husky sigh. Ariane tensed, waiting for his eyes to open and focus on hers. The alarm that sang through her body did nothing to quench the heat of awakened desire. Even now, bracing to fight free of his arms, she felt her heart begin to race with forbidden excitement.

"Ariane," he whispered again, turning his head on the pillow. His hands moved down along the curve of her spine. Ariane shuddered, and his body trembled in sympathy. The potent symbol of his desire pushed up between her thighs.

But his eyes remained closed. He held her tightly, but still he slept; it was as if their bodies communicated on some plane beyond thought or reason. Ariane closed her mind and locked it away. She let sensation take her again, relaxed her muscles one by one, lulled by strange contentment as powerful as any drug.

The first touch of the returning nightmare faded almost as soon as it began. The walls never closed around her; space stretched out on every side, brilliant with stars. They formed luminous paths that reached to places beyond infinity, beckoning with silent songs of hope.

"This is yours, Ariane. Take it." The voice was deep, low, exultant with victory. A hand clasped hers, dwarfing it like a child's. She turned to look at Rook, his black hair limned by starlight. Copper eyes burned. "Don't be afraid to take it," he urged. He reached out, and the stars fell into his hands. "Don't be afraid."

"Don't be afraid. . . ."

Ariane jerked awake, Rook's voice ringing in her ears. His eyes were open as they'd been in the dream, locked on hers, burning—burning and frightening and tender.

Inexplicable panic tore at her, and she pulled away with all her strength. Rook let her go instantly. Stumbling away from the bunk, Ariane crossed to the opposite bulkhead and turned her back to him, folding her arms tightly across her chest. The heat and scent of his body filled her nostrils with every indrawn breath.

"Ariane," Rook said. She heard him shift, painfully aware of each small sound he made. She knew when he sat up on the bunk, when he paused for a moment at some lingering discomfort and straightened again.

She swallowed heavily. "You were having a nightmare," she said. "You—might have hurt yourself. I was afraid—" She fell silent, afraid to turn and find the mockery in his eyes.

"A nightmare?" Rook moved again, and Ariane braced herself for his approach. But he remained on the bunk; she could hear the whisper of his fingers stroking the sheets in a maddening rhythm.

"It was no nightmare I had, Ariane," he murmured. "You were there, in my arms. And you were touching me—"

"No." She squeezed her eyes shut as if such a small act could bar him from her senses.

"No?" he repeated, without a trace of mockery. "Did I imagine it, Ariane? The desperate, pitiable dreams of a condemned man?"

Ariane caught her answer before it left her lips. *Yes,* she wanted to cry. A dream; all it could ever be.

It was not too late. The decision was not irrevocable. She had touched his mind, the deepest workings of his body, and still he did not know her for what she was. He would not force her; they could go on as they had, poised on the edge of the abyss, until death came for them.

She could die with honor. Honor that meant less than nothing, when her great-grandfather's grand plans would die with her. She could remain a proud Marchand until the bitter end.

Or she could take what had been given her in these final hours. She could know, fully, what it was to be a woman. Savor what she had only tasted, set her desire free of its feeble bonds.

Marchand and Kalian, savage and aristocrat—such labels had surely become meaningless at last.

Here, in this ship, were only Rook and Ariane.

The shrill tocsin of the proximity alarm pierced Ariane's thoughts like a duelist's mortal blow. She whirled to the computer terminal.

Rook was only a step behind her. "How close?" he said

against her ear. The fine hairs along her neck stirred at his nearness, but she kept her eyes and her attention locked on the screen.

"Same as before. A flyover." She held her breath, counting out the seconds. And when the alarm died and they were still alive, it took every iota of her will to keep from falling back into Rook's arms.

Instead, she balled her fist and smashed it down onto the smooth, shiny surface of the desk. "Why?" she whispered. "Why don't they just end it?"

Rook touched her arm, almost snapping her control. "I don't know. Perhaps they mean to take you hostage after all." He moved away, his feet almost soundless on the deck. "We can send out a message beacon, offer terms—"

"Never!" She pivoted to face him, perilously close to tears. She fought a fierce inward battle until her voice was almost calm again. "Never. I'll die before I let *canailles* like these hold Marchand honor in their filthy hands."

Rook came to a halt in midstep. His eyes were shuttered and wary, utterly unreadable.

Marchand honor. Those words still came so easily, after all her struggles. She swallowed her despair, unable to meet Rook's steady gaze.

She almost felt she could read his thoughts, the words he would speak when he threw her precious honor back at her. But he only shook his head, a slow and deliberate gesture of resignation.

"Of course," he said, his mouth turning up in a self-mocking smile. "Forgive my presumption, Lady Ariane."

Her heart tightened in her chest. Alternate tides of hot and cold surged through her as she looked into Rook's metal-bright eyes.

Pride made a last attempt to sway her course from surrender. "I'm not afraid to die," she said, lifting her chin. Even to her own ears the words rang false. "I'm not afraid—"

She turned away from him before he could read the lie in her eyes. Leaning heavily over the desk, her loose hair nearly brushing the surface, she listened to Rook's deliberate footsteps.

"I know," he said softly. "I may question your devotion to honor, Lady Ariane, but never your courage. Never that."

Ariane flung back her head; a laugh strangled in her throat. "You *should* question it, Rook Galloway." She looked around; he stood a safe distance away, far enough to give her the courage to continue.

"I hate being trapped, Rook," she whispered. "I've always hated confinement." Shame made her meet Rook's eyes at last. "I grew up always testing the limits of proper behavior. I dreaded the thought of a life bound to Espérance, a proper woman of the Elite, and so I convinced my great-grandfather to give me this ship so that I could escape. But until I first saw you on Tantalus, I didn't know what it was to be a prisoner." Tears stung behind her eyelids. "Until now—I didn't realize how much a coward I truly am."

She sensed his protest before he voiced it, and raised a hand to forestall him. "You were right to mock my honor, Rook. Whatever I have left of it isn't worth the price." Her wry smile slipped back into place with deceptive ease. "If I were still a proper Marchand, I'd never admit my weaknesses to an enemy. *If* I were a proper Marchand. But I'm not, Rook. Perhaps I've never been."

Rook looked up at her sharply. She could almost believe he knew. Something changed in his face.

"Not a Marchand?" he said, almost lightly. "Oh, no, Lady Ariane. You've convinced me too well."

Ariane refused the escape he unwittingly offered her. "I'm not running away from what I am, Rook. Even though everything I said about being afraid was true." She found it surprisingly easy to take a step forward. Rook almost flinched, disquiet in his copper eyes.

"Yes, I'm afraid, Rook. Afraid of letting go before I've known what it is to live." She took another step, and Rook went as still as an animal being stalked. Once she might have felt satisfaction, turning the tables on the Kalian savage; now she felt another kind of power, acceptance brilliant as sunlight flooding every part of her being.

Rook. She wanted to reach for him, but she stopped and held her distance. "You've taught me so much. You've forced me to face things in myself—things I would have lost without ever knowing they existed. And now it's almost too late. We might die anytime—in an hour, tomorrow—"

Rook found his voice at last. "The ship—" he began hoarsely.

"She's almost ready. As ready as I can make her. I've initiated the final reconfiguration of the hyperspace network. She'll be spaceworthy again within twenty-four hours." Relief flickered across Rook's face, but she cut him off with a shake of her head. "But what will happen when we lift? Will they be waiting to blast us out of existence the moment we leave atmosphere?"

"They won't take us so easily," Rook growled.

Us. She lost the sense of his reply, cherishing that one word, losing herself in the austere beauty of the man who stood before her.

"No, Rook. They won't take us easily." Stubborn pride curved her mouth into a smile. "We aren't so different, Rook. You lived with the reality of death every day on Tantalus, and you didn't let it destroy you. You fought, and you took what you wanted, knowing you might have to die to get it."

"Ariane—"

"Listen to me, Rook." She took another inexorable step forward, daring him to retreat. He held his ground, but his eyes were almost all pupil, copper swallowed in black.

At last she reached out, across the small, infinite space between them. "A few minutes ago, when you woke, you—asked me if it was a dream. The dream of a condemned man." Her fingers brushed his arm; a current of blinding emotion arced from his flesh to hers and back again.

"It wasn't a dream." She swallowed, taking the final step. "I want you, Rook. I want you to make love to me."

CHAPTER TWELVE

"*I want you.*"

The words rebounded in Rook's mind, nearly severing his hard-won control.

Ariane looked up at him, her gaze frank and unafraid. Instantly he relived the last time she had spoken those words, words he had forced her to speak: lost in the heat of passion, her body open under him, his for the taking.

His own body was already responding, even when she met his eyes so calmly, as if she'd asked him to make some minor repair on the ship. When he'd wakened, hard with desire, to find her in his arms, he had nearly forgotten everything but the need he had never driven from his heart.

Until she'd spoken words of fear and loss, sacrificed her pride to open herself to him again. Her soul this time, not merely her body. And as she had made her admissions, silently begging for his understanding, he had looked into her eyes and seen himself. His own fear, his bewilderment, his futile, all-too-human defiance of death. And the need that could not be denied.

Ariane wet her lips, and his eyes moved to follow the motion. Blood beat fast in his veins and gathered in his groin, clouding his thoughts.

Victory. He should have felt triumph, seeing a Marchand break before his eyes. Ariane Burke-Marchand, renouncing her heritage—the very pride that she'd taken in with her Elite mother's milk.

Ariane, speaking of a past he had never touched, had never known. Ariane, echoing his own unspoken terror of confinement, of walls closing in, of isolation blacker than space itself.

Ariane, honor forgotten, asking him to make love to her just once before they died. . . .

"I'm flattered, Lady Ariane," he said, emphasizing the title with deliberate cruelty, "that you might find some use for me in your final hours. Or is it that I left you unsatisfied?"

He felt her shock as if she stood in his own skin. He waited for her furious reply, but the silence held, stretched second by unbearable second.

"I may be a coward, Rook," she said at last, only a faint tremor marring the evenness of her voice, "but I'm not afraid of you."

Rook laughed harshly. "You said you'd die before you let me touch you again. Wasn't the last lesson sufficient?" He kissed her then without a trace of gentleness. She went rigid as he plunged his tongue deep into her mouth and ground his hips into hers, pushing her down against the desk.

He let the fear take him, fear and rage and need like a star gone nova. He felt his teeth bruise Ariane's lips, heard her gasp for breath. Desperation drove every trace of pity from his heart.

"Is this what you wanted, Ariane?" he rasped. He tangled one fist in her hair and pulled her head back, exposing the arched column of her throat. Her eyes were tightly closed, but she made no move to escape.

With a soft curse he let her go. Ariane remained where she was, bent back over the desk, her hands braced behind her. The look in her eyes held no censure, no hatred. Only a deep sadness.

"Does your hatred run so deep that you won't accept anything freely given?" she whispered. "Anything you can't seize in the name of revenge?"

She advanced on him with ruthless determination.

"We're here, Rook," she said fiercely. "You and I. Two people wanting each other, facing death. What we were before doesn't matter."

"Doesn't matter?" he echoed. He tried again to summon the shield of rage, but it slipped through his grasp. He could no more temper the heat in his blood or the need in his soul than he could alter the laws of space and time. "When I'm the last of my people left alive?"

Ariane caught her breath, the sheen of tears glazing her eyes. She held out her hand, palm up; soft skin, pale and beautiful and fragile. "We're the same, Rook. Human. Needing to forget how alone we are."

Alone. Rook closed his eyes and let himself drown in his aloneness, tasted it and molded it and tried to wrap it around himself. But there was light shining through the shadow of his isolation. Light that pulsed with Ariane's heartbeat, Ariane's breath, Ariane's life. . . .

The soft pads of her fingertips rested on his clenched fist. And he thought he could hear her voice filling the hollows of his soul.

We are the same.

Something within him gave way, understanding he had no strength left to deny.

He was Kalian no longer. He had lost the sense of who he was, every bitter purpose he had nursed in his heart since Ariane had come to Tantalus. Ariane had stolen it away from him.

"Do you know what you want, Ariane?" he asked softly, unfolding his hand to hold hers.

Her smile flared into brilliance, and Rook felt her joy as if it were his own.

"I know." Her hand tightened with surprising strength.

"And if we live?"

Ariane shook her head. "There is no future, Rook. No past. I almost saw you die—" The smile faded, and she rested her other hand flat against his chest as if she could catch and hold his heart. He watched her struggle for words and find them. "I want to be a part of you, Rook. And I want you in me."

The image evoked by her words flared in Rook's mind: flesh on flesh, bodies joined to form a perfect whole. The release he had denied himself before.

"I have little to give you, Ariane," he said hoarsely.

Her fingers curved to cup his cheek, stilling thought and fear with sensation and desire.

"I ask nothing of you, Rook. Nothing more than this." And she pulled him down, meeting his lips with her own.

Ariane knew she had won, and her own lingering doubts were swept away in Rook's response. There was no harshness in him now, no desire to hurt or drive away. His arms closed around her, lifting her off her feet—cradling her like something infinitely precious. And his mouth moved softly, almost hesitantly, on hers.

She held back from seeking his mind, knowing it was too soon. This was a time for the physical, the knowledge that she could touch and be touched by him without pain or anger. That death would not be meaningless after all.

Rook ended the kiss long before she was ready, letting her slide back to the deck. He cupped her face in his big hands.

"I've never stopped wanting you, Ariane," he said. His voice was rough with emotion he refused to show, but she could see the wonder reflected in his copper eyes. Callused fingers stroked her skin, returning the caresses she had given him while he slept.

She laid her hands over his. "Why didn't you finish it before, then?" she whispered. "I wouldn't have stopped you."

The memory of his sensual touch, his heated demands after the duel, seized her mind and body. His breath caught as if he read her mind. For a moment she thought he would reveal his inner thoughts as she had done, make himself vulnerable to her at last.

But he only smiled, more sadness than cynicism in the expression. His fingers drifted down her face to rest on her lips.

"No past, Ariane," he said softly. He searched her eyes. "No questions, no demands. Only now."

Only now. That was all she had asked, and it would have to be enough.

"Only now," she agreed. Hesitantly she parted her lips, touched his fingers with her tongue. He shuddered. There were heavy shadows beneath his brows, lines carved into his forehead under the ragged fall of black hair; she drew her thumb down the deepest crease in the center as if she could smooth it away.

He closed his eyes, and his hands moved from her mouth to settle behind the curve of her neck.

"Ariane," he breathed. He bent to kiss her forehead, her eyelids, the arch of her cheekbones. He had never been so gentle; Ariane tilted back her head and bathed in his warmth. His touch spoke of the things he would never admit to her or to himself.

Lacing his hands in her hair, Rook found her lips parted and yearning. His mouth firmed, became gradually more demanding. Ariane felt his tongue slide along her lower lip and dip inward. Not like before, when he had meant only to possess. This was new, a tender exploration, as if there had never been another time.

His fingers, tangled in her hair, pulled her closer. She melted into him and clutched his shoulders when he bent her over his arm. She knew he would never let her fall, but she was already tumbling, relinquishing authority over her body and her heart.

Almost reverently he eased his tongue fully into her mouth. He tasted like some exotic alien wine, heady and powerful. Each gentle thrust of his tongue drove the intoxicating heat deeper through her body.

Rook made a sound low in his throat, half growl and half groan, as she curled her tongue over his. Suddenly the kiss grew fierce and hungry. His teeth closed over her lower lip and pulled; he worked his mouth on hers as if he could devour her. His desire pulsed through her at every point their bodies touched.

"No past," he had said, but she remembered: how it had been when his mouth had caressed every intimate part of her, how powerfully and treacherously she had wanted him, how her need and his had mingled and become inseparable.

It was happening again, but now she grasped it with all her strength. She answered his wordless cry with one of her own.

Rook pulled away. Ariane blinked up at him, her lips

aching with the loss. The copper of his eyes had become a thin corona around the black pupil, like a sun in eclipse.

"Did I hurt you?" he said. The question was almost incomprehensible, lost in the harsh rasp of Rook's breathing.

Ariane touched his mouth as if she could capture the words. "Hurt me?" She gave a soundless laugh. "No, Rook. Never."

But his eyes narrowed to slits, searching her face. A faint flush stained his skin under the tan. Suddenly he dropped his hands to her shoulders, flexing his fingers open and closed.

"I forget who I am, Ariane," he said. "When I touch you —" He broke off, and she felt the shame and self-contempt that he struggled to hide. "If I lose control—"

Ariane closed her eyes and leaned forward to rest her forehead against his chest. His heart beat heavy and fast.

"I've already lost mine, Rook," she admitted softly. "Nothing you do can hurt me now."

Rook's hands slid down her arms. With a tenderness that belied his warning, he lowered his cheek to her hair.

"When I take what you offer," he said, "there will be no going back."

A bone-deep shiver coursed through Ariane. No going back. She offered her virginity to Rook, and he knew what that meant to an unmarried woman of the Elite. He had known all along.

He had won it from her before and refused to take it.

Wynn's handsome, aristocratic face rose in her memory; she pushed the vision away with almost frightening ease. But she could not be afraid; fear and guilt existed in a world she could no longer touch.

Rook still remembered what she had been in that other world. It took all of Ariane's resolve to keep from revealing herself for what she was, what she had become. The time was not right—not when the man who held her had given her the gift of his own vulnerability.

She breathed in the scent of his skin, turned to brush her lips over the warm, hard contours of his chest.

"No past," she breathed. "No future." Her mouth

searched by instinct for the nub of his nipple and closed over it lightly. "Only now. Teach me, Rook. Take me——"

He swept her up into his arms, making her gasp, and kissed her urgently. She felt herself suspended between heaven and earth, shivering and burning, as Rook carried her to the bunk.

Ariane let him ease her down. Rook knelt at the foot of the bunk, a powerful masculine shape in the cabin's dim light. In spite of her vows to forget the past, she felt every part of her body tighten in anticipation of what was to come—remembering the last time, when Rook had been the victor and she the prize.

She had abandoned herself then, to the savage part of herself she hadn't learned to accept. Now she welcomed Rook with acceptance and full control over her own heart.

Rook looked down at her, motionless. His gaze was intent and hungry, moving over her as if he thought she might vanish at a touch.

Claiming the moment of silence, Ariane let her own eyes trace the hard, powerful symmetry of his form. From the first time she had seen him, she'd found him beautiful—in the Warren, and on Tantalus.

It was not the elegant beauty of pure blood and perfect breeding, refined by generations of arranged marriages among the Elite. It was something far more compelling: dark, exotic, charged with the harsh mystery of Kali and the Shaper's legacy. The beauty of a predator that could never quite be tamed.

He had said he found *her* beautiful, in the heat of battle. And passion. Suddenly shy, Ariane closed her eyes.

Work-roughened fingers drifted across her eyelids. "Second thoughts, Ariane?" The strain in his voice was evident.

She stretched her body on the bunk, deliberately opening to him, and caught his hand against her face. "This is still new to me, Rook. I've never been with a man. Not before——"

Before you. The unspoken words hung between them; Rook withdrew his hand and closed his eyes. Ariane studied the way the tendons of his neck flowed smoothly into his shoulders, the shadowed arc of his chest, the ridged muscle of his abdomen. Thick hair tumbled over his back like the pelt of a shadowcat. The pulse beat very fast beneath the skin of his throat.

Ariane raised herself on her elbows, eased into a sitting position, and dropped her legs over the side of the bunk. She knew Rook heard her as she rose and moved away, but he made no attempt to stop her.

He would let her escape, after everything she had done to overcome his strange reluctance. But Ariane's thoughts were far from flight. She worked at the fastenings of her shipsuit, eased the soft garment down over her shoulders and hips, and let it pool at her feet.

The shiver that raced through her had nothing to do with the cabin's carefully regulated temperature. Abandoning the shipsuit where it lay on the carpet, she walked to the antique chest where she kept her clothing and opened the carved lid.

The firesilk of her sleeping gown slid sensually over her fingers as she lifted it above her head and let it fall and settle into the curves and planes of her body. She hadn't worn it since that first night out from Agora; the almost erotic feel of it had been too much for her hypersensitive nerves when the Fahar had filled the entire ship with the essence of their loving.

After that night she had always imagined she could smell Rook's compelling scent locked into the delicate weave, and she had buried it deep in the trunk.

Now the time had come to reclaim it, an Elite woman's garment worn to seduce a Kalian. *No,* Ariane thought, crossing the deck to stand behind Rook. *Only a woman loving a man.*

Her hands shook as she reached out to stroke the black hair that veiled the heavy, tense muscles of his back. She gathered the coarse strands and let them sift through her fingers like dark water. And then she leaned into him, pressing her face to his hair.

Only a single breath of his scent filled her lungs before he turned, swift and graceful, to grasp her bare arms. He half rose from the bunk and pulled her to his chest, between his thighs, so that her mouth was level with his.

The burnished brilliance of Rook's eyes darkened further as his gaze swept over her. Pushing her back gently, he skimmed his hands down her arms and inward, molding the firesilk to waist and hip.

Heat gathered under Ariane's skin—where his hands traveled, in the pit of her belly, along the arch of her cheekbones. She grabbed at Rook's shoulders.

"I thought you were having second thoughts, Rook," she said, reaching absurdly for humor. "I'm no expert at seduction. . . ."

His answer was a groan as he dragged her mouth against his.

Leaning into him, Ariane shuddered at the possessive hunger of his kiss, the exquisite friction of firesilk caught between her nipples and his chest. His hands worked slowly down her back to cup her buttocks, and she met the demands of his lips as if that contact alone could keep her from falling.

He stole his name from her mouth just before he released it and then gave her the gift of her own, in a voice husky with wonder and desire.

"Ariane." With a deft adjustment he shifted her body so that her hips remained trapped between his thighs and her back bent over his supporting arm. His gaze was almost tangible as it caressed her neck, her bare shoulders, the plunging neckline that ended between her breasts.

"Does it meet with your approval, Rook Galloway?" she asked.

His eyes snapped back to hers, and his mouth curled. It was the familiar half-mocking smile, stripped of hostility and strangely precious to her.

"I've only seen you in a shipsuit, Ariane," he said. "This is something of an improvement." As if to illustrate his words, he feathered his hand over her hip, up her belly, and pressed it just under her breast. Her heart lurched.

She lifted her chin with a shadow of the old pride. "I

never saw the use for elaborate clothing on a working ship," she retorted.

His smile faded. "Or for the pleasure of an enemy," he countered softly.

Without thinking Ariane bunched her fist and brought it down on his shoulder, hard. "Damn you, Rook Galloway. There are no enemies here." She cursed herself as her eyes filled with tears. "Or would you rather have me struggle and hate you until the bitter end?"

He stared at her, stricken. Of a sudden he caught her by the waist and plunged down, burying his face between her breasts. Rough, impatient fingers plucked at one narrow strap of her gown, working it over her shoulder.

This was the only reply he could give, and it was enough. Ariane knew what would come next, but when his tongue stroked her nipple through the silk she gasped aloud.

Abruptly abandoning the strap, Rook gave his full attention to her breasts. He lifted her to straddle him as he settled back onto the bunk, and the skirt of the gown rode up around her thighs.

He kissed the swell of bare skin above the gown's neckline, worked his way down to the shadowed valley between her breasts. Cupping one hand under the soft, curved weight, he lifted her breast and pressed his lips to the taut fabric that covered it.

The sensation was not new, and yet it might have been the first time—freely giving herself, freely wanting. Ariane arched up into his caress, and Rook took her nipple in his mouth and suckled, wetting the silk to transparency. His other hand nestled in the small of her back, supporting her as she shuddered and trembled.

She was only partly aware when Rook worked the straps free and pushed the sheer fabric down over her breasts, his hand following in its wake to cover her bare flesh. Warm breath skimmed across the damp skin of her neck as he buried his face in her hair.

"It would be better," he said, a catch in his voice, his hand massaging her breast, "if you could hate me."

Tears spilled free of Ariane's lids, tears of sadness and need and tenderness. "No, Rook," she whispered. "Hate is never better." And she gasped again as he licked the corner of her jaw, the hollow of her neck, the slope of her breast until he found her nipple again.

She could sense the moment when, somewhere amid the tangle of her own feelings, she began to touch Rook's mind. It started as awareness of desire not her own, built steadily to an intensity of emotion that belonged uniquely to him. There were no litdisks to explain how this sharing worked, or why Rook was so blind to the connection. And to what she was.

She had been grateful for that blindness. But now she wanted to open herself, make him feel it, find the shadow that guarded his soul and pierce it with the light that she knew, instinctively, waited to be born between them.

He drew deeply on her nipple and she lost her focus, caught up in a maelstrom of sensation. "Did I tell you," he murmured, his lips tracing the words on her skin, "how beautiful you are?"

Ariane shook her head, but it was not in denial of his words. She arched again as he pulled the gown lower beneath her breasts and kissed the underside of each.

"Beautiful," he repeated, kissing the arch of her ribs. "By the Shapers, I can't—"

But he let the sentence trail into caresses that sent spirals of erotic pleasure arcing down from her belly to the place he had not yet touched. When he could reach no further without bending her almost to the deck, he lifted her hard against him and turned so that she lay half on the bunk and he knelt above her.

"I want to taste you, Ariane," he said hoarsely. Copper eyes locked on hers, molten, questioning. His hands settled on her parted thighs, and she could no longer separate memory from the heated images that seemed to flow directly from his mind to hers.

"Rook," she groaned, reaching for him, but he had already caught the hem of her gown, tumbled just above her knees, and was sliding it up with his palms. She was aching and moist before his hands cupped her hips, her intimate flesh taut with anticipation.

His breath touched her first, heat on heat, and his fingers followed. They met no resistance as he drew them slowly from the soft brown curls down into her liquid warmth, stroking between the delicate petals. Ariane lifted her hips with a cry; Rook's mouth replaced his fingers and he slipped his hands under her buttocks to hold her still.

And as he tasted her with his lips and caressed her with his tongue, giving her the gift of pleasure without demanding anything for himself, she laced her fingers in his hair and reached out once again for his mind.

She plunged into chaos. Rook's inner self was a whirling darkness, pierced by shafts of contradictory emotion she could not touch long enough to name. She could feel the pulse of his blood and the rush of air in his lungs, the taut ache of his desire, newly healed bone and muscle and flesh beating with strength, but the storm in his mind pushed her back again and again. And then Rook's intimate stroking broke her concentration utterly, hurling her into another tempest of physical sensation.

Rook's mouth had found the center of pleasure, teasing it with a firm, gentle rhythm that carried her closer and closer to the ecstasy she yearned for with an ancient and elemental need.

But something stopped her as she trembled on the brink of fulfillment.

With an effort she pulled free of the dizzying spiral of pleasure, caught Rook's hair in both hands, and lifted his head. He made a soft sound of protest, looking up at her from beneath his brows, eyes almost black.

Ariane rose, shifting to grasp his taut shoulders. A deep, unsatisfied ache throbbed in her, but it was not hers alone. Rook's need was so intense that it was like pain—pain that she alone could heal.

"Together, Rook," she said, her voice a raw whisper. "I want it to be together, with you inside me."

Rook stared at her face—flushed with arousal, soft with

the pleasure he had given. He had almost felt her physical joy within his mind and soul, as if the taste and feel of her could convey far more than the simple responses of her body.

He was hard and heavy with the longing to bury himself deep within her, pushed to the point of pain by the sweet tang of her readiness. He flexed his hands on her thighs, unwilling to let go, afraid of losing control.

Ariane was not afraid. She fixed him with that deep, clear gaze and leaned forward, using his shoulders for support. "This is for both of us, Rook," she said. She lifted one hand and drew her finger across his lips, still wet with her feminine mist. "I want you to teach me, Rook. How to touch you—" She feathered a caress from his shoulder to the inward slope of his waist, wringing a shudder from him. "How to bring you pleasure. . . ."

Her words intensified his hunger almost beyond bearing. Mutely he gathered her to him, lowered her from the bunk so that they knelt face to face and thigh to thigh.

He rested his forehead against hers, trying to focus on the silky texture of her skin and hair, the soft sigh of her breath. This was not merely lust, brought to fever pitch by days of frustrated denial and years of abstinence, or a hunger to possess driven by bitterness. But he did not dare think beyond the physical; to do so would drive him to the edge of sanity.

Her small, elegant hands flattened on his chest, slipping in among the dark curls. Tilting her head, she kissed the corner of his mouth. Her tongue slipped out to trace his lips.

Rook swallowed a deep growl and trapped her mouth, drawing her tongue inward. He kissed her until she gasped for breath and let her go, sucking fire into his own lungs.

"I have nothing to teach you," he whispered through the inferno.

She smiled, shy and bold at once, and her hands moved from his chest to cup the hard swell of his arousal.

Only the most rigid control of his body's functions kept him from release as she began to stroke him through the pliant fabric of his trousers. Her fingers were knowing, expert, as if she had experienced this intimacy many times before. He made no move to stop her when she unfastened the fly and released his shaft into her palm.

The ability to speak anything but her name deserted him utterly. He caught a glimpse of the triumphant wonder in her eyes before he closed his own and gave himself to the exquisite torment.

Without conscious awareness he came to be lying on his back, carpet under him and Ariane above him, straddling his thighs. Her hands worked their magic; a highly charged image of Ariane taking him into her mouth formed amid the turmoil of his thoughts, and an instant later her lips enveloped him.

She held him down with surprising strength as his body reacted and surged against her. Firm, gentle hands pulled his trousers lower, trapping his thighs. Afraid to touch her, he clenched his fingers into the carpet and gasped in time to the rhythm of her caresses.

He nearly cried out when she withdrew. But then she slid up over him, her gown bunching at her waist, her breasts brushing his hips and his belly and his ribs, trapping his slick hardness at the apex of her thighs. Her lips traced patterns across his chest, lingered at the nipples as if she were fascinated by the differences between them. She shifted her body so that her thighs cradled his hips, and liquid heat begged him to enter.

"Now, Rook," she gasped softly, rocking back, bracing her hands on his chest. "Now."

Her soft command pulsed through him as he rose to grasp her waist, lifted her, and used his own body to carry her onto her back where he had lain. Urgency flared like a supernova, arcing from Ariane to himself, denying restraint. Yet Rook fought for control and regained enough of it to cradle her face in his hands, kiss her gently, look deeply into her brilliant eyes.

"I'll try to make it easy, Ariane," he murmured, laying his cheek against hers. "There may be pain—"

She drew him down in answer, parting her thighs. "I want

you, Rook," she said, and smiled. Trembling, Rook balanced his weight on his arms and settled himself against her.

Her body yielded to him, wet and hot and tight, as he eased inside. He heard her breath catch, though her smile never faltered; when he would have stopped she flattened her hands in the small of his back and held him within her.

"All of you, Rook," she commanded. "Now—"

And he let himself go, plunging in, meeting the slight resistance of her virginity and piercing it with one deep thrust. Ariane arched up, her knees tightening around his hips as he began to move. He watched her face, searching for pain or fear, but it was alight with joy.

Elemental triumph, masculine and savage, gripped his mind at her wanton surrender; he savored it, drinking gasps from Ariane's parted lips and knowing he alone had claimed her innocence. For an instant he remembered the face of the man who would have taken her, smiling so arrogantly from the holopic; possessive fury whipped at Rook, and he plunged deeper still as if to mark Ariane his for all time.

But Ariane yielded, accepting his assault, returning pleasure without restraint. When she began to move with him, grasping him fully within her body, locking her arms around his back to draw him closer, he felt himself disarmed and defeated by something stronger than desire.

He reached between their bodies and touched the soft, slick flesh that centered Ariane's pleasure. Her mouth opened in a silent cry; she tightened around him, bringing him perilously close to release.

Amid the sensual pleasure, dark and hot, Rook felt the stirrings of light: like stars piercing the blackness of space, luminescence pulsed at the edge of his consciousness. Tangible brilliance that seared without pain. Light that bore Ariane's essence as surely as she bore his body within hers.

Rook. A voice came with the light, suddenly there within his consciousness. *Rook, I'm here.*

Instinct held him to the ancient rhythms of coupling even as he reeled inwardly at the unmistakable touch of Ariane's mind.

Her eyes were closed, the rich flow of her hair spread on the carpet as she arched her neck and undulated beneath him.

Hear me, Rook. See me. Know me. . . .

And he knew. He knew what only his body had recognized from the first time he had laid eyes on Ariane Burke-Marchand.

There was no time to absorb the revelation. Rook felt the light spread outward, pulsating to the beat of Ariane's heart. And then it exploded in ecstasy, blinding him, banishing every trace of shadow. He felt himself spin free of his body, hang suspended in radiance, bound to another whose very soul cried out with his.

Brilliance dimmed to a warm glow, caressing Rook like a lover. Ariane was with him—in mind, in spirit—joined in a wholeness deeper than reason or instinct.

His body was drained of strength when he found it again. Ariane stirred beneath him languorously. She looked up at him, unafraid, tranquil, brown eyes limned with copper.

Kalian eyes.

She touched his face and cupped his jaw in her cool palm.

"I didn't know how to tell you, Rook. I didn't know how to accept it myself until—" She broke off, smiling with a tenderness that twisted Rook's heart in a knot. "There will be time to explain all of it. Plenty of time."

Rook tried to gather his thoughts, to contradict her, but she pressed her finger to his lips. "No future, Rook. Whatever happens—we're together. We aren't alone anymore. And I—"

The words she didn't speak came to him on a tide of emotion. Rook rolled onto his side and held her tight in the curve of his arms.

She never saw the shadow in his eyes.

Chapter Thirteen

"*I*t happened the first time we touched."

Ariane stretched on the bunk, easing a cramp in her bare leg, and entwined it with Rook's. The mental contact had faded now; she could no longer sense his thoughts, breach the barrier around his mind so effortlessly. But she could feel him, more deeply than ever before—on an emotional level that needed no words. Through a bond forged between their minds by the act of love.

Rook turned his head. The slight distance in his eyes didn't alarm her; he had much to accept. With a sigh she laid her cheek against his chest.

"I promised not to speak of the past, but if I'm to explain—to understand everything that's happened—"

His jaw cupped over her forehead. "The past can't touch us now," he said. There was a sadness in his voice, but she would not search his heart for the source. It was enough that she was no longer his enemy. Enough that they were lovers.

Enough that she loved him.

"Years ago," she said hesitantly, "when I came to the Warren and met you there—" She paused, waiting for a reaction.

"Go on," he said evenly, rubbing his cheek against her hair.

Ariane swallowed. "I came to the Warren, following Jacques—but that night, before he'd ever left the mansion, I was feeling something I couldn't explain." She shifted, remembering. "Now that I look back on it, I know I'd been feeling things like that all my life, and dismissing them—as hunches, or imagination. Little things." She smiled sadly, Finch's face before her. "Mostly it was with Finch, sometimes when I went down into Espérance. A sense of emotions not my own."

"The Sharing," Rook said. Ariane looked up, reading emotions so tangled that she could make no sense of them at all.

"I'd heard," she continued softly, "that Kalians had some mental powers. No one seemed to know quite what they were, and Finch never spoke of them. Another reason to hate and fear the aliens." Sighing, she nestled against Rook's chest again and savored his nearness. "The night of the riots, I couldn't sleep. I felt—angry, restless, afraid—and when I saw Jacques leave, and you go after him, I knew I had to follow."

Rook's breath caught, and Ariane felt a spiral of pain twist in that part of her where Rook resided. "I never understood why you'd come," he said.

"There was another reason." Ariane's voice grew muffled as she hid her face. "I'd seen you when you returned from Tolstoy, training with the other educated Kalians, walking in the park." Heat rose to her cheeks, and she knew Rook would feel the warmth on his skin. "I was a child then, and it seemed safe and romantic to want someone I could never have. So I fell in love with you."

Muscles went tense under her and relaxed again. "Loved me?" he echoed.

"I was very foolish—then," she whispered. "And proud, and uncertain. And you were handsome, strong, exotic. Nothing like the Elite men I knew. You were part of a world—a future—I knew I could never have. You were the dream of freedom."

"Freedom?"

The word carried an edge that startled her. She pushed away from Rook, reaching for the defenses she'd almost forgotten.

He looked down at her, eyes shuttered. "You were raised as a Marchand, born to a life of ease and privilege. What freedom was denied the great-granddaughter of the most powerful Patriarch in Lumière?"

Ariane felt as though she'd been slapped. Instinctively she

shielded her own mind and heart, closed down the newborn connection between them. Rook flinched in turn.

"Freedom?" she repeated, pulling free of his embrace. "You asked me once what I knew of Kalians. What do you know of my family, Rook, other than what you've wanted to believe?" Struggling to keep her voice even, she rolled away from him and rose, stalking away. She snagged a blanket from the bunk and wrapped it about herself.

"I don't pretend to have suffered. My lot wasn't a hard one. I had everything—everything your people didn't have." She blinked, feeling a stab of shame and sorrow at the loss of Rook's people. *Her* people.

She folded her arms across her chest and stared at the bulkhead. "But it wasn't what I wanted, Rook. I lived in a gilded cage. Even when the Patriarch gave me more freedom than most females of my caste, let me train as a duelist and bend the rules of propriety, I was always destined to become a proper bride in some advantageous marriage. I knew it from childhood. But when I was young, the future I dreaded seemed very far away."

Loose hair drifted about her shoulders as she shook her head. "All my life I dreamed of traveling the stars, finding new worlds. I would stare up at the sky and know I belonged out there—on the frontier, fighting battles for far greater things than honor. And I knew it was forever beyond my reach. Then Jacques died—"

Old guilt surged up in her, trapping the words in her throat. Because Jacques had died, she'd been destined to take his place in the marriage that would bind the Slaytons and Marchand. She had been wild with grief, consumed by anger; the future seemed to close in around her like a cage, swinging shut far too soon. And so she'd fought—negotiated for the right to a few years of independence, a taste of the life she could never have.

And her great-grandfather hadn't denied her. He'd sent for private tutors to teach her piloting and navigation; she'd lost herself in her studies, trying to forget pain and loss. For three years she'd piloted a Marchand courier ship—the *d'Artagnan*—and had lived the life of adventure and freedom she had craved.

The life to which her hidden Kalian blood had called her.

"After Jacques died," she continued, fighting past the knot in her throat, "I was given the chance to spend a few years as an interworld courier for my family, in this ship. It was all I ever wanted, even though I knew it would end." She gave a short, sad laugh. "For a few years I followed my dreams. But I never got over my obsession with you. And so I came to Tantalus."

A shiver caught her unaware, coursing down her spine. The silence in the cabin was absolute, yet she felt Rook leave the bunk and come up behind her.

"Ariane." His hands closed gently on her arms, pulling her back against him.

"I would never have known you," she said softly, leaning into him. "If not for the terrible things that happened, we would never have met. And I would never have known myself."

She left unspoken the thought that beat in her brain: *The price was far too high.* Rook wrapped his arms about her tightly.

Quiet settled around them, peaceful at first, then tightening gradually into tension. Ariane was not yet ready to speak of Rook's vendetta, and yet it still hung between them—in spite of the emotional bond of Sharing, in spite of death that might descend any time to claim them both.

It was Rook who provided the escape. "Finch told you," he said into her hair. "On Agora, when she sent me away."

Ariane accepted his change of subject gratefully, pushing the most dangerous issue into the hidden part of her mind. She twisted to look up into his eyes.

"Yes. She told me—about my grandmother, and my mother, and about my real father." Finch's words came back to her as if they'd been spoken only moments before. Of Kestrel Tremayne, Sedge Allen—Kalians who had loved Marchand woman and passed on their blood before they died.

"And you never guessed," Rook mused, his gaze distant.

"No. Not even when I felt the Sharing—without knowing what it was. The night of the riots in the Warren. And with you."

He shook his head. "I felt it. In the interrogation room, on the ship—countless times." His eyes came back to her, touched with wonder and wry, self-deprecating humor. "I was blinded by my own emotion, my determination to see what I expected to see. I ignored what I felt, dismissed it as a kind of madness—"

"As I dismissed my little differences in all the years I was growing up. And all the days I was with you."

"But the Fahar knew," Rook said, his voice low and intense. "Kamur sensed it from the very beginning, when he asked us if we were mates—" Color flooded the tan of Rook's high cheekbones. "He knew I wanted you—and why."

Ariane understood. He had wanted her—not merely out of lust or hatred or eight long years' celibacy. It had been far more than that from the very beginning.

His body had known her for what she was. *His* kind. Kalian.

"Surra knew as well. She asked me—" Ariane laughed, struck suddenly by the absurd humor of it. "She asked me why we had not mated—"

Rook silenced her with a kiss. She felt as if she weighed nothing at all, lifted in his powerful arms with only the blanket between them.

"It was madness," Rook said when he released her, his voice breathless and rough. "Wanting you, and trying to stay away. . . ."

Why? The question hovered on the tip of her tongue, but she bit it back. "And I wanted you," she said softly, "even when I didn't understand."

For a moment she was sure he would sweep her up and carry her back to the bunk. But he only pressed his face into the curve of her shoulder, hot breath caressing her skin as his arousal pushed the blanket against her thigh.

"The Fahar knew," she said, a little breathlessly, "and so

did Finch. She was finally able to tell me, after all those years of caring for me, after escaping Espérance. When we arrived on Agora, I *saw* her on the Concourse but didn't recognize her. She was—*Changed*."

"And she knew me, even Changed," Rook murmured against her skin. He pulled back, brushing Ariane's hair away from her forehead. "She recognized me before we met. A rare skill among Kalians." His eyes grew bleak. "For most Kalians it would require—would have required physical contact. But she knew me."

Grief washed over Ariane, as much Rook's as her own. "She told me how she—helped my body to hide what it was from the moment of my birth." Slowly she reached up, wound a strand of her own hair around her fingers so that she could see the unremarkable brown of it. "She made me look like a proper Marchand. A kind of healing, she said."

Rook caught her hand and enclosed it in his. "To protect your family's honor," he said with a touch of bitterness. "If your Elite knew you had Kalian blood. . . ."

"Rook," she whispered, reaching blindly for his heart.

He released her hand and closed his eyes. "I'm sorry," he said at last. "It's—difficult—for me to understand. . . ."

Ariane wrapped her arms around him, aching at the vulnerability in his voice, knowing what that cost him.

"It was hard for me to accept, even after Finch—Shared with me and I knew it was true," Ariane murmured. "I was ashamed at first—afraid, because I didn't want to lose myself, what I'd always believed I was. My pride in my name. My honor. And I was afraid because I thought you would see the difference, know what I was."

Rook moved his hands across her back restlessly, and she could feel the possessiveness in his touch. "If you had told me . . ." His voice constricted into a thin whisper.

Ariane hugged him fiercely. "Part of me wanted to. Knowing how alone you were, how you must feel when Finch died. But I couldn't risk it, because I didn't know what you would do. I couldn't trust you, or myself. Because—"

Because you were my enemy. . . .

Rook stiffened. His hands stilled on her back. "Can I blame you for that?" he said.

Finch's words rang in her ears above Rook's low voice. *"Do not fear to trust Rook Galloway, or your own heart. . . ."*

Trust. They were lovers, allies against a common foe, but they were not ready to trust. She felt her own doubts like a constant ache pushed far to the back of her consciousness; in Rook there was an ever-shifting wall of shadow that hid a part of himself she could never quite touch.

She could not tell him what Finch had said—that she, too, could learn to Change. *I'm not ready to be Kalian in every sense,* she thought with a sharp pang of realization. She was not ready to reach inside herself, alter the color of her hair to black, the pigment of her eyes to copper. . . .

She shied away from that shameful fear. Carefully, slowly, she freed herself from Rook's light hold.

Rook hardly seemed to notice. "She was a woman of great power, great wisdom," he said distantly, following his own thoughts. "An Elder who would have been honored on Kali."

"She was my great-grandmother," Ariane whispered.

Rook's gaze focused on her. "So," he murmured. She wanted him to reach for her, hold her again, but she was almost relieved when he turned away. He paced across the room, stopping to stare at the Anubian tapestry on the bulkhead above the bunk.

It was impossible not to feel him. Though the connection was less powerful without physical contact, Ariane sensed Rook's emotions—sorrow she could not ease, despair over the loss of an entire people. She alone was not enough.

Except for us, they are gone. . . .

"Rook," she said softly. "If Finch did it, if she left Espérance on her own, there may be others—"

"Others?" He turned to confront her. For the first time since they had made love, he looked like a stranger. "Finch had the old knowledge. She was able to hide what she was. The man who taught me to Change was an Elder himself, born on Kali. The ability to channel Healing to Change—so much was lost when we left our world." His voice was bitterly cold. "Our identity, our freedom. Even the Sharing became rare."

Ariane looked up at him, knowing she could not follow where he had gone. She ached with his pain, with his silent rejection of her comfort.

He spoke of the Shaper's gifts. All those things the Espérancians—ordinary humans—had feared in the Kalian refugees. Healing, superhuman vitality and speed, animal-keen senses. And other talents few had known existed—the ability to Change, the Sharing.

"You have such strength," Finch had told Ariane. Strength that had remained hidden within her for so many years. Strength that had enabled her to reach into Rook's body and help him to heal—that she still did not know the limits of.

And Finch had said she and Rook might be the only hope. . . .

Hope. Ariane closed her eyes. Hope of what? Finch had died too soon, leaving too little explained. Ariane could not speak of hope to Rook when so much lay unresolved between them. When she was only beginning to believe in it herself.

Her gaze drifted to the locker at the foot of the bunk as she remembered the ring Finch had given her; the enigmatic gift she'd been too afraid to acknowledge. She crouched beside the locker, rummaging through the books and litdisks and holopics until she found the ring at the bottom, wrapped in a scrap of soft cloth. Clutching it in her fist, she rose and padded quietly back to Rook.

"Finch—gave me this," she said.

He looked at her and at the ring she held on her open palm. Slowly he took it from her, turned it over and over. It was large enough to fit around his finger. The cheap cabochon in the center gleamed dully in the cabin's dim light.

"I don't know why she gave it to me," Ariane said, to fill the silence. "Does it—mean anything to you? I never saw her wear it on Espérance."

Rook shook his head and tried to return the ring, but Ariane stepped away. "I want you to have it, Rook."

He looked at her fully, searching her eyes, and something in his face relaxed. "She gave it to you," he said, catching her hand and curling her fingers around the ring. "It's yours, Ariane."

There was returning warmth in his voice, in the burnished metal of his eyes. Ariane felt her pulse begin to race as he moved closer. He worked the ring from her grasp and walked to the desk, setting it down carefully. Then he returned and enfolded her in his arms.

"I'm sorry, Rook," she whispered.

"It was never your doing, Ariane," he said, his lips brushing her hair. "Finch gave you her blessing. You carry her blood. You were always one of us."

One of us.

Ariane leaned into his embrace and lifted her face for his kiss. This time it was gentle, almost hesitant, as if he were rediscovering her after long separation. Tenderness, Rook's big hands stroking her back, his mouth caressing hers, transformed slowly to desire. The blanket slipped free of her shoulders and tumbled about her feet.

The strain that had held them apart vanished. The Sharing wrapped them in its invisible fetters, drawing them closer still. Isolation gave way to wholeness, pain submerged once again in joy.

Wordlessly Rook lifted her and carried her to the bunk. He made love to her almost reverently, as if to compensate for his earlier coldness. Ariane accepted his body into her own, taking with it his heart and soul.

They moved together as one. And when they reached the apex of fulfillment, Ariane dared to whisper four profound, simple words into the brilliant storm of rapture and light.

"I love you, Rook."

Ariane's impossible declaration echoed in Rook's mind as he secured the double panels shielding the hyperdrive module and made his way down the outer hull to the ground.

The sun was setting—reddish, dust-filtered light that cast long shadows from the rocky outcrops surrounding the ship. Rook stared up into the darkening sky and brushed the dust from his clothing.

This lull in the storm, this endless waiting, had become a blessing and a curse. A blessing because he and Ariane were together, sheltered in their own world, out of time, free of past and future.

"I love you," she had said.

Denial warred with acceptance for control of Rook's heart, claiming his body for a battlefield. Deep shudders racked his muscles. He reached into himself and slowed his heartbeat, moved the thin air carefully in and out of his lungs.

A blessing and a curse. The curse was in knowing he could do nothing to save Ariane from death if and when it chose to come.

Stepping into the air lock, Rook could feel her waiting just beyond the inner hatch. She was never far from his awareness, and when they touched—when they touched . . .

His arousal was immediate and powerful, the physical expression of a need that never left him. He leaned against the bulkhead to quiet the turmoil in his mind before releasing the inner hatch.

She was there—beautiful, serene, unafraid. Her dark, brilliant gaze pulled him into her arms like the gravity well of a star.

Ariane broke the embrace, reaching up to smooth his tangled, dusty hair back from his forehead.

"The cycle is almost complete," she said softly. "The computer shows most systems back on-line."

Rook breathed in the clean scent of her skin and nodded. "Only a matter of hours now."

Neither of them spoke of the decision they had come to almost without discussion. There was no need, when they could feel each other so deeply.

In a few hours the *d'Artagnan* would leap spaceward, Ariane at the helm and Rook at her side. They would cry defiance to the enemies who thought them trapped, make a last bid for freedom against impossible odds.

"We won't roll over and die at their bidding," Ariane had told him fiercely after they had loved. And he had held her, silenced by pride and by fear for her that closed his throat and froze the blood in his veins.

No, they wouldn't roll over and die. They'd challenge death head-on, warrior-lovers bound by the same desperate passion for liberty.

But it was too soon. And too late. Rook pulled Ariane close again and concentrated on every surface of her body that touched and molded to his own.

Ariane made a muffled sound against his chest. "I'm a damned good pilot, Rook, even if I'm no expert at hyperdrive repair."

Her uncanny response to his feelings still had the power to startle him. He caught her face between his hands.

"I know." He forced himself to match her wry smile, cherishing her courage. It was impossible to forget the way she had evaded the League ships at Agora, or landed the disabled ship safely on this nameless world. Still, a part of him wanted to seal her in the lifepod, hide her away as if a few extra centimeters of adamantium could protect her, while he took on every hostile force in the universe that would do her harm. . . .

Ariane's brown eyes flashed copper fire. "Forget it. This is *our* battle." She tangled her fingers in a lock of his hair and gave it a gentle tug.

"I'm not afraid, Rook," she murmured. "I don't think I'll ever be afraid again—"

Rook captured her lips before they closed on the last word. He bent to cradle her in his arms, wanting her closer than any kiss would permit.

Brave Ariane. She was everything he could have wanted in a mate, if he had ever believed in such a brilliant destiny. She was a true survivor. A true Kalian, like those who had learned to flourish on a hostile and alien world.

Until fate had outwitted them at last.

No. Without breaking the kiss, Rook carried her through the cockpit hatch and set her down in the pilot's seat, kneeling between her legs. He locked his arms about her waist and slid her forward until her thighs embraced him and her heart raced against his.

No. There was a desperation in him beyond anything he had known—even in the Warren when he had been sentenced, even on Tantalus. A desperation to hold what he could before it was taken from him.

Ariane's hands slid up his back and laced behind his neck. "You'll never lose me, Rook. I love you. . . ."

Her unveiled emotion dispelled the beckoning shadow of despair. Rook surrendered to the pulse of life, blood beating warm under Ariane's translucent skin and the soft rhythm of her lips and tongue meeting his own.

His hands trembled as he opened the fastenings of her shipsuit, and she pushed him away to finish, dropping a kiss on the tensed muscle of his arm. Finch's ring swung on a cord between her breasts, polished by smooth white flesh. Rook licked the warm hollow of her throat as her fingers moved to open his shirt and slip beneath it. When the lush swell of her breasts was bared to his gaze, he bent her back and took her into his mouth.

He felt her pleasure as he felt his own, sensation mingling beyond separation. Her nipples were firm under his stroking tongue. Strong, delicate hands arched into his chest, stroked the new skin that covered his shoulder, pressed the clenched muscles of his belly.

She sighed his name as he lifted her to strip the suit free of her body. He felt her readiness before he touched her; the moist, tender flesh between her thighs quivered at his caress. A single swift gesture freed his arousal. Ariane stroked him once, lingeringly, before he eased her down on top of him.

The loving was never the same, never old. Rook closed his eyes, clasping her hips to steady her; she drew him deep within her. There was no taking, no giving as they moved, face to face, need to need; only Sharing, soul entwined with soul and heart with heart.

And Healing. Rook felt his desperation shatter with the force of their release. Ariane drew his face into her shoulder, shuddering, and her tender joy left no room for fear in the purity of their union.

Her lips brushed his forehead. "No matter what happens," she whispered, "they can never take this away."

Rook raised his head to meet her gaze. He gathered the words he had guarded so carefully, symbols of the one thing he had never let her see. Emblems of a weakness that was weakness no longer.

"On Kali," he began softly, "in the old days, it was said that the Shapers opened human minds to the Sharing as a means of survival. To draw the colonists closer together, give them the ability to see into each other's hearts and stand as one against the forces that could destroy them."

Ariane cupped his cheek in her palm. "The Shapers were very wise."

"Yes. And it was said that the Sharing once worked on another level—to draw men and women together as mates."

"Like the Fahar." The softness of her thighs slid over his hips as she shifted, and he felt himself growing hard within her.

"Like the Fahar," he echoed hoarsely. "Though it never became canon as it did on Harr. It was something—unspoken. . . ."

Ariane rubbed her cheek against his shoulder. "Perhaps because no words were needed."

Rook groaned under his breath. Without conscious thought he began to move in her, cupping her buttocks in his hands. "No. But when my people—our people came to Espérance, the old ways were forgotten."

The liquid heat of Ariane's tongue traced his jaw. "But not the oldest ways—"

With rigid self-control he held himself still, drawing back to look deep into her eyes.

"Ariane," he grated, capturing her face in his hands. "If we were on Kali, I would have asked you to be my mate."

She closed her eyes. Her silent exaltation poured light into his soul as he spilled his seed into her body.

"If we were on Kali," she breathed, "I would have said yes."

Rook crushed her to him, letting emotion free of its bonds at last. Emptiness filled, bitterness conquered, completion found in the arms of only one woman. Ariane. Her name, her being filled him to overflowing, and he gave her the sum of all he was to every last cell and thought and dream.

From some great distance he thought he heard her voice, persistent and low, calling him away from heaven. It wasn't until she pulled free of his embrace that he came back to reality.

"Rook, the comm . . ." Her words trailed off as another voice, dark and masculine, invaded the cockpit like a marauder bent on destruction.

"This is Perséphone *out of Espérance.* D'Artagnan, *do you copy?"*

Ariane scrambled away, her face drained of color. Cold air raised gooseflesh on her damp skin.

"Rook Galloway, do you read me?"

The hackles rose at the back of Rook's neck, primitive, violent energy coursing through his muscles. He rose slowly, turning to stare at the blinking control panel.

Ariane stood absolutely still, tensed as if to fight or run. The smell of alarm grew thick in the ship's recycled air.

"Wynn," she whispered.

CHAPTER FOURTEEN

*W*ynn Slayton.

The name wrote itself in burning script behind Rook's eyelids—an aristocrat's elegant hand on fine paper, hidden between holopics in Ariane's cabin. Bound with the image of an arrogant, handsome face, icy gray eyes turned possessively on the woman at his side.

Wynn Slayton. Commissaire of Lumière's police force during the time of the riots. Chief witness against Rook at the trial that had condemned him to a death sentence on Tantalus.

The man Ariane was promised to marry.

The timeless, intimate world Rook and Ariane had created shattered like Nirvanan crystal. He felt the walls snap back into place around his heart, between him and Ariane, built of instincts more powerful than an emotion as treacherous as joy.

Or love.

A shadow of rage darkened Rook's vision as he closed his trousers and stalked to the control board. Ariane stepped aside, crossing her arms in front of her chest as if to shelter herself from his gaze. Her face was blank with shock.

Slayton's arrogant voice broke the silence. "D'Artagnan, *this is Wynn Slayton of the starship* Perséphone. *I have you on my scanners.*"

Rook dropped his clenched fist and let it hover over the commlink switch.

"*Rook Galloway, I know you're there, presumably alive. And I know you have Lady Ariane Burke-Marchand.*"

The sound of her name—her full, Espérancian name— made Rook's stomach knot and the bile rise in his throat. Possessiveness surged through him, hot and barbaric.

Ariane had never spoken of Wynn Slayton, had never mentioned the betrothal to the man in the holopic—believing Rook knew nothing about it, unaware that he had searched her personal files.

And now Slayton was here.

He turned back to Ariane, deliberately masking his emotion from her eyes and her senses.

"A friend of yours, Ariane?" he said softly.

Naked and shivering, Ariane looked achingly vulnerable. It took all of Rook's will to keep from going to her and holding her hard against him. Instead, he bent to snag her shipsuit from the deck and tossed it to her.

She dropped her eyes and slipped into the shipsuit, fastening it to the top of her neck. When she looked up again, her gaze was wary. Rook felt the last remnants of Sharing stripped away as she shielded her own emotions from him and retreated behind her own instinctive walls.

But not before he caught a glimpse of the feelings she wanted to hide: shame, regret, fear.

Rook clenched his fists. Her betrothed, one of her Elite peers, had found her—after she had expected to die. After she had given away her honor and admitted her savage Kalian blood.

Shame and regret and fear.

Rook forced his thoughts into cold, practical channels. "Wynn Slayton," he said. "I remember him, Ariane. One of the most powerful men on Espérance eight years ago."

Her throat worked, but she met his gaze steadily. "I wouldn't expect you to forget," she whispered.

"No," Rook said, smiling grimly. "Is his family still allied with yours? Espérancian politics have been somewhat—beyond my reach."

Ariane's half-choked reply was lost in the buzz of the commlink. Rook reached out to lower the volume of Slayton's demanding voice.

"The *Perséphone*," Rook mused, as if to himself. He sat down in the pilot's seat and called up registration records on the ship's computer. "Wynn Slayton's private ship. Strange coincidence that he should be here now."

Ariane shook her head. "I don't understand. The drug-runners . . ."

"An interesting question," Rook said. "How did he get by them? Unless he has certain inside information—"

Her chin lifted in the old gesture of Marchand pride. "No! The Slaytons are an honorable family, beyond reproach. Wynn would never be part of—"

"You'll forgive me," Rook interrupted softly, "if I presume to question Elite honor."

As if the past hours had never happened, as if they had never been lovers, they stared at each other in taut silence. Rook needed no Sharing to know what went on in Ariane's mind: memory of the trial eight years ago, of Rook's accusations against the Marchand when he'd taken her hostage on Tantalus, all the things they had pushed away in the face of death.

Wynn Slayton was as much his enemy as the Marchand had ever been. More, because he claimed Ariane as one of his own, reminded her of all she had been: a woman of the Elite, an aristocrat who could not be tainted by Kalian blood.

Shame, regret, and fear.

Slayton had already begun to steal Ariane away.

Rook leaned back into the seat with deceptive calm. "Perhaps the more pertinent question is how he found us here. By now they'll have my escape posted on every major world, including Espérance. And they know about you." His voice shook under the control he tried to impose on it. "Did your Patriarch send him out to search for you, Ariane?"

She only stared at him, her skin nearly transparent, shadowed under the dark wells of her eyes.

"But no one should have known we were here, in this isolated system. It would take months to search every possible route between Agora and Espérance, even if they guessed my destination. The odds against meeting us at all . . ."

He closed his eyes, considering the possibilities with icy

rationality. "No one knew the route I planned. Not even the Fahar."

"Rook—"

His eyes snapped open. "How did your betrothed find us here, Ariane?"

Ariane caught her breath and leaned heavily against the back of the copilot's seat.

"You knew," she whispered.

"Yes, I knew. I saw the holopics in your locker, Ariane. I found the letter—"

"And you searched my personal files, of course." Ariane's voice was suddenly cool and utterly Marchand, though the color rose fiercely in her cheeks.

"Of course." It was all too easy—too safe—to fall back into the old habits, taunting her and playing the part of remorseless captor. "If you were afraid I'd find out, you should have done a better job of hiding the evidence."

The sharp report of Ariane's hand striking the edge of the control board echoed through the cockpit. "Damn you, Rook, I had no reason to tell you. I would have been a fool if I did. We were enemies—" Color ebbed from her face again.

"Were, Ariane?" He let the word hang for a moment and turned to look blindly at the console. "I wonder what else you didn't tell me. But I should be grateful that you chose to bestow the gift of your body on me in spite of your pledge—"

The force of her blow was strong enough to turn his head.

"You bastard," she rasped, tears thick in her voice.

"Perhaps you should remember that you are the bastard, Ariane," he said, touching his cheek. "Will Wynn Slayton still want you now?"

For a moment Ariane seemed to hover on the edge of attacking him, her fingers curled into claws and her eyes lambent with fury and pain. Rook felt an unwelcome surge of hope. Her pain was real, as real as the shame and regret he had sensed earlier. The tears that spilled from her eyes were brilliant tokens of her vulnerability. But he ruthlessly beat back his uncertainty.

"It doesn't matter. The fact remains that he found us. How, Ariane?"

"You believe—" she choked. Her face was flushed and incredulous. "You believe that I—"

"I don't know what to believe," Rook said hoarsely.

A screeching blare of static whistled over the comm. Rook broke away and flicked a row of switches on the control board, snatching up the commlink headset and looping it over his head.

"I hear you, Wynn Slayton."

Incomprehensible noise resolved into the voice of his rival.

"So we meet again, Rook Galloway." There was a long silence. Rook heard Ariane move up beside him, almost Kalian-quiet.

Almost.

"—you have Ariane Burke-Marchand—"

Rook focused his attention and adjusted a control. "Yes, I have Lady Ariane. Well and—" He stopped himself short of the word *whole,* battling the primal urge to throw his possession of Ariane into Slayton's face.

"That is fortunate, Kalian. If she had come to any harm—"

Rook smiled, though Slayton couldn't see. "Threats, Slayton? Most unwise." Against his will he glanced aside at Ariane. She was staring fixedly at the comm, deathly pale. Rook looked away. "She's still my hostage, Slayton. I don't know how you found me, but if you want to see Lady Ariane alive . . ."

He let the words trail off, despising himself. If Ariane could believe he meant the threats he spoke for Slayton's benefit . . .

"You want your freedom, Kalian," Slayton said. The comm transmission conveyed a trace of strain in the deep, mellifluous voice. *"I want Lady Ariane returned safely. A simple exchange."*

Simple. Rook laughed bitterly deep in his throat. Once things had been simple for him—escape and revenge. The time for simplicity was long past.

"A bargain, Slayton?" Rook said. "Why should I trust any of your kind?"

Rook heard the sharp sound of Ariane's indrawn breath.

"What do you propose, Slayton?" he asked.

He could almost feel his enemy's triumph, like some malignant Sharing. *"As I said, a simple exchange. You will release Lady Ariane unharmed, and I will permit you to take the d'Artagnan out of the system."*

"Very generous of you, Slayton," Rook murmured. "You'll forgive this Kalian if he doubts your generosity."

There was another long pause. *"You have nothing to lose, Kalian, and everything to gain. If you refuse, or if I find any harm has come to the Lady, I will hunt you down to the ends of the universe."* Slayton spoke with the absolute certainty of a man whose power had never been challenged. *"But if you release her, you will have your freedom, and a ship to carry you out of League space."*

Freedom. Rook repeated the word and nearly choked on it.

In a few brief days his life—everything he had lived for—had come apart, shattered by a woman's touch, and had reformed into a new wholeness he'd never dreamed could exist. And now it had shattered anew, leaving him adrift and lost and alone.

Rational thought was beyond him now. The decision he was asked to make was impossible.

Slowly he raised his head. "What do you think of your fiancé's bargain, Ariane?" he asked tonelessly. "Should I trust him? Do you want—" His teeth clenched shut on the question he couldn't speak. *Do you want to go back to him?*

There was no answer but silence. Ariane was gone, fled with Kalian soundlessness. Rook shut off the commlink and sat down heavily, dragging the headset free of his hair.

He remembered light and her body cradling his, two souls joined in ecstasy.

"I love you, Rook."

Her mind, her heart could not have lied. But he was

afraid; afraid of losing what he had almost never found. Afraid that his deepest, most fragile hopes could be wrong.

Fool, he cursed himself. *Fool and bastard.* Ariane had been right. He had become no more than a savage, lost to the Kalian virtues he prized so highly. He had hurt Ariane beyond bearing, rejected the love she had freely offered. He had refused to trust.

Trust the woman he loved.

Rook got to his feet, studying the control panel with new purpose.

Ariane would be safe. She would be safe and free to make her own choices.

He would let her go.

A strange lightness came to Rook then, and his fingers moved swiftly over the controls. The *d'Artagnan* began to hum a starship's arcane melody, running through the pre-flight checks one by one.

Ariane would choose.

There was no choice at all.

Ariane dragged her hand across her face, smearing the tears she had shed for impossible dreams.

She had mastered the shock at last, reaching instinctively into herself with newfound Kalian senses and adjusting her body's reactions until she felt almost calm. But the hurt remained in her soul. Nothing, no one, could heal that.

No one but Rook.

Ariane leaped up from the bunk and resumed her pacing. Incredible enough that Wynn had shown up. Wynn was no drug lord, whatever his family's business. He was a good, honest man. A man who had made a terrible mistake eight years ago, just as she had done.

Ariane stopped in front of the cabin hatch. *How did Wynn find us?* The way Rook had looked at her, touched her, suspicion and pain in his voice and eyes and emotions . . .

Rook could believe she would betray him.

She groaned softly. He'd never had time to learn trust, even of her. When Wynn had arrived, she'd been shocked—

and a storm of conflicting emotions had overwhelmed her control.

Shame. Because she had lost her honor, and they would learn the truth: her great-grandfather, who held honor above everything, and Wynn, who had not deserved betrayal. Regret, because the world she and Rook had made in the face of death was gone forever. Fear, because she could not bear to lose the man she loved above life itself.

She had begun to lose him from the moment the commlink had relayed Wynn's first words.

Ariane slammed her palms against the cool metal of the hatch. The fact remained that Wynn had found her. He would have gone to Agora to meet her, would have learned of the kidnapping and Rook's escape. Somehow he had located the *d'Artagnan,* coming boldly to her rescue.

Rescue. Ariane choked on a laugh. Death might have been preferable. Bound to Rook for all time. . . .

No. I won't give in so easily. She raised her head and set her jaw. She had both in full measure: Marchand pride and Kalian stubbornness—the will to survive and conquer.

There was no choice at all. She had given herself to Rook, and she could not, would not, let him push her away. Somehow she'd convince him of her love. Somehow she'd confront her own fears and help him find justice, make a future for them both.

A future in which Rook could find peace and lay the old bitterness to rest. A future in which they would be together, Sharing, whole within themselves and each other. . . .

The hatch slid open under her palms, and she fell forward against Rook's hard body. His hands came up to steady her and then pushed her away roughly.

He walked by her without a word, turning only when he reached the far bulkhead. His eyes were utterly inhuman.

"You are a consummate actress, Lady Ariane," he said in formal Franglais. "It's a pity the stage is no place for a Marchand." He opened his hand, and something small and metallic fell to the deck, bouncing twice on the carpet before coming to rest at Ariane's feet.

The air froze in her lungs. Slowly she bent to retrieve the object, refusing to believe the obvious.

A tracer. Small, elegant, prohibitively expensive. Almost impossible to detect by ordinary means, it worked by eavesdropping on navcomp flight data and transmitting that data to a pursuing ship just before a jump into hyperspace, allowing the pursuer to determine the probable destination of its quarry.

"I found it quite by accident," Rook continued. "I might have overlooked it entirely if I hadn't been taking considerable care in the preflight checks." He smiled for the first time, mechanically. "You hid it very well—but, then, this is your ship, Lady Ariane."

Ariane released her breath and let the tracer fall from bloodless fingers. "I didn't put it there, Rook," she whispered.

His smile twisted. "You *are* good, Lady Ariane. You know what you want, and you'll stop at nothing to have it. A true Marchand." He shook his head. "Perhaps in the end you even convinced yourself—the Sharing doesn't permit lying easily."

Without thinking Ariane started across the cabin, reaching for him. He stepped back and raised his hands to ward her off.

"I've learned something of your strength, Lady Ariane. On Kali you would have been an Elder at a very young age. But you never had the benefit of learning the moral limits of the Shaper's gifts."

Tears gathered in Ariane's throat at his rejection of every good, gentle thing that had been between them.

"I never lied to you," she managed at last. "I never planted that tracer. I don't know how it got on the ship. You have to believe me." She searched frantically for some logic that would pierce his harsh certainty of her guilt. "I got you away from Agora, Rook. When the drug-runners almost killed you, I saved your life." *I gave you myself. . . .*

His mouth thinned to a rigid line. "No need to be afraid now, Ariane. I won't hurt you, though I'll let your would-be lover believe you're in peril of your life." He turned his face away from her immediate protest. "We struck a bargain, he and I. One I don't expect him to keep."

Ariane kicked savagely at the tracer. It skipped across the carpet to strike the bulkhead with a faint clang. "Damn you, Rook. I love you. I think I've loved you from the first moment I saw you." Her voice compressed to a whisper. "I would rather die than betray you. . . ."

Rook's eyes grew distant. "I can't blame you, Ariane. Your Marchand blood makes you what you are. The Patriarch's great-granddaughter, true to your kind." His gaze came back to her, remotely curious. "I was the one who laid the course for this system. You couldn't have known rescue would come in time after the drug-runners disabled us. Unless that was part of the plan, and you knew they were allies all along. They *are* Espérancians." He shook his head. "Or did you truly believe you might die, Ariane? You may even have convinced yourself you made your sacrifice for love. Easier to accept."

Silenced by his indifferent recital, Ariane felt desperation build to fever pitch in her blood. He was willfully blind, walled in by eight years of hatred that a few hours of love could never breach. Not even *her* love.

But there must be some way to reach him. Some way beyond words. Some way to drive beyond the shadow and find the light again. . . .

Before Rook could sense her intentions, Ariane gathered herself and charged him, hands spread to grasp and hold. His bare chest was burning hot, and his reaction to her touch drove through the contact like a disruptor blast.

Violence. Rage. Despair. The emotions raged out from his mind, sucking her in like a black hole. She struggled for balance, clutching his rigid arm, as other feelings rose to the surface: jealousy, possessiveness, self-contempt, the pain of soul-deep wounds almost too grave for Healing.

From some great distance she heard an animal roar, felt herself flung back with such force that she came up hard against the bunk and tumbled back, the breath knocked from her lungs.

Rook stood over her, trembling, wild-eyed. He worked his hands, opening and closing them convulsively. "No more," he rasped. "It's over.

"You're going back to your own kind, where you belong."

CHAPTER FIFTEEN

"*I*'m all right, Wynn."

Ariane's voice was calm as she spoke to her intended husband over the comm. She might have felt no emotion at all, so close to rescue and the culmination of everything she had schemed for.

Rook heard the drone of Slayton's reply fade to a dull hum. A few moments ago, in her cabin, he had almost been convinced of her innocence. Ariane Burke-Marchand had nearly won him over with a few sweet words and anguished looks. And a touch that had nearly burned a fatal pathway into his soul.

Now she was every inch the dispassionate aristocrat, slipping so easily back into her old part. *Remember, Rook,* he told himself. *This is what she is.*

"I haven't been harmed in any way. Listen to me, Wynn. . . ."

Rook closed his senses to the lingering scent of their last lovemaking—to the pounding need that still made him weak in her presence—and snatched the headset away from Ariane. "Enough," he grated. "Slayton, do you hear me?"

"I hear, Kalian." So superior, his enemy, so certain of victory.

"You know your terms have been met. Now you'll meet mine. I'll lift at seventeen thirty standard time. Your lady will be in the lifepod. At eighteen hundred I'll eject the pod in range for your retrieval. If you hold to your end of the bargain, she'll reach you safely. If not . . ." He let the silence hang for a moment. "If not, I'll have nothing to lose, as you so accurately pointed out. There is enough armament on this ship to destroy the lifepod before you take me."

Ariane made no sound, but Rook was compelled to look

at her. "No, the discannon isn't repaired," he told her softly, "but your fiancé won't know that—unless you find a way to tell him, Lady Ariane." Even now it sickened him to think she believed he might carry out his threat. He smiled bitterly. "I gave you my word I won't harm you. But I feel the need for added insurance that your would-be lover will keep his."

He turned to the control board and completed the last preflight procedures with a few swift gestures, readying the engines for sublight and hyperspace flight. All the preparations had been made, everything he could do to increase the odds of survival and insure Ariane's safety.

Because no matter what she had done he could never let her be hurt. She had won something of him that couldn't be recalled, and he was fool enough to know he'd give his life for hers.

She was watching him, dry-eyed, when he turned to her again. "I understand the lifepods in Caravel-class ships are quite comfortable, Lady Ariane. With any luck you won't be confined too long." He gestured toward the cockpit hatch with a mocking bow.

Her smile was strained but defiant. "You may doubt that I'm a true Kalian, Rook, but I've accepted it all too well. You'll have to physically force me into that lifepod."

Without thinking, he advanced on Ariane. His hands were within a centimeter of brushing her arms when he halted.

"You're afraid to touch me, Rook," she said. "Afraid because I might force you to see the truth. Because what we Share is too powerful to deny."

Rook stepped back sharply and stationed himself with the pilot's seat between them.

"I have one more use for you, Lady Ariane," he snarled. "Take the ship up. Now."

She might have defied him again, but she only dropped her eyes and slipped into the pilot's seat. Her skilled fingers darted over the console and grasped the control stick.

"Why are you trusting me with the controls, Rook?" she murmured as the engines hummed to full power.

"I don't trust you, Lady Ariane," he answered grimly. "No more than I trust your betrothed." While she took the *d'Artagnan* carefully up into the dust-laden winds of the planet's lower atmosphere, Rook worked at extinguishing the stubborn weakness within himself. By the time they were in space, he would be ready to do what must be done. His blow would be swift and painless. Ariane would be safe within the lifepod, conscious again when Slayton picked her up.

He stared at the back of her head, at the soft hair he still longed to sift through his fingers and hold against his face. He braced himself, mentally and physically, as the *d'Artagnan* cleared atmosphere.

Now. It must be now. He clenched his fingers into a fist and set his other hand on the back of the chair to spin it around.

The ship lurched, and he lost his balance. Rook had only a moment to register that Ariane had made a sudden change in course before he darted forward to grasp her arms.

The Sharing exploded through him, a wash of luminescence that paralyzed him like an animal transfixed by a disruptor beam. He felt Ariane's mind instantly—powerful, more powerful than he had ever dreamed—locking his own in bonds woven of light.

Rook. Rook. Listen to me—

He fought back blindly, heedless of the consequences. This was torment, to have her within him, part of him, loved and hated, betrayer and betrayed— Something black and utterly without warmth exploded within him, extinguishing the light wherever it touched, shredding it to nothingness.

Get out, the savage screamed. *Get out of my mind—*

And suddenly he was free. Nausea nearly made his legs give way, but somehow he kept his feet and caught Ariane as she slumped in her seat.

For a moment he could only listen for her heartbeat, frozen with dread until he was certain she lived. He eased her back gently and turned to the console, readjusting the course setting with clumsy fingers and slowing the ship to a crawl.

Numb and half-blind, Rook lifted Ariane in his arms and carried her from the cockpit. He made his way to the stern of the ship, opening the hatch to the lifepod bay off the cargo hold. He settled her into the couch, webbed her in, and knelt beside her in the cramped, claustrophobic space.

"You nearly succeeded, Ariane," he whispered, brushing her tangled hair away from her forehead.

The lump of ice his heart had become seemed not to move at all.

One last time he drank in the sight of her, memorizing the stubborn beauty of her face until the lifepod's adamantium canopy sealed her from his gaze.

He rose and retreated, sealed the hatch and cleared the air lock, pausing for a few precious seconds to lean heavily against the bulkhead.

Somehow his hand found the release lever. He listened to the lifepod disengage and tumble free of the ship. Pain twisted in his chest as he felt his heart go with it—with *her*—leaving him barren and empty.

Ariane.

Rook turned and walked slowly back to the cockpit.

"We have the lifepod on our screens, sir."

Wynn looked up from his inspection of the *Perséphone*'s weapons system, laid out in a color-coded schematic on the console before him. With a casual gesture he cleared the screen and walked across the bridge to lean over the first officer's shoulder.

"And?"

The first officer looked up. "Scanners show one passenger. Alive, sir."

"Excellent. Take her in as close as you can and send Johnson and Champetier to retrieve the pod."

Straightening, Wynn locked his hands behind his back and moved to the wide glasteel canopy. He could not see the *d'Artagnan*, but he knew the ship was there, waiting. He could almost feel the presence of the barbarian who had dared to abduct his promised bride.

The Kalian savage who dared to mock *him*.

He waited with practiced patience while his crew brought the lifepod in, working to ease the tension in his shoulders. Waiting was something he was very good at, but the Kalian had almost cracked the composure he had perfected after so many long years.

He turned to the officer behind him. "Status?"

"Our men have the pod, sir. They've got it in the hangar now."

Wynn tilted his head, as if he could hear the activity from the bridge. "And the *d'Artagnan*?"

There was a slight pause as the officer consulted his board. "She's moved out of range, sir. But she hasn't broadcast intent to jump."

The officer's voice betrayed his puzzlement, and Wynn smiled. He wasn't surprised. They played a game, he and the savage; it amused him to let it continue as long as possible. And the Kalian was obliging him.

He listened as the ship's medic sent up his report: the Lady Ariane was well, uninjured, psychologically sound. She was demanding to see Wynn right away, in spite of the medic's recommendations.

Wynn smoothed his hand over his hair. "Send her up," he ordered, "and have Dr. Champetier accompany her."

So his little bride was longing to see him. How would she behave, having been the hostage of the very man who had been convicted of killing her brother? How grateful would she be for such a timely rescue? How deeply would she feel the dishonor of her captivity?

And if the Kalian had touched her . . .

Wynn's smile faded as he strode to the gunner's station. "Be ready for my signal," he told the crewman quietly. "You know what to do."

He schooled his face to joy and solicitude as the bridge chimes sounded and the hatch slid open. Ariane stood in the hatchway, her face pale and haggard, hair tangled.

He held out his arms and she came to him slowly, as if the weight of the universe rested on her slim shoulders. The analytical part of Wynn that was never still noted how changed she was; they had met seldom in the three years she'd been running courier for her family. She had matured, developed a unique, compelling beauty he did not remember, apparent even under her visible exhaustion. But that was only part of the change.

Ariane Burke-Marchand had been beaten. There was no pride in her face, the arrogance born of twenty generations of pure Elite blood. The baggy, rumpled shipsuit she wore belonged on one of the Laborer caste, and she carried herself like a woman who has lost every last vestige of honor.

The great-granddaughter of the Patriarch of the Marchand had been humbled. In her bleak eyes Wynn saw the future of all her family and everything Bernard Marchand valued.

Wynn kept his expression serene and welcoming as she came at last into his arms.

"Ariane," he murmured. *"Mon petit amour.* You're safe now."

She pulled free almost at once, clutching his sleeve tightly as she looked up into his eyes.

It was like a dream, or a nightmare. Ariane swayed and would have fallen if not for her fingers wrapped in the expensive fabric of Wynn's braided sleeve.

You're safe now. She wanted to laugh, or cry; she could do neither with Wynn searching her face, looking for hurt or signs of mental unbalance after her ordeal.

She could not let Wynn see her pain or her fear or the desperation that locked all the reassurances in her throat. So she stared at Wynn silently—at this man she was to marry, whose life was to be bound to hers.

For a moment she saw two faces, one superimposed upon the other: Wynn, almost flawlessly handsome, his short dark hair fashionably curled, his smooth skin almost unmarked by any evidence of his years; and Rook, rugged and harsh, skin burned under a hot sun and scarred by hardship, black hair like a wild creature's mane about his broad, bare shoulders.

She trembled with the urge to turn and run, commandeer

a scout ship from the *Perséphone*'s hangar and follow Rook to the ends of the universe. . . .

"You have what you wanted, Slayton."

Rook's voice stalked the *Perséphone*'s bridge like a shadow-cat among sheep, deep and menacing.

Wynn pulled gently away from Ariane's grasp and signaled to the medic who had followed her up from the hangar. Ariane shook off the doctor's hesitant touch and followed Wynn as he stopped in the center of the bridge, bracing his hands on the back of his elegantly padded captain's chair.

"I have the Lady Ariane, Kalian. But not everything I wanted."

Something in his smooth, cultured voice made the hairs rise on the back of Ariane's neck. She could almost smell Wynn's hatred—hatred he hid so perfectly under his well-bred mask.

"We never get everything we want, Slayton."

Ariane came up to Wynn just in time to catch the smile that curled his aristocratic mouth. "Speak for yourself, Kalian." He looked aside at one of his officers. "Have you got him in range, Webb?"

The blood surged in Ariane's ears, nearly deafening her. She lunged at Wynn and pulled him around to face her. For a moment his expression revealed shock at her strength, and then it settled into a mask of concern.

"Ariane, you've been through a terrible ordeal, but it's over. You must rest." He stroked his hand over her hair as he would a child's. "We'll speak of it later. You have nothing to fear now. Let me take care of you. Champetier—"

"No!" She shook her head, fighting down panic. "What are you going to do, Wynn?"

His elegant dark brows drew down in puzzlement. "Only see to it that the Kalian pays for what he's done. It's none of your concern, *ma petite.*"

"None of my concern?" She jerked away. "I was the hostage, Wynn. And Rook Galloway did me no harm—"

"No harm?" Wynn looked her up and down intently.

"He killed your brother. *Mon Dieu,* he's a murderous savage—"

"He didn't kill my brother." She watched Wynn go utterly still. "I can't explain how I know, Wynn. Not now. But he's innocent."

The first officer's voice cut between them. "Sir, the *d'Artagnan* is moving toward the sun."

Toward the sun. Not to the edge of the system, where the ship would be clear of solar and planetary gravity wells with plenty of room to make the jump to hyperspace.

Jumping too near a star was risky at the best of times. And the *d'Artagnan* was not in perfect condition. . . .

Why, Rook? Why?

"Stay on top of her, Webb," Wynn ordered, still staring at Ariane.

She reached for Wynn and grasped his hand as if she could make him believe with her touch. "Listen to me, Wynn. He let me go safely, according to your bargain. You gave your word of honor to let him go—"

For an instant she looked out the canopy, searching for a ship that should have been long gone. *Go, Rook,* she cried silently. *For God's sake, go—*

"Let him go?" This time there was no mistaking the incredulity in Wynn's voice. He caught her shoulders, gentleness barely masking something less benign. "What did he do to you, Ariane? When did Elite honor ever apply to his kind?"

Ariane remembered Rook's scathing denunciation of Marchand honor. Grimly she lifted her chin and met Wynn's gaze. *"My* honor applies."

Wynn looked over her shoulder at the medic who shadowed her. "You're ill, Ariane."

"No. Not ill." She bent her arms to grasp Wynn's biceps, rigid under the rich fabric of his uniform sleeve. "Please, Wynn. I gave my word. Let him go."

Abruptly Wynn's hands loosened on her shoulders. His face was uncharacteristically grim. Cold, like a stranger's. He signaled to the communications officer with one upraised finger.

"Rook Galloway, this is Wynn Slayton. You have five minutes to leave the system. If you fail to depart in that time, I will destroy you."

"He's still headed for the sun, sir," Webb said.

The medic murmured something in Ariane's ear, but she ignored his entreaties. She planted herself in front of Wynn. "The *d'Artagnan* was badly damaged by drug-runners and forced to land several days ago. She's still not in perfect condition. He may be having trouble. . . ."

Wynn gave her a look that turned her blood to ice. "He's mocking us, Ariane, playing his mad Kalian games. They were always a primitive race. Dangerous and worthless." He shook his head and sighed. "Very well, Ariane. He'll escape —this time." He signaled to Webb. "Lay in a course for Espérance."

When he turned to Ariane again, the threatening stranger's face was gone. "It's done. Consider it an early wedding present." He smiled, and his gaze burned suddenly with hot possessiveness, flaring and dying within the same instant. "Now, go with Champetier, *chérie.*" He stroked her cheek with the back of his hand. "We'll soon be home."

Exhaustion slammed into Ariane, and she let herself lean on the arm the doctor offered as he moved up beside her. She glanced out the canopy one last time, praying for one glimpse of Rook before he left her in limbo.

Wynn followed her gaze, but she was too intent to see the silent gesture he directed at Webb. Wynn nodded to the crewman at the gunner's station, felt the faint vibration under his heels as the ship picked up speed.

The Kalian had flown very near the sun, but whatever his intention—some simpleminded trick or suicide—he would have no chance to carry it out. Wynn pretended deliberate disinterest as the *Perséphone* drew within range of the *d'Artagnan*. Ariane was at the hatch, oblivious to the maneuver, leaning against the bulkhead and half-hidden by Champetier's body.

She never saw the *d'Artagnan* appear within the frame of the canopy, limned by sunlight. She never saw Wynn give the signal to fire. But she turned as light flared and debris spiraled outward from the center of the blast, and her mouth formed a silent scream before she toppled to the deck.

CHAPTER SIXTEEN

$\mathcal{E}$spérancian sunlight streamed down through the high mullioned windows of the Patriarch's private study, painting a pattern of bars across Ariane's face and shoulders and the parquet floor behind her. She stared out at the small walled garden, lush native foliage carefully tamed by the hand of man.

Once she had loved that garden. Bernard had occasionally let her and Jacques play there while he worked, if they were quiet and well-behaved. And she had loved this study with its smell of antique books and polish, the half-hidden alcoves with their exotic trinkets brought from distant worlds.

Now it felt like a cage.

Her mind touched briefly on the unbearable and flinched away. A day or an aeon—it would have made no difference. Her heart had been ripped living from her body, and the void left in its place sucked and pulled at her sanity like a black hole in lifeless space.

Strange—even now she could almost feel him, as if in their brief time together he had become part of her. In her imagination he remained stubbornly alive, waiting, standing in judgment, demanding that she finish what he had begun.

Her vision blurred, and she blinked. She had stared too long into the sun; her eyes had no tears left to give up. They had all been shed on the voyage back from the Louve system, a lifetime's worth in a few brief days. She could not remember what she had said or done or thought, confined to the richly appointed cabin Wynn had given her. She knew she had gone on living. She had answered questions and submitted to the doctor's care, surviving in spite of herself.

Because of what she was: the heir of survivors, descended

of a breed that had left Earth millennia ago and tamed unknown worlds.

She had arrived on Espérance and walked into Bernard Marchand's restrained embrace. Her old life had wrapped about her like a shroud, as if she could still be protected from hurt and pain. And for a while, numb, she had hidden within these high mansion walls as if she'd never left them.

But one morning she had awakened in her old suite and rose, pulled on the lounging suit a silent servant had left, looked into the ornately carved mirror over her dresser, and seen a face that was no longer truly her own.

Now Ariane waited for Bernard to receive her message and return from one of his innumerable meetings. She knew he would come as quickly as he could; the servants he had set to watch her since her return would have given him continual reports on her condition, would have informed him the moment she had ventured from her rooms.

He could not know what had driven her out after so many days of silent hiding, though he would have learned from Wynn every last detail of her rescue and the death of the man who had held her captive. He would have expected that his great-granddaughter needed this hiatus in order to recover from the trauma she had suffered at a barbarian's hands.

But the time had come for her to face the universe again, even though all she wanted was oblivion.

The massive ebonwood door swung open behind her with a whisper, and Ariane turned slowly to face her great-grandfather.

He strode toward her, drawing her into a brief and formal embrace. "Ariane," he said, his keen, dark gaze sweeping her from head to foot. "You are well?"

She let herself be guided into a chair opposite his desk and looked up at Bernard Marchand. He was dressed impeccably in a severely cut, expertly tailored suit that matched his eyes and contrasted dramatically with his white hair. The Patriarch of the Marchand needed no ostentation. His only jewelry was the wide Patriarch's ring on his right hand, black diamond glittering with reflected sunlight.

He still had the commanding appearance of strength and vigor, though Ariane could sense beneath his vitality the inevitable deterioration that Slayton drugs held at bay.

"I'm well, Grand-père," she answered. The tonelessness of her own voice no longer shocked her. Bernard's dark brows drew down; abruptly he turned away to look out the window as Ariane had done earlier. His long-fingered, blue-veined hands clasped at the small of his back and tightened.

"Wynn gave me the physician's report," he said, the words measured and distant. "I know the only remedy for what you've suffered is time, and rest. As much time as you need. Wynn has agreed." His silhouette was stark against the window. "Nothing has changed, Ariane. The marriage can be postponed for a few weeks. As far as Lumière is concerned, the stories of your kidnapping were nothing but rumors with little basis in fact. I've—taken care of the Families. Nothing will be said against you, Ariane, that I promise."

Ariane listened to his reassurances with only half her attention, her innermost self focused on a voice only she could hear. She dropped her eyes to stare at her clasped hands, remembering the rough-smooth texture of Rook's skin and his fingers caressing her.

"Our honor will suffer no lasting damage from this debacle, Ariane. The marriage will quiet any lingering—questions." His voice took on the edge that cowed even the most arrogant among the Elite. *"Dieu,* if I had only been there to punish the savage myself—"

"Grand-père."

She spoke softly, but that single word stopped him like a shout. Silence hung in the study, as deceptively solid as the broken beams of sunlight.

"Everything has changed, Grand-père," she murmured.

The Patriarch lifted his head. His body tensed, but still he did not turn to face her. For a moment Ariane only gazed at him, drifting on a tide of memory.

Bernard Marchand. In her years of growing up he had been her guardian, her ideal of honor, the arbiter of wisdom and justice. He and Jacques had been her only family, and she had adored the Patriarch with a child's unquestioning love, fiercely striving to win his in return. When she had grown old enough to understand that shared Marchand honor bound them more deeply than any emotion, it had seemed enough.

And even when she had defied him, fought with him for freedoms her rank should have made impossible, she had never forgotten her duty. Bernard had raised her to be a true Marchand. He had known she would settle down in the end and follow the dictates of her blood. That she would achieve what House Marchand demanded: an advantageous marriage, heirs to carry on the name, where his children and grandchildren had failed.

Bernard was a man who could intimidate the most powerful of the Elite, who had won the respect of major powers throughout the galaxy, but he waited for her to speak as if he knew what she would say. As if he were afraid.

Bernard Marchand, who feared nothing.

"I know what I am," she said softly.

The steady sound of Bernard's breathing stopped and shuddered out again. He walked with slow, deliberate steps to his desk and leaned over it, bracing himself as if he feared he might fall. His hands curled into fists on polished surface, every tendon standing out in harsh relief under the weathered skin.

The man who faced her across the desk had outlived children and grandchildren, opened Espérancian trade to the other worlds of the League, held the reins of a growing empire in his blue-blooded hands. He was Patriarch of the most powerful and ancient family in Lumière, last of the original Marchand line. His hawkish face was proud and stern, carved and seamed by experience and loss. Of the few who had been permitted into his most private sanctuary, none had ever seen him utterly vulnerable.

Ariane saw him fade into an ordinary old man before her eyes.

Sorrow touched her distantly, that she should be forced to bring him pain after what they had both endured. If it had been only a matter of her own future—a future that held little meaning—she might have let it go. But this was the man who had both saved and condemned Rook and his people. The man who might hold the key to finding the answers Rook had died for.

"I know—what I am," she repeated, and Bernard Marchand did not pretend to misunderstand.

"How did you find out?"

Ariane gathered her inner awareness and focused it, ignoring the tearing pain that came with touching the place she had once Shared with Rook. "Do you remember Finch, Grand-père?" she asked tonelessly. "She didn't die along with the other Kalians eight years ago. When we—when Rook Galloway took me to Agora, I found her there."

Bernard made a sound that might have been denial and sank into the heavy carved chair behind him.

"Finch," he whispered. He caught himself abruptly, and his eyes focused again, lifting slowly to hers. "My God, Ariane—"

She met his gaze. "Finch told me everything. She was dying, Grand-père."

"Dying," Bernard echoed. Ariane could see the emotions move in rapid succession behind his eyes, shock upon shock.

"She was here after the riots, after the trials," Ariane continued softly. "But none of us knew it. She Changed—made herself look like a common Marchand servant. To stay with me. Until she could stay no longer."

Color returned to the skin stretched so tautly over Bernard's high cheekbones. "Alive. I did not know—"

"But you did know the rest. About what I was. About Anne-Marie, and Chantal. My mother. And my Kalian father."

Bernard passed a shaking hand over his eyes. "Yes. I knew. I was there when my daughter took her lover on Kali, during the peace talks with the Fahar. I was with her when Sedge Allen died in an accident."

"And you brought her back to Espérance, saw to it that our people never knew the truth."

Slowly Ariane's great-grandfather drew himself up with the old pride, assuming the mantle of his rank and power. "Yes. For the sake of Marchand honor. And for her sake, and the sake of her child-to-be."

"Chantal," Ariane said. "But it didn't end there."

"No." Bernard's voice was as emotionless as her own. "Your mother had only a trace of copper in her eyes, and Finch—took care of that. She understood the necessity. She agreed to keep her silence."

Ariane closed her eyes. All the memories were painful now, part of a wound in her soul that would never heal. "Until Agora," she murmured.

Bernard stalked across the study to stand by the windows again. "When Chantal came of age, I gave her in marriage to the heir of a cadet branch of our family, a tie that would strengthen her Marchand blood."

"My—" Ariane choked on the word "father." "Pierre Burke-Marchand."

Bernard made a low sound. "It should have been enough; Chantal was always dutiful. But after Jacques was born, she changed. She was never content with Pierre. One day I had my men follow Chantal into the Warren when she was meeting her—Kalian lover."

Kestrel Tremayne. Ariane clenched her hands in her lap, unable to speak.

"I had no choice," he continued. "I brought Chantal back and confined her to the mansion. Tremayne"—he drew a deep breath—"ran. I didn't know what I would do with him, but when my men found him in a Warren warehouse, he was already dead. Apparently murdered."

Opening her eyes, Ariane stared at the perfect, polished surface of his desk. She was too numb to feel any horror. "By whom, Grand-père?"

His very silence told her that he understood what she implied. "I had nothing to do with his death," he said at last. "I could learn nothing. Shortly afterward Chantal—told me she was pregnant. She claimed the child was Tremayne's.

When she was due, I sent your fa— Pierre away on Marchand business. Only Finch and myself attended your birth."

Ariane got to her feet. They supported her remarkably well. "I was born with black hair and copper eyes," she said, turning to face him. "Finch Changed me, just as she Changed Chantal."

Bernard's stance was unflinchingly erect. "Yes. You were perfect in every way. A perfect Kalian."

"And you never told Pierre." She moved to his side by the window, light bathing her face as she turned it up to the sun. "I know why you had to keep it hidden, Grand-père. Even the Marchand name would be irrevocably damaged by a hint of mixed blood."

"So you do understand." Black eyes glittered like Anubian jade. "You would never have been accepted, Ariane. Never. I did everything I could to help the Kalians. But you and Jacques had to inherit an untainted name." His voice roughened. "No one else knows. You are safe, Ariane. You're home."

Home. Ariane gazed into the sun until her eyes watered and burned. Home had been a Caravel-class starship and the arms of a man who was gone forever.

"Why didn't you tell me?"

"There was no need for you to know," he said harshly. "If I had kept you here by me, where you belonged, none of this would have happened. I should have realized—"

He closed his mouth with a snap. Ariane smiled sadly. "Realized that my Kalian blood would reveal itself in time?"

His answer was in his eyes. Had he seen that Kalian blood in her every time she'd tested the bounds of Marchand propriety, stood up to his authority as no one else would dare, family or otherwise? Had he waited, dreading the lapse that would reveal her mixed heritage—and his daughter's and granddaughter's shame—to the world?

Bernard Marchand, so perfect in honor, had deceived everyone to protect his name. Ariane had carried that false pride like a banner every day of her life, until Finch—and

Rook—had shown her the truth. Once she might have wept at the irony of it.

"You need think of it no longer, Ariane," Bernard said suddenly, as if he heard censure in her silence. As if her feelings had bearing on anything he did to protect House Marchand. "The past is dead, and your future is assured."

The future. "My marriage to Wynn?" she asked. "Does he know what he'll be getting, Grand-père?"

He stiffened, but Ariane refused to look away. "I haven't told you everything that happened when Rook Galloway took me captive. Learning what I was . . . that was only a small part of it. The smallest part."

Bernard tilted back his head, the tendons working in his jaw. For a moment Ariane thought he had guessed the truth, that she had given herself to a Kalian criminal. Wynn had shown no sign that he suspected, but Bernard—Bernard knew of her Kalian blood, her Kalian wildness. . . .

"I heard the other side of the story," she continued steadily. "The part I never knew, about the riots and the imprisonment of the Kalians. Rook Galloway believed that they had been the ones betrayed from the very beginning."

"What?"

"He was not a savage, Grand-père. He was wrongly convicted. I had a part in condemning him for killing Jacques—but when I went to question him on Tantalus, I think I already knew he was innocent."

"Innocent!" he spat. "He was a murderer, a barbarian with no conception of honor, like all his—"

"Like all his kind. Like me." Ariane regarded his face as the color drained out of it. "But he didn't kill me, Grand-père. When he captured my ship, he didn't know I was Kalian. He didn't hurt me at all, when he could have, when he had every reason to hate what I was. Even though he believed our family was responsible for the murder of his entire people."

Bernard's expression betrayed him, his mask of outraged pride vanishing in an instant. Ariane felt the world heave under her.

"Was he right?" she asked hoarsely. "Did you hate them so much, Grand-père? Enough to want revenge on all of them?"

Bernard brushed past her and stumbled against Ariane's chair, grasping the carved back for support. "What are you saying?"

She wanted to close her eyes and retreat to some empty place where no one could ever find her again, where she could live with Rook in her memories until her body faded away. But *this* was why she was here, why she would go on. For Rook. For their people. For justice.

And so she told Bernard, all that Rook had revealed to her: how he believed that Marchand guardsmen in plain uniforms had attacked Kalian households without warning, taken people away into the night; how Kalians had attempted to defend themselves; how another guardsman—an Espérancian—had killed Jacques as Rook held him, leaving Rook to take the blame.

"It was easy to believe Rook was the killer—for me, for Wynn, for all of us, after what had happened. We were all lost in grief and shock, and they were the savages who had turned on their benefactors."

Bernard's hand slammed on the back of the chair. "There was proof! Proof of their betrayal, the very Kalians we'd educated at our own expense—they planned to steal Marchand ships, kill personnel, blackmail us—"

"Yes. Proof. Is that why you sent covert operatives down into the Warren that night? Did it get out of hand, or was the riot intended all along? A way to get rid of all of them when they had become too difficult to control?"

He stared at her as if she were a stranger. "I sent no men. I was sleeping when Gaston woke me to tell me of the riots. Wynn sent the gendarmes, and I authorized the use of Marchand troops." His fingers flexed. "We didn't learn of the Kalian plot to commandeer Marchand ships until after the riots were put down. Wynn's investigation uncovered the sabotage of the ships' systems, found Kalians who would talk. But I sent no men!"

Ariane forced herself to continue, moving across the room to confront the Patriarch. "Yet Rook's people saw them. Kalians died. And the trials—did the Kalians ever get their rightful measure of justice, even under League law? Was there any hope of impartiality then, with the entire city against them, and Jacques dead?" She leaned forward mercilessly. "Was the explosion on the ship carrying the Kalians to Agora truly an accident, Grand-père?"

Sinking heavily into the chair, his face chalk-white, Bernard shook his head. "Is it possible that you believe this, Ariane?" he rasped. "One convict's word against all you've ever known? *Dieu.*" He closed his eyes. "I saved them. I intended to repay what they had done for Espérance. Even after they took my daughter and granddaughter away from me, I risked much for them. I put Marchand resources behind them when the other Families refused to lend their aid. I sent their brightest to be educated at the finest universities. When all of Espérance despised them, *I* protected them."

Once Ariane would have been stunned at the open pain in Bernard's voice. This was emotion he would show no one— had never shown her, his heir, the last of his direct line, who had been closer to him than any other.

But too much had changed within herself. She was no longer a young girl struggling to win the Patriarch's approval, caught between honor and her own need for freedom. That Ariane was dead.

"No," she said. "Even when I came to realize that Rook had been wrongly condemned, I couldn't bring myself to accept that our family would have committed willful acts of genocide."

"Genocide?" Ariane watched Bernard shed his vulnerability and retreat into himself, drawing a shield of pride and reserve between them again. "Our family preserved their race from extinction when Kali was devastated, and I would have set them free again. The destruction of the *Bonaventure* was an unfortunate accident." He looked up from under his heavy brows, suddenly fierce as a hunting eagle. "It was no more than that, Ariane."

"But it was, Grand-père. Some great injustice destroyed an entire people." She lifted her chin. *"My* people."

The Patriarch surged to his feet. *"We* are your people," he rasped. "What happened to the Kalians was a tragedy, but you can do nothing to bring them back. After all you've endured—"

"I've endured nothing. I've had a life of ease and privilege." Her gaze blurred and turned inward. "Rook gave *his* life trying to find answers. He thought he was the last of his kind. But he wasn't. *He wasn't."*

Her words hovered like an unanswerable challenge. Bernard's expression hardened into comprehension.

"What did he do to you, Ariane?" he demanded. "Did he touch you? *Mon Dieu—"*

There was no shame in her, no lingering regret over what she might lose by telling him the truth. She had already lost everything that mattered.

"He was my lover," she said.

Bernard's reaction was a palpable thing, agony that shivered in the air between them. He turned his face aside as if he couldn't bear to look at her. "Again," he whispered harshly. "Again. Like to like. Inevitable. . . ."

"Perhaps it was." She drew herself to her full height, pulling his eyes back to her with the sheer force of her will. "But I knew he and his people had been wronged before we— stopped being enemies. Rook was one of the most honorable men I have ever known. I was proud to have been his mate."

Bernard's gaze turned icy with contempt. "Proud?" he repeated incredulously. "So easily you discard Marchand honor—"

"This is a matter of Marchand honor," she said. "I swore I would find the answers, and the truth, no matter what the cost. That's why I'm here, Grand-père. Why I'm not with Rook now."

He understood. Like ritual dueling to the death, suicide had once been an honorable course among the Elite. Ariane saw the beginning of realization in his face—not acceptance, never that—but the knowledge that she meant every word she said to the depths of her being. Her pride had always matched his.

"So. Do you think to—abandon your name and blood as you threw away your honor, Ariane? Is our ancient line to end with you?"

"I am still Marchand. I can no more deny that blood than I can abandon what I've sworn to do."

"And your duty?"

"I haven't forgotten that either, Grand-père." She drew in a deep breath. "You said Wynn was still eager for the marriage."

Bernard stiffened.

"He knows nothing of my true relationship with Rook— no more than he knows of my Kalian blood."

She could almost feel the change in Bernard, bleak despair transforming to wary hope. Ariane placed her palms flat on his desk. "I know this marriage is vital to the family, Grand-père. Essential to the future of all we hold. Has that changed?"

She knew it had not. Bernard had never divulged all the complex political and financial reasons for the marriage, but she knew well enough what lay behind the ancient tradition of marriages of alliance. To abandon the contract now would be unthinkable.

Once duty and honor alone had bound her to the contract. Now she would bargain like one of the Merchant caste for what she must have. To find the answers, she must bring her great-grandfather pain, and dishonor to one of her oldest friends. To find justice, she must betray the memory of the man she had loved more than life itself.

"You would go so easily from Kalian lover to marriage with Wynn, who believes you are untouched?" Bernard asked hoarsely.

"You deceived Wynn when you failed to tell him of my mixed blood. Which is the greater dishonor?" She leaned forward. "When does honor give way to expediency and necessity? When did Marchand honor fail the Kalians?"

They stared at each other, Marchand and Marchand, human and Kalian. Bernard was the first to look away. "The marriage must take place," he said through clenched teeth. "What do you want, Ariane?"

She swallowed, asking silent forgiveness of the copper-eyed man who lived only in her memory. "I will do my duty, Grand-père. I will marry Wynn and bear his children and carry on the Marchand name. Wynn will never know the truth about Rook Galloway. I ask only one thing: complete access to all Marchand and city records dealing with the Kalian riots and the aftermath, including all classified files, and the full support of all Marchand resources. Whatever I need to make a complete investigation of the events leading up to the death of the Kalian people."

"And what if you don't find your answers, Ariane?"

She had no response to his question. This was her last link to Rook, this quest she had set for herself. This goal would keep her alive, sane, give her the purpose she needed to draw in one breath after another. Failure was not a possibility.

"Let me have what I need, Grand-père," she said. "And it will be as if nothing had changed."

"Very well." He looked at her dispassionately, all Patriarch once again, giving her the attention due a respected enemy. "You have your—bargain."

The numbness that had enshrouded her since Rook's death saved her once again. Her great-grandfather's shame, his unmistakable rejection of her, touched her only from a great distance.

"Thank you," she said quietly. "I will be discreet, Sieur Marchand. You have no reason to fear for our name." She gave him a formal bow. "Please inform me when the arrangements are complete."

She turned to go, knowing she had done what she must. At the door she glanced back at the old man who leaned over his desk, arms trembling under the weight of Marchand's hidden disgrace.

Forgive me, she said silently to the Patriarch who had taught her the meaning of honor—and again to the Kalian who had taught her the power of love. *Forgive me.*

• • •

Wynn had been expecting this meeting. He had spent the past several days considering how far to push the game, how much to make Bernard Marchand suffer.

He rose as a servant directed the Patriarch into his study, offering his hand with a smile. Bernard's face gave nothing away, but Wynn saw the tension in the old man's big frame and smiled secretly.

Had he guessed, then? Or had the girl told him? Wynn's brief amusement faded. Under other circumstances he would have delighted in ruining Ariane's good name among the Elite just for the pain and shame it would bring to her great-grandfather. But there was far too much at stake, and a far more thorough revenge in the offing.

"Bernard," he said softly. "Will you try this excellent cognac?"

The Patriarch was distracted enough that he took several seconds to answer. "Thank you," he said, seating himself in his usual place by the black diamarble mantelpiece. Wynn could feel Bernard's hawklike eyes following his movements as he poured out the brandy and offered a fine crystal glass to his guest.

"Ariane is well?" he asked, all solicitude. "She has recovered from her ordeal and is in good health?"

"Yes. She is—completely recovered," Bernard said. He took a measured sip of his drink as Wynn sat down across from him. "If it weren't for your intervention—"

Wynn waved away Bernard's gruff words. "You've thanked me enough, old friend. I'm only grateful that I was in the system investigating the rumor of illicit drug production at the time. It was my place to save my betrothed, and my honor to restore her to you." He smiled around the rim of his snifter. "Few women would have survived what she did and come through unscathed. Ariane is quite—remarkable."

Bernard seemed to look right through him. "Yes," he murmured.

"I know she will bear fine, strong sons to bind our families," Wynn said, strolling over to the sideboard to refill his glass. He lifted it in a silent toast. "The marriage will be the greatest celebration Lumière has seen in a century. Our blood united at last, Bernard. Think of it!" He drank with an extravagant gesture. "As it was always meant to be."

Leaving his glass untouched on the side table, Bernard rose. He paced toward the hearth and leaned against it, staring at the intricate carving as if he'd never seen it before. At this moment the Patriarch looked his age: old, worn, and weary in ways the longevity drugs could never ameliorate.

Wynn went back to his chair and sat down, stretching his legs before him. He drained his glass, savoring the heat of the potent liquor and his secret triumph. Bernard's uncharacteristic silence was more telling than any diplomatic words.

"I admit I was concerned for a short while after I found Ariane," Wynn said, turning the empty snifter in his hand. "She seemed quite—disoriented. Confused." He shook his head ruefully. "She even insisted that I spare the life of the savage—that it was a matter of honor. *Her* honor. Of course, she never learned I'd destroyed him. She believed the ship exploded when the savage attempted to enter hyperspace too deep in Louve's gravity well." He sighed. "If I didn't know her better, I would almost have believed she had lost her enthusiasm for our union."

Bernard's gaze jerked sharply back to Wynn. "Ariane knows her duty."

"I am relieved to hear it. I would be quite devastated if anything were to come between us now."

Bernard returned to his chair and sat down stiffly. A muscle in his rigid jaw twitched. "She's well now," he said. "The contract will be fulfilled." He reached for his glass, nearly upsetting it, and drained it in one swallow. "We have only to set the date."

"Excellent. More brandy?" Wynn noted the way Bernard's hand shook as he set down the glass. "Of course, there is the small matter of adjusting the contract to—compensate for the change in circumstances since Ariane's adventures."

The old man went utterly still. "Change?"

"The minor detail of Ariane's loss of virginity."

The delicate crystal, still clenched in Bernard's fingers, shattered in a spray of light. Wynn sighed, his face a mask of sympathy.

"You will, of course, understand why I considered it essential to learn the full truth of what had happened," he said. "Oh, I have no doubt that Ariane was forced. The brute had her in his power for many days. For all her courage, Ariane is only a woman, and only human."

"Dieu," Bernard whispered.

"I had my physician run . . . a few extra tests. Ariane wasn't aware of them. I'm sure you intended to tell me of this, Bernard, at the right time. Perhaps this very hour?" He smiled, rose slowly, and retrieved an embroidered napkin from the sideboard. He offered it to Bernard.

The Patriarch clenched the napkin in his fist until the tendons stood out in the back of his hand. "You'll still have her, Wynn?"

"Of course." Wynn resumed his seat and made himself comfortable. "Would I hurt my dearest friends by bringing shame and scandal down upon their House? The advantages of the unsullied Marchand name are far too great an asset. Should the marriage be called off, I might find it necessary to —recover some of the assets I've invested in Marchand enterprises throughout the League." He stroked the elegant wooden arm of his chair. "The timing would be most unfortunate for you, Bernard. I rely on your influence to expand my—our—interests."

The old man looked at Wynn as if he'd never seen him before. *Are you beginning to understand?* Wynn thought. *Are you beginning to be afraid?*

"And, after all," he continued aloud, "I know the meaning of scandal. My family suffered through it. I wouldn't wish it on you, Bernard, or on Ariane. No, I think we will proceed as planned, with perhaps a few adjustments."

He saw Bernard remembering the affair of Ria Santini-Slayton, understanding at last what Wynn implied. The old man had nothing to say. His eyes fixed on his most trusted friend as Wynn proceeded to outline the additional concessions he wished, deliberately chosen to weaken the Marchand empire.

When it was finished, and Bernard had made not a single protest, Wynn offered him another drink to seal the bargain. Bernard drained the glass.

"Now that we've put these tiresome details behind us," Wynn said, looping his arm around Bernard's bent shoulders, "we can turn to far more pleasant matters." He shook his head as he guided Bernard toward the door. "It's a fortunate thing that the Kalians are gone. They have caused entirely too much trouble, haven't they, *mon cher ami?*"

He carried on a one-sided conversation with the Patriarch for the next hour, finalizing plans for the wedding, and bid the old man a pleasant adieu. Afterward he sat in his favorite chair and contemplated the fruition of his plans.

The breaking had begun at last. First Wynn would claim Bernard's most treasured possession—his great-granddaughter and heir, whom he entrusted to the man he believed his closest ally. And then the problems would begin: debts called in, business deals gone bad, shipments lost. One by one the Marchand's offplanet holdings would begin to fail. Only Wynn Slayton could save them—but he would not. Not until they were his alone.

And when the first phase had ended and the Marchand withdrew to Espérance to recoup—turning to allies and the base of power that had been theirs for centuries—they would find those allies turned against them, and the structure of power on Espérance forever changed.

The Kalians would make the second phase simple. Carefully conditioned Kalian impostors were already settled in the households of the greatest families in Lumière, masquerading as servants and guardsmen. Through them Wynn knew more damning secrets of the Elite than he could ever use—but enough, more than enough, to bend the great Families to his will. Some of Bernard Marchand's supporters would fall to Kalian assassins; others would succumb to carefully engineered blackmail.

In the end the Marchand would have no allies. Only then

would Wynn himself turn to his mentor and reveal what he had done. Marchand power would be destroyed, and it would be the Slayton name that ruled in Lumière. And, in time, all of Espérance.

Wynn smiled and called for a second bottle of brandy.

CHAPTER SEVENTEEN

Nothing.

Ariane pushed an almost transparent slice of meat across her plate and stared blankly at Wynn's empty chair. Only two weeks until the wedding, and she had learned nothing.

The breakfast room was unbearably cheerful with the sky-lights opened to spring sunlight and birdsong profuse from the garden behind the screens. Wynn had been a perfect gentleman, serving her with his own hand. And every mouthful of food she'd forced herself to eat had become ashes on her tongue.

She hadn't let Wynn see it. If he noted her reserve, he attributed it to nerves or the aftereffects of her ordeal. She was the dutiful bride, and she had lived up to her part of the bargain.

But there was little to show for it, for all the resources Bernard had put at her command. The computer records held little that she didn't already know. If there were classified documents she was missing, she couldn't locate them, even with the help of House Marchand's most skilled technicians.

The things she had learned had only added to the puzzle. Rumors and vague reports of Kalians disappearing from the Warren in the years just prior to the riot; brief accounts of unpublicized clashes between Kalians and Espérancians along the Fringe; a buried memorandum by some Marchand agent of odd behavior among the refugees. The follow-up had been negligible.

Transcripts and recordings of the trial had been no better. All the proof Bernard had cited was there—proof that certain educated Kalians had intended to sabotage and take over Marchand ships and personnel. Kalian denials in the wake of that proof seemed almost pathetic.

Until she had found Rook's face among the recordings and played back his testimony.

Ariane set down her fork and swallowed the bile in her throat. He had been young—young and handsome and desperately eloquent in the face of overwhelming odds. And she herself had spoken out against him, her face frozen with hatred.

She had been coldly indifferent when he'd been sent to Tantalus.

With perfect outward poise Ariane moved to the open doors and sucked in lungfuls of sweet-scented garden air. No servant looking on would guess that every memory, every moment she lived, was torment.

Footsteps whispered on the tiled floor behind her. Warm hands touched her shoulders gently.

"What are you thinking, Ariane?" Wynn murmured. She held herself very still as his breath caressed her temple.

"Of—our future," she answered, closing her eyes as he brushed his lips against the side of her neck.

"Impatient, my Ariane?" he said. He turned her in his arms. "Only two more weeks. Does it seem so long?"

An eternity would be too soon, she thought, forcing a smile to her lips. "We'll have a lifetime together, Wynn."

"So we will." He pulled her close, pressing a kiss to her forehead. "But I do confess to a certain impatience."

Ariane felt nothing, held in his arms. She looked right through him and saw another face, framed in a mane of heavy black hair; another pair of eyes, hot as liquid copper.

She remembered Rook's touch with aching intensity— the hard planes of his scarred body, his mouth on hers, his fingers caressing her naked breasts. . . .

But it was Wynn's hand cupping her, teasing her nipple through her blouse with his thumb. At the last minute she kept herself from jerking away, lashing out at the man who dared claim what belonged forever to one who was dead.

"Wynn," she whispered. "Please."

He withdrew his hand. "Shy, my Ariane? There is no need to be." His eyes dropped to her puckered nipple. "So innocent, so untouched. But I believe you will enjoy our wedding bed, *ma chérie.*"

Her shudder was invisible to his eyes, locked deep within her body. Since she had begun to see Wynn again, he had shown clearly how much he anticipated the consummation of their wedding contract. He insisted on accompanying her to every Elite function her rank and duty demanded, attended her at almost every meal, played the gallant suitor constantly. And he revealed his desire in subtle touches, long looks, a thousand ways that challenged her ability to hide her despair.

She could not hate Wynn. He was blameless in this. He would have let Rook go, at her word. He stood by her now, when he could reasonably have protested the dishonor of her capture by a Kalian savage.

Unable to meet his eyes, Ariane stared at the pulse beating in his neck above the collar of his expensive morning suit. He didn't know. He couldn't. Even when he lay with her, he wouldn't guess the truth.

And her heart, her soul, would remain untouched.

Wynn sighed. "You have become a very desirable woman, Ariane," he said. "But it is, after all, only two more weeks." He flicked his finger playfully against her chin, as he'd done so often when she was a child, and stepped away. "I have business to take care of this morning, but I hope you'll permit me to attend you at luncheon." With a smile of absolute confidence, he bowed lightly and left the room.

Ariane stood for a long time looking after him. There were five hours until luncheon—five hours to access the records and go over them for the thousandth time.

But when she retired to her suite on the second floor overlooking the private courtyard, she went to the armoire by the north windows in her sitting room and pulled out the shipsuit she hadn't touched since her return to Espérance.

Her Kalian senses were overwhelmed by Rook's lingering scent as she drew the cloth against her face. She knelt on the floor and listened as if she could hear his heartbeat in the heavy silence of the room. It seemed as if the very walls were beginning to close in around her—bound there forever, bound to Wynn's bed, living out her life in shadow.

Kai-horo, the Fahar called it—pain of the soul that would never end.

She bent over, gasping for breath, until her loose hair brushed the Anubian carpet. Something rolled free of the shipsuit in her arms.

A man's inexpensive ring hung on a thin cord came to rest by her knee, and she reached for it blindly.

Finch's ring. She had worn it around her neck since the day Rook had learned what she was; the ring and the shipsuit were all she had carried away from the *d'Artagnan,* save a shattered heart.

She turned the ring over in her hand, convulsively rubbing the cheap black stone with her finger. She had tried to give it to Rook, and he had refused. He had died believing she had rejected her Kalian blood. He had died believing that she had betrayed him. . . .

A voice shattered the stillness.

At first Ariane's mind refused to grasp what she was hearing. Finch—lost Finch, speaking softly from the ring between Ariane's cupped hands.

Instinctively Ariane touched the stone again, feeling for the hidden catch that had activated the recording. She found what she was looking for at the edge of the setting. The voice stopped in midsentence.

She struggled to keep her fingers steady as she experimented with the tiny recorder. Careful manipulation of the almost invisible controls brought her to the very beginning of the narrative.

Finch's voice gave the date as Avril 28 of the year the *Bonaventure,* bearing its Kalian refugees to Agora, had been destroyed.

"Take this, my child. It is all I have time to give you now. . . ."

Closing her eyes, Ariane remembered Finch's final, urgent words. How she had pressed the ring into Ariane's hands.

All along it had been far more than a mere keepsake.

"I pray this has reached the right hands," Finch's voice began. *"The testimony I give in this recording is truth, and by the Maker's will justice will be served."*

Ariane stopped the recording, rose, and moved to her private computer, setting it up to make a transcription of Finch's testimony. She sat on the edge of the chair and listened as the old Kalian's ghostly voice filled her ears with the painful and terrible truth.

When it was over, after the shock had run its course, Ariane felt strangely light. Now she knew. It had all been there in front of her from the beginning.

The one thing she didn't know was *why.*

But her purpose now was clear, as it hadn't been during the fruitless search for facts that had eluded her again and again. She understood what she had to do. The cost was unimportant. Finch had kept herself alive to see that this account went to someone she could trust. And Rook had died searching for what had lain within his grasp.

Ariane shut off her computer, dumped the new data in a restricted-access file, and looped the ring on its cord over her neck, hiding it beneath the collar of her blouse. The evidence she needed might be hidden behind the high walls of one of Lumière's premier estates—within secured computer cores inaccessible to outsiders. In the next hour she had just enough time to visit Marchand Security and talk to old Gaston about obtaining a Key capable of infiltrating the most sophisticated systems on Espérance. If Gaston balked at giving her an illegal program, she would go straight to Bernard.

That she didn't want to do. Not until she had incontrovertible proof—proof that would hold up in an Espérancian court.

And as for Wynn— Ariane smiled without a trace of humor. He would find her inexplicably changed at luncheon, and she would have to use every bit of skill, every trick her time with Rook had taught her, to make him believe she could no longer wait for their wedding night.

•   •   •   •

Ariane led Wynn into the garden after luncheon, dismissing all the servants except the one expressionless footman who followed with the dessert cordials.

She knew when Wynn recognized the change in her behavior. She took great care during the meal to begin subtly, with long looks such as he had given her, and smiles hinting of seduction. Wynn's gaze had become frankly speculative; by the time he rose to escort her from the table, his touch held the heat of possessive anticipation.

They found a quiet corner of the garden far from prying eyes, where no one would interrupt their tryst. They were to be married; few among the Elite would fault them for sampling the physical delights of their alliance, but Wynn had always observed the proprieties. He looked around quickly before joining Ariane on the narrow, decorative Nirvanan laceweave bench.

"I asked you this morning what you were thinking," Wynn said softly. He lifted a tendril of hair that had escaped her coiffure, and this time she turned to him with heavy-lidded eyes. "You said it was about our future."

Moving her hand on the bench so that her fingers brushed Wynn's, Ariane smiled. "That was this morning," she said. "Now I'm—thinking about other things."

"Such as?"

Ariane wondered bleakly what he would do if he could read her mind. He was handsome, and rich, and powerful; many women among the Elite would have been overwhelmed by the honor of wedding him, even the daughters of Families that would have cut his a hundred years ago.

But they could not see what lay beneath his flawless facade, just as they would be unable to look beyond the taint of Kalian blood.

She sighed meaningfully, glancing at Wynn through her eyelashes. "Such as the things you said to me," she said huskily. "About being—impatient." Immediately she dropped her eyes with appropriate modesty.

Wynn caught her chin in his hand. "So," he said. "I knew you couldn't deny that hot Marchand blood, my Ariane."

For a moment she struggled desperately with her revulsion, with the desire to confront him with everything she knew and guessed, with the truth of her own mixed heritage. But she held her silence and let her face carry the lie, let her resolution feed her courage.

"I've never known what it's really like," she told him softly. "I've been afraid. But now I realize that I—want to understand what it is to be loved. . . ."

Something strange flickered in Wynn's expression, just as quickly gone before Ariane could make sense of it. And then he tilted her chin to meet her lips with his own.

This was not the brief kiss he had bestowed on her after the contract had been signed three years ago. This was hot, possessive, hungry; Ariane knew at once that his words of ardor had not been feigned. He desired her as Rook had desired her.

"Ariane," he said, hard against her mouth, "I want you."

She remembered Rook's voice saying those very words; Rook was all she could hear, all she could feel as Wynn deepened his kiss and began to caress her body. With a little effort she put herself beyond awareness of Wynn's demanding touch, making her body a puppet that obeyed her will and melted in Wynn's arms.

"Wynn," she whispered. "Wynn, I want—"

Abruptly Wynn released her and jerked away, his face flushed as he stared up at the footman standing over them.

"What are you doing here?" Wynn snarled.

The servant's proper, expressionless mask never wavered. He bowed and presented the silver tray with the cordials. Wynn's eyes narrowed dangerously; Ariane put her hand on his arm and smiled.

"I—ordered cordials to be brought after the meal," she said. She glanced at the footman, a man she didn't recognize, and gestured casually. The servant extended the tray; Ariane took one tiny glass and offered it to Wynn. His expression relaxed. Ariane took the second glass and waved the footman away.

Wynn had almost emptied his glass before Ariane realized

the footman hadn't withdrawn. She looked up sharply and met eyes that were neither humble nor downcast, but blazed into hers with a wealth of contempt and hatred she could not misinterpret.

"You are dismissed," Ariane snapped, unnerved in spite of herself. All the things Finch had revealed whirled in her mind. After a last hard glance the footman retreated, and Ariane memorized his face. Later she would check up on him. Later, when she was sure of the rest. . . .

"Your servants are poorly schooled," Wynn remarked, setting down his empty glass. "I'll speak to Bernard about it." And then he smiled, his eyes intent on hers. "Where were we?" He pulled her into his arms, claiming her mouth once again. Ariane stroked his shoulders like an automaton. The servant's condemning stare hovered in her thoughts, even as Wynn began to whisper heated promises against her ear.

Forgive me, Rook. This is something I must do. . . .

When Wynn let her go, she was ready with her own innocently seductive words, the ones calculated to get her into Wynn's private chambers. He was more than eager to accommodate her. In his arrogance Wynn never questioned her change of heart.

He left her with a promise to meet her in his garden pavilion at midnight and an admonition to arrange a discreet escort. Ariane waited until he had disappeared and turned her head to wipe the taste of his mouth from her lips with the back of her sleeve. Gathering her shaking legs under her, she went back into the private dining parlor and sat down heavily at the cleared table.

"Café, my lady?"

Ariane looked up with a jerk. It was the insolent footman, the man she hadn't remembered seeing before. He gave her a shallow bow and smiled.

She thought later that she should have known, should have recognized him instantly. Her heart alone should have told her. But she only stared up at him blankly, unable to gather the words of reproach for his behavior. Until he began to Change.

The bland face transfigured before her eyes. Brown hair darkened to black, clubbed at his neck; eyes paled from brown to copper, fixing on her with dark intensity.

For the briefest moment she thought she had gone mad.

And then she knew. She *knew*.

"Rook," she whispered. Her heart drummed a frantic tattoo as she attempted to rise. "Rook!"

It was impossible, and yet it was real. Far more than her eyes confirmed the miracle of his presence. She *felt* him, that distant sense she'd dismissed as an echo of their brief time together bursting into a conflagration within her.

Rook was *alive*.

She braced her hands on the table and pushed herself up, absorbing him with every newly discovered Kalian sense. The smell of him, musk and all things wild and exotic; the bronze beauty of his skin, the hot depths of his eyes.

She saw nothing of what those eyes told her. Joy carried her beyond questions, beyond doubt or fear or pain.

Laughter and tears mingled in her throat, quelling any hope of rational speech. Ariane forgot the game she must play, the plans she had so carefully laid only moments before. She took a shaky step toward Rook, but he retreated as if he were the mirage she knew he could not be.

Rook! she cried from her very soul.

The door that led from the servant's hallway opened with a faint hiss. A young, uniformed maid walked into the room, her arms full of exotic hothouse flowers.

"Lady Ariane," she began. "Lord Slayton sent these—"

Ariane choked on her laughter and stopped, her hand half lifted toward Rook. But Rook was gone, the stoic and non-descript servant back in his place. He bowed perfunctorily and backed away to stand at his station beside the garden doors.

The maid hesitated, glanced aside at the footman and dipped a curtsy to Ariane. "If you please, Lady, I'll put these in water."

Ariane hardly heard her. She nodded and sank back down at the table, fighting the overwhelming need to turn and gaze at Rook. Even so, she couldn't keep an absurd grin from her face, and the maid smiled shyly back as she removed yesterday's flowers from the vase on the table and replaced them with Wynn's gift.

"A lovely day, Lady," the maid offered.

"A miraculous day," Ariane breathed. Suddenly, heedlessly she sprang to her feet and grabbed the young maid's hands. "I want you to take the afternoon off. Annike—that is your name? You'll find a bonus in your credit balance. Use it on something frivolous. Go have fun!"

Annike's eyes widened. "My lady!" She bobbed awkwardly, flushed with puzzled excitement. She tugged her hands free of Ariane's. "I—we all wish you *un bon marriage,* Lady Ariane. *Merci—Merci!"*

Ariane watched her vanish through the servant's door and followed, locking it behind the maid. She made a swift circuit of the room to make certain all other doors were closed and sealed against further interruptions, and turned to face Rook with her heart in her eyes.

He was himself again, watching her across the length of the room. "Ariane," he said softly, caressing her name. "That was a touching scene. Your lowly servants must appreciate your condescension."

His words—all but her name—were lost to Ariane's exaltation. She nearly floated to him, as if her feet were encased in antigrav shoes.

"Rook," she said hoarsely. "You're—alive. Alive." Her voice broke. "I thought you were—"

"Dead?"

He walked to meet her, graceful and feral and whole, incongruous and beloved in his servant's livery. His lips lifted in a smile.

She knew that smile. It held a cynical edge that she had seen so many times, so much a part of the man she loved. The man who had come back to her in defiance of all hope.

"Sorry to disappoint you, Lady Ariane," he said.

He made no sense. Nothing did. This would not be real

until she touched him, felt the light of Sharing burst through her mind and soul.

"Rook," she repeated. Her fingers grazed his arms, slid up to his shoulders. He was solid; no phantom, no mad dream. She trembled, and he trembled too—linked as they had been before their terrible separation. "You've come back to me. . . ."

She caught his face between her hands, loosed the hair he'd drawn back and let it fall about his shoulders, pulled his head down to hers. She kissed his mouth, his jaw, tasting his skin and her own tears. Her body throbbed with elemental need, with emotion so deep no words had ever been created to encompass it.

To be within his body, his soul—to be part of him again was her single purpose. She wrapped her arms around his waist and pressed her cheek to his chest. His heart beat fast and strong.

But she was not close enough. She reached for the fastenings of his shirt with clumsy fingers.

His hands caught her wrists and held them still. Closing her eyes, she gloried in the hot roughness of his skin on hers.

"Indiscreet, Lady Ariane," he said. "What if we should be interrupted again?"

He was absurd, beloved and absurd. Ariane flung her head back and laughed through her tears. "Is that all you can say, Rook?" she said thickly. "No one will come. You're safe, Rook. Safe. *Dieu Merci.* . . ."

Still he held her back. "No questions, *cherie?* Don't you wonder how I escaped the jaws of death?"

"It doesn't matter," she said. "You're here. *Dieu, you're here.*" She leaned into him, and he released her wrists. His hands touched her back, and his breath shuddered out across the crown of her head.

"Ariane," he whispered. "Even now you almost make me believe."

For the first time she felt the wrongness. Through the brilliant haze of her elation his bitter words on the *d'Artagnan* came back to her, as if from a forgotten nightmare: his cruel accusations, the rejection of all her protests. And she remembered the terrible image of the ship exploding before her eyes as she waited, safe, aboard the *Perséphone*.

"Mon amour," she cried softly. She caught his jaw and forced his eyes down to meet hers. In his gaze she saw at last the bitter contempt, the overwhelming pain that had followed him back from death itself.

But that time before had no meaning. Now there was a second chance. Life was everything. Life, and Rook. She had only to reach him. Once she touched him, soul to soul, mind to mind, it would all be right. . . .

Her fingers clutched his shoulders. She closed her eyes and summoned all her Kalian strength, envisioning the light that had always bridged the abyss between them.

It was like hitting a wall. Rook raised his hands and pushed her away. Staggering back, she felt the power of dark emotion within him, emotion that sucked all the light from the world.

"So fickle, my lady," he said harshly. "Only a moment ago you were in the arms of your betrothed. Or is it merely your 'hot Marchand blood,' as Slayton so aptly put it?" His eyes narrowed to slits. "It seems I taught you too well."

He would not let her in. Not yet. But the fierce strength of her love and hope were more than a match for that darkness he clung to so desperately. Not even his contemptuous words could hurt her now.

Nothing could take him away from her again—

"I apologize for the inconvenience of having reappeared at such an inopportune moment," he continued in a flat, dead voice. "I managed to avoid the torpedo your lover intended for the *d'Artagnan*. It was a simple trick to eject debris and make it appear that the ship had been destroyed—just before I maneuvered behind the sun and out of range of Slayton's scanners."

A trick. It had been a trick. Ariane wanted to laugh, but the sound came out as a croak.

"Listen to me, Rook" she pleaded, clenching her fists to keep from touching him. "You're here. That's all that matters." She gave him everything she felt with her eyes, her face, willing him to see. "I didn't want to go on—" She swallowed and began again. "I've learned so much, beloved. Enough to help us find justice. It was all I had left. But now you're here—"

"Do you wonder how I managed that, Lady Ariane?" he said, staring over her head. "It was no simple matter to make my way here, but I had a very powerful incentive." He glanced around the parlor as if he were mentally cataloging every detail. "Do you remember what we discussed before our unfortunate encounter in the Louve system?"

He wasn't listening—refused to hear her, to feel her joy and gratitude. Once again he was blinded by his drive for the terrible thing their loving had not purged from his heart.

Revenge.

"Rook," she whispered. "I love you."

He laughed soundlessly.

"I never betrayed you," she said. "I didn't know Wynn intended to fire. I told him—"

"That we'd been lovers?" Rook looked down at her, his eyes empty. "That would have been an interesting scene. Or did you simply act the helpless victim? I know how brilliantly you play your roles."

A thousand words tangled in Ariane's throat, explanations and warnings and pleas. None would come clear in her mind. Hope could not be crushed, not even by Rook's impenetrable hatred.

"You won't listen to me," she said, trembling. "Let me touch you. Please—let me touch you, and you'll feel the truth." She swallowed, acknowledging her own compulsion to hold his living body against hers. "I need to touch you."

He took a step back. "Oh, no, my lady. You are far too powerful. That much *is* truth—the inescapable taint of your Kalian blood." His head jerked up, and his nostrils flared as if to sift the air for the scent of enemies.

Kalian blood. The blood they shared in spite of the barriers he threw up between them. While his attention was distracted, Ariane marshaled the arguments that could reach him where her love had failed.

"Yes," she said. "And I've learned that everything you guessed about the fate of our people was right."

His eyes snapped back to hers.

"There *was* a plot, Rook," she said. "A plot to discredit our people, weaken them, use them for a terrible purpose." The icy facade of Rook's expression never wavered, and she forced her way past the bleakness of despair. "The ring, the ring Finch gave me—it contained a recording of her testimony from the year following the riot. She saw and heard things that prove the Kalians were innocent." She fumbled for the ring under her blouse and drew it out. "It's all here. Tonight I'll get the rest of the proof we need to go to the Elite Council and—"

"Tonight, when you meet your lover?"

She nearly wept then. He had seen her in Wynn's arms, kissing him, whispering words of seduction to the man who would be her husband.

She closed her eyes. "You—you are my only lover, Rook."

The force of his hostility washed over her like a solar flare. "I was the first," he said tonelessly. "And I did enjoy your sweet body while it was mine." She heard him move away, opened her eyes to watch him pace the room and turn back to her, fluid and dangerous. "I could take you hostage and have it again. Your Elite bridegroom might be somewhat annoyed." He cocked his head consideringly. "Or should I go directly to the Patriarch . . ."

Ariane felt her world slip from her grasp. This couldn't be happening. She wouldn't let it happen. Not again—never again.

She strode across the room, staring up into Rook's alien eyes.

"No, Rook. You won't hurt him. I know you too well." Tears burned her eyes, but she ignored them. "I've seen into your soul."

"I have no soul," he grated.

She summoned Kalian speed and reached for his hand before he could stop her, turning the palm against her lips. "Hate me, if you must. But don't destroy yourself—"

He worked his fingers free one by one. Sorrow washed over her, and with it the first stirrings of desperate anger.

"You admitted your blindness once, Rook. We've been given another chance." She raised her clenched fist. "Is this all you'll take from that chance? Is this the legacy you'll leave in memory of our people—a legacy of vengeance and death? Oh, my love."

His eyes changed, dark lashes dropping to shield them from her gaze. She thought she had reached him then. With a deeper vision she could see the light he denied, the bond between them he was afraid to acknowledge—afraid of losing all he had left of himself.

But the bond still existed. . . .

"*Our* people?" he said at last, softly mocking, shattering her hopes. "You've made your choice. I should congratulate you on your forthcoming marriage, Lady Ariane. You seem well enough satisfied in your Elite lover."

With a deep growl, he closed the space between them and jerked her into his arms. The shock of his embrace reverberated through her body. "Will he touch you as I touched you?" he whispered hoarsely.

Ariane fought to control the sensations that were spinning her into chaos. She was touching him—she could reach into his mind, make him understand, make him believe—

His mouth came down on hers violently. His tongue plunged deep into her mouth, thrusting and withdrawing. His teeth grazed her lips.

"When you're with your high-bred lover, think of me," he rasped. "Remember when I was inside you, when you were mine in body and soul." He lifted her hard against him, cupping her hips to his arousal. She grasped at his shoulders and focused desperately on the elusive Sharing that was her only remaining hope.

"Rook," she groaned, lacing her fingers in his hair, holding him to her. Coarse, knotted strands came loose in her fingers. She reached deeper, deeper into his mind with her own and drove past the wall he had set against her.

It almost worked. Rook went rigid, his entire body reacting to her invasion. "No," he snarled. He severed the fragile connection with another bruising kiss.

"He'll never truly have you, Ariane," Rook rasped as he let her stumble to the floor. "I've marked you forever." With a gesture of deliberate contempt, he drew the back of his hand across his mouth. "Enjoy your pleasures while you can."

Then he was gone. Dazed and blinded, Ariane never saw him walk away.

He was Kalian. She knew she wouldn't find him, no matter how swiftly she ran or how desperately she searched.

And she had not *reached* him. His kiss, her last chance of reopening the bond between them, had been turned into a weapon of revenge. He would hear no explanations, no words of love from the woman he had learned once again to despise.

But he was alive. That miracle remained. And there was something within her Rook's rage could not touch. Her love for him beat strong and fierce, more real than any emotion she had known in all her life. He was alive, and she would protect him even if he hated her to his last breath. Even if she must lose him forever.

Rook. My love. . . .

Ariane found her way out to the garden and stood in a shaft of velvet sunshine, gathering her shattered thoughts. Rook was bent on revenge, and he must be stopped—for his sake, and for the sake of her Family.

He wouldn't hurt an old man, she thought. She would have sworn it on her soul. But there was enough Marchand in her to refuse the risk. And if Rook got to the Patriarch, the Marchand Guard would kill him without hesitation.

No. You'll live, Rook. You will be free.

Though it sickened her, she knew one thing had not changed. She had to go through with her plans to obtain the proof she needed—proof of the treachery that had destroyed an entire race.

And she had to warn the Patriarch to be ready if Rook came for him.

Forgive me, beloved.

Ariane walked slowly from the garden and through the parlor, her mind composing the message she would send her great-grandfather.

But her Kalian heart was with Rook, and it wasn't defeated yet.

He wandered what had once been the Warren, a casteless beggar invisible to Espérancian eyes.

They walked past him, these ambitious Laborers who had begun to reclaim the abandoned quarter, never knowing what he was. He never stayed long enough in one place to attract the attention of the bored gendarmes.

After so many years the lure of inexpensive real estate had worn away the taint of the former Kalian presence. Rook crouched in the shadows and watched machines constructing new dwellings over the bones and ashes of his people.

"Our people," Ariane had said. He struggled to summon the hatred that had sustained him through that terrible reunion and felt nothing at all. She had flayed him with a touch, with soft words designed to bend him from his purpose.

She had very nearly succeeded.

As the day waned, Rook left the Warren behind. He altered his appearance to that of a respectable Merchant and made his way through the neat, prosperous neighborhoods that ringed the gated walls of the Haute-Ville. Another Change and stolen livery gave him entrée into the privileged realm of the Elite.

There were no special checkpoints at the gate. No one questioned his stolen identification. Ariane had not warned them against him. He had given her all the time she needed to betray him again.

I never betrayed you. She had looked into his eyes and

claimed it so fervently, so eloquently. And all the while his mind, his thoughts, had been filled with the vision of Ariane in Wynn Slayton's arms.

Rook's feet carried him back to the Marchand mansion in its elegant setting at the crest of Côte des Arbres. The other Marchand servants saw only one of their own kind, and to the Elite he didn't exist. Only as he approached the inner sanctum of the Patriarch's suites did he find it necessary to make use of Kalian stealth. Even then he slipped by Bernard Marchand's House guards with almost ridiculous ease.

The Patriarch passed within a few meters of him in the wide hallway that led to the Family quarters, oblivious to his danger. When Rook trailed him to his study, a handsome room lined with books that smelled of rich wood and alien worlds, the old man dismissed his personal guard and left himself utterly unprotected.

A hundred years ago no member of the Elite would have dared even a moment of such vulnerability. The age of assassins had ended, but if Bernard Marchand realized the last full-blooded Kalian was alive and on his trail . . .

Rook stood just outside the door, senses straining for a trap. Ariane would have warned her great-grandfather. They should have been waiting to take him. He had expected it, wanted it, anticipated the final struggle. To end it all as a true Kalian, fighting in memory of his people.

But the hall was silent, and Bernard Marchand sat with his head bent over steepled fingers. An old man who had once saved the Kalians from certain destruction, whom Rook had faced across an Espérancian courtroom. Ariane's great-grandfather. His enemy.

"You won't hurt him," Ariane had said. *"I know you too well."* She had looked up at Rook with those glorious eyes and told him he could not bring harm to someone she loved.

Again and again she had dared to meet Rook's gaze and tell him she loved him.

Rook leaned his head against the wall, trapped in a prison of his own making. In a few brief strides he could have

Bernard Marchand at his mercy, chant the Passing of his people, and follow them into infinity.

But Ariane's voice bound him still. *"Hate me, if you must. . . ."* He wanted to hate her, *had* hated her until the moment he had held her once again in his arms and met her lips with his own.

Because in that one moment, when she had almost touched his mind, he'd known they were truly bound forever: neither treachery nor time nor anything but death could ever set them free of each other.

Only death could set him free.

Let me go, Ariane. Let me return to my people at last.

He was mad enough to think he heard her answer.

CHAPTER EIGHTEEN

"*A* toast."

Wynn raised his glass to Ariane, smiling into her eyes. "A toast to our coming union."

He watched her lift her glass, savoring his arousal as her tongue darted out to flick against the rim. She had dressed with exquisite care this night: her gown shimmered with the near transparency of iridescent Nuevo Tokyo silk, her earrings and matching necklet were elegantly simple, and her hair was caught up in a deceptively elaborate coil that a single touch would free to fall about her bared shoulders.

Why had she changed her mind? Wynn had let that idle thought amuse him through the hours of the day, though her reasons hardly mattered. Even if she had, with some finely tuned Marchand instinct, sensed the faint shadow of treachery, she was helpless to affect any part of his plan.

No. Far easier to believe that she had realized how much was at stake, and how much in his debt she—and her family —truly were. She had cunning enough to bind herself to him in the way women had done since the first humans had walked on distant Earth. But she had carefully concealed her loss of virginity, apparently believing he had been deceived.

Perhaps she was simply eager to resume the forbidden pleasures initiated by her dead Kalian lover.

Ariane looked at him over the rim of her glass, dark eyes veiled. Wynn let his gaze wander boldly over her. She had almost mastered the art of seduction, this hot-blooded little wanton who had let a savage possess her elegant body. But she had yet to learn how little the Kalian's touch would matter in the end.

It would be his pleasure to show her.

Wynn crossed the space between them and whisked her

empty glass from her hand. "Can I get you anything more, *chérie?*" he asked softly. *"Nectar d'amour,* perhaps?"

The hint of a blush touched her pale skin. He would have expected such a reaction from a pure young debutante, but not from Ariane. The rare and potent aphrodisiac was one of House Slayton's specialties. But Ariane only shook her head, freeing a tendril of hair to curl against her neck.

"But I forget," he said. He slipped his hand around her waist with casual possessiveness and felt her skin twitch through the silk. "You have no need of such—props, do you, my Ariane?" Pulling her hard against him, he kneaded her buttocks with his palms. "You're as eager as I am to consummate our alliance."

He forced her to prove her sincerity then, grinding his hips into hers and kissing her without a trace of gentlemanly restraint. Her body went still and then became liquid fire in his arms. Wynn thought of the Kalian and pushed his tongue deep into her mouth. She groaned. Her fingernails pricked his shoulders like delicate claws.

Abruptly he released her, making no attempt to conceal his triumph. "I am pleased, Ariane," he said, raking his finger across her flushed cheek. "Perhaps there is something to be said for taking an experienced bride."

Her shock was sweeter than any aphrodisiac. So, her so-honorable Grand-père hadn't told her that Wynn knew of her disgrace. True aristocrat that she was, she covered her dismay quickly and gave him a cool, unapologetic smile.

"So you know," she said, stepping away. "But you still want me. We can be honest with each other."

Wynn laughed. "Always straightforward, my Ariane. Never content to follow the rules. In that we're two of a kind." He leaned against the sideboard, admiring her athletic grace in the dimmed light of his private sitting room. "I admit I am . . . curious. What was it like to be taken by a Kalian?"

If the blunt question offended her, she showed nothing of her true emotions. She arched her neck lazily.

"Do you really want a description, Wynn?" Gliding across

the carpet, she swayed very close. "Or would you rather teach me what the savage could not?"

Her husky words were so close to his own thoughts that he almost betrayed himself. Instead, he accepted the offer of her parted lips. When he let her go, her eyes were glazed with passion, hot and hungry.

His mind touched briefly on Sable, her supple Kalian body and fierce jealousies, and dismissed her completely. There was no reason he couldn't have both women for as long as he wanted them. Perhaps he would merely postpone his original plan of disposing of Ariane and replacing her with Sable. Eventually Ariane would become more trouble than she was worth, a rallying point for her broken family. But until then . . .

Ariane gasped softly as he grasped her hand and pulled her toward the bedchamber. He ached with wanting her. For too many years he had denied himself what he wanted, waiting for the moment when his plans would come at last to fruition.

With an effort he pushed aside the tempting image of Ariane bound to his bed, helpless, as he performed a thousand subtle, sexual tortures on her lovely body. That could come later, when all Marchand was his. It would be enough to brand her now in a way she would never forget.

She made no protest as he bore her back onto the scented sheets. The faint flicker of alarm in her eyes when he tore the fragile silk at her shoulder excited him almost beyond control. His teeth closed over one bared nipple; she arched and cried out.

"I'll teach you, Ariane," he grunted, forcing her gown above her hips. All Marchand lay beneath him, waiting to be ravished. "And you'll never forget the lesson—"

"Sieur Slayton."

He jerked up his head, freeing Ariane's breast. The voice was disguised, but he knew who spoke in the doorway behind him. Black rage shuddered through him.

Sable. Sable dared interrupt him now.

Ignoring Ariane, he pushed away from the bed. Sable

wore the guise of a common servant, drab and humble, but her eyes blazed with a telltale hint of copper.

"Forgive me, Sieur Slayton," Sable whispered, bending nearly double, "but there is an emergency. Security—"

Wynn fought down the desire to cross the room and back-hand Sable against the wall. The little bitch was ready for another lesson in humility.

But he knew Sable too well. She was telling the truth, whatever personal satisfaction she might have gained by inter-rupting his liaison. Flashing a look of grim promise at his mistress, Wynn turned back to Ariane.

In her disheveled state, the gown half-ripped away from her body and her hair torn free of its coiffure, she looked even more alluring. She stared at Sable blankly and glanced at Wynn, her swollen lip caught between her teeth.

"Forgive me, *chérie,*" Wynn murmured, bending to cap-ture her hand. It was trembling. "A minor interruption. I will return as soon as I can. In the meantime I'll see that you're brought refreshments." He turned her hand and licked her palm. "Patience. . . ."

He gave Sable a curt order as he left the chamber, pleased at the naked pain that flashed across her counterfeit face. Let Sable wait on her rival and learn how little worth she had except whatever Wynn chose to give her. Wynn entertained himself with thoughts of both women in his bed, pleasuring him, as he strode toward Security.

It might be only a matter of minutes before the servant returned.

Ariane tugged once at the torn bodice of her gown, kicked off her delicate, impractical sandals, and put the past hour from her mind. Luck had been with her; Wynn was gone, and the servant had been sent off for wine and delica-cies. Ariane had been careful to demand a very specific, very rare wine from the Deux-Rivières lowlands. Wynn undoubt-edly had it, stored in his vast cellars, but the servant would be well occupied tracking it down.

Stroking the seam of her gown under her arm, Ariane

released the tiny pouch that contained a single dose of a potent sleep-inducing drug. She retrieved two glasses from Wynn's private sitting room and filled them with brandy, dumping the contents of the pouch into one of them. If Wynn returned too soon, she would resort to that dangerous method of keeping him out of the way. If her luck held, she wouldn't need it.

Her fingers were shaking as she bent her head to remove one delicate crystal earring. She had seen Wynn admiring her jewelry, oblivious to its true nature. The crystal itself was the very pinnacle of Marchand's data-storage technology; she could dump the entire contents of Wynn's computer core files into it and have room to spare.

If she could break into that core. The crystal also contained a program called the Key that should permit her to bypass all cybernetic defenses, masquerading as an authorized part of the Slayton computer network.

Though the Key was an illegal device, more powerful than anything like it on Espérance, Wynn's computers were extremely well protected. She had to be on-site to use it. Here, in Wynn's inner sanctum.

The nearest terminal was only a few meters from the bed where Wynn had hoped to claim her. Ariane clenched her teeth. It had been far too close.

You were right, Rook, she thought grimly. *I should have been on the stage.* But she put her fears for Rook and the Patriarch from her mind, settling at the terminal to begin the process of breaching Wynn's most closely held secrets.

Ariane pressed the crystal into the depression below the screen. Her fingers flew over the keyboard, releasing the Key into the system. She waited, holding her breath, as the program slipped by the first security barriers. By the third barrier the screen's standby pattern wavered; it seemed the Key might not be powerful enough to overcome Wynn's defenses. Ariane sighed as the last gate opened and the danger passed. No alarms sounded to bring Wynn running back.

Ariane allowed herself a moment of profound relief as the screen flashed the symbols that indicated the Key had done its work. She was in. One by one she entered the code words of her carefully devised retrieval program, drawing every bit of data about the Kalians from Wynn's files. Within seconds the program had dumped the information into the crystal, and she knew she had everything she'd come to find.

But it wasn't enough. Ariane lingered, staring at the screen. She had to know now if Finch had been right, before Wynn returned and she looked into his triumphant eyes.

She began a second search, focusing on a single query. The scrolling list that appeared on the screen froze her blood.

Kalian names. There were hundreds there, grouped with birth and death dates. In most cases the date of death was missing. And following each name was a list of symbols, and locations—Houses of the Elite, Council offices, gendarme precincts. All the bastions of power in Lumière, including Slayton's own estate. More Kalians were here in this very mansion than anywhere else on Espérance.

Except for the vast majority of lines that listed only one location: the polar continent, an uninhabited chunk of ice-bound land far to the north no Espérancian had ever bothered to name.

Ariane snatched up the crystal and began to reassemble her earrings, eyes fixed on the screen. There was a chance she misunderstood. But taken together with Finch's revelations, the meaning seemed stunningly clear.

The Kalians were still alive. And Wynn Slayton had them in his power.

Rook, she thought, dizzy with shock. *Finch was right. You aren't alone. We aren't alone. Now we know, we know—*

A faint sound behind her rang like a siren of doom just as her hand slapped down to blank the screen. She swung around and leaped to her feet, crouched and ready. A woman stood just inside the doorway.

The face Ariane looked into was her own.

"Lady Ariane," the mirror image purred. Tossing thick brown hair, she glided into the chamber. "Do you remember me?"

Ariane's thoughts tumbled over one another, sifting and

discarding. She knew what this woman must be. Kalian—Kalian like Rook, able to shift her appearance. A ghost returned from simulated death. One of the Kalians Wynn controlled for his own unknown, sinister purposes.

Brown Marchand eyes narrowed on the terminal behind Ariane. "How thoughtless of me to interrupt you a second time," the Kalian woman said. "But I think Wynn will be pleased." The pseudo-Ariane's face shifted, flowing into the guise of the servant Ariane had sent away earlier, settling at last into familiar lines.

Eight years vanished in an instant as Ariane recognized the Kalian woman. Sable. The Hawk rebel Rook had argued so bitterly with during the riots, who had vanished after Jacques's death. Who now reappeared in Wynn's mansion, symbol of a conspiracy Ariane had only begun to uncover.

"Surprised, Lady Ariane?" Sable said mockingly. "No—I'd advise you to stay where you are. I am Kalian, and you're only human. Wynn would be displeased if I—hurt you before he has had a chance to question you."

Ariane shifted her weight on the balls of her feet and cursed the confining gown she wore. Sable was Kalian, but she was unable to sense that Ariane was one of her own blood. Sable's open hatred, undimmed after so long, blinded her just as Rook's had done.

"Don't think that Wynn will overlook your spying, Marchand," Sable continued, moving around the bed. "He only wanted you while it was convenient. Now you're far too much of a liability."

Fragments of fact and supposition began to come together in Ariane's mind. "Why?" she asked. "Why did you ally yourself with Wynn, let everyone believe all the Kalians were dead?" She edged away from the terminal, giving herself more room to move. "What did he do to you, Sable?"

"Do to me?" Sable laughed. "He saved me from the fate of my slaughtered people. He gave me my life."

She didn't know the truth. Ariane could see it in her eyes. Wynn had deceived her, just as he'd deceived the Marchand, Espérance, and the entire League.

The full extent of Wynn's treachery had yet to be revealed.

"In exchange for what, Sable?" Ariane said, measuring the distance between them. "What has he promised you? What did he offer in return for your loyalty?"

"Revenge." Sable bared her teeth. "What else?"

"Against—who? My family?"

"The murderers of my people," Sable snarled.

"Even though Wynn was the one who engineered the riots from the very beginning?" Ariane said quickly. "The man who arranged to intercept the refugee ship headed for Agora?"

Sable never even blinked. "You lie, Marchand bitch. You wanted our deaths. Wynn tried to help us—"

"No. It was Wynn who wanted your people—alive, to use as his agents." Ariane readied herself for attack. "And you are only one of them. Why, Sable? What are his plans? Why would he promise you revenge against the Marchand?"

Ariane never expected answers. Finch had been right—whatever means Wynn had used to bind the Kalians to his will was extremely effective. There was madness in Sable's copper eyes, incomprehension of the logical questions Ariane asked. Sable recognized no truth except the one Wynn had given her. But Ariane saw that her rapid words were confusing the Kalian, and she needed that tiny edge.

"How many others are there, Sable? How many under Wynn's control?"

"Control?" For an instant Sable sounded lost, her expression contorting. "There is no—"

Drawing on every Kalian reflex, Ariane jumped. Sable recognized her intent an instant too late. Ariane's momentum carried Sable to the floor as her hand grasped at Sable's sleeve, slid down to circle the Kalian woman's wrist.

In a burst of light their minds touched. It was the Sharing, unmistakable but entirely different from what Ariane had felt with Rook. Ariane reeled at the unexpected assault of a foreign mind, a jumble of violent thoughts and colors and emotions, laced throughout with something terribly wrong, alien, evil. . . .

"*No!*"

The deep-throated protest seemed to come from within Ariane's mind, severing her contact with Sable just as the other woman wrenched free. Scrambling up, Ariane's eyes fixed on the figure at the other end of the room.

"Rook!" she cried. She watched the final moments of his transformation from nondescript servant in Slayton livery to Kalian warrior, her heart suspended between joy and fear. He looked at her only for an instant before his wild eyes fixed on Sable.

"Sable," he whispered hoarsely. "Impossible—"

The two copper-eyed Kalians froze into a perfect tableau, like a scene out of an old-Earth melodrama. Sable's mouth worked silently. Ariane gave herself no time to think. She hurled herself at Sable again, countering the Kalian woman's ferocious strength. As Rook broke his paralysis and moved toward them, Ariane caught sight of the shadow that appeared in the doorway and leveled a small, deadly weapon at Rook—

Ariane's cry of warning came just in time. Rook spun and ducked as the 'ruptor beam sliced over his head. Sable twisted violently in Ariane's hold and slammed her fist into her stomach. Gasping for air, Ariane staggered back as Sable leaped the bed to join the guard in the doorway.

"Take her!" Sable screamed, pointing at Ariane. The Slayton guard, his face devoid of emotion, swung his 'ruptor toward Ariane.

The weapon went flying from his hand. Rook had the guard pinned against the wall and helpless before Ariane caught her breath. Sable went at Rook with fingers curled into claws, raking at his stunned face.

But Sable's savagery was no match for Ariane's desperation. With a soundless roar she rolled across the rumpled bed and slammed into Sable's back. It was like trying to hold fire, but she caught Sable in a wrestler's hold as they careened to the floor.

This time there was no lessening the impact of Sable's mind on her own. Ariane felt an almost physical jolt when

Sable recognized Ariane's Kalian nature. Sable struggled to pull her mind free as she fought with her body.

But the Sharing between them had gone beyond anything either could control. Helpless to prevent it, Ariane felt her thoughts become inextricably tangled with Sable's, her memories locked with the Kalian woman's, a flood of knowledge that could not be stemmed pouring through the unwanted link. For a few blinding moments their minds became one—Ariane was Sable, Sable Ariane. And Sable/Ariane felt the alien thing within their minds, a disease, an evil presence that must be driven out. . . .

With a jolt Ariane found herself free, her mind still touching Sable's but separate once again. The wrongness in Sable's brain was burned into Ariane's own by Kalian senses that knew without seeing, understood without words.

This was the center of Wynn's control, this chemical sickness that altered Sable's cells and warped her very thoughts.

Instinct guided Ariane where logic could not. The need to Heal overcame every other demand. Her very being lashed out at the wrongness in the mind touching her own. As she had done with Rook when he had hovered so near death, Ariane reached deep into Sable's body with powers of Healing she could not begin to comprehend, searching out and excising the alien chemicals that held Sable in thrall.

A third presence joined them, a warm, vital strength that flowed into her when she began to falter. Strong arms supported her body. Ariane felt the wrongness in Sable recede and vanish. Her outward senses returned in a rush, awareness of Rook's firm grip on her shoulder and Sable's shudders under her hands.

And then Sable's copper eyes were staring into her own, blank with horror.

"Shapers," she gasped. "I'm free—"

Rook rested his hand on Sable's forehead. His fingers trembled. "Free," he echoed. "Here." He stared at Ariane, inarticulate with shock. "Why? How?"

Ariane would have given the world to answer Rook's questions then, tell him everything, explain the unbelievable facts and terrible misunderstandings that had driven them apart. But there was no time, and he was here, for whatever reason—with her, the contempt and hatred gone from his face.

He had not gone after the Patriarch. He had come after her instead. . . .

She reached automatically for the necklet she had worn, an expensive bauble that held a miniature commlink in one segment. It was gone; she remembered Sable clawing at her throat. Her gaze raked across the room and caught on a glimmer of gold.

The necklet was broken, the delicate commlink smashed in the struggle. There would be no reaching the Patriarch that way now.

"No time," she said aloud. She swallowed, staring fiercely into Rook's eyes. "We have to get to my great-grandfather— for *our* people. You have to trust me, Rook."

She would not beg for his trust. Not as she had begged him to listen before. She had pushed the pain aside where it couldn't hamper what she had come to do. The rest was in Rook's hands. She watched his face—scarred, grim, beloved —and concealed every trace of hope.

He didn't know what she had learned from Finch and in Wynn's private chambers, why she had gone to Wynn in the guise of seductress. The shock of seeing Sable, of witnessing the Kalian woman's bizarre behavior, had given him proof enough of the danger Ariane was in. His own peril had always been obvious.

Distant shouts cut off any answer he intended to give. Rook scrambled into a crouch beside the unconscious guard, shoving the guard's disruptor into the waistband of his trousers.

"He must have transmitted an alarm," Rook muttered.

"They'll kill you." Sable struggled into a sitting position, glancing swiftly from Ariane to Rook. "Betrayed—all lies—" She shook her head. "I'm no longer your enemy. Go. Go now."

Torn by indecision, Ariane knew she had no choice but to

trust Sable as she'd asked Rook to trust her. Her brief link with Sable had made her understand why the Kalian woman had hated the Marchand with such intensity. But she knew Sable was free of whatever had kept her under Wynn's spell. The devastating knowledge was in Sable's eyes as it had been in her mind.

Every unsettled emotion Ariane felt was mirrored in Rook's face. He touched the Slayton guard with strange gentleness. "Heron," he whispered.

Ariane joined him, staring down at the man's still form. He had *Changed*, and his face was a Kalian's.

"I saw him die," Rook said. "In the Warren eight years ago. I thought he was dead—"

The voices in the hallway grew louder. Rook sprang up. He ran to the doorway and pressed himself against the wall, muscles tensed and ready.

Before she could follow him, the guard stirred at her feet. His eyes fluttered open and focused on her face.

"You. Kalian," he mumbled.

She realized with a start that this man, unlike Sable, had recognized her Kalian blood without touching her—just as Finch had recognized the disguised Kalians under Wynn's control eight years ago, and had known Rook for what he was on Agora.

Heron was still under Wynn's control—unless she could enter his mind. She laid her palm gently on his wrist.

The counterfeit guard's pulse jumped under Ariane's fingers.

"Enemy—" he rasped, lunging up at her violently.

Whatever else he might have said was lost as Rook gripped Ariane's arm and jerked her away. Rook set Ariane behind him, standing over the Kalian guard with clenched fists. "Forgive me," Rook murmured. In a blindingly swift move he struck Heron a calculated blow, and the Kalian lapsed back into unconsciousness.

Another strong hand grasped Ariane's arm. "If you don't leave now," Sable said, her voice a low thrum of fury, "it will all be for nothing. There's a hidden exit some long-dead

Slayton Patriarch had built into these suites that Wynn never bothered to hide from me." Sable led them away from the bed and into a small antechamber, moving unerringly to one of the walls. Her palm swept over the wall a few centimeters from its surface, and a panel slid open near the floor.

Sable stepped back. "The passageway leads into the servant's quarters." Muffled footfalls drummed on carpet, very close. She shot Rook a wild look. "Get out of here! I'll delay the guards."

"Sable—" Rook began.

"Do you care nothing for your precious Marchand?" the Kalian woman snarled. "Run!"

Rook's gaze caught Ariane's and held, piercing to her very heart. As if they had never been apart, as if they were joined beyond any sundering, they turned as one toward the promise of escape. Ariane plunged into the narrow passageway on hands and knees, Rook just behind. Stifling darkness closed around them as Sable sealed the panel. Ariane struggled with blinding panic, her old fear of confinement; she felt her muscles locking, refusing to carry her farther.

But Rook was there. His hand brushed her back; she moved forward again, and suddenly there was a faint glow suffusing the passage before them, lighting the way.

Ariane breathed silent thanks to the Slayton who'd combined paranoia with common sense. The rest of the journey was tense and uncomfortable, but Ariane's mind was already on the obstacles ahead. The chances they'd beat Wynn's forces to the garage where her private runabout was parked were not good. If they had to cross the Haute-Ville on foot . . .

"Ariane," Rook whispered sharply. She blinked at the glowing square drawn on the wall that ended the passage only a few meters away.

The exit. If Sable had been right, they'd be in the servant's quarters, below the main levels. If Sable had kept her word, Wynn's guards wouldn't be waiting for them.

Ariane reached for the square, brushing it with her fingers.

Immediately it grew transparent, offering a clear view of the storage room into which the passage opened.

Empty. No one to see them at this early hour of the morning; the night staff would be on duty on the higher levels.

Rook shouldered up beside her. "I'll go first," he said. In the faint light his features were unreadable, but Ariane felt a flare of indignant rage. Without a word she touched the square again, and a panel opened into the storage room close to the floor. She crawled headfirst into the room. Rook followed, jaw set with familiar grimness.

They had exchanged little more than looks since that painful parting at the Marchand mansion, and nothing had been resolved. The tension between them sang in the air, raising the fine hairs at the base of Ariane's neck. The copper blaze of Rook's eyes told her that his anger, his bitter mistrust of her, had not abated.

She scanned the room quickly as Rook sealed the passageway behind them. Neat stacks of linen and cleaning supplies filled the shelves; several black unisex servant's smocks hung on one wall. Rook snatched two of them from their hooks and tossed one to Ariane.

"We'll have to Change," he said, jerking the smock over his head.

Even though he put no inflection on the word, Ariane knew what he meant. If they were to have any chance of getting out of there, they'd have to use every Kalian advantage they possessed. And that included taking on another form, another identity. . . .

"I've never done it," she whispered, crumpling the smock in her fists. "I don't know how—"

His hands closed on her shoulders; the brief and involuntary Sharing that passed between them made her sway.

"But you can do things only the most powerful Elders could do," he said roughly, shaking her. "You can Heal. I felt you in Sable's mind. You Shared with her."

His words were almost an accusation, and his expression was savage. Ariane kept her voice perfectly calm.

"She was under Wynn's control. Like Heron and all the others—"

He cut her off. "Listen to me. I'm going to show you how to Change. In your mind."

Through the Sharing. Ariane stiffened. When they had Shared before, there had been profound emotion and word-less knowledge, but nothing so explicit. Yet at the Marchand mansion she had desperately wanted to reach him that way, the only way that could not be corrupted by deception and mistrust.

Now he offered it to her. What he gave would alter the last human distinction Ariane had clung to: the Marchand appearance she had lived with all her life. The features that had protected her, marked her as the Patriarch's great-grand-daughter and Elite, one of the ruling class of Lumière.

She had feared this moment from the time she'd looked in a mirror aboard the *d'Artagnan* and seen a trace of copper in her own eyes.

Lifting her gaze to Rook's, she gave him the full measure of her Marchand pride. "All right," she said. "Do it."

His hesitation was almost imperceptible. Raising his hands to her face, he cupped her jaw with loverlike tenderness. She opened her mind to his, guided by the memory of what they had Shared before their parting.

And then he was with her, inside her, pouring images into her mind. She tried to catch the simmer of emotion impris-oned behind the thoughts he conveyed, but he eluded her. He would not let her into his own mind—he gave only what he had promised, and nothing more, until he released her.

Amid the dizzying echo of his thoughts she found what she needed to know. The fear was gone.

"Now," Rook said softly. His eyes had grown strange, almost gentle, as he dropped his hands from her body. He gave her a pattern to follow, Changing himself into the guise of a servant. Reaching within her own mind, Ariane turned her Healing skills to the job of altering her own cells—envi-sioning the face she would wear, making the image real.

A deep and certain instinct told her when it was finished.

Rook confirmed it, gazing at her with something very like pride in his eyes before he turned away.

"You know this place better than I do," he said as she pulled the smock over her head and removed her earrings, dropping them into one capacious pocket. "Can you get us out of here?"

"Yes." She drew a mental map of the servant's level; one mansion would be much like another in that respect. "There will be a servant's entrance in the back, near the supply docks. It's too early for anyone to be there now, unless Wynn's guards get to it first."

"Then we'll run." Rook flashed her a grin—reckless and fierce—and grabbed her hand. It was like Agora or the Louve system all over again, when they had changed from enemies to allies. Unexpected joy pumped new energy into Ariane's body; she pulled Rook to the doorway and paused only an instant before leading him into the hall at a sprint.

As she had predicted, there were no servants abroad at that hour. The halls were featureless, punctuated with unmarked doors leading to quarters or storage rooms or other parts of the mansion, but Ariane had lived among the Elite and their servants all her life. They paused at each junction, straining Kalian senses; the place might have been deserted. And when they reached the servant's entrance, it was unguarded.

Rook set himself in front of Ariane, scanning the empty supply docks and deserted lane. The dark silhouettes of trees in Wynn's terraced garden rose above a high grillwork fence; the only sound was the hum of night insects. Ariane imagined the Kalians on their lost world, fighting every day for survival, existing in an ecosystem that rewarded carelessness with death. She could have been one of them.

Perhaps this was her final initiation.

"We have to find a comm terminal," she said, catching her breath. "Some way to reach the Patriarch, to warn him."

Rook's eyes caught a sliver of dim light and reflected it back in red. "Didn't you warn him before, Ariane?" he said softly.

Against *him*, he meant. He didn't know the very specific

things she had said to the Patriarch when she had alerted him to Rook's supposed intentions.

"It's gone beyond that now," she snapped. "If you can't trust me—"

"I heard what you said to Sable, before you Healed her," Rook interrupted. "I was there when you were in her mind."

The explanation was brief, but it was sufficient. Whether or not he believed what Ariane had told Sable, he knew the answers lay with her. Whatever he felt for her—feelings he kept so carefully locked away, even from her mental touch—would not interfere with this new and fragile alliance between them.

For now, it would have to be enough.

Their eyes locked once more, and by one accord they fled into the night.

Wynn controlled his fury, but his remaining guardsmen—Kalian and non-Kalian alike—cringed and would not meet his gaze.

Only the Kalian guard once known as Heron, swaying on his feet, dared to face his master.

"She was Kalian," he said hoarsely. He had repeated that incredible statement several times, but Wynn was only just beginning to absorb the significance of it.

Rook Galloway wasn't dead. He had survived to make his way back to Espérance. Worse, he had come here—broken Wynn's careful security and penetrated his private chambers. At the very moment Ariane Burke-Marchand, Wynn's bride-to-be, had been breaking into his personal files.

And Ariane was Kalian.

It never occurred to Wynn to doubt Heron's words. He had a small cadre of Kalians, Heron among them, who had the skill of being able to identify other Kalians from a distance, even those who were Changed. Until now that skill had been of little use.

But Heron, who had come to Wynn's chambers at the

bidding of some Kalian instinct, had recognized Ariane—heir of the pure Marchand line—for what she was.

He shook his head, frowning so darkly that several of his guardsmen stiffened to rigid alert. The new revelations had come almost too suddenly to be absorbed. And he must absorb them quickly, turn them to his own use, or everything he had worked for would be obliterated by a changeling Kalian bitch and her renegade lover.

Wynn strode to his computer and regarded it with self-imposed calm. The moment he'd checked it he'd known Ariane had found everything; all the security systems had been breached. The pertinent data had been downloaded. How she had come to suspect him remained a mystery. Why she had chosen to betray him was now crystal clear.

Ariane—a Kalian. Bernard must know.

Slow blackmail of Bernard Marchand would have been Wynn's method of choice, if he'd learned of Ariane's heritage before she'd uncovered his secrets. That was no longer an option.

His most trusted men were already out searching for Ariane and her lover; he knew his non-Kalians would have little hope of finding them. The prey were swifter and stronger and more cunning than ordinary humans. And he could not discount the possibility that both had Changed. . . .

Abruptly he turned to Heron, who was staring blankly at nothing.

"Where is Sable?"

"Here."

She glided into the room, radiating heat and energy, her copper eyes alight. Alone among his Kalians, she did not cringe from his hard gaze.

"After I called you, I sent the first guards who responded to the alarm after them," she said, coming to stand beside him. "They lost them." Her lip curled, and she nodded at Heron. "He'll tell you that the Marchand bitch and the renegade were working together. She sent me away for wine, and I obeyed her, as you ordered me to. When I returned, she was at your private terminal."

Wynn had pieced most of it together from Heron's broken explanations. "But the two of you couldn't stop them," he said softly, watching her face.

"*I* didn't know she was Kalian," Sable said, the hint of a whine in her voice. She glared at Heron. "*He* knew, and he let the renegade disarm him—"

"Silence."

Sable dropped her eyes. Wynn dismissed the non-Kalian guards and told them to await his orders outside. The Kalians that remained—three Changed men in Slayton uniforms—were still as automatons.

Moving to his terminal, Wynn transmitted a series of commands to Slayton agents posted in various parts of the city and in the Gendarmerie. He'd already sent another contingent of men to watch the gates to the Marchand mansion. He had to make sure Ariane couldn't reach her great-grandfather by any means. He must have time to alter his plans and set them in motion.

But if he were too blatant, he'd give himself away before he was ready. He couldn't risk alerting the Haute-Ville or those gendarmes he had been unable to buy or blackmail. As it was, he'd have no chance to reach his offworld contacts, the inside men poised to create chaos in Marchand's interstellar empire, unless he could gain another week. Soon he would activate his Kalian operatives hidden within the great Houses, but not yet. Not until Ariane Marchand was safely neutralized.

"They're on foot," Sable offered quietly, as if she'd read his thoughts. "I made sure they couldn't get to the Marchand woman's runabout."

On foot. The Slayton and Marchand estates were on opposite ends of the Haute-Ville, several kilometers apart. There were virtually no public communication terminals in all the district; within the next few minutes he'd have men posted at every House between. And Kalian hounds to hunt down his enemies.

"Matthews," he said.

The Kalian guard came to stand just behind him.

"Summon any Kalians who can identify **Marchand** and the renegade as you did and have them assemble here immediately."

Matthews was gone before Wynn turned around. He looked at Sable and felt a surge of arousal. The adrenaline pumping through his body demanded an immediate outlet; for an instant he was sorely tempted to throw Sable down on the carpet and take her there, expending his rage and frustration between her parted thighs.

Cold intellect prevailed. Later he would indulge himself. Sable would serve a far more essential purpose; after this was over, she would take Ariane Marchand's place long enough to deceive her great-grandfather and the rest of the Elite. She would play the part well enough for the short time he'd need to set Marchand's downfall into inevitable motion.

The first reports began to come in on his private comm, hesitant admissions of failure. So far Ariane and Galloway had managed to evade their human pursuers. Wynn clenched his fists and envisioned the punishment he'd inflict on these incompetents. When he was in power—

"Sieur Slayton."

He turned to face Heron Matthews, who stood ready with four other Changed Kalians, three men and a woman, all but one in neutral servant's dress.

"Excellent," Wynn breathed. "Listen carefully. You are to use any means, any resource at my command, to track down and stop the Kalian woman who calls herself Ariane Marchand and the convict known as Rook Galloway. They may be wearing other forms. You will have unrestricted license to command my forces wherever you find them." He smiled coldly. "If you succeed, your rations of Euphorie will be doubled. If not—"

He had no need to complete the threat. His Kalians knew, though they revealed nothing in their altered faces.

"Terminate Galloway and dispose of his body," Wynn continued. "Stop Ariane Marchand at all costs. She must not reach any comm terminal, any estate, any person who can help her. Bring her here to me if at all possible. But if not—"

Something made him glance at Sable, who watched him with a strange and intense fascination. He reached out to stroke her cheek.

"If not," he said softly, "kill her."

CHAPTER NINETEEN

"*H*e knew," Ariane gasped.

She didn't show a trace of fear, even when capture had come so close. It was breathlessness that made her words tremble as she leaned against Rook in the darkness.

He closed his eyes and breathed in the scent of her, himself trembling for a thousand reasons. The gendarme who had approached them so casually a few minutes ago had seemed unaware of anything amiss. Even at this hour occasional servants could be seen crossing the great square on the Hill, on errands for their Elite masters or returning from off-time visits to the Low Town.

Until the gendarme had spotted them walking toward the gates of the Lambert estate, Rook and Ariane had managed to avoid the pursuit Wynn Slayton had sent out after them. In spite of their training, Wynn's human troops had been easy enough for two Kalians to evade. What he and Ariane did now was little different from Rook's childhood in the Warren—existing among shadows, slipping past the Fringe into the Espérancian quarters for clandestine excursions after curfew on a bet or a dare.

But the penalty for capture then hadn't been fatal. When the gendarme had called out to them, apparently bored with his shift, Ariane had behaved exactly as a servant should and waited passively for the man's approach. "If we run, we'll give ourselves away," she'd whispered. Rook's instincts had screamed fight or flight, but he had done as she asked.

At first it had seemed that Ariane was right. The gendarme saw them as nondescript servants in cleaning smocks, muttering dull but plausible answers to his indifferent questions.

Until the gendarme had dismissed them and they'd turned

to go. Rook had been ready when the gendarme pulled his 'ruptor. He'd whirled and downed the man in one move, acting without thought or emotion.

And had known at a touch that the gendarme was Kalian. Changed, like Heron.

"He knew," Ariane repeated, looking up at Rook. She winced as the sharp branches of the shrubs in which they hid scraped her skin. "He was Kalian, and he recognized us the moment he saw us."

Rook looked out through the heavy foliage at the tree-lined street. "Yes," he said tonelessly.

"I'm a fool," Ariane whispered harshly. "The man you called Heron—*he* knew I was Kalian, before I touched him. The same way Finch knew you were Kalian, on Agora when she saw you with me in the Concourse."

He closed his eyes, remembering. Finch, who had always known Ariane for what she was. Sable, Heron, the unknown Gendarme: Kalians under Espérancian control. Alive but warped almost beyond recognition.

"You and I, we don't have that ability," Ariane said. Her voice was a center of rationality amid chaos. "I didn't know Heron was Kalian until I touched him. I didn't have time to —" She swallowed audibly. "He must have told Wynn what I was, and about you. If Wynn has other Kalians like Heron or that gendarme, they'll be able to find us before—"

Something snapped in Rook—helpless rage he had kept too long in check. He grabbed Ariane's arm and dragged her against him brutally, seeing Heron's face, hearing Heron's voice: *"Enemy—"*

"Should I have killed him?" he rasped, shaking her. "Should I have silenced him, and the gendarme, because they would betray their own people?"

Ariane's gaze locked on his. Her dark eyes swallowed him, heart and soul.

"Heron was never the traitor," she answered softly. "You were there when I Healed Sable. They can't fight what Wynn has done to them."

Abruptly Rook let her go, folding in on himself. Wynn.

Wynn Slayton had been behind it from the beginning. The Marchand had been part of it, but perhaps the evil had all been Slayton's.

Perhaps Ariane was, in every way, innocent. . . .

Her touch slid over his back, sending racking shivers through his body. He remembered how Wynn had touched her in the garden—Ariane's torn gown when he'd found her in Wynn's chambers. He had never hated more than he hated in this moment.

"Slayton," he growled from deep in his belly.

"There's so much—" Ariane began. "So much to tell, but I can't explain now," she said. "We have to reach the Marchand mansion. I'd hoped, if we could get onto the Lambert grounds—" Her fingers grasped a handful of Rook's smock. "We can't risk it. We can't risk approaching anyone. We don't know how many agents Wynn has all over the Haute-Ville. Our only chance is to get to House Marchand and—" Her breath warmed his skin through the smock. "And hope."

Hope. Rook straightened, and Ariane withdrew her hand as if she expected him to push her away.

A thousand things had yet to be resolved between them. Under the powerful influence of her emotion Ariane's features Changed, shifted back into their proper planes. Rook looked at the tangled hair loose about her shoulders, the firm stubbornness of her jaw, the calm challenge in her eyes.

If he could have done it—in spite of everything, if he could have done it—he'd spirit her away from this world and abandon his own people. He would sell his soul for Ariane Marchand.

But she would not demand it of him. She offered her hand and he took it, nearly crushing it before he remembered himself. They rose as one, scenting the air for the hunters. Now they would run from their own kind.

The final kilometer that lay between them and the Marchand estates might have been the distance from Espérance to old Earth. Again and again they dodged shadowed watchers, men and women who waited on every street, by every gate, in every place of refuge. Some must have been Kalians; twice they knew themselves pursued by hunters almost as swift as they.

Ariane knew the way, but it was Rook who set their path, calling on the Kalian gifts he'd had a lifetime to develop. Ariane was beside him, unquestioning, a brilliant presence that made Rook's blood sing and his senses razor-sharp. Free; he and Ariane were free, and while they remained together, the hope she spoke of survived.

But when they reached the great park that bordered the Marchand estates, they found a gendarme patrol skimmer waiting across the boulevard.

"Too late," Ariane whispered, no surprise in her voice. She crouched beside the wall of the small townhouse opposite the mansion and breathed deeply. "We won't get in that way."

Rook settled beside her, shielding her with his body like a shadowcat with its mate. He scanned the patterns of dark and light cast by the widely spaced lamps along the street. What his eyes couldn't see his other Kalian senses revealed: more watchers, ranged all along the estate's high walls.

"Too many," Ariane murmured, echoing his thoughts. "There is another way. The servant's entrance, on the other side."

"Which they'll be watching," Rook said harshly.

"Yes." She shifted, glancing up at the sky "It must be near four in the morning. In about an hour the Chef's staff will be going into Low Town for the daily market. There's a chance that if we intercept them, take their places when they return—"

"Slayton's Kalian slaves"—Rook nearly choked on the words—"can identify us no matter what form we take."

"But Wynn's men can't be open about what they're doing, either. By six, servants will be moving around the estate, potential witnesses to anything Wynn attempts." She looked into his eyes. "It's the best chance we have, unless we walk straight up to the gates now and call their bluff."

For a moment he imagined it, Ariane striding boldly

across the boulevard, throwing her life away on a gamble that Wynn's men wouldn't kill her openly so close to sanctuary. But he had heard Sable's harsh warnings, knew in his gut that Wynn Slayton, a man who could coldly enslave a race, would never allow Ariane to defy him and live.

"No," he said softly. If Ariane's unlikely plan failed, there would be yet another way. Ariane had to get inside, to the protection of her great-grandfather. But Rook had no need to go with her. He could draw their enemy's fire, lead them away just long enough for Ariane to reach safety.

"Then all we have to do for the next two hours is keep Wynn's men from finding us," Ariane murmured. Her eyes shifted to the park with its dark masses of native foliage, bordered in the distance by Lumière's richest and most powerful estates. "The park. I know it like the back of my hand. Jacques and I played in it as children." A sad smile touched her mouth. "I think I know a place where they won't look."

She led Rook away, backtracking the way they had come, retreating until they found a place where the boulevard narrowed and the park extended a strip of vegetation almost to the gates of the adjoining townhouses. The park welcomed them with its silent darkness, unlit save for a single meandering path.

Rook had learned to survive in the jungles of Tantalus, the closest he had ever come to the savage nature of the world on which his people had been touched by the Shapers. This park was Espérancian wilderness tamed to human use, yet it called to Rook in an ancient and unmistakable voice. Ariane felt it as well. Her eyes glowed copper when distant light touched them; her breath hissed in a soft, primitive melody. The two Kalians ran lightly amid the undergrowth, unhindered and unpursued.

The place Ariane took him was in the center of the park. There were clusters of boulders arranged to form a maze; on every side were enormous trees that might have been part of an ancient forest before the coming of man.

Ariane smiled at him oddly when she paused at the trunk of one giant. "Follow me," she said. Her nimble fingers found holds on the rough bark; strong legs pushed her up until she stood among the lowest branches. And then Rook saw the remnants of something man-made among the leaves.

"We built a tree house here, Jacques and I," Ariane said softly. She perched on a broad limb, perfectly at ease, her hands touching an old, peeling board still attached to the ridged bark with an ancient nail. Others like it created the broken outline of a platform, walls, portions of a roof. "We were always exploring. I guess it was the Kalian in us."

Rook found nothing to say. While Ariane had played there, secure in her name, unaware of her heritage, Rook and his people had struggled to survive in a cold prison of gray walls and despair. Only the stars had promised freedom.

He looked up at the pattern of sky and leaves far above his head. The stars were still visible. The past could never be regained: Ariane's innocence, his own, the life of her brother and the Kalians who had been sacrificed for some Elite game of power he had no hope of understanding.

But the future remained.

"We can see almost the whole park from here," Ariane said. Suddenly she shivered, wrapping her arms about herself. "If they come, we'll be ready."

Rook saw the memories flash in her eyes, mirroring his own. They had waited like this on the unnamed planet in the Louve system, enemies allied against a greater threat. In that crucible everything had changed. They had become lovers, inextricably bound. Rook had dared to believe there might be wholeness, healing, justice, the possibility of love. Until Ariane had betrayed him—

"I didn't betray you, Rook."

He did not meet her eyes, but his hands clutched a heavy branch and nearly snapped it in two. How many times had she made that claim? On the *d'Artagnan* before he had sent her back to her treacherous Elite betrothed—in the Marchand mansion, when Rook had been blinded by rage at the sight of Ariane in Wynn Slayton's arms. And again in Slayton's chambers, when Rook had touched her mind and Sable's in the Sharing.

"I don't know how that tracer got onto the *d'Artagnan,*" she continued stubbornly in the wake of his silence. "But everything else has become very, very clear."

"Slayton," Rook whispered. The thickness in his throat made it impossible to say more, to offer a single word of reassurance.

"Yes." She shifted her balance and unsealed the pocket of her smock. "Wynn Slayton. He was behind all of it, Rook. And now I have all the proof I need." She held something small and pale between her fingers. "All here, everything he planned, everything he did to our people."

Rook hardly heard her. Behind his closed lids he could see Slayton fondling Ariane, watched her ardent response.

"That was why I went to him, Rook. Why I had to get into his private chambers, and into his computer. Once I suspected—"

"I wanted to kill him," Rook snarled. His heart slammed against his ribs with the need to release his grief and confusion and rage. "When he touched you—"

Ariane moved, and he never saw her coming. Her breath gusted against his cheek.

"Because you believed I enjoyed it? Or because you couldn't bring yourself to kill *me?*"

He made an inarticulate sound. Even now he wanted her.

"You wouldn't listen to me then. Damn you, I thought you were dead. You didn't give me time—" She gritted her teeth. "Do you think I had anything else to live for but to find the truth?"

Anything to live for. After Ariane's supposed betrayal, he'd thought the only thing left to live for was revenge, and he'd been wrong. Wrong about everything.

"Or do you still believe I wanted Wynn to kill you?" she demanded.

Rook opened his eyes. Her face was a pale blur. Self-contempt and the need to protect his battered heart fought for dominance. He wanted to drive her away, he wanted to take her mouth and possess her body and join her soul to his. . . .

"I followed you," he said, ignoring her question. "I came after you tonight, but not until I'd found your Patriarch."

She froze.

"I got into your estates just as easily as I got into Slayton's. I was within arm's reach of Bernard Marchand. But there were no guards waiting for me, Ariane."

Dark lashes shielded her eyes. "They were there," she said calmly. "I couldn't risk that you might—" She broke off, but her quiet words ripped into his gut. "I couldn't let you be hurt. I explained it to the Patriarch, and he saw to it that if you came after him, you'd be—detained."

So the old man had known. Rook remembered the lined, weary face, a face he had hated for so many long years.

"They didn't catch me, Ariane," he said. "They couldn't have stopped me if I'd chosen to kill him."

She flinched at his bald words, but her gaze fixed on his with such intensity that he nearly forgot the need to breathe.

"But you didn't, Rook," she said. "You didn't."

"No." His mouth twisted. "You made me weak, Ariane."

"Weak," she said. She dropped her head and laughed with a kind of weary helplessness. "When I thought you were dead, gone from me forever, I didn't think I'd have the will to survive. *That* was weakness. The only thing I had of you was the need to find the answers I thought you'd died for. That was the only strength I had left." She looked up. "And then you came back. What I felt then—It hurt, that you hated me so much, but *that* I could survive, because you lived. And it wasn't just your life or mine anymore." Her fingers spread over her smock's sealed pocket. "I had to get the proof, and then I had to find you again. I had to make you understand what Finch knew all along."

"Finch—"

"That ring Finch gave me was the key, but I didn't realize it until just before you confronted me in the breakfast parlor."

"You told Sable that Slayton was behind it all," he said harshly, digging his fingers into the rough bark when he would have reached for her.

"Yes. And Finch guessed it, when she was hiding on the Marchand estates after the riots, disguised as a common servant. Everything she observed she recorded on a tiny device set in the ring she gave me on Agora. We had it all along, Rook."

All along. He had been blind all along to things he hadn't wanted, hadn't been able to see, just as she had told him.

"Finch was one of the few Kalians who escaped the fate of the rest of her people," Ariane continued. "Long after the Kalians had supposedly been taken from the city to the internment camps, she saw Wynn Slayton on the Marchand estates—in the company of a Changed Kalian."

Like Heron. Like the nameless gendarme. "She recognized one of us—"

"Yes. And she followed Wynn and the Kalian, and heard things she didn't understand. So she watched, and waited, and slipped out of the mansion to follow when she could. That was when she learned that Wynn Slayton had more than one Kalian working for him—that he had many, Changed to hide their race, hidden on his estates. When all the Kalians were supposedly barred from the city."

Rook shook his head. "How?"

"Finch listened, and she learned. How Wynn Slayton had engineered the riots very carefully, for his own ends, by using a certain drug devastatingly effective on Kalians alone, making them pliable to his commands and suggestions, obedient to his will." In spite of her calm recital, Ariane made no attempt to hide the emotion that blazed in her eyes. "How he learned that some Kalians had the ability to shapeshift—twisted and manipulated our people, gained control of certain Kalians and hid them before the rest were sent away, without any of the Elite knowing it was even possible."

Drugs. Ariane had Healed Sable; he had felt some part of that in the instant when the three of them had Shared in Wynn's chambers. She had reached into Sable's mind and instinctively eliminated the chemical taint she'd found there.

"I'm free," Sable had said.

"Sable," he said aloud. "She was his agent."

"Yes. And he made her, and the other Kalians under his control, believe the Marchand were behind the riots and everything that befell our people."

Rook jerked up his head. "And did your family have no part in any of it, Ariane?" he asked grimly.

She closed her eyes. "My great-grandfather trusted Wynn. He knew only what Wynn told him as a result of his supposed investigation. Bernard never sent his guardsmen into the Warren to persecute the Kalians. I have no doubt that those were Wynn's agents."

"But your Patriarch wasn't interested in listening to the testimony of mere savages," Rook said. "He chose to intern our people like animals."

Ariane looked as though she might deny his accusation; her face was flushed and taut with emotion. "Yes," she said at last, bowing her head. "He made mistakes. He was wrong. We all were. But Bernard tried to set the Kalians free when he provided a ship to Agora." Her eyes lifted. "Finch was still on the Marchand estates when the plans were made. She learned that Slayton planned to intercept the *Bonaventure*. She heard only enough to believe that he intended to destroy it."

Rising abruptly, Rook balanced on the broad branch and paced its length as far as he could go. "For what reason?" he said sharply. "Why would he do this? What did he have to gain?"

"Finch never learned that. She was afraid to approach any Espérancian with what she'd heard—not even me, knowing that I blamed a Kalian for Jacques's death. She'd seen the trial broadcasts; she didn't know whom to trust. So she went to one of Wynn's disguised Kalians, hoping to break through. The man turned on her and tried to kill her. She barely escaped with her life, and she knew she had to flee."

Kalians against Kalians; Kalians traitors to their own. Rook leaned heavily against a vertical branch, resting his cheek on the ridged surface. "So she went to Agora," he murmured.

"Yes. And she waited. All that time she had faith that someone would come, someone she could tell the truth to.

Someone who would listen. She heard about the destruction of the *Bonaventure,* but I think she believed until the very end that Kalians survived. She held on to that hope until the day she saw us and gave me the ring. And my heritage."

"Take care of her, Rook Galloway. Take care of my Ariane." Rook heard Finch's wise, warm voice as if she stood behind him. He had failed Finch utterly. He had turned on Ariane, too ready to believe she was part of what he hated. Because hatred had kept him alive for so long, and he was afraid of everything else. . . .

"Yesterday, when you came to me in the mansion and I learned you were alive," Ariane said softly, "I'd just heard the recording on that ring. But it wasn't enough. I had to learn more. When Wynn brought me back from the Louve system, I made a bargain with my great-grandfather—I'd go through with the contracted marriage to Wynn if I had full access to all Marchand resources so that I could learn exactly what happened so many years ago." The words trailed into a whisper. "It was all I had left to—"

Live for. He heard the rest of her sentence as if she'd spoken it in his soul. All the hatred he'd ever felt turned on himself in that moment, corrosive and bitter, strangling any hope of reply.

"Most of the rest you know." Ariane caught at nearby branches and levered herself up to face him. Leaves rustled and sighed. "I arranged to meet Wynn privately before our marriage so that I could gain access to his computer systems from inside. Marchand security provided me with a device to break into his core. That was when Sable found me, and you arrived."

Just in time to see Sable's Healing at Ariane's hands, find the world he had known and accepted crumbled again, as it had when he'd been an innocent boy just returned from Tolstoy.

Only one thing remained solid in this universe of chaos.

"Ariane," he rasped.

She poised there, meeting his eyes, this woman who was

his only true mate in all the universe—waiting, holding his heart in the palm of her hand. She had never once let it fall.

With the smooth efficiency of a hunter he sprang across the bough to catch her up in his arms. Her mouth opened willingly beneath his, and her sweet breath gave him back his life.

His kiss held all the desperation, the hurt, the anger he had held within himself far too long. But it was not the cruel assault he had forced on her in the Marchand mansion. It was completion, and need, and questions he could not ask. It was a silent plea, and Ariane answered it.

Her body was neither passive nor resistant but molded itself perfectly to his, the other half of a whole that had been brutally torn apart. A delirious rush of pure joy arced between them, taking the form of light—light like a blade piercing deep and true. In the brilliance of that light no secrets, no falsehoods, could be hidden.

"Rook," Ariane said against his shoulder, his neck, his lips. "I thought I'd lost you." Her small hands clutched his back with fierce strength. "Twice I thought I'd lost you. Once to death, and once to your own hatred."

He closed his eyes and his forehead to the cool skin between her neck and shoulder, feeling the caress of her hair on his face. "I almost lost myself," he said hoarsely.

Suddenly she drew back, and her eyes flamed with copper fire. "You couldn't, Rook. What you are"—she rested her palm over his thundering heart—"can't be taken away, or enslaved, or imprisoned. You are all of Kali. But even if you'd died—" She blinked and shook her head. "Even if you'd died, you would have gone on living. In the others who are still alive and can be Healed and set free. In me. Everything you fought for would have been realized, if it took me to the end of my life to achieve it."

Rook caught her face between his hands, stroking the tears away with his thumbs. He kissed her eyelids one by one, savoring the taste of her courage, her profound loyalty. Her love.

"Ariane," he said. The word cracked like something infinitely fragile. "Forgive me."

Until this moment he would have died before asking forgiveness of a Marchand. And Ariane was still Marchand, would always be, loyal to her Patriarch and her great-grandfather's blood. That she was Kalian couldn't change that. He wouldn't demand it of her. Not ever again.

"No," she whispered. "No forgiveness. Not from me. There's been so much pain on both sides. We have to be the ones to set it right. Together, Rook."

Humbled, shaken to the depths of his being, Rook could only hold her, touching her mind in a Sharing that left him shattered. Ariane gathered up the pieces, shaping him anew with loving hands. When he was complete again, she burned at the very core of him, like a nurturing star at the end of a thousand-year journey.

"I haven't told you," she said at last, cradled in his arms among the leaves, "the miraculous part of all this."

Rook knew what a miracle was. He rested his cheek on her hair and breathed it in, felt it pulse under his hands, against his heart.

"The Kalians here—under Wynn's control—they aren't the only ones who are left alive," Ariane murmured. "The *Bonaventure* didn't go down with all its crew and passengers."

Rook went very still.

"Finch never knew Wynn's true intentions. Somehow he deceived the League and my family, brought them back here, to use for his own evil purposes. And they're still here. On Espérance." She twisted in his arms to meet his eyes. "I haven't seen most of the data on this crystal, but I did find a list. A list of Kalians—living Kalians, scattered throughout Lumière in estates allied to my family, in the Gendarmerie, the Council precincts. And hundreds, perhaps thousands more—hidden somewhere on the polar continent.

"They didn't die, Rook. Our people—live."

He had no words in answer to her final revelation. Instead, he clung to Ariane with all his strength, thanking the

Maker—the Mother of all life—as he hadn't since those long-dead years of childhood innocence in his parents' arms.

"There are still things I don't know," Ariane continued, nestling her head in the hollow of his shoulder. "Why Jacques died, and who killed him. What Wynn intends with all this. But I know he betrayed our people, the Marchand, the Elite—all Espérance." Her voice grew hard. "The crystal will reveal the rest. He'll be stopped, and everything he's done will be exposed for the world to see.

"Wynn Slayton will be punished for his crimes."

"Oh, yes," Rook murmured, staring blindly among the stirring leaves. "He will be."

Ariane understood. Like a she-cat she twisted in his arms and glared at him with narrowed eyes. "But not by you, Rook Galloway," she growled. Her hands gripped his shoulders, bearing down fiercely. "I won't lose you again—even if I have to lock you in a cage somewhere and throw away the key until this is over."

And Rook knew she would try. Her eyes were full copper now, unwittingly Changed to reflect the nature she'd hidden all her life. Against the power of her love he had no defense, no hope of open rebellion.

He had only necessity. If it became necessary, he would defeat her and do what he had to do. But until that moment came, he had the universe and all eternity here in his arms. . . .

Ariane's head snapped around toward the park below them.

"Someone's coming," she whispered. Rook got to his feet, pulling her up with him. A whisper of sound came to them on the breeze—almost imperceptible, a hunter's guarded steps. Two sets of footfalls—two shadows that broke away from the silhouette of wild shrubs twenty meters away. Rook knew who these pursuers must be.

"Slayton's Kalians," he said grimly. "They've tracked us."

Ariane glanced at him without a trace of fear. "Then our work starts now. All we have to do is catch them—long enough for me to get inside their minds and Heal them."

Rook nearly laughed. "So simple, Ariane?"

"Is there any other choice?" She looked into his eyes, caressing him with the warmth of a thousand suns. Her lips parted, and he bent to kiss her, hard and swift, before letting her drop back to the wide branch.

But he was not prepared for what she did next.

With natural grace Ariane crouched low, gathered her legs under her, and leaped into the air. She had already rolled into a perfect fall before Rook could follow; she sprang up and assumed a fighter's stance at the base of the tree just as the Kalian trackers saw her and began to run.

Rook grabbed the disruptor from his waistband under the smock and aimed it precisely at the first of the men to reach Ariane. The glint of the Kalian's own 'ruptor provided the target. At the last possible instant Rook fired; the hunter's disruptor shattered and exploded from his grasp to the man's muffled cry of pain. Ariane moved in a blur, tackling the unarmed man and pinning him to the ground.

The other Kalian had no chance to go to his partner's aid. Rook flung himself out and down, his heart in his throat. A 'ruptor beam narrowly missed him before he had the man's wrist in a crushing grip and forced him to drop the weapon.

"Rook," Ariane cried from behind him. "I need you—"

Without thought Rook smashed his fist into the disguised Kalian's stunned face. He sprang to Ariane's side, crouching to hold the struggling Kalian while Ariane closed her eyes and began to reach within herself for the Sharing that could save them all.

Rook felt only a faint vibration of mental contact as she entered the man's mind, his senses tuned to the unconscious man behind him and the silent park. But as Ariane went deeper, began the Healing that would set the Kalian free, he slipped into the Sharing with her, touched the taint of Wynn's foul drugs as she expunged it, knew the triumphant joy of her success as the Kalian accepted release.

Copper eyes blinked up at Ariane, dazed and fearful. "Where—" the man began.

Ariane smoothed her palm over his forehead. "You have

nothing to fear now. You're free." Rook felt her open the Sharing once again, and the man's rigid expression eased. He looked at Rook and closed his eyes, breathing in harsh gusts.

"Are you strong enough to continue, Ariane?" Rook asked softly, taking her arm as she drew back. He jerked his head toward the prone man who was still Wynn's creature. He could feel Ariane's weariness as if it were a part of himself; the Healing drained her, and she had already been through so much.

But she smiled, serene and brave. "We can't stop now," she said, "when we've come so far." Briefly she rested her forehead against his, drawing on his strength, before turning to the second Kalian.

When Ariane touched him, her expression flickered in surprise. "Heron," she murmured. And after she had finished, the face looking up at them had returned to that of the man Rook had known in the Warren so long ago.

"Healer," he said in wonder, staring at Ariane. Copper eyes shifted to Rook.

"Heron," Rook said, crouching beside him. His throat was unexpectedly tight. "I thought they had killed you." He glanced automatically to the hand that had been shattered by a Gendarme's disruptor in the Warren eight years ago; it had been replaced by an expensive synthetic, almost indistinguishable from the real thing. Such a loss would be beyond any Kalian's healing. Heron followed Rook's gaze and flexed artificial fingers, his homely face cracking into a pained, lopsided grin.

"A gift from our master," he croaked. His eyes were fever-bright. "For—services rendered." He shuddered and flung his head to the side. "I—didn't remember. I didn't know. Maker's Tears—"

Rook bent over his friend, grasping the flesh-and-blood wrist above the false appendage. The Sharing came easily now; Ariane had made that possible.

"You're free now, Heron, and we need your help," he said softly. "Hundreds of our people are under Wynn Slayton's yoke, as you were. We must free them and stop Slayton. He was the man who set out to destroy our people."

"Destroy—"

"Yes. For reasons of his own. Ariane—Ariane Marchand"—he nodded at her—"has the proof to bring him down. Wynn will stop her any way he can, using our own people, as he tried to use you. But we must reach the Marchand Patriarch, who has the power to act on what she's learned."

Heron's gaze drifted back to Ariane. "I remembered I called you—enemy. But you're Kalian, a Healer." He reached blindly for her hand, and she took it gently. "I'll do whatever you ask."

No more words were spoken. Rook and Ariane exchanged glances; they helped Heron up and left him to deal with his dazed partner.

To Wynn's guardsmen who watched the servant's entrance to the Marchand mansion, Heron would appear as a Slayton agent triumphantly delivering two valuable prisoners. The guards would be deceived until they dropped their vigilance—just long enough. Human soldiers were no match for four driven Kalians. One way or another they'd break through Slayton's net and reach the Patriarch.

And then the reckoning would begin.

By the time they entered the rear gates of the Marchand mansion, dodging wide-eyed servants laden with fresh produce from the Low Town market, Ariane, Rook, Heron, and the fourth Kalian, Marten by name, had two non-Kalian Slayton guardsmen in tow. The guardsmen, disguised as a strolling Gendarme and idle porter, hadn't had time to call for help before they'd fallen to Heron's ruse. Now Slayton's men stumbled between Heron and Marten, stunned by their sudden capture.

There was no one else to prevent the Kalians' entrance. Servants melted silently out of their way; Ariane knew Marchand guards would be summoned, and she anticipated their coming. She moved boldly through the corridors, hardly acknowledging the hasty bows of Marchand retainers. Rook stalked at her side, restored to his true form; behind him Heron and Marten had reverted as well. The sight of three members of a supposedly dead race must have been startling.

The first guards to intercept them skidded to a halt, weapons half-drawn, as their eyes took in the bizarre group. The officer saluted awkwardly, his gaze flickering between Ariane and the Kalians.

"Lady Ariane," he said, clearing his throat. "We received an alert—"

"I imagine you did," Ariane said softly. "Your eyes don't deceive you, Lieutenant. These are Kalians, and they are with me. The other two are prisoners. If you'll be so good as to escort us to the Patriarch immediately—"

The officer's momentary confusion vanished at her smooth, self-assured command. He holstered his disruptor and signaled to his men, who fell in around Ariane's party. By no outward sign did the guardsmen display their shock at the presence of the Kalians; they kept their eyes locked smartly ahead while the officer spoke softly into his wrist comm, relaying Ariane's message to the Patriarch.

So it was that Bernard Marchand was waiting for them in the hall just outside the second-floor conference room, his hawklike features perfectly composed.

"Ariane," he said evenly. His hard gaze took in her dirty black servant's smock, her wildly tangled hair—and moved deliberately to focus on the Kalian who stood beside her.

"Rook Galloway," he acknowledged. "I have been expecting you."

"A long time, Bernard Marchand," Rook answered. He took a single step forward; the two men stared at each other across the hall. The tension was so palpable that Heron and Marten shifted and murmured, and the guardsmen stiffened to either side.

Ariane broke the silence before it could stretch to the breaking point. "Introductions can come later," she said sharply. "Grand-père, these men—these Kalians—are with me. Until an hour ago they were under Wynn Slayton's control—as are all the rest of their people."

Bernard didn't so much as blink. "The rest of their people," he said flatly. "Then they are—alive."

She crossed the room to stand before him. "Alive, yes, and here on Espérance. They weren't destroyed aboard the *Bonaventure*. Wynn only made it appear that they had been, so he could bring them back here to use for his own purposes." She caught her breath. "Last night I finally learned the truth of what happened eight years ago. Wynn was behind the Warren riots; he forced the Kalians into everything they did. He betrayed them, and all of us."

For the first time Bernard's face revealed a flicker of shock. The lines of age creasing his face deepened in parchment skin. "Wynn," he whispered. Ariane knew him too well; she ached to go to him, comfort him in this moment of profound loss—loss of the man he had trusted and regarded as a son, loss of his own certainties. She knew what it was to feel the very earth give way under your feet.

But there was no time for solace, and the Patriarch would have been shamed by any acknowledgment of his weakness. He drew himself up proudly, throwing off the weight of his years. His eyes passed briefly over Heron and Marten and came to rest on the Slayton prisoners.

"And these men?"

"Slayton agents sent out to stop us from reaching you," Ariane said, plunging her hand into the pocket of her smock. "With this." She rolled the tiny crystal in the palm of her hand. "Everything is here, all the proof of what I've told you. Last night, acting on other evidence, I went to Wynn's mansion and broke into his personal computer. He didn't suspect me. I read enough of what I dumped into this crystal to know my suspicions were correct. I saw several of the Kalians he'd drugged and enslaved—shapechanged to look like ordinary Espérancians."

She almost heard Bernard's thoughts. *Yes, like me,* she said silently. "We managed to rescue Heron and Marten, but Wynn sent others after us."

"To what purpose?" Bernard muttered, his gaze turned inward. "What does he want?"

"I don't know. Not entirely. But he has Kalian agents in at least six houses allied to Marchand—and in the Gendarmerie and Council chambers as well. The rest of the Kalians are being held on the polar continent. Whatever he plans is something he'd kill to hide." She swallowed, remembering Wynn's triumphant lust. "He has to be stopped, Grand-père—and the Kalians have to be set free."

He almost seemed not to have heard her. "Jacques?" he asked.

Ariane tightened her fist around the crystal, glancing behind at Rook's unreadable face. "I told you I'd realized that Rook had been falsely accused of his murder. If Wynn had any part in Jacques's death, it'll be here." She unclenched her fingers and held out her hand. "Run it through, Grand-père. We must act quickly."

Bernard's hesitation was almost imperceptible. With a glance at the guards he moved quickly through the double doors into the conference room and to the computer terminal at the head of the great clairewood table. Ariane and the others followed, the guards taking charge of Slayton's men, who watched the proceedings in dazed silence.

Rook moved up beside Ariane as she watched the Patriarch scan the contents of the crystal on the wide screen. Sometime during her explanations Rook had stripped off his servant's smock and the Slayton tunic he'd worn beneath; he was defiantly bare-chested, as he'd been on the *d'Artagnan*, flaunting his savage origins in this civilized Marchand domain. Ariane shivered; even now his nearness made her forget everything but the joy of his presence. She wanted to turn into his arms, feel his strength, press her mouth to the hard curve of his chest, give herself up to barbaric and elemental pleasures. . . .

"I've seen enough."

The Patriarch's voice carried through the room with all the authority of undisputed power. The guards came to attention; Ariane felt Rook's callused fingers slide through hers possessively.

Bernard rose from his seat before the screen and turned to face them slowly. "You were right, Ariane. Wynn must be stopped, and we have no more time to waste." He looked at the officer of the guards. "Take these prisoners to Security. They're to be thoroughly questioned. I'll transmit the pertinent data directly to Captain Wolf." His hard stare settled on the Slayton agents. "If they cooperate, see that they're made comfortable. I will have answers."

The officer glanced uneasily at the Kalians. "Sieur Marchand, shall I send more men to—" He broke off when Rook turned to him with narrowed eyes and hard-set jaw, blatantly menacing.

Bernard smiled without any trace of humor. "Have no fear for my safety, Lieutenant. Now, go."

The guards saluted and withdrew, escorting the nervous prisoners. Bernard shifted his attention back to Ariane.

"The priorities are clear to me, Ariane. We must neutralize these hidden Kalian agents—"

"Neutralize—" Rook growled. His muscles tensed and rippled as he started toward Bernard. Ariane caught his arm and held on.

"Forgive me, Mr. Galloway," Bernard said with a twist of his aristocratic lips. "We have much yet to discuss, but these men under Slayton control must be stopped before Wynn can activate them for whatever purpose he intends."

Ariane felt the mental flare of Rook's hostility and put herself deliberately between the two men. "That, Grand-père, is my job. Mine and Rook's and theirs." She jerked her head toward Heron and Marten, who had come to stand behind her. With a few swift, well-chosen words she explained her newfound abilities as a Healer, able to reach into Kalian minds and remove all trace of the drug Wynn had used to control them.

"That's why we have to go, Grand-père—into those estates to find the Kalians and Heal them. Heron has the ability to recognize them, whatever form they've taken. If—"

"Out of the question," Bernard interrupted. "You've already put yourself in danger without bothering to inform me. That was no part of our bargain." He struck his clenched fist against the tabletop. "There must be another way."

Ariane stepped back until she came up against Rook's solid strength; his arms closed around her. She shook her head. "No. No other way that will protect those agents and remove them quickly. All four of us have the ability to take on any identity we need. No one will recognize us—if you can get us into the estates without setting off panic and endangering the Kalians."

The Patriarch gazed at her for a long moment, his eyes impersonal and calculating. Ariane was achingly aware of Rook's body against hers.

"Very well," Bernard said heavily, leaning back against his chair. "The Houses affected are all allied to Marchand." His brows lowered. "If you pose as Marchand Security, I'll tell them just enough to get you inside on the pretext of looking for covert operatives. But if you get into any trouble, you are to inform me immediately."

Closing her eyes, Ariane breathed silent thanks. "We'll be ready the moment you've arranged it." She straightened, pulling free of Rook's arms. "There's no telling what Wynn will do when he's told we've escaped him. We must begin now."

"Yes." Bernard spun his chair around and sat down, punching keys rapidly. "I'm sending covert agents to surround Slayton's manor immediately. I'll personally speak to Captain de Funès about the counterfeit gendarmes—he can be trusted. I won't raise a general alarm unless it becomes absolutely necessary."

"And the others?" Rook's voice was hoarse and strange. Bernard turned in his chair, and Ariane looked up into his stony face. "Our people who remain enslaved on the polar continent, under Slayton's power? What of them?"

Another strained silence fell over the room. Heron and Marten came to flank Rook on either side.

"Rook is right," Ariane said. "They must be protected, no matter what the cost."

The Patriarch met Rook's gaze steadily. "Very well. Marchand honor owes them that much." He faced the screen again. "It will spread Marchand forces thin, but I'll send a contingent of House Troops for reconnaissance at the polar continent. I must know the situation before I risk my men."

There was no other way. Ariane knew that well; she waited for Rook to protest, marshaling explanations to make him understand. His emotions came clearly to her through the Sharing; after so many years believing he was the last of his kind, he was not entirely rational on the subject. She understood; how well she understood.

"Trust him, Rook," she asked, squeezing his hand fiercely. "Trust *me*."

Rook bent his head, meeting her eyes with copper heat. "Yes, *chérie*," he said. His free hand cupped her chin. "Always."

Bernard joined them, almost of a height with Rook, his expression unreadable. "Shall we call a truce, Rook Galloway?" Slowly, deliberately, he extended his long-fingered aristocrat's hand to the Kalian he had once condemned.

With equal deliberation, gaze never wavering, Rook took the Patriarch's hand in his own.

CHAPTER TWENTY

*A*riane woke to the sound of birdsong from the open terrace doors. Breathing in the scent of early-morning air, she curved her body against the man who lay at her side and cherished this moment of peace for the miracle it was.

Rook slept soundly, his chest rising and falling in a deep and regular rhythm. His face was almost relaxed, free of yesterday's tension. But his loose hair lay tangled over the overstuffed pillows, and his big, scarred body was incongruous in Ariane's ornate bed.

She had never seen anything so beautiful in all her life.

They had loved on the *d'Artagnan's* narrow bunks, lost in their own world amid the stars—but never here, in her domain. Not even when Ariane had seen the wanting in his eyes and felt the fierce answer of her own undeniable need. Not since Marchand and Kalian had cried truce.

Rook slept on as Ariane spread her hand over his heart, resting her head on his shoulder. Strange that she should be the first awake after all that had passed the day before. Rook had worried last night over her exhaustion; ten of Wynn's Kalian agents throughout Lumière had been located and Healed and brought back to the Marchand estates in the space of a single day. Only Ariane had possessed the ability to free those men and women from their drug-induced bondage. She had been unaccustomed to using those rare Kalian gifts.

But Rook had always been there to lend his strength when she'd faltered. He had all but carried her home from their last mission; she remembered him settling her in this bed, covering her, murmuring words that echoed within her mind through the bond between them.

She was safe; she was home. Home in House Marchand; home in Rook's arms. Rook's people—*her* people—had been set free, brought here to makeshift dormitories set up in the mansion's second-story ballroom. They would be properly cared for until she'd recovered enough to make certain she had done her work well and thoroughly.

Soon the other Kalians, Wynn's prisoners on the polar continent, would join their brothers and sisters in freedom. . . .

Rook stirred, muttering as he turned his head toward her. His grim mouth curved upward, as if he was aware of her presence. Ariane closed her eyes and reached into his mind, Sharing on a level deeper than conscious thought.

I love you, Rook.

The muscles in his bare arms bunched and flowed as he reached for her. She caught his hand and kissed his rough knuckles gently before slipping out of the bed. She could have lain there beside Rook forever, but too much remained undone. Too many duties demanded her attention, and she was still Marchand by training if not by blood.

Slipping into a plain lounging suit a servant had left by her armoire, Ariane glanced around the elegant room. After three years in the cramped quarters of the *d'Artagnan,* her bedchamber seemed almost foreign. While she'd believed Rook dead, it hadn't mattered. Now—now she felt herself shivering for reasons she couldn't begin to understand.

Only a moment ago she'd been thinking that this was home, because Rook was there.

Her feet carried her with Kalian silence across the richly carpeted floor, through her private sitting room and out into the tiled hall. The two guardsmen discreetly placed to either side of the door straightened at her passing; she nodded and they relaxed.

They still did not know. None of them knew that their mistress was a savage. Perhaps it was only a matter of time, but she found herself unable to think beyond the immediate future.

She had only just won that future back.

Ariane strode down familiar hallways, past the family suites and guest chambers and through the sitting rooms and salons set aside for family meetings and intimate social gatherings. A remote staircase took her to the third floor, where Marchand Operations, Security, and Administration offices echoed with soft voices and the near-subliminal hum of machinery.

She knew the Patriarch was there, overseeing the reconnaissance operation he'd promised. Ariane slowed as she approached a curve in the corridor and heard the low tones of her great-grandfather's voice.

"Slayton got through our net with ridiculous ease," Bernard whispered harshly. "He managed to escape Marchand's most highly trained operatives. And now you tell me that five of my best pilots have been shot down over an installation that shouldn't even exist."

"The installation is remarkably well protected, Sieur Bernard," another man's voice answered. "Slayton has pilots of his own. My best man reported that he'd never seen maneuvers like those. Slayton's fighters are suicidal."

There was a long silence. "Kalians," Bernard muttered. He uttered a pungent curse.

The other man cleared his throat. "We can plan an all-out assault with a higher allocation of troops, but we don't know what countermeasures Slayton may throw against us. His shielding is tight, and he's well armed. Casualties of any prisoners he has in the installation may be—very high."

Prisoners. Ariane thought of the names she'd seen on Wynn's computer screen—Kalian men, women, and children locked away and forgotten in a land of perpetual cold that no Espérancian but Wynn had ever bothered to exploit. She clenched her fists and leaned against the wall, listening.

"And none of the alternatives are acceptable," the Patriarch said softly. "Lady Ariane is to hear nothing of this— particularly nothing of Slayton's message—until we have resolved this problem. One way or another."

The Security officer mumbled a reply as the Patriarch dismissed him with a few soft commands, but Ariane's mind was racing. *Slayton's message.* Wynn had escaped the Patriarch's cordon around his estates, had clearly been prepared for Bernard's attempt on his polar base. He had Kalian fighters under his command. If he had gone to ground there, he could hold Marchand forces at bay and threaten thousands of Kalian lives. And her great-grandfather didn't want her to know about it.

Ariane spun on her heel and headed back for her suite. She noted that Rook was no longer in bed, but her attention focused immediately on the screen before her as she settled at her private computer.

All the reports that had come in from the reconnaissance party were classified, but Security had not yet had time to lock the data into files her password could not access. Within minutes she had the past twenty-four hours' communication transmissions from the polar continent on her screen. Everything she had overheard was correct.

And there was a message from Wynn Slayton—addressed to Ariane Burke-Marchand.

She scanned the brief transmission, her lips tightening into a grim line.

"I will kill him."

Rook's voice was perfectly level, without a trace of emotion. It sent a shock coursing through Ariane even before he rested his big hand on her shoulder, just beneath the fall of her hair.

Blanking the screen, Ariane swiveled to face him. He towered over her, looking in that moment as threatening, as alien, as savage as he'd been the day he'd taken the *d'Artagnan* and changed her life forever.

She caught his other hand. "You think I don't feel what you feel, Rook?" she said, staring up into his glacial eyes. "You think I don't know what has to be done?"

His gaze cleared a little, lost that blindly dangerous look. He focused on her slowly. "If we do what he says," he said, "he'll have all of us. He won't keep his word, Ariane."

She fought the absurd desire to laugh. "Of course he won't keep his word. But I do know he'll kill all of *them* if we don't agree to his terms."

Rook's teeth bared. "I won't let—"

She laid her palms flat against his bare chest. "I said I'd put you in a cage before I'd risk losing you again. You'd do the same thing to me in a second—and we'd both be wrong." She reached up to curl her hand around his neck. The coarse weight of his hair lay warm on her skin. "You weren't meant to be caged, Rook, and neither was I. No matter what the price of freedom."

His silent protest held an edge of violence, rejecting the unintended image in her mind. She closed her eyes.

"You might stop me, Rook. You're still stronger than I. You could keep me safe in my gilded cage simply by telling my great-grandfather what I intend to do." Leaning into him, she wrapped her arms around his waist and pressed her ear to the beat of his heart. "But our people need me. Just as I need you."

A deep sound rumbled in Rook's chest, a groan and a protest that needed no words. His arms closed about her, and the emotion that passed between them vibrated with his fear for her. His instincts demanded that he keep her from all harm, a Kalian man with his mate against a hostile world.

But his mind knew otherwise. His mind acknowledged her strength, her courage, the honor she had never abandoned. His mind understood the devil's bargain that his heart could not condone.

"For our people, Rook," she said, humbled by the wonder of his fierce admiration. "For us."

"Yes," said a light, familiar voice.

She and Rook turned as one. Heron Matthews stood in the doorway, flanked by two other Kalians and the uneasy pair of Marchand guardsmen. Ariane reassured and dismissed the guards with a nod, and they retreated reluctantly just out of sight. Heron and the other two Kalians, one of them Marten, walked softly into the room.

Rook was the first to speak. "Have they let you run tame in these fine halls, Heron?" he said, turning Ariane in the crook of his arm.

Heron, tall, gangly man that he was, gave a crooked grin that encompassed them both. "We have the Healer to thank for that," he said.

Healer, he'd said, not Lady Ariane, though he understood clearly who and what she was in this place. She'd seen to it that the Kalians had the freedom to move about the mansion, knowing full well they'd had their fill of captivity. Ariane looked into Heron's clear, honest eyes.

"Has there been trouble, Heron?" she asked softly.

The Kalian shook his head. Aside from his dark hair and copper eyes, he was as near Rook's opposite in build and appearance as was possible to be. A day ago he had been set on killing them both; now he looked utterly harmless.

But no Kalian was ever truly harmless.

"No trouble, Healer," he said. "But we have been listening, and learning. Our former master taught us well." He glanced back at his companions. "We know about the rest of our people, the danger they're in. And that you and Rook are going after them."

Ariane dismissed her brief surprise. The Kalians she and Rook had rescued had been there only a day, and already they understood the situation with frightening clarity. If Wynn had been able to use them as planned, he might well have succeeded in whatever aims he'd nursed since the riots.

Now, however, an entire race was at risk of being wiped out.

Heron took a step toward her, his hand—his real hand—extended. "Those of us who are well enough wish to go with you. We'll fight for you, Healer—and for our people."

There wasn't any question of refusal. By the same logic she'd given Rook, they needed any advantage they could take. Heron's eyes were devoid of hatred, but she knew he'd give his life to free those still in Wynn's hands. Just as Rook would. Just as she would herself.

She glanced up at Rook, feeling his answer before he spoke. "Slayton expects only the two of us," he said to Heron. "We'll have to leave you some distance from the installation and try to get you inside once Wynn admits us. It won't be possible to make any plans."

His meaning was clear. Any or all of them might die; what

they attempted would have to be improvised from beginning to end. His arm tightened around Ariane almost painfully.

Heron's teeth bared in a predator's grin. "The Healer gave us back our lives, but we must fight for them as our forefathers did on Kali. We will go."

Without another word the Kalians gathered in Ariane's chamber for a council of war. When it was finished, Heron and his brothers went to rejoin and gather their fellow volunteers, while Ariane set about securing a personnel transport that would carry them to Wynn's polar stronghold. Once again they would use their ability to Change to evade the Patriarch's surveillance; her great-grandfather wouldn't know where she'd gone until it was too late to stop her.

She grieved for that. It was another small betrayal of the man who'd protected her name and raised her as his heir, let her taste the freedom of the stars. A man she honored, and to whom she owed so much. The one thing she feared more than the final confrontation that lay ahead was the choice she would be forced to make when it was over.

If she survived.

Endless white stretched below the transport, almost as pristine as the day the first colonists had landed on Espérance.

Even after all the years since the first colonists had arrived, there was still enough untouched arable land on the planet so that no Family or mercantile interest had bothered to claim or develop this bleak terrain. Wynn would have found it easy, with his wealth and influence, to set up his clandestine operations with no one the wiser.

The first reconnaissance reports said that the installation was almost entirely underground. From above, the place was invisible. Only when the first disruptor cannons had opened fire from hidden turrets had the Marchand troops realized what they faced. Then the sleek, unmarked fighters had appeared from nowhere, forcing the Patriarch's men into retreat. Now the Marchand men awaited further orders, safely beyond the reach of Slayton's defenses.

Ariane had piloted the transport past the loose Marchand

cordon with a false coded message from the Patriarch, and her great-grandfather's troops hadn't presumed to question her. A little beyond, Ariane landed the craft to release the eight Kalian volunteers several kilometers from Wynn's stronghold. They dropped into the snow, anonymous shapes in bulky cold-weather gear, and instantly disappeared. It was up to them to make their way past any ground defenses and be ready if and when Ariane and Rook were able to get them inside.

With Rook grim and silent at her shoulder, Ariane took the transport up and began to transmit the code Wynn's message had provided. Two sleek one-man fighters streaked through the icy blue sky to flank her. A voice she didn't recognize gave a terse order over her comm; she pulled into a hover and waited while Wynn's people scanned her ship to determine that only two people were aboard.

The fighters escorted them down to a flat gray landing strip recently cleared of snow and ice. The men who emerged from the unmarked craft fell in beside Rook and Ariane, their eyes blank and distant. Ariane guessed them to be Changed Kalians. Just past the landing strip a featureless gray block rose out of the ground, and two more guards appeared at the dark square of an opening. Bitter air whistled in Ariane's ears and tugged viciously at her heavy parka; Rook gathered her close, his eyes constantly tracking the guards who surrounded them.

Darkness swallowed them as they stepped up to the gray block and through the doorway. Ariane heard a low hum as the tiny room in which they stood withdrew into the ground and continued down, deep under the ice-locked earth.

When the door opened again, Wynn Slayton was waiting on the other side.

If she hadn't been standing in front of him, Ariane knew that Rook would have gone for Wynn then and there. His body went rigid at her back; a growl rumbled deep in his chest, and the emotion that beat out from him was almost overwhelming.

Rook, she thought silently in warning. His breath shuddered out explosively, but he only grasped her elbow and held her to his chest. The Kalian guards urged them out of the lift into a small room, and Wynn stepped back, his eyes fixed on Ariane's face as if Rook did not exist.

"I am pleased, Ariane," Wynn said softly. "Very pleased that you could join me here."

She'd had too long to think about this meeting, too long to fall prey to crippling emotion when she could least afford it. That she despised her one-time betrothed was a given, but she couldn't let her hatred cloud her mind. Or fear.

What Wynn felt for her—that was far more critical.

His eyes raked her from booted feet to the top of her head as she brushed her fur-lined hood back from her hair. "You left us very little choice, Wynn," she said calmly. "Will you let the Kalians go as agreed?"

Wynn smiled. "Straight to the point, Ariane, as always. But there is no need to rush." For the first time his gaze flicked to Rook. "It occurs to me that this is our first meeting in—eight years?" he said. "You proved to be a more intelligent opponent than I gave you credit for."

Rook pushed in front of Ariane. "You may have a thousand Kalians under your control, Slayton," he said, "but if you touch Ariane, I'll still have time to kill you."

Glancing at the impassive Kalian guards, Wynn cocked his head. "Perhaps. There are certain disadvantages to Euphorie —it does tend to slow those remarkable Kalian reflexes somewhat." His eyes turned back to Ariane. "I admit I was prepared for threats and barbarian bluster from your lover, Ariane. Your—taste in sexual partners is less of a surprise now that I know you are one of them." He laughed. "Irony of ironies—that the Marchand heir is of tainted blood, while my own family had to fight for the honor of becoming one of the Elite."

Ariane refused to rise to his bait. Rook's muscles bunched and released, but his rage had dropped to a steady simmer well under his control. In the silence that followed, Ariane saw Wynn's expression shift almost imperceptibly as he considered the man he had helped condemn to eight years of hell.

"If I had known, Ariane," Wynn said at last, "if only I'd known what you were— I admit that wasn't a factor I'd allowed for in my most far-reaching calculations. You, also, proved to be a formidable opponent when you should have been merely a pawn. But I've never allowed regret to weaken me. I will have at least some measure of my revenge."

Ariane took an unconscious step forward, restrained by Rook's hard fingers on her arm. "Revenge," she repeated. "Against whom, and why?"

Her question echoed in the featureless gray room. Wynn nodded to his guards, and they herded Rook and Ariane through a second doorway and into a dimly lit corridor.

"Why?" Wynn said, half turning to address her as they walked. "I am surprised that you would need to ask that question, Ariane. Or hasn't your great-grandfather explained it to you?"

Ariane sifted through her brief conversations with Bernard since her return with the evidence. There had been no time for lengthy discussions; the Patriarch might have had that piece of the puzzle all along.

"All this is revenge against us," she said. "Against the Marchand."

"Of course. I'll be happy to explain in detail when circumstances permit. Perhaps to you it would be—ancient history, Ariane. But I'm certain your great-grandfather already understands very well."

Bernard. By now he would be aware that Ariane and Rook had taken Wynn's offer to exchange themselves for the Kalian captives. She looked up at Rook, and he met her gaze with a strange, almost triumphant smile. His hand tightened on her arm; through the Sharing his warmth, his strength, his faith in her, burned itself into her mind and heart.

Rook believed in her. Wynn's menace was nothing against the power of that belief.

"Somewhere along the line you must have miscalculated badly," she said to Wynn's back. "By involving the Kalians you've set yourself up against not only my family, but all Espérance and the League." She breathed deeply to keep her words level. "I used to admire you, Wynn—your confidence and your intelligence and your impeccable sense of honor. But I think this time you've overreached yourself. You've sacrificed too much. The price you'll pay for this so-called revenge—"

"No barbarian bluster from you, Ariane," Wynn interrupted, sounding amused. "You might ask your lover about the price of revenge."

Rook laughed, drawing Wynn's startled gaze back to him. "I gained something beyond price when my pursuit of revenge led me back to Espérance." Suddenly he stepped forward and caught Wynn's arm. "The mistakes I made nearly cost me everything I fought to survive for all those years on Tantalus. What will you have left when this is over, Slayton?"

The two men stared at each other, ignoring the Kalian guards who moved in with weapons trained on Rook. The air seethed with hostility that set Ariane's hair on end. Awareness flared in Wynn's eyes—the understanding that Rook could snap his neck with a single blow if he lost his thin veneer of control.

But Rook stepped back lightly, dragging his palm against his thigh as if he'd touched something noxious. His utter contempt was more devastating than any open assault.

Wynn's momentary shock vanished, and his face lost its aristocratic refinement behind a mask of feral rage. "Is Ariane the prize you won, Kalian?" he snarled. "Whatever price I pay will not be nearly so high as yours."

He turned on his heel and the guards shoved Rook and Ariane forward. Rook caught Ariane's hand and held it tightly, communicating a message beyond the reach of words.

They came suddenly to the end of the corridor, where it opened out onto a wide metal platform overlooking a cavernous chamber. The air was cold, and Ariane's breath plumed in front of her face, momentarily obscuring the scene before her.

Then she realized what she was seeing.

It was like a vast prison, row upon row of cubicles, cramped rooms with narrow bunks and primitive facilities. In each cell were several people—women and men, young and old, all dark-haired. Kalian. Thousands of them, caged like beasts. The musky smell of their bodies rose on the cold air, and a child's wail pierced the eerie silence.

Ariane swayed with the overwhelming sense of countless minds in bondage. Rook choked back a cry, his measureless grief adding to her own.

"What do you think of my collection, Ariane?" Wynn said, leaning against the railing. "Will your thin Marchand blood be recompense enough for my loss?" He smiled coldly. "Perhaps in time I would have found some use for all these who didn't have your gift for changing. Kalians make excellent fighter pilots; as soldiers they would be nearly invincible."

"If not for your drugs—" Rook began in a rough whisper.

"Yes, that was a fortuitous discovery," Wynn said. He reached out to catch Ariane's chin, ignoring Rook's aborted lunge. "I have reason to know that Euphorie works just as effectively on those of mixed blood." His wrist comm buzzed; he released Ariane, and she scrubbed her face against the collar of her parka. Rook stood trembling between his Kalian guards, eyes bleak and fixed on Wynn as the older man turned away.

Moving to a small console at the edge of the platform, Wynn touched several buttons in sequence. All at once the view of imprisoned Kalians disappeared behind an illusory wall that seemed as solid as the plasteel it resembled. A moment later Ariane sensed a new presence and followed Wynn's welcoming gaze.

"Ah, Sable—"

Sable moved among them like a shadow, and Wynn drew her close. Staring into the Kalian woman's eyes, Ariane felt a chill of uncertainty. Until this moment she hadn't known what had become of Sable; she and Rook hadn't been able to risk counting on her help. Now Sable returned her look with her lips twisted in contempt, seemingly unaware of what lay behind the opaque screen.

"We meet again, Marchand," Sable purred. "Or should I call you 'sister'?"

There was no hint of what truly lay behind Sable's words. Ariane flexed her fingers convulsively. Her Kalian abilities were still too limited. She needed to touch Sable to be sure she was still free of Wynn's control, still an ally to be trusted. . . .

"Ah, yes. Sisters in more than one sense," Wynn said. "Metaphorically speaking. After all, Pierre Burke-Marchand was not your father at all, was he, Ariane? Yes, I was able to find that information once I knew what to look for." He shook his head. "So much irony. Pierre was not your father —but he *was* Sable's."

He clearly expected Ariane to betray her shock, but Ariane had already touched Sable's mind too deeply in Wynn's chambers. There had been a moment when the two women had become one—no secrets, no barriers between them. Ariane found the knowledge lodged within her own memory, where she had pushed it aside, one more shock among too many.

Sable strolled forward casually.

"He raped my mother one night in the Warren and left her with his seed in her belly," she said tonelessly. Her gaze flickered to Rook. "You never knew that, did you? My mother hid her shame well. But I never forgot it."

Rook pulled against his guards' restraining hands. "It was no shame, Sable."

She ignored him, all her attention focused on Ariane. "You had the privileges, the fine meals, the easy life. I hated your Family, your name, everything you stood for, Ariane Burke-Marchand. And yet all along you were no better than I was."

The pain in her voice was genuine. In spite of the drug that had controlled and deceived her, Sable's hatred of the

Marchand had been real from the beginning. Perhaps it ruled her still. Ariane searched desperately for some hidden message behind Sable's bleak stare.

"Can you blame her for wanting revenge, Ariane?" Wynn asked. "And I was there to give it to her." He nuzzled Sable's cheek with blatant sensuality. "Have you anything more to say to your 'sister' before we proceed, *minette*?"

Tossing her hair back from her shoulders, Sable moved with dizzying speed. Her hands closed like vises on Ariane's arms.

A flood of invective spilled from between Sable's clenched teeth, but Ariane heard none of it. From the moment Sable's hands touched her, she was lost in the Sharing—another mind joining hers, filling her with knowledge that needed no words or human symbols. Automatically her brain translated the storm of images and feelings.

Trust me. Whatever I do, trust me. Be strong.

And then Sable released her, shoving her back against the guards with a final curse.

"Sable's temper was always chancy, Ariane," Wynn said, pulling Sable back to his side. "But you have no need to fear it now. You'll be in my tender care."

"Slayton—" Rook growled.

"As for you, my blustering savage, Sable will make you—comfortable, until I have further use for you." Sable drew a disruptor from her belt and took Rook's elbow to draw him away. The guards closed in around them both.

Ariane hid her alarm behind an expressionless mask. "The Kalians, Wynn," she whispered. "You will let them go." She glanced back at Rook, cut off from view by Sable and the guards. "All of them."

"Of course, *ma petite*. Even your ferocious lover. I have no use for them now, and every use for you." He held out his elegant hand to Ariane, smiling. "Come, Ariane. Your life for all these; surely your honor recognizes the necessity."

Swallowing the fear that strangled the breath in her throat, Ariane took his hand. A wave of sheer emotion rolled over her before she had taken a single step. Wynn jerked her roughly across the platform; behind them the violent sounds of struggle echoed and rebounded in the charged, frigid air. Ariane wrenched free and turned in time to see Rook crouched opposite Sable and the guards, his body gathered for attack. One guard raised his disruptor, taking careful aim.

"Rook!" Ariane screamed. His blazing eyes flashed to her; Sable rushed forward, turning the disruptor in her hand and bringing the butt of it crashing into Rook's forehead.

He fell in utter silence. Ariane's sight blurred; she fought like a wild thing against Wynn and the guards who tried to restrain her.

"Well, Sable?" Wynn asked, his breathing a little rough from the brief struggle.

Sable rose and reversed her disruptor calmly. "He's not dead, but he may wish he was." Abruptly she turned and stared straight into Ariane's eyes. "Do you want it to be worse for him, Marchand?"

Trust me. That unspoken message flashed again through Ariane's mind. If she lingered now, she would gain nothing for herself or Rook and might lose any hope of Sable's aid. In stopping Rook so thoroughly, Sable had saved him from his own reckless desire to protect Ariane—and probable death.

But it was the hardest thing she'd ever done to turn away, go quietly with Wynn, leaving Rook in the hands of a woman who still nurtured an old and powerful hatred. A woman Wynn Slayton still trusted, and might have reason to. . . .

"A wise decision, Ariane," Wynn said, tucking her arm through his elbow as if they were still courting. The guards fell into step behind them. "A pity you weren't able to say a proper good-bye to your lover—but clean breaks are often the easiest."

Forcing one foot in front of the other, Ariane walked with him submissively. Her ears strained for Rook's voice, her mind reached for the touch of his, but all was lost in the terrible silence.

She had her own job to do now—whatever it took to keep Wynn off guard and give Rook a chance to recover. It seemed that a thousand ghostly footsteps dogged her heels: the chained, disembodied souls of the Kalians who waited to be set free.

CHAPTER TWENTY-ONE

*R*ook wiped blood from the corner of his mouth with the heel of his hand and tried to focus his eyes on the woman who stood over him.

"You can go," Sable's voice said to someone Rook couldn't see. The rap of boots retreated across the metal floor and receded into silence.

It took only a moment for Rook to remember. "Ariane," he rasped, battling vertigo as he scrambled to his feet. His head still rang with the force of Sable's blow. "Ariane!"

Sable took a single step and calmly blocked his path to the corridor into which Ariane and Wynn had vanished. The sound that came from deep in Rook's throat was hardly human. He lowered his head and bared his teeth, seeing only an enemy who stood between him and his mate.

"Don't be a fool, Rook," Sable said. "You can't save her that way."

Something in her words broke through the blind instinct that held Rook in its grip. He straightened, shaking his head to clear the lingering dizziness.

"She's with Slayton—" he said hoarsely.

"Yes. And as long as you don't go charging to her rescue, she'll be able to take care of herself until we've done what *we* have to do."

Rook exploded into motion, dodging to the side. Sable mirrored his movements. He outweighed her by many kilos, but she was a warrior trained. Even so, his desperation would have shifted the balance if not for the disruptor she pointed steadily at his heart.

Her mouth curved in a grim smile at his patent shock. "No, I haven't reverted to Wynn's creature, even though he believes I'm still under the influence of his drug. My mind is my own, and I don't care to throw my life away—or yours, or Ariane's—because of your muddleheaded notions of gallantry."

Rook forced himself to a semblance of calm, gauging Sable's hold on the disruptor. "Slayton will do anything—" he growled.

"He might, but he is far too methodical to abandon all his plans." Sable shifted her weight, staring hard into his eyes. "Listen to me, Rook. Wynn still trusts me. He has kept me—so he thinks—ignorant of what he's done to our people. He thinks I still believe that all but a few he chose to save—like myself, and Heron—are dead. He was careful to prevent me from seeing *that*"—she jerked her head at the illusory wall behind them—"but I've known from the moment he brought me here, and I've watched and waited. Now the moment has come." Her eyes closed in a sudden revelation of pain. "While he's involved with Ariane, you and I have a chance to free our people. I know how to do it, but unless you and I act together, we'll have no hope of getting them all out in time."

Rook shook his head. "In time for what? Time for Slayton to escape and take Ariane with him?" *Or worse,* his mind screamed. But Sable only sighed, unutterably weary.

"He won't leave without me. Of that I'm certain. Yes, he wants Ariane, and he plans to drug her to make her malleable—"

"Drug—"

She aborted his sudden lunge with the muzzle of her 'ruptor. "In your blind emotion you seem to have forgotten that Ariane is a Healer—a Healer such as our people haven't seen in a century. She wiped the drug out of my mind as if it never existed. She can surely neutralize the worst effects of the drug as Wynn gives it to her. She knows I'm on your side, and she's bright enough to realize what she has to do."

Rook heard her explanations without comprehension. His senses strained for a hint of Ariane's scent, the whisper of her voice, the essence of her mind.

"Ariane is Kalian, yet you seem to have no more respect

for her than these Espérancians have for their fragile, pampered females," Sable said, openly contemptuous. "Damn you, Rook, would you sacrifice all our people for one woman?"

Yes, the savage within him cried. *Yes.* But his questing mind had touched something—something attenuated but unmistakable, a presence that had become a permanent part of his soul.

Ariane. She was well, and whole, and in the very depths of his being he knew what she was trying to tell him.

"Or will you grant her the honor of doing what she came here to do?"

Rook's vision sharpened to sudden, liberating clarity. "Yes," he said, as if answering Ariane's distant, silent voice. He looked at Sable. "Yes."

Jerking back the disruptor, Sable grabbed his wrist. "We've already lost too much precious time." She began to turn away, but Rook twisted his hand to catch hers.

"Wait," he said. "Can you get me to a hatch leading outside? We brought eight of our people—Slayton's agents that Ariane was able to Heal. They're waiting outside. With their help—"

Sable gave him no answer. She spun on her heel and ran along the platform, away from the corridor from which they'd come. Rook shot a glance at the opaque screen that concealed the rows of cages and their dull-eyed inhabitants, his emotions too tangled to acknowledge.

But Ariane was with him. She was with him as he followed Sable through the echoing corridors, past Kalian guards with blank faces, to the heavy sealed portal that opened onto the barren surface. She was with him as he found Heron and the others and led them inside, returning to the place where their people were imprisoned.

And Ariane was with them all when the Kalians she had Healed began to set their people free.

·　·　·

"I have wondered, Ariane," Wynn said, examining the hypodermic injector in his hand, "what made you suspect me."

Ariane watched him from the table where he and his guards had bound her, stripped almost to the skin, muscles taut against shackles designed to resist full Kalian strength. Wynn measured out a precise dose of the drug and glanced back at her, one eyebrow arched.

"I should have known long ago," she said quietly.

Wynn smiled. "Something in your tone suggests that you find me—evil? Is that the quaint word for it? Such purity as you possess should surely have been able to detect my treacherous nature. Or is it, in retrospect, some Kalian sense you might have utilized?"

Refusing to look away, Ariane answered with the contempt in her eyes.

"Your lover couldn't have known that his people survived here on Espérance, even if he'd heard of their supposed destruction aboard the *Bonaventure* during his time on Tantalus," Wynn continued, unfazed. "Certainly the Patriarch was ignorant of my intentions." He turned to face her, holding the injector carelessly. "No matter, Ariane. If you don't feel inclined to talk now, you will later. My curiosity can wait."

Ariane let her thoughts return to Rook as they had done again and again since Wynn had brought her to this cold, sterile medlab with its sinister banks of consoles and equipment designed for experiments she could hardly begin to imagine. She knew Rook was safe; once, straining with all her might, she had felt the whisper of his emotions—rage, frustration, fear for her—and tried to reach him with the sheer force of her will. The contact had been brief, but it had been real.

Rook was with her now, and nothing Wynn said or did could abolish his presence.

"Your performance was quite superb, Ariane," Wynn said. "I was almost prepared to believe you were only the hotblooded little whore you pretended to be. What a pair we might have made, *chérie,* had things been different."

Ariane flexed her hands in their restraints. "Which of us was the greater actor, Wynn? The Patriarch trusted you with everything—his business affairs, his wealth, his affection. Even with his heir." She spoke without a trace of emotion, yielding him nothing. "He saw you as the son and grandson he never had, the future hope of both our families, perhaps all of Espérance."

"Ah, yes. Bernard was ever the idealist, but he overlooked his own sins. He made the mistake of forgetting the lessons of the past. But you are ignorant of all that, aren't you? I doubt your beloved great-grandfather would ever admit his youthful iniquities." He strolled closer, resting his hip against her cot. "I did promise to explain. But first—" Dismissing the two Kalian guards with a jerk of his head, he smiled down at Ariane. "First we must see to the small matter of your continuing cooperation."

Before Ariane could prepare herself, Wynn jabbed the injector against her arm. She felt the effects of the drug almost instantly. Something obscene and inimical flowed into her veins, coursed its way into her brain. Turning inward, Ariane traced its progress and prepared to battle the insidious invasion.

Wynn watched her, oblivious. "There. Soon you'll feel quite—relaxed, Ariane." He drew his finger lightly across her lips. "It won't hurt at all, I promise."

But it did. Had she let go, it might have been easy and peaceful. But she fought the drug and its enslavement with all the Healing powers she had discovered within herself, and the struggle was agony. When she opened her eyes, the room spun and flexed wildly, and her body seemed to rise above the cot.

"I think we'll deal very well together when we've left this world, my Ariane." Wynn's voice grew attenuated and strange, as if he spoke at the far end of a tunnel. "You won't even mind what I do to your great-grandfather and his precious family name, or what becomes of these barbarians."

Ariane let his words wash over her, stripped of horror by the more immediate battle. A small, involuntary sound escaped her throat, and Wynn took it as a sign of his imminent victory.

"I've planned this so long, Ariane. In spite of what you've done to interfere, I'll still be able to accomplish a great deal. With your help, of course." He sighed, and his face seemed to double and triple in Ariane's vision. "In the days of the assassins these matters were much easier to arrange. Kalians were born to be the perfect operatives. With just a little more time I would have been able to activate my agents among Marchand's allied Houses."

Ariane swallowed painfully. "Assassination—"

"Only as a last resort. My Kalians had collected information on members of the Elite that would have been highly useful in—persuading Bernard's allies against helping him when I brought him down. He would have found himself entirely alone, your family isolated." He looked away, his fingers absently stroking Ariane's face.

"The Kalians were only part of it, of course, though in time I might have found more diverse uses for them. That illegal drug operation you and your lover so unexpectedly discovered in the Louve system—that was mine. I found you there because one of my runners contacted me when he realized who you were." He laughed softly. "Most convenient. Bernard believed I was investigating rumors of that very operation; he was disturbed that Espérancians might be involved in such a crime. But while that little venture was earning me a considerable sum in the interstellar black market, I was also carefully planting rumors and evidence throughout the League that the Marchand were the ones behind it."

Why? The single word rebounded in Ariane's brain, but she didn't realize she'd spoken it aloud until Wynn smiled down at her with undisguised triumph.

"Ah, yes. I did promise to explain. The roots lie far in the past, and it all began with your beloved Patriarch. The irony of it—that all this came from his devotion to the sacred purity of your Marchand blood and Caste."

While Ariane listened in numb, helpless silence, Wynn

began to weave a tangled story of old resentments long believed forgotten, of a young Bernard Marchand's arrogance and his rejection of his Slayton bride on their betrothal day so many years ago. He told her how the Slayton family had been humiliated and Tyler Slayton, Wynn's father, had hurled himself to suicidal death in the first Fahar Conflict.

"Your Patriarch believed," Wynn said hoarsely, "that nothing outweighed the purity of Marchand blood and honor, no matter what the price. So when he became convinced that Ria Santini-Slayton was tainted with the illegitimate blood of the Laborer Caste, he cast her aside. In so doing he dishonored the Slayton name for years to come, drove my father to his death, and slowly destroyed my mother."

Ariane shook her head. "I never—knew—"

"Of course not. The Patriarch had his own secrets to hide, didn't he? He thought to make up for my losses by making me his adopted son in all but name." He choked on a laugh. "His pangs of conscience came too late. The damage was done. I have waited all these years, used whatever fate put in my path to make certain of his downfall."

"Including the—Kalians. An entire people nearly—destroyed because of your desire for revenge." Ariane swallowed back the heaviness in her throat. "You are—insane—"

"No more insane, perhaps, than your Patriarch when he put so much power into my hands, blinded himself to everything he didn't wish to see." He sighed, shaking his head. "Bernard was the first on Espérance to treat with the League, gaining influence that would make Marchand a name recognized on nearly every civilized world. Under the umbrella of that name I established my own agenda. In every Marchand operation I placed my own people, loyal only to Slayton interests. Marchand ships carried the illegal drugs that the Louve operations produced. I obtained controlling interests in several of the banks that hold Marchand debts. Without Slayton support and the backing of its major Elite allies on Espérance, the Marchand empire will cease to exist."

A wave of nausea passed through Ariane. "You still won't win. Bernard—has the crystal—"

"Fortunately, I didn't keep all my records in the core you penetrated in Lumière, Ariane," Wynn said. "My diverse League interests—the ones your great-grandfather's influence so graciously opened up to me—remain quite safe. And the many transactions and ventures I handled for the Patriarch—" He twisted a lock of Ariane's hair around his finger. "Quite a number of them are so delicately balanced that a word from me will send them crashing to ruin."

With a hollow, detached dread Ariane realized that Wynn's scenario was all too plausible. Bernard had left too much in Wynn's hands, relied too much on that pragmatic, ruthless acumen that had won House Slayton its place among the Elite. After Jacques's death he'd leaned on Wynn even more, knowing he was to be Ariane's husband. . . .

"Jacques," Ariane whispered. "You were—behind the riots. You were there when Jacques died—" The horror of what she envisioned threatened to obliterate her tenuous control. "You—killed Jacques."

Wynn sighed again and looked down at her, a mockery of regret on his handsome face. "An unfortunate side effect of the business. Your lover made himself unexpectedly useful by interfering and drawing the full blame onto himself. It did insure that Bernard would feel little pity for the Kalians and be quite amenable to sending them away where I could gain control of them. It also took another variable out of the equation—by replacing Jacques's marriage to my sister with yours to me, I gained a far more direct control of relations between our families."

No. Ariane tried to jerk her head free of Wynn's lingering touch, but what will remained to her was focused entirely on neutralizing the drug singing so seductively in her blood.

"Jacques was a sacrifice, a partial payment of the debt your great-grandfather owes my family," Wynn continued, his voice grown suddenly harsh. "The Kalians he fought to save will be another when I activate the warhead that wipes this compound from existence."

"No," she whispered aloud.

"I do regret it, Ariane," he said. "You may hate me now, but that will change. When you have nothing left—not your Patriarch nor your name nor your barbarian lover—you will be grateful enough for whatever I give you." He bent to kiss her rigid lips. "And now I think we've lingered long enough." Pushing away from the cot, he lifted his arm and began to speak into the comm band around his wrist. Ariane heard him speak Sable's name.

"You've dealt with Galloway? Excellent. Join me in the medlab immediately and see that the remaining guards return to the compound."

Dealt with Galloway. Ariane reached frantically into that place inside herself where she'd felt Rook before and found him still there. He had been with Sable, and Sable had asked Ariane to trust her. She had to be ready. . . .

She took the final risk, withdrawing her consciousness into the very core of her being and shutting everything else away. As she had done with Rook, with Sable, with the other drugged Kalians, she reached for the wrongness within her very cells and commanded her body to reject it.

From another world she heard sounds—voices, a sudden shout, the scuffle of feet and muffled thud of striking objects. A shadow loomed over her; living warmth brushed her wrists and ankles and swept her free of her bonds.

Rook. His essence blended with hers and the last of the drug vanished from her system. Powerful arms lifted her, cradled her against the driving rhythm of his heartbeat.

She opened her eyes. Rook's hair veiled her face, his rapid breaths mingling with her own. The sudden heat of his kiss infused her with life and strength.

"Wynn—" she began as he released her lips, but he was already letting her slide to the floor, one arm clamped around her waist.

"You're safe," he said softly. Ariane forced her eyes away from him and followed his gaze.

The medlab was filled with Kalians. She recognized Heron at once, and Marten, and the others they had brought from

Lumière. Sable stood at their head, a disruptor in her hand. And Wynn—Wynn Slayton crouched alone in the corner of the room, his expression blank with shock.

Rook pulled Ariane against him as if he could meld her body with his. "Sable showed us how to set the others free," he said, showing her through the Sharing what he did not explain in words. "We came as quickly as we could."

Ariane took from his mind the image of hundreds of bewildered Kalian faces, men and women and children who meekly followed Sable and Rook out of the cages in which they had lived for so many years. Then the view shifted to Rook's first glimpse of Ariane, pinned to the cot, her face pale and drawn as she fought the drug for mastery while Wynn caressed her still body. The scene was hazed with the tinge of Rook's violent and helpless rage.

Turning into his arms, Ariane caught his rigid jaw between her hands. "It's over, Rook," she whispered. "I'm all right. Our people are free."

But his eyes were fixed on Wynn. And Wynn's were locked on Sable's disruptor, aimed at his heart.

"Sable," Wynn whispered. In all the time she had known him, Ariane had never heard his voice betray the astonished vulnerability it did now. "You betrayed me."

"Did I, Wynn?" Sable smiled, bitter and sad and mocking. Her grip tightened on the 'ruptor. "Who betrayed whom all those years ago?"

Wynn shook his head. "The drug—"

"Ask Ariane. You thought I knew nothing of what you had hidden behind these walls. I've known how you used me —used all of us—since she came to your estates and unlocked your secrets."

Ariane watched Wynn's expression change as he grasped the enormity of what had happened. "Both of you," he said, glancing at Ariane. "And the rest—"

"Free. All of them," Rook cut in. Pushing Ariane roughly behind him, he stalked across the room. "You're finished, Slayton."

Straightening slowly, Wynn regarded Rook with a twisted smile that matched Sable's for bitter pride.

"You hate me, Galloway, but you've been as much my pawn as all your people. It was easy to manipulate you." He laughed. "You'll never be other than what you are—a barbarian. But you and I have at least one thing in common. We both understand the drive for revenge that eclipses every other desire."

Rook's fingers worked into fists. "Yes. I understand revenge." He took another step forward. "But that isn't why you won't leave this place alive."

The icy ruthlessness of his words shattered Ariane's paralysis. She reached out for Rook, knowing she had to penetrate the deepest part of his mind before he committed an act that would destroy him as surely as it did Wynn. His hatred defied her, beat her back just as his muscles bunched in readiness for a lethal charge.

But Sable was there first. "No, Rook," she said. "I can't let you do that." Her disruptor fixed on Rook as her eyes flickered to Ariane. "Stay where you are. I don't want to hurt either one of you." She half turned to address the Kalians behind her. "Keep back. I will fire if I have to."

Rook went very still, his hand catching Ariane's in a crushing grip. She welcomed the pain even as she reeled in the chaos of his emotions.

"Sable," Rook rasped. "Why? You know what he is—"

"Yes." Sable drew in a deep, shuddering breath. "I know. And I also know myself." She met Ariane's eyes. "You did me no favor, Healer." Slipping along the perimeter of the room, she drew close to Wynn. "This was always my intention since you Healed me—to free our people and see Wynn safely off this world."

Wynn breathed a harsh laugh. "Who betrays whom, Sable?" he said.

Her face lost all expression. "I'm the only chance you have," she said. "You won't get another one." Before he could answer, she turned to Ariane and Rook. "Get our people out of this place and as far away as you can. The rest is out of your hands."

There was no question of arguing with Sable. Ariane saw the subtle madness in her eyes, a madness that she knew all too well. Through the Sharing she felt Rook rebelliously accept the same unalterable facts.

Wynn Slayton would escape, his sins unpunished, his threats unanswered.

Sable backed toward the door, Wynn at her side. "Give me ten minutes. If anyone follows within that time, I'll shoot to kill."

The Kalians in the doorway parted silently before her. Running footsteps receded down the corridor.

With one accord the Kalians joined Rook and Ariane. Rook swept them with his gaze, pulling Ariane to his side again.

"It seems we have no choice," he said grimly. "Heron, you and the others get our people out of the compound. There are still Kalian guards who might offer resistance; take no chances with any of them. Ariane and I—"

"Will go directly to the landing field." She looked up at Rook. "We'll use the transport's comm to contact the Marchand troops. They'll get word to the Patriarch."

He jerked a nod, and the Kalians turned for the door. Ariane began to follow, but Rook tugged her back into his arms. His mouth came down hard and hot; Ariane buried her fingers in his mane and matched him kiss for kiss.

And then they ran. The lift was waiting for them, taking them up to the surface and the hidden entrance through which they had first arrived. Rook paused as icy air hit them, his eyes scanning the barren landscape. There was no sign of Sable or Wynn, but hundreds of dark, huddled figures were emerging from another hidden exit a half kilometer away.

Hard-packed snow cracked under Ariane's boots as Rook urged her forward; the landing field was empty of ships except for their transport and the two fighters that had escorted them in. No one tried to stop them. Ariane jumped into the pilot's seat of the transport and slipped on the com headset while Rook waited tensely beside her.

"I'll send for more transports immediately," she told him as her fingers worked the controls. "Whatever House Marchand can beg, borrow, or steal. We can send our people to the Patriarch's country estate near Nouveau-Quebec; that's the best place I can think of at short notice. We'll send up supplies, medical personnel, everything—" She broke off as she made contact with the Marchand forces. Rook leaned close to her, listening as she gave the necessary commands and peeled the headset free of her hair.

"It's done," she said. "They're on their way."

Without a word Rook dropped into the copilot's seat and webbed himself in. Ariane lifted the transport in a cloud of ice and swung it around toward the place where the Kalians were gathering. She set it down carefully as close to them as she dared come; Rook sucked in a breath, echoing her emotion as they watched the blank, bewildered faces of a people too long lost to freedom.

"Dieu," she murmured softly. Rook slipped up behind her, dropping his chin onto her hair.

"We'll take care of them," he said hoarsely. "They'll be Healed, and free—"

A deep, chilling rumble silenced him. Together they stared out through the canopy, searching for the source of the sound. A geyser of snow and ice fountained into the air a kilometer away, catching the sun in a blinding storm of light. Something sleek and dark emerged from white chaos; a ship, bursting free of some underground berth, slicing skyward in a scream of engines.

"Slayton," Rook rasped. Within moments the ship was lost to sight, space-bound; Ariane swung her eyes back to the ground and saw the Kalian refugees picking themselves up, milling in confusion.

Rook's grip shifted to her shoulder. "We must go to them," he said. His mingled grief and rage came to her clearly, blending with her own. "They need our help—"

Ariane had just risen to accompany him when a chime

from the comm drew her back to the console. She picked up the headset again, listened in growing shock as the Marchand troop captain gave her the grim, impossible news. Her fingers slipped three times on the headset before she was able to remove it.

"What is it?" Rook's voice came from a great distance, drawing her slowly back to herself. She struggled for words, and he gripped her hand in his own. "Ariane, tell me."

"The Patriarch—" Swallowing, she began again. "The Patriarch has been attacked. He's in critical condition."

"Attacked," Rook echoed. "By whom?"

Ariane forced herself to meet his eyes.

"By a Kalian assassin."

CHAPTER TWENTY-TWO

*R*ook leaped to his feet, still clenching her hand. "How?"

Ariane let herself be drawn up and into his arms. "I don't know. We—must not have found all of them—all of Wynn's agents. Wynn—he must have had time to—"

He muttered a curse. "The assassin?"

Her answer was muffled against his chest. "Dead. The Patriarch's guards—killed him."

Rook closed his eyes. "But the Patriarch lives."

"Yes." Pushing back, she looked up, heedless of the tears that glazed her dark eyes. "But he's on full life-support. God, this is my fault—" Hot moisture spilled onto her cheeks. "My fault—"

"Your fault for trying to save our people?" Rook caught her chin and tilted her head back. He struggled to suppress his own sudden and profound fear. "I won't let you take that burden."

Tangled emotions reached him through the Sharing, nearly overwhelmed by her self-contempt. "I have to get back," she said painfully. "Back to Bernard. He needs me—"

And I need you. Our people need you— But he kept the protests locked in his throat, stroking her hair, staring out the canopy at the blinding snow. That burden, too, he could not give her now.

"Yes," he said at last. "And I must stay here, with our people, and see them to safety."

Suddenly her fingers were clutching him fiercely, and her eyes grew fully lucid through the tears. Her own protests worked behind the delicate skin of her throat; the Sharing conveyed the words she would not say, begging him to go with her.

And then she dropped her hands. "Yes," she echoed softly. "Yes. I'll see you get complete authority to direct the troops and get those transports to the country estate. The moment I'm back in Lumière and have—seen to the Patriarch—I'll send everything you'll need."

All the cool efficiency of her training was back to save her when she most needed it. Rook felt her withdraw, slipping away from him until the Sharing was a mere shadow of sensation, too distant to grasp.

Inwardly he raged at the necessity of what she did. Of what they both must do. "For a day," he told her roughly. "Two. No more."

She had moved away to lean over the console, her back to him. Her head lifted. "Come when you can," she said without inflection. "When the Kalians are—safe."

The Kalians. Not "our people." Rook shivered, fighting the urge to go to her and trap her in his arms. "I will," he promised grimly. He tried once again to find words to comfort her, to bind her, to make the world around them vanish. But it was too late. Ariane slid into the pilot's seat and began to speak in the measured tones of authority, directing the Marchand troops and preparing the way for Rook.

When the first of the troops arrived, Ariane commanded them with practiced efficiency. The officers hardly blinked when she set Rook over them and gave them their orders. And then Rook was gathering his people, preparing them for the journey ahead, Heron and the other Kalians from Lumière at his side.

He didn't look up as Ariane's ship lifted, scattering snow and ice like tiny prisms on the bitter wind.

"Lady Ariane!"

The young man's voice was vaguely familiar, his face more so as Ariane paused just outside the doors of Bernard's suite. He hurried toward her, a comp tab in his hand, his expression stern and relieved.

She remembered him suddenly—Pascal Leigh-Marchand, one of her numerous cousins from a cadet branch of the

Family. He had lost his parents at an early age, and along with several other cousins had been tutored with Ariane on the Marchand estates. As children they had played; as adolescents they had fought and fenced, but he had left for Tolstoy's university some time before Ariane had taken the *d'Artagnan* for her three-year sabbatical. He would have returned to Espérance before she had, but they hadn't met again until this moment. She had been far too preoccupied since her return to note the comings and goings of the innumerable relatives who lived or worked on the estate.

"Pascal," she said gravely. "It's good to see you again. How is he?"

Pascal accepted her abruptness with a slight bow, acknowledging her authority. "In good hands," he said. "I've had Dr. Adler waiting to answer your questions. Specialists have already seen him; they say he'll recover with time. I've—taken the liberty of doing what I can to ensure that the reins pass easily." He gestured with the comp tab. "I'll have the major domo and Guard captain at your disposal when you're ready."

Ariane had no time to indulge her surprise at Pascal's presence, or his very welcome efficiency. She nodded and walked by him, past a small crowd of murmuring cousins, servants, and House troops waiting in the anteroom, and through a second set of guarded doors.

Dr. Adler bowed as she entered and began to speak as she moved quickly to Bernard's side. The Patriarch was in a life-support hood, pale and drawn, his chest entirely covered in medical webbing. From a distance Ariane heard the doctor's explanations, his reassurances, his careful warnings. She rested her cheek against the clear hood and watched Bernard's shallow breathing, struggling to hold back the tears.

Bernard would live. That much was clear. The rest of it sank in by painful increments. He would take time and profound rest and quiet to recover; in spite of the longevity drugs, his body was weak and far beyond youth.

My fault, she keened silently. *Mine.* Bernard's blue-veined, sunken lids fluttered. The readings on the bedside monitor wavered. Dr. Adler swept by her to adjust a control, muttered incomprehensibly.

"Don't—" Bernard's voice rasped, hollow through the hood. "Don't leave me—"

Smearing tears against the hood, Ariane shook her head. "I won't leave you, Grand-père," she whispered. As if he had heard her, he subsided, his chest shuddering in a deep sigh. Ariane pushed herself up on rubbery legs and exchanged glances with the doctor. He nodded gravely and disappeared through the door to an adjoining room, leaving her alone with an old, frightened man.

Thoughts forced their way through the dullness of her brain. Just outside the doors the others were waiting—people who depended on Marchand for their livelihood, their purpose. It was incomprehensible to them—to her—that the Patriarch could cease to be. He *was* Marchand. In many ways he was Lumière itself, the beating heart of Espérance. A heart Wynn had almost stopped, that she had left vulnerable in pursuit of her Kalian blood.

Bernard was Marchand as she could never be, and yet she was all he had. She was his heir, the only one left of his direct line, even tainted as she was. She had been raised to duty, to responsibility, to the things she must know to step into his place.

Once her duty had been to become Wynn's wife, to stand at his side as he took the power of two of the greatest Houses on Espérance. Now she was utterly alone.

Ariane stared at Bernard's slack face. She could not, would not think beyond the moment. She had survived everything else; this was no different. Emotion became too overwhelming to bear, so she shunted it aside and focused on what must be done.

Pascal was waiting for her outside, ready as he had promised. Between his unexpected efforts and those of the major domo, the Guard captain, and the head of House Security, Ariane found it almost easy to slide into her new role. She saw the relief on worried faces as she issued orders and set things to running again as they must. She sent out the transports and supplies she had promised Rook, reassigning personnel to help get the Kalians settled at the country estate. She delegated authority where she could to Marchand cousins and agents, making Pascal her official aide as he'd been Bernard's during the years of her absence. Together they saw that Marchand business on Espérance and throughout the League continued without interruption, and reassured members of allied Houses and press representatives who flooded the estate's comm lines.

Pascal came to her during those first hours with the transmission Bernard had received just before the assassin had struck. She read the transcript once and then again, too exhausted to react. Pascal stared at her with concern when a bitter, bubbling laugh forced its way from her throat.

The League had found out about Wynn. Oh, not everything—not about the Kalians or the extent of his evil plans— but enough. Enough that they'd been on their way to Espérance to question him about a certain illegal drug operation in the Louve System.

She tried contacting the League Patrol ship that had put into orbit when the transmission had been relayed. It had already left Espérance, without warning or explanation. Ariane dispatched a message ship to Agora with the news of Wynn's treachery and escape, knowing there was little more she could do.

Twelve hours passed before Ariane was forced to accept her body's demand for rest. Pascal, ever at her side, took over where he could. Twice she talked to Rook by comm, grasping at the sound of his voice as at a lifeline to sanity; when she lay in her makeshift bed in the sitting room adjoining Bernard's, she let herself think of his return, and the feel of his powerful arms holding her close.

Beyond that was nothing.

In two brief days she had changed.

Rook paused in the doorway to the study, drinking her in with his gaze. Her brown hair was knotted haphazardly at the base of her neck, and there were blue-gray crescents under her eyes. The weary slump of her body over the desk cut him to the heart.

"Ariane," he said softly.

She looked up, and her face was transformed. Joy flared like a nova in her eyes.

"Rook," she choked, pushing up from the chair. The strength of her emotion preceded her, enfolding Rook just before he took her in his arms.

The kiss began with quiet desperation and gradually transformed, gentling into a ceremony of reunion. They had been worlds apart for the past two days, each bearing the burden of responsibility alone.

But Ariane had suffered more. Rook held her away from himself, examining her face grimly. Her lips smiled, but her eyes were haunted with a fear she refused to let him feel, even through the Sharing. The supple strength of her body had visibly faded, and she felt to him unbearably fragile, as if she might break at a stronger touch.

The anger he had never let go flared in him again, dark rage at the ordeal she had to endure because of what she was. Because she refused to turn her back on the chains of her past. . . .

Her head jerked against his palm, and he knew she had felt his anger. He drew the emotion back to the deepest part of his mind, concealing it as she hid her fear.

"Is he all right?" Rook asked, stroking her cheek with his fingers.

Ariane relaxed, closing her eyes at his caress. "Yes. He'll recover—in time."

Biting back the compulsion to demand what she couldn't promise, Rook guided her back to the chair. "This—" He gestured around the study, at the stacks of comp tabs and transcripts scattered over the huge desk. "This is too much, Ariane." He knelt before her and gripped the armrests of the chair, trapping her in it.

"Look at you," he continued harshly. "Do you think I can't feel it?" He grasped her hand and turned it over, palm up, in his. Her fingers trembled. "In two days they've drained you, made you into a shadow of yourself. What will happen in a week, a month?" He bit back his greatest fear, refusing to voice it. "This is a prison, Ariane—no more nor less than Tantalus. If you go on—"

"Is it more than what you've been doing, relocating and caring for several thousand Kalians?" she interrupted. She leaned back, gazing up at him through lids weighted by exhaustion. "This is what I was bred—trained—to do."

Inwardly he flinched at her calm acceptance. "Is it, Ariane?"

She looked down at their joined hands. "Kalians are good at survival," she said at last, hesitating over her words. "I'm fighting for the survival of my world, my House, my family. And the Kalians we're trying to save."

"And what of *your* survival, Ariane?" he whispered.

Her smile was warm as she touched his face, running her fingers over his jaw as if to ease the clenched muscles under the sun-bronzed skin.

"I'll be all right, Rook. I'm strong. Wouldn't you have done anything to save your people if you could? Haven't you already?" She cupped his face in her hands. "Can you expect any less of me?"

Sable's words in the compound came back to him then. *"Ariane is Kalian, yet you seem to have no more respect for her than these Espérancians have for their fragile, pampered females. Would you sacrifice all our people for one woman?"*

"By the Shapers," he hissed.

Ariane rested her forehead against his. "You're here now. That's all that matters."

All that matters. A sound of despair and need forced its way from Rook's throat, and he silenced it against Ariane's lips. They let the kiss take them to a place where birth and honor and blood—the future itself—had no meaning.

And then a soft chime rang from the comm terminal at Ariane's desk. She broke away, eyes dazed. She settled at the comm to answer; Rook sprang up to pace the confines of the study, listening to the weary cadence of Ariane's voice as she dealt with some new crisis.

"I'm sorry," she said. Her footsteps whispered behind him, and her arms settled around his waist. He closed his eyes and flung back his head. Her touch still made him tremble, but the moment of unity had passed.

"You'll want a full report of my progress in Nouveau-Quebec," he said tonelessly. "The supplies and personnel you've sent are enough for the time being, but it may take several weeks for most of the people to recover."

"Yes," she murmured. Her hands flexed at his waist. "I can't Heal all of them personally. I wish I could. But with nearly all our Med staff there, we're doing what we can." She sighed. "Without the regular doses of Euphorie that Wynn fed them, it's only a matter of time and rest. I promise you they'll have everything they need."

They. Rook heard the way she detached herself from the Kalians, refused an emotional involvement that could only distract her from her duties. Deliberately he unclenched his fists, covering her hands with his own.

In the two days they'd been apart, he'd thought of Ariane in every spare moment left to him. He remembered the part her selfless courage had played in Wynn's defeat and the freeing of their people. He thought of her fierce loyalty to him, never faltering in spite of his blind distrust and hatred. He dreamed of making love to her again and again, burying himself in her sweet body until nothing could separate them.

But she was too far away. Even as she clung to him, she held a part of herself locked in a place he couldn't reach. Just as *he* had done for so many years.

As if she caught the echo of his thoughts, she drew back, pulling her hands from beneath his.

"There's something I've been waiting to show you," she said, crossing to the desk. Paper rustled. She came to stand before him, holding a multipage transcript in her hand.

"Bernard received this message from a League Patrol ship just before he was attacked. The ship had just arrived to request Marchand and Council aid in taking Wynn Slayton into custody for questioning."

"Questioning—"

"Yes. It seems they've been investigating illegal drug activities in the League for some time—suspecting Marchand involvement." Her tone grew thin and hard. "Wynn succeeded in that part of his plan. But he didn't know that Patrol agents would put a tracer on the *d'Artagnan* when we berthed at Agora, and follow us to the Louve System."

Rook went very still. "A tracer—" The memory of his bitter accusations against Ariane made his stomach knot. That had been the one element of her supposed betrayal that had never been resolved.

Looking up at him, Ariane smiled sadly. "We weren't alone when Wynn confronted us. A cloaked Patrol ship was listening in and observing everything that went on. When the *Perséphone* left the system, the ship moved in and managed to capture a few drugrunners who weren't fast enough to escape. Over the next weeks they managed to learn enough from Wynn's less loyal employees to implicate him and clear Marchand of any involvement in the Louve operation."

Rook took the transcripts from Ariane's hand. He read them through and tossed them onto the desk almost violently.

"Damn them," he whispered. "Damn them all." Because of the League's indifference, his people had been lost and enslaved. Because of the League's callous disregard for justice, innocent people had been condemned to living hell on Tantalus. And because of the League's reticence, Ariane had been put in terrible danger and faced Rook's own unjustified wrath.

He looked down at Ariane, turning his rage inward again. "They came too late," he said harshly.

"The Patriarch had no time to send a reply before he was struck down," Ariane said. Her eyes were very bright. "I tried to contact them when I returned, but the ship had already left orbit."

"And now Slayton's gone."

Moving closer, Ariane touched his arm. Only the flutter of her eyelids revealed how much she felt of his emotion, in spite of all his efforts. "But the League is after him now. He won't be able to carry out his plans. He'll be a fugitive. He's lost everything, no matter where he goes."

And what of us, Ariane? How much have we lost? A thousand scathing words caught in his throat. What retribution would the League mete out when they had failed in all the rest? When would there be a resolution, an end to the years of suffering and injustice?

"I'm sorry, Rook," Ariane whispered.

He flinched and turned to catch her arms. "Sorry? After all you've done?" He laughed hoarsely. "They've hurt you as much as they have me and our people, Ariane—the League, your family, this world—and they'll go on hurting you. This isn't your place."

Ariane did not want to hear it. Her muscles hardened under his hands, resisting with Kalian strength. "Bernard—"

"Do you truly believe that out of all the members of your extended clan only you can hold Marchand together?"

Brown eyes took on the tinge of copper. "I'm the heir, trained all my life to do this," she said fiercely, twisting in his hold. "I was responsible for what happened to Bernard. I was sworn to uphold the honor of this family long before I ever knew you—"

"Or what you truly are?" Rook bared his teeth. "In all your aristocratic pride you've forgotten you're more Kalian than Marchand." She turned her face aside, and he caught her chin to pull it back. "If your Elite ever learned the truth, they'd cast you out as they did the rest of our people. What use would you be then?"

Her stricken gaze cut him to the quick, making him despise the desperation that drove him to such cruel measures. But now that he had begun, he could no more stop himself than he could halt the stars in their motion; the thought he could not voice, the thought of losing Ariane when they had both survived so much and come so far, drove him inevitably toward the brink of madness.

"I won't let them destroy you, Ariane," he said. *Even if I must steal you away from this, from Bernard Marchand, as I once stole your ship and your honor. . . .*

His voice softened as his grip did, becoming a caress. "You don't belong here, not anymore. Listen to me, Ariane—"

Someone cleared his throat, and Rook jerked his gaze up over Ariane's head. A young man—a Marchand—stood in the doorway, his expression carefully neutral.

"Forgive me, Lady Ariane—Sieur Galloway—but I have an urgent message from the Patriarch."

Ariane whirled, the color draining from her skin. "He's awake?"

The young man inclined his head. "Dr. Adler thinks it best that you come at once. With Mr. Galloway."

The guarded expression Ariane turned on Rook was enough to make him stifle a curse. "Why Mr. Galloway?" she asked quietly.

"The Patriarch is very insistent about speaking to him," the man replied. Shifting his weight in the doorway, he met Rook's eyes. "He's asking for you."

They would never take him alive.

Wynn stared out the canopy at the curved, pitted surface of the asteroid, listening to the static that crackled on the comm.

The League Patrol ship was waiting. He knew it; he felt it with the instincts of a hunter become the hunted. They had been waiting before, poised in distant orbit, when he fled Espérance's atmosphere; why they had been there or who had alerted them hardly mattered now.

The first battle had been brief but decisive. The Patrol ship had already disabled his hyperdrive, preventing him from leaving the Espérancian system; he had eluded their pursuit through normal space to find this sanctuary where he could recoup and repair the damage they'd done.

But the hyperdrive hadn't been repaired. The damage was too great. He could huddle here in the asteroid belt for days before they tracked him down, waiting meekly for the inevitable.

That was not the Slayton way.

Smiling grimly, Wynn got up from the pilot's seat. Sable

was leaning against the bulkhead at the other end of the cabin, watching him. Always watching. His little traitress, his savior, his kitten turned shadowcat.

She had been at his side when they lifted from the polar continent, aided him in the skirmish with the Patrol ship and the flight afterward. Her silence had never been broken in all that time. No explanations, no protestations, no excuses. Only silence. Even his imprecations had dried up after the first shock had passed. What he felt now was far beyond the reach of words.

The 'ruptor she'd turned on him in the compound lay within easy reach on the copilot's seat. She had put it there without a word when they'd hidden here in the belt.

He wondered if she wanted to die.

"We're going out," he told her softly.

Her eyes slid up to meet his: clear, copper, beautiful. Unafraid. "To fight?" she asked. Her voice was hoarse, as if she'd almost forgotten how to use it.

"Yes." He crossed to her and lifted his hand, drawing a finger down her face from cheekbone to chin. She moved not at all. "Do you regret your choice, Sable?"

"No."

He smiled, pulling his thumb from her chin with a jerk. "You're a strange creature, Sable, but I've enjoyed having the use of you." He pushed his body hard against hers. "Why didn't you stay with your people? Is it that you've become too accustomed to being my plaything?"

His desire to punish her, to make her hurt and cry out, foundered against her steady, silent gaze. "Curse you," he hissed. "Damn you to hell—"

He brought his mouth down on hers without warning, grinding her lips against her teeth. Her breath flooded out in a rush, and suddenly she was responding ardently, without inhibition, as she had done in the grip of Euphorie.

There was only anger and lust in him as he took her, pulling her down to the deck and tearing away her clothes without pity or hesitation. She let him do what he would, soundless, biting her lip when he thrust inside her, wrapping her legs about his waist as he pounded out his rage.

He came with a deep groan to a shuddering climax. A moment later he left her where she lay, sealing his trousers and striding to the control panel without a backward glance.

One by one he primed the ship's weapons systems, preparing the engine for normal space flight. When he guided the ship away from the shelter of the belt, he knew the wait would not be long.

He fired immediately on sight of the League ship. The first shot hit; the second went wide of the mark.

The League vessel's returning fire caught him a glancing blow. He made no effort to web himself into the seat; there was no point to such precautions now.

The comm crackled with voices demanding his surrender. He ignored them and finally shut the audio off entirely. In the profound silence he heard Sable's soft gasps, the rustle of clothing, the uneven rhythm of her footfalls as she came up behind him.

"Are you ready to die, Sable?" he mocked bitterly. "Did you enjoy our final moments of passion?"

Gripping the back of the copilot's seat, Sable looked at him. "I'm not afraid," she said. She reached for him, her fingers curved in supplication. Copper eyes burned through the tangled veil of her hair. "What are you afraid of, Wynn Slayton?"

Wynn cursed. Wrenching the control stick, he turned the ship deliberately toward the League vessel, setting a collision course. Sable touched him. Not to stop, not to demand. She merely touched, and he shuddered uncontrollably, watching the League ship grow larger and larger in the canopy.

Until he could bear no more, flung himself out of the seat and away from the woman who remained to gaze on the face of death. When the next shot struck the ship, it was Sable who took the brunt of it, flung like a rag doll across the console and violently to the deck while Wynn slammed against the opposite bulkhead.

The scream of emergency sirens deafened Wynn where he

lay on the deck. The alarms died as the secondary life-support system dropped the cockpit into near darkness, broken only by the rows of red lights on the console.

Wynn pulled himself to his knees, favoring the arm that ended in a broken wrist. A shadowy form lay crumpled on the deck, mere meters away; Wynn crawled to it awkwardly, bereft even of curses.

Sable lay on her side, utterly still. Bending over her, Wynn heard the faint rattling hiss of her breath.

"Sable," he whispered. With his good hand he caught her shoulder, rolled her gently onto her back. Blood soaked her midnight hair. She coughed, and another bubble of blood formed on her lips.

"Wynn," she croaked. Her hand lifted, fell again; Wynn stretched out his legs and lifted her head across his thigh.

Her lashes lifted slowly. "I'm dying—" she began.

"No." Wynn laid his palm against her faint heartbeat as if his will alone could keep it going. "Damn you, no."

Sable's lips curled. "There are some things—even you can't control." Her eyes closed. "You never—owned me, Wynn Slayton."

He wanted to rage, to scream, to beat back death with his own hands. He bent his head close to hers.

"You're wrong, Sable. Wrong. You're mine—you'll always be mine—"

She gasped, lurching up in his arms. He tasted blood as her lips brushed his. Copper brilliance flared in her eyes. "Kiss me, Wynn," she demanded.

He did. He felt her life fade, fleeing her body through the gate of her parted lips. Her fingers tangled in his hair, tightening in a grip only death could break.

"I hate you," she whispered, staring into his eyes as the spark died in her own. "I—love—you. . . ."

The Patrolmen found him hours later when they boarded the silent ship, but he never heard them.

CHAPTER TWENTY-THREE

"*G*alloway."

The old man's voice was hoarse and thin, though the hood of the med unit had been drawn back. His skin was pale and deeply lined, his eyes sunken, his long aristocrat's fingers clutching the sheets like bony claws. No sign now of the most powerful man on Espérance.

Rook did not want to pity him.

"Galloway," the Patriarch repeated. He lifted his hand. "You—know why I've asked to see you."

Chilled by that very certainty, Rook stared down at the old man and refused to answer. Their truce was at an end; let this prince of the Elite suffer, as Rook and his people had suffered.

As Ariane suffered now.

The Patriarch's lips curved up in a raw smile. He gasped and caught his breath; Ariane moved swiftly to his side, and his pain-dulled eyes flashed to her.

"Leave us, Ariane," he said. "Please."

She left, looking at Rook in wordless entreaty. He would have given the world to follow her out.

But he stayed. The Patriarch gazed at Rook, a shadow of the old command in his eyes. "You—won't make it easy for me, will you, Galloway?" he whispered.

"Should I?" Rook answered with equal softness.

Bernard closed his eyes. "No. I wouldn't . . . expect it of you. Not after all—" He breathed deeply. "Not after all that's passed."

Rook reluctantly acknowledged his respect for this man, this final and most deadly adversary. "It seems we understand each other, Marchand," he said.

"And you . . . know what I want."

Oh, yes, Rook knew. His body hummed with the mindless instinct to fight, but his rational mind held him still with the bleakness of despair.

"Don't take her from me, Galloway."

It was more a command than a plea. The words hung between them; Rook looked away, working his fists into knots at his sides.

Bernard breathed a bitter laugh. "Do you think I . . . don't know? You could take her, Galloway. You have that power even now. You could . . . steal her away as you did before."

The admission must have been profoundly difficult for this proud old man. Rook met Bernard's eyes, and the pain in them was as vivid as if it had come through the Sharing.

"She is my mate," Rook rasped.

"Yes. That, too, I . . . understand." Bernard's features tightened in distress. "I . . . don't expect you to do anything for—my sake. But for Ariane's—"

"Ariane's sake?" He paced the length of the med unit and back again. "I've seen her, what the past few days have done to her. You'd destroy her little by little, starving her spirit in this gilded cage, just as Slayton tried to destroy our people." He leaned over the Patriarch, nostrils flaring at the scent of his adversary. "Knowing what she is. Knowing she understands what she would have to deny for the rest of her life— her Kalian blood. You'd destroy—"

"Shall we . . . speak of destruction, Galloway?" Rising on his elbows, Bernard met Rook's gaze fiercely. "You'd force Ariane to turn her back on everything she's known." With a gasp he settled back to the bed, face waxen. "She . . . may be Kalian, but she was raised a Marchand. To Marchand duties—Marchand honor. Not to the life you would give her."

Ariane's haunted eyes seemed to come between them, Marchand brown touched with Kalian copper.

"Must I beg?" Bernard's words were thready with pain. "Will that give you satisfaction? I lost all of them. My daughter, my granddaughter—Ariane is all I have left." He moved his hand across the bed, closing his fingers on Rook's wrist. "Don't force her to . . . make a choice she'll regret for the rest of her life."

His voice lost its edge, softening to vulnerability. "I raised her as my heir. I have . . . known her from the day of her birth. You have had her only months. What can you give her, Galloway?"

Rook lifted his head, staring blindly at the rows of monitor lights on the console beside the med unit. Bernard's fingers dropped from his wrist.

"Would you stay here at her side . . . Lady Marchand's tame Kalian?"

Rook pushed away from the bedside and leaned heavily against the far wall. The Patriarch knew. He knew the Kalians could not stay on Espérance—that it held too many memories, too much pain. When the people were sufficiently recovered, they would find some way to leave this world behind them forever.

But they needed someone to lead them—

"She nearly gave her life for your people," Bernard rasped. "Isn't that . . . enough?"

Rook whirled, seeing only a blur where the Patriarch lay. He backed against the wall and trembled there like an animal at bay. It would never be enough. Not in an eternity.

"The . . . decision is yours, Galloway," Bernard said. "But if you make no effort to . . . influence Ariane, I will see to it that your people have . . . ships, supplies, the best Marchand has to offer in finding and . . . colonizing a new world. A new home."

"As you did before?" Rook said bitterly.

"I—accept my mistakes, Galloway. There will be no more. This on my word, and my honor."

Rook thought of his people, their bewildered faces as they fought free of the drug and eight years of slavery. There would be no going back. Only forward—to a new life.

The Patriarch could make it simple.

"Damn you, Marchand," Rook whispered.

The old man closed his eyes. "Damn me . . . if you wish, Galloway. But leave me my heir."

The door hissed open at Rook's back, and he turned to face the white-clad doctor who had been waiting just outside.

"He must rest," the doctor said. "Is your business concluded, Mr. Galloway?"

Rook never looked back at the old man behind him. "Yes. It is concluded."

He strode from the room, brushing by the doctor and the hovering servants. Ariane waited in the outer chamber, her eyes fixing on his in mingled hope and dread.

Rook hardly slowed his pace. Taking Ariane by the hand, he pulled her with him into the hall. She fell into step beside him, accepting his urgent silence. He found his way through the maze of corridors to the elegant ebonwood doors leading into Ariane's private suites. A startled servant bowed herself out of their way as he swept Ariane into his arms and carried her over the threshold.

"Let me love you, Ariane," he said.

He eased her onto the bed—*her* bed, where they had nestled in exhaustion once before, too weary to do more than sleep.

But Rook's eyes were hot, demanding and promising fulfillment, stripping the weariness from Ariane's body as his touch stripped her of reason. She watched him gaze down at her, his harsh, beloved features naked with desire and agony. With a single swift gesture he pulled his unadorned shirt over his head and tossed it onto the floor.

"Let me love you," he repeated hoarsely. His weight came down beside her, and she ached with the memory of their last lovemaking—aboard the *d'Artagnan,* before Wynn had effected his betrayal to drive them apart.

Their reunion had become a mockery of her naive dreams.

"Rook," she whispered. His heavy mane brushed her face, her neck, as he kissed her, mouth and chin and cheek and forehead. His fingers traced her features, speaking eloquently of quiet desperation.

What had passed between him and the Patriarch had driven him to the edge; the pulse beat heavy in his throat, and his need swept through her like pain.

She had known when he'd emerged from Bernard's rooms. The look on his face had confirmed all the unvoiced conclusions she had reached in the silence of her heart. It was the look of a man facing his own certain death.

Rook had never been afraid to die. What he feared now was far more terrible.

Deep within both of them was knowledge they could not face. She and Rook had skirted around it, thrusting and parrying like duelists. Until now they had kept the truth at bay.

It was a truth that could not be spoken; it would rend and tear them apart like a Kalian predator, devouring what little they had of the future.

Rook rolled Ariane against him, one hand tangled in her hair and the other curved about her waist. His fingers worked almost clumsily at the fastenings of her blouse; he needed to feel her, skin to skin. She helped him, wriggling to free herself, but his urgency was too great. He slipped his hand underneath to cup her breast.

Ariane arched into his touch. Her nipples hardened as his palm stroked over them. Rook's breathing grew ragged; he cradled her breast in his hand as Ariane pushed the blouse from her shoulders and pressed into him.

She wanted him. She wanted to be one with him, whole, complete once again; wanted to feel him move within her, empty himself into the very center of her being. In the duel of love she could forget, as she had done aboard the *d'Artagnan*.

Rook wanted that same oblivion.

"Shapers," he groaned as she kissed his chest, her skin tingling with the teasing brush of his hair. Her tongue found his nipple; he gave himself up to the caress for a moment, his head flung back, the wild locks of his mane dark against the richly embroidered pillows.

But he was not content to remain passive. His deep-burning anger, so much a part of him, demanded action. Ariane felt his intentions before he rolled over, bore her back on the bed, and covered her breast with his mouth.

She surrendered willingly. Always, when they'd made love, there'd been a level of ferocity, a stormy passion born of their Kalian natures. She had accepted that at last. But desperation had driven them when they'd loved aboard the *d'Artagnan,* just as it drove them now. Perhaps it was all they would ever have.

Laving her nipple with his tongue, Rook pinned her to the bed with his body. She thrust upward, and he suckled her almost violently, as if he could draw her into himself. His hand curled over her other breast, kneading it rhythmically. Ariane opened her mouth on a soundless cry. Rook surged up to take her lips, his tongue thrusting deep.

The Sharing pulsed between them with every touch. Ariane welcomed the mindlessness of physical passion, afraid to look beyond the frantic desire that beat through flesh and bone and nerves and blood. Even that fear was lost as Rook's hand swept down over her belly and pushed her loose trousers low about her hips. His hot fingers moved unerringly; he sucked her gasp into his own mouth.

He stroked her, dipping and seeking, drawing a flood to drown them both. His kisses dropped to the hollow of her throat, her shoulders, once again to her breasts. Ariane gripped his shoulders; his muscles were taut under his skin as his arousal strained against the fabric of his trousers.

Dropping her hands to his rigid belly, Ariane pushed against him to work at the fastenings. He twisted to give her access, never ceasing his caresses. When she freed him and took his hot length in her hand, he gave a deep, shuddering sigh and cupped her womanhood with fierce possessiveness.

"Ariane," he said raggedly. His eyes caught hers and held, giving her all of himself in that one look. Pain and triumph, anger and joy, denial and acceptance. Not for Rook the courtier's way, the words Wynn had used to seduce her in the garden an eternity ago. He needed none. His body spoke for him with unmatched eloquence.

He pushed her trousers down until she lay open to him, welcoming him, demanding him with that same eloquence. He covered her, braced on his powerful arms. Only at the end did he close his eyes, plunging inside her with one sure stroke.

Ariane arched to meet him. With each thrust her ecstasy increased a thousandfold. Her fingernails curled into the muscle of Rook's back, marking him as he marked her; deeper and deeper, moving hard and fast, merciless in his need. She lost herself in him—*became* him, knew his primal instinct to claim her in the most ancient of ways.

There was no division between taking and giving, possessed and possessor. They were perfect equals, mates by definitions unknown among her great-grandfather's people. Rook filled her to the brim and then filled her again, endlessly renewing, reaching into her soul.

When she thought he could go no further, he took her again, until she felt the violent tension that quivered from his taut shoulders to his hard thighs cradled between hers. He went suddenly still; she felt him cry silently for release, but he bent his head to hers and whispered the words he had never spoken.

"I love you, Ariane."

And then he drove into her, carrying her with him to the summit and beyond to the place where stars were born out of darkness.

Ariane held him within her as they came to earth. Rook, breathing rapidly, laid his cheek against hers while she stroked his damp hair. After a moment he rolled to his side, pulling her into the curve of his body with her head tucked under his chin.

They lay together, limbs entwined and hearts beating in perfect tandem. Ariane closed her eyes, shutting out the rich appointments of her rooms, the symbols of wealth and privilege that closed around them like a cage. In her mind they were still aboard the *d'Artagnan*—free because they had nothing to lose, no future to bind them.

I love you, Rook had said. He repeated it soundlessly as he stroked her cooling skin, kissed the tears from her cheeks, held her tight within the circle of his arms.

I love you. The gift of that admission broke her heart and put it back together again. In the wake of their loving was completion, a circle of body and soul bound by the Sharing. Ariane refused to feel anything, know anything else.

Until Rook spoke the words to shatter her anew.

"Our people can't remain on Espérance, Ariane."

Ariane went very still. She knotted her fist against Rook's chest, hating him for destroying their fragile peace, loving him beyond reason or regret.

She had known. Without thinking it through, she'd known there could be only one denouement to the tragedy played out by the people of Kali and Espérance. Even with her influence and the Patriarch's support, the Kalians would never again find a home on this world. They had suffered too much; the final healing must come with freedom. Freedom and a place where they could make their own way, their own future.

"I know," she whispered.

"The Patriarch has agreed to help our people find a new world."

"Yes," she said. "If he hadn't, I would have—" Her throat knotted, refusing to give voice to what could not be borne.

Rook's hold tightened. "He saved our people once." His fingers laced through her hair, clenching and unclenching. Ariane felt the tension build through his body and release in a sudden, harsh breath. "And you've saved them again. I may never understand your—Marchand honor. But I understand now that you are of his blood."

Ariane tasted Rook's skin as her lips parted. *I am Kalian,* she cried silently. She knew Rook heard; he curled himself around her like a living shield, holding her fast through her inner struggle.

"Our people will need someone to lead them, Ariane."

Her body shuddered with reaction, but she reached into herself and slowed her heartbeat, stanched the flow of adrenaline that made her muscles knot and tremble. The Sharing made his statement profoundly, bitterly clear.

There was no hint of a question in it. If Rook still hoped she would abandon her duty, he would not torment her with that longing.

The Kalians would need a leader, one who had known more freedom than any of those who had been Wynn's chattel. They would need a symbol of their new life; a man who knew the ways of the League, whose courage and strength would hold them together in the face of every challenge that was to come.

They needed Rook.

I need you. Ariane caught the frantic thought and smothered it before it could slip through the Sharing. But Rook felt her agony; it was the reflection of his own, doubling and redoubling into a wordless cry of torment.

No. Ariane rolled away from Rook and flung herself from the bed. A few blind steps carried her to the wall; she stood there, forehead pressed to the cool paneling.

She wanted to beg him to stay. She wanted to rant and scream and tell him that the Kalians could survive without him. That *she* could not survive without him. . . .

Abruptly she turned, impaling him with her eyes. He hadn't moved; he remained where she had left him, a lithe predator crouched on tumbled silk sheets, incongruous amid the elegance she had been born to. He was a Kalian shadow-cat in a gilded cage. His gaze was unblinking, brilliant with wisdom and anger and pain and desire.

And love. . . .

She could bind him still. She could use that love, the power of the Sharing, and make it impossible for him to leave her. *Kai-horo,* the Fahar had said. She could make him know a pain of the soul that would eclipse his will and keep him by her side forever.

Slowly, deliberately, she returned to the bed, kneeling on the edge. Rook's eyes swept over her with undisguised hunger. Once he had made her know her own weakness, her own savagery, the instinctive power that was hers by right of her Kalian blood. He had mocked her Marchand honor, though he mocked it no more.

Now she would abandon her honor again as once she'd rejected it for the ecstasy of his embrace. No guilt, no shame, only need—savage and uncaring of anything but the driving necessity to hold what was hers.

"I love you, Rook," she breathed, leaning forward to brush his belly with her breasts. His arousal was already full and ready for her touch; she caught it in her hand and watched him shudder. "You are my mate."

"Ariane—" Her name was a plea, hoarse and raw, as if he recognized her intent, the mercilessness with which she would shatter his resolve.

She hardly heard him, listening to an inner voice that beat out commands in an ancient, savage rhythm. *My mate,* it said. *Mine. No one will take him from me. . . .*

Rook reared up, grabbing her wrists. His eyes were bleak and tormented, his face a mask of anguish. They stared at each other, trapped in a cycle of emotion that held them immobile and deadlocked.

The distant chime of the comm in Ariane's study drove them apart.

Swaying in confusion, Ariane backed away from Rook and lurched from the bed, her fingers clutching at the bedding. She dragged the duvet with her as she moved, wrapping it around her body. The chime sounded again; she stumbled into the study and silenced the signal with a slap of her hand. She listened to the Security Chief's report and sat very still for a long time afterward, her head bowed to the desk.

By the time she returned to the bedroom, Rook was dressed and standing by the French doors, staring at the sheer curtains as if he could see through them into the darkened garden beyond.

"Rook," she said softly. He tilted his head without turning, and she moved to sit wearily on the edge of the bed.

"Wynn has been captured, Rook. They caught his ship

just outside the asteroid belt." She closed her eyes. "And Sable is dead. She was killed in a skirmish when Wynn tried to attack the Patrol ship."

Rook's reaction was hidden from her sight, and even his emotions were shielded from her. He might have been light-years away.

"I've asked that—Sable's body be returned to us—to her people," she said. "League officers will bring her down to Espérance within the next few hours." Her heart labored with the strain of waiting for his response. "You have cere-monies, rites of passing—"

His footsteps whispered on the carpet. "Yes."

"There's more, Rook. When Finch—died, she was still in Kalian guise. The League authorities who investigated her death put her body in freeze until they had time to conduct a full inquiry as to why a member of a supposedly dead race was on Agora."

"Finch—"

Ariane opened her eyes and stared at Rook's clenched fists. "I've also requested that they send Finch back to us on the next available ship from Agora. She'll return to her people at last."

"And Slayton?"

The hatred was back, the anger, all trace of weakness erased from his voice. Ariane drew the duvet more tightly about herself.

"I've transmitted a full report of Wynn's conspiracy to the Patrol ship that captured him. The League will negotiate with the Elite Council regarding punishment for his crimes. He's broken League as well as planetary laws. They also want to speak to you, Rook—about your experiences on Tantalus and here on Espérance since your return. They're opening an investigation on the Kalian tragedy, and we—the Marchand —have promised full cooperation."

The flat recital served to distance her as Rook had dis-tanced himself, cutting her free of emotion. "Too late," Rook murmured, and though she heard his bitterness, she could not feel it.

"Not too late for justice," she said tonelessly. "It isn't only the League behind this investigation, Rook. Others had a hand in it as well." She looked up. "A party of Fahar have asked permission to speak in person to the acting Head of House Marchand—and the Kalian known as Rook Galloway."

"Brother!"

The Fahar who came forward to greet Rook was glossy of coat and bright of eye—and painfully familiar.

"Kamur," Rook said softly. Ariane murmured something unintelligible.

"Brother—and Sister," Kamur repeated, his bright-emerald gaze bathing them both in his obvious delight. "I knew the Gods spoke truly when they sent me here to find you."

The private conference room seemed too small to contain Kamur's enthusiasm, and suddenly there were others—Surra, coming up behind him to rub against his shoulder, and two older Fahar, one wearing the surplice of Harr's priesthood, the other bearing a chain of office marking him as Lawmaker. Kamur and Surra melted aside respectfully.

Ariane moved deftly into the silence, greeting the Fahar elders with respectful bows, making introductions and offering refreshments. The Espérancian honor guard that had escorted the Fahar to the Marchand estates left the room to take up positions outside.

"You must wonder why we are here, Lady Ariane."

The deep, purring voice was that of the Wise, the Fahar priest, who gazed at the humans unblinkingly from golden eyes. Rook glanced at Ariane, who was cool and attentive, utterly Marchand. Gone was the erotic intensity she had turned on him before the interruption, the wild longing that had nearly broken his resolve. Now she was entirely what she must be—the Patriarch's representative facing members of a once-hostile alien race.

There had been no Fahar delegation on Espérance since the Kalian trials. Ariane's expression revealed nothing; if she took any pleasure in the reunion with Kamur and Surra, she did not show it. Rook felt only numb acceptance.

Oblivious to Rook's thoughts, Ariane inclined her head to the Fahar priest. "I know only that you accompanied the League Patrol ship when it arrived to take Wynn Slayton into custody, and—"

"Yes. We were aboard when the battle—" Kamur's eager voice subsided at one slow glance from the Wise, and his ears flattened in chagrin.

"As the young one says, we arrived with the Patrol ship. But our reasons for coming had nothing to do with this Slayton, though we have learned much since leaving Agora." He twitched his ear in the direction of the Lawmaker. *"Arrim* Rhoan and I came at the request of this Farseer"—he nodded aside at Kamur—"when we found him and his mate on M'nauri."

Rook looked carefully at Kamur. Surra sat close beside him, and it was clear they were still well and truly mated. The resemblance between Surra and the Lawmaker was noticeable enough that Rook knew the elder Fahar must be her father— the man who had objected to her mating with Kamur. It was clear that Kamur and Surra's pursuers had caught up with them after the *d'Artagnan* had dropped them off on M'nauri, but the Lawmaker seemed accepting enough now.

"I see you understand," the Wise said to Rook, smiling human-fashion. "We learned Lady Ariane's ship had granted passage to these young ones when they fled Agora. My vision told me they would be found on M'nauri. When we arrived—"

The Wise broke off as Kamur's ears twitched frantically. "I see the young one is driven to speak," the priest said dryly. "Suffice it to say that when I and *Arrim* Rhoan arrived, we saw at once that the sealing between Surra and Kamur could not be broken. The Gods had made their will clear, and we had but to accept. The young ones had much to tell us—"

"I had had a vision—" Kamur began, squirming in his seat in spite of Surra's calming touch.

The Wise made some subtle Fahar gesture that silenced

the boy. "We had already learned that you, Brother Galloway, had fled League imprisonment with the aid of Lady Ariane. It was said by the League authorities on Agora that the Lady was your hostage, and we feared the same of Kamur and Surra. But we soon learned matters were not so easily understood. All Harr had believed the Kalian race destroyed—until Kamur told us of you both." His gaze moved from Rook to Ariane. "It was only one of many puzzles. And then Kamur told us of his vision."

Another subtle gesture of ears and face granted Kamur the right to speak. He sat forward in his chair, eyes wide.

"When Surra and I reached M'nauri, we could not forget all you had done for us," he said. "On the second day after planetfall, I had a vision—that you, Brother, were in great trouble, and that your fate was bound with that of the Kalian people."

Rook studied Ariane's still face, wondering if she understood what such a vision meant among the Fahar, especially those trained for the priesthood. If Kamur was in truth a Farseer, his vision would be regarded as fact by all other Fahar.

Kamur had known from the beginning that Rook and Ariane were destined to become mates. Did Ariane remember what Kamur had said to her on Agora? *"Do not fear what must be."* And what he had said to Rook: *"You will find what you seek, but do not let it destroy you."*

Clenching his fists, Rook looked away. Kamur had been right, and terribly wrong.

"I did not understand all that lay behind my vision," Kamur continued, "because you did not tell us the nature of your difficulty. But the vision showed clearly that the Kalians were not dead—and that I must find you again."

For the first time the Lawmaker spoke, rising gracefully to his feet. "Even when we reopened diplomatic relations with the League over a year ago, we did not know that Kalians had been sent to the League's prison world. The League diplomats hid that fact from us." He flashed his teeth briefly in an expression that had nothing in common with a human smile.

"Because of Kamur and Surra, we quickly learned the truth. We had remained aloof too long, believing we had no part in human affairs after the Kalian tragedy. Kamur's vision made it clear we must become involved again."

"So we returned to Agora," the Wise said calmly. "Rhoan and I spoke at length to the League authorities, who found it expedient to be—more forthcoming with our delegation. They told us all they knew of you, Brother, and the Lady Ariane. They also told us of the Kalian woman Finch, whose body they had found. They would have scoffed at Kamur's vision, but the discovery of a Kalian on Agora, and Kamur's recognition of Lady Ariane as Kalian, aroused their interest."

For the first time a flicker of reaction crossed Ariane's schooled features. Rook knew her thoughts as if they were joined in the Sharing. If the League officials had believed anything Kamur and the Fahar elders had told them, they knew Ariane bore Kalian blood. And if the League knew, all Espérance might know in time.

Rook envisioned a bleak future in which Ariane faced the humiliation of having her taint revealed to her Elite peers. She would be rejected and shunned by the people the Patriarch had ruled so long. If Rook were not here at her side, to protect her from all harm and sorrow . . .

"—we made it clear that we would go to Espérance with or without their aid," the priest finished, unaware of Rook's blind stare. With an effort Rook repressed the compulsion to touch Ariane and focused his eyes on the Fahar.

"In the end," Kamur put in, grinning, "they agreed to take us aboard a Patrol ship bound for Espérance, warning us that their business with the great Families must take precedence over ours. But it all became one and the same, as we learned when Lady Ariane sent her report to the Patrol captain following Slayton's capture."

The conference room grew abruptly silent. Ariane lifted her head, nostrils flaring like a Kalian scenting the winds of the home world.

"Then you know everything now," she said, her voice

very strange after the rich Fahar inflections. "How Rook was wrongly convicted, how Slayton was behind what happened to the Kalians—"

"And that, thanks to your intervention, the survivors are now safe and healing." The priest inclined his head. "Kamur's vision was true. You and Brother Galloway were bound up in the destiny of all your people and freed them from a fate none of us were wise enough to see. We of Harr will always regret that we chose to withdraw from human space rather than seek to learn the truth after the *Bonaventure* incident. Much must still be resolved, but the League and the Marchand"—he bent his golden gaze on Ariane—"have agreed to our request for an investigation and unrestricted Fahar access to our brother Kalians. All Harr will rejoice in this reunion." He glanced at Kamur and Surra, huddled together in utter contentment. "The Gods work in mysterious ways, do they not?"

"Yes," Ariane murmured, her face turned carefully away from Rook's gaze. "Yes."

After that arrangements were made to settle the Fahar in their own suite of rooms, Ariane speaking quietly of future discussions and the establishment of a new Fahar consulate in Lumière. She promised the Fahar that they would be taken to Nouveau-Quebec to see the Kalians as soon as possible. The Lawmaker and the priest, offering hope of restored health for the Patriarch, were escorted to their quarters by the Marchand honor guard; Surra retired to the rooms set aside for herself and Kamur. But Kamur lingered in the conference room, watching Rook and Ariane with too-knowing eyes.

"I regret that Surra and I were not able to arrive in time to give you more direct aid," the young Fahar said. "We would have repaid you and helped save our brothers. If only my vision had come sooner—"

"You've more than repaid us, Kamur," Ariane said, real warmth in her voice. She extended her hand, and Kamur took it gingerly, retracting his claws. "There will be no more estrangement between Fahar and human from this day forward."

Kamur blinked. "May it be so," he intoned.

Turning away, heedless of the discourtesy, Rook paced across the room and leaned against a chair with his back to Ariane as she asked Kamur about his life with Surra and their plans for the future. He was too lost in his own chaotic thoughts to note the sudden silence and Kamur's approach.

"Brother Rook."

Rook tightened his grip on the back of the chair. He knew at once that Ariane was gone.

"Your heart is still troubled. Yours, and the Lady Ariane's. I know this."

Even a being with half Kamur's sensitivity would have felt the unbearable tension between Rook and Ariane. And Kamur had seen so much more aboard the *d'Artagnan*. Rook smoothed his expression to one of calm acceptance.

"Much has happened, Kamur," he said. "Much has yet to be done."

"It is not of your people I speak—"

"There is nothing else to be spoken of," Rook cut in harshly.

Kamur's ears flickered and settled into a forlorn sideways position that hinted of sorrow. He did not pretend to misunderstand. "I had hoped it would all be settled between you. I had no clear vision in this matter, but Surra and I knew you had mated truly the moment we saw you again. It was meant to be."

Meant to be. Rook closed his eyes. "You still don't understand humans, Kamur. We don't have your faith in destiny."

Kamur gave a sigh that was nearly human. "Even now?" he said, laying an elegant furred hand on Rook's shoulder.

Rook had no answers. If he had never kidnapped Ariane and taken her ship, saved Kamur from the lifepod, returned at the Fahar's request to Agora and met Finch—if Ariane hadn't discovered and acted on the truth for love of Rook Galloway —his people would never have been freed. It was all inextricably intertwined. But personal happiness meant nothing in the final scheme of things. There must be sacrifice, a price to pay. . . .

"Even now," he whispered.

Kamur was silent so long that Rook looked up to stare at the young Fahar. The emerald eyes had narrowed to dreamy slits, and his ears had pricked as if listening to some distant sound.

"Yet you are still bound together," Kamur said slowly, "tied to the fate of your people."

Rook jerked free of Kamur's light hold and was halfway to the door before he turned. "Tell me, Farseer," he said at last. "Can such a binding reach across the void between stars and hope to survive?"

This time it was Kamur who had no answer.

CHAPTER TWENTY-FOUR

*T*he ceremony of Passing ended as it had begun, brought to completion by the chanting of a thousand voices.

Ariane breathed in the scent of smoke and let the tears fall unchecked. Rook, at her side, lifted a handful of ashes and released them to drift on the wind. Sable had burned as brightly in death as she'd done in life, all bold colors and defiance; Finch had returned to her people at last. Kalian faces looked heavenward, into the sunset.

Into their future.

Kalian faces. Ariane gazed around the vast circle, at elders and children and young men and women, clear-eyed and growing strong with rest and nourishment and hope. The Kalian ceremony of Passing was more than the giving of honor to those who had saved their people; it was a binding, a coming together of those who had been held apart by walls and drugs and enslavement.

It was a renewal of a heritage denied so long—not only in the past eight years but all during the Kalians' time on Espérance. The voices that rose in the chant spoke the Kalian language without fear, surrounded only by those who understood.

And everywhere was the Sharing—in simple touches, in joyful embraces. The people had rediscovered that greatest of all the Shaper's gifts. Ariane sensed the vibrant hum of Kalian emotions in the very air around her, more potent than any Espérancian drug.

The last echo of the rite faded into silence. Ariane felt a big, callused hand take hers; a moment later smaller fingers clutched her other hand. The Kalian child to her left looked up at her with perfect trust. Ariane was swept into the Sharing on a tide of color and light that transcended physical boundaries. Rook was with her, and the child, and all the others who surrounded the pyre and kept vigil over those who had Passed.

Ariane closed her eyes and let the Sharing enfold her. Her own Kalian nature beat through her in a wordless song, in soul-deep knowledge reflected in a thousand minds. Minds that welcomed to her, accepting without hesitation.

Accepting. The Kalians had accepted so much. Ariane flung up her head, scattering tears. She was Kalian, and yet she could not accept what must be. Could not accept that all this must end.

That Rook must leave her. . . .

Wrenching free of the Sharing and the hands that held her, Ariane fled. She ran across the great wooded park set aside for the rite, away from the vast country estate that housed the Kalian survivors. Warm evening wind, redolent of the scent of smoke, dried her face. She rejected the touch of Kalian minds, sprinting like a wild thing until she found herself utterly alone.

In the silence of the summer woods she let herself remember.

Since the coming of the Fahar one week ago, she had fought a fierce and desperate battle. It had been fought during wild lovemaking with Rook, in silence that could not be broken with talk of an unthinkable future. And it had been fought within herself. In this past week she had known she still had time to convince Rook to stay with her.

It lay within her power, to twist Rook's love for her and turn it against his devotion to their people. *Their people.* Ariane laughed bitterly. She could never forget, not for a moment, even joined with Rook body and heart and soul.

Especially not then. And to force him to choose would tear him apart. Once he had mocked Marchand honor, Marchand duty; but Kalians had their own honor, just as deep and abiding.

She could seduce him into abandoning his honor forever.

The last rays of the sun bled down through whispering leaves. Ariane crouched and pushed her fingers deep into

Espérancian earth, as if she could force the world, and time itself, to stand still.

Three weeks, the doctors said. Ariane knew it to be true, had felt it when she'd touched the Kalians who were slowest to recover and needed her personal help. In three weeks, perhaps a month, the Kalians would be fit enough to travel, and the Elders had already agreed that to leave this world with all its sorrows outweighed any other consideration. The people would be ready.

The colony ships were already set aside, provided by the Marchand and laden with supplies donated by the League. This time there would be no possibility of disaster. The Kalians would have only the finest with which to locate and colonize a new world—a world of their own. A new Kali.

On another world they would find their healing, put the past behind them forever. Being what they were, they would become part of that new world and thrive, raising their children in peace and hope.

And Rook—

"No," she whispered.

"Healer."

The child's voice came to her soft as the rustle of leaves. Ariane lifted her head slowly. It was the girl Wren, who had stood beside her during the ceremony, whose small fingers had clutched hers.

"You ran away, and we were worried," Wren said. The child reached out to stroke Ariane's cheek with chubby fingers. Her open face, framed by raggedly cut black hair, crumpled in sorrow. "I'm sorry, Healer. Can I help?"

Ariane closed her eyes. She could no more hide from the truth than she could from this Kalian child. With a low, inarticulate sound she pulled the girl into her arms.

Comfort came to her, and love that made no demands. Small hands clutched the back of her shirt fiercely. "Don't be sad, Healer," Wren murmured. "It hurts when you're so sad—"

"Ariane."

She froze, holding the child a moment longer before letting her go. Wren's hand felt for hers; together they looked up. Rook stood over them, very still in the hushed twilight.

"Are you well, Ariane?" he asked. The question was a shield against all the things that couldn't be said, hadn't been said between them since the Patriarch had left Ariane with the burden of House Marchand. His expression was unreadable, and his eyes reflected nothing but the dying sun.

Ariane rose, holding Wren's hand like a lifeline. "I'm all right." She managed a smile, stroking the girl's glossy dark head. "I have someone looking after me."

Rook's gaze dropped, and his face relaxed. "Wren," he said gently, "did you come out here to find the Healer?"

Wren nodded solemnly. "She hurts."

Ariane stared helplessly at Rook, watching his throat work, feeling the echo of anguish he struggled to conceal. Suddenly he dropped to his knees, engulfing Wren's tiny hand in his own. Not even the Sharing could pierce the emotional armor he'd set about himself.

"I know," he said, his voice a rough whisper. "Sometimes life makes us hurt, but we find the strength to go on. The Shapers made us that way."

"That's why they gave us the Sharing," Wren added. "So that we won't be alone."

Rook closed his eyes. "Yes. So we'll never be alone."

Wren let go of Ariane's hand and touched his face gently. "Don't be afraid, Rook. We won't leave you."

Ariane turned away, her throat knotted and aching. The wood became a blur of shadow. She heard a faint rustle as Rook rose.

"Can you find your way back to the people, Wren?" Rook said softly.

"Yes. Will you take care of the Healer?"

"I promise."

Ariane glanced back just as the little girl flung her arms around Rook and was swallowed up in his embrace. "I love you, Rook," Wren whispered.

Riven by pain beyond bearing, Ariane pressed her palms

to her belly and watched the girl disappear into the growing darkness.

"I think—she'll be a Healer one day," Rook murmured. She forced herself to look at him. "She'll be needed on the new world."

They stared at each other, trapped in the familiar, agonized silence. Rook moved suddenly, a sharp lunge in her direction that ended short of a touch. His hand swung back to his side, clenching air.

"I have something for you, Ariane," he said at last.

He moved away and she followed, through the wood and back the way they had come. But Rook turned aside before they reached the park, following a route Ariane recognized when she saw the line of trees that marked the border of the estate's private landing field.

And she recognized the ship that rested among the bulky transports and escort craft, its sleek lines unmistakable even in the faint glow of the runway.

"The *d'Artagnan*," she whispered. Unthinking, she reached for Rook's hand. "How—"

His fingers closed around hers convulsively. "She was never destroyed, Ariane," he said. "I flew her directly to Espérance when I escaped. I landed in a wilderness area where she would never be found before I made my way to Lumière." He gave a rough laugh. "She'll need more repair than I could give her. But I wanted—" He broke off, slamming down on his emotion before it could reach Ariane unbridled through the Sharing. "I took it from you, Ariane, and I wanted to give it back."

The rest of his words hung unspoken between them. *Before I leave you. Before we are parted forever. . . .*

It had all begun aboard the *d'Artagnan*—the battle of wills, the passion, the love, the sorrow. The discovery of everything she was in the deepest part of her soul. Rook had stolen her ship, and now he surrendered it to her. But he had stolen her heart as well, and that could never be returned.

She almost spoke the words then, begging him to stay.

With a despairing cry Ariane turned into Rook's arms.

The barriers vanished between them, and Ariane felt the whole of Rook's being, all the things that made him what he was. His fierce love for her, his rampant desire; his strength and courage in the face of overwhelming odds; the heart-wrenching need for belonging, the deep-burning anger that had driven him so long; and the unutterable fear of aloneness.

In the fiery crucible of that moment every last self-delusion was lifted from her eyes. Because she was truly a Healer, she knew.

Rook could never be bound to this world. Not even for her sake; not even by all the inhuman power of their love. Rook, too, needed Healing, but it was a healing she could not give him alone. She knew with blinding clarity that if she asked him to stay, he would do it, even at the cost of his soul. But if she asked him to stay, she would with those simple words destroy the man he was, the man she loved more than her own life. Loving him, even for so short a time, had been worth the price.

He, like his people, must be free.

Tangling her fingers in his hair, she traced the corded tendons of his neck and looked up into his face. One by one she memorized his features: the hard planes and angles she had once thought so alien, the beauty of a wild creature never meant to be tamed. He was a reflection of the deepest and truest part of herself.

Wherever he went, her heart would go with him.

A strange, profound acceptance worked its way through her. She stepped free of Rook's arms and he let her go, unresisting. Knowing, as she knew, without words.

"Thank you, Rook," she whispered. "Thank you for this gift."

He bowed his head, black mane veiling his face. When he looked up, his eyes were molten with unshed tears. She pressed her palm to the taut muscles of his jaw.

"It's time to return to our people," she said.

Rook stared through the porthole of the shuttle until Ariane was no more than a blurred speck against the spaceport landing field. Even then he watched, frozen, as the landing field became one pattern among many and the city of Lumière vanished altogether under the clouds.

The taste of her was still on his lips, the scent of her in his nostrils, the silken patterns of her touch branded into his flesh. Her voice blotted out every sound.

"I love you, Rook. Remember me."

The vibrations of the shuttle's engine shifted as it left Espérance's atmosphere. Rook noted the change distantly, his concentration turned to forcing one breath after another to fill his lungs, holding the pain to a level that would not drive him to madness.

When Espérance itself became a blue-and-white ball, Rook leaned his head against the cold glasteel and turned inward, clutching at what remained to him of Ariane, the sense of her that grew more fragile with every passing kilometer.

From this moment on he must learn to survive as he had never done before. His heart would continue to beat, his brain to function as it must so that he could lead his people ably and well.

The Shapers had altered the Kalians to live where ordinary humans would die. But the Shapers had not gifted their Children with the ability to stop feeling when emotion and need demanded too high a price.

Rook dug his curled fingers into the shuttle's upholstered bulkhead. Wynn Slayton had been right in the end. *"Whatever price I pay will not be nearly as high as yours. . . ."*

"Mr. Galloway."

Rook lifted his forehead from the porthole slowly. The Marchand shuttle pilot didn't touch him; the man had that much sense. "We rendezvous with the *Kali* in one hour."

The low sound Rook made satisfied the pilot, who returned to the cockpit without another word. Rook pushed away from the bulkhead and leaned against the nearest seat. He was the only passenger; the others were already aboard the *Kali* and *Shiva*. Waiting for him.

The courses were laid in. Within twelve hours both ships

would be far from this world and this system, launched on the first leg of their journey. A journey that would carry them beyond League space, into uncharted territory. But the Kalians would not go alone; at the border of Fahar space the Espérancian crew and pilots would be replaced by Fahar eager to join their brothers in the great adventure. Kamur and Surra would be among them.

Somewhere in the vastness of space a new world, unsullied by sorrow and hatred, awaited the first footfalls of the Shaper's Children.

Dropping into the seat, Rook leaned back and closed his eyes. He whispered her name like a chant of Passing, consigning his heart to its own quiet death.

His life belonged to his people. But his soul was Ariane's for eternity.

Ariane stared skyward until the shuttle was no more than a point of darkness against blue and was lost among the clouds.

Her tears had long since dried. Loose hair whipped about her face, stinging in the stiff breeze. Starship passengers and crew and spaceport officials came and went, intent on their own business, but she never saw them. The world was swallowed up in the memory of Rook's eyes, his final, desperate embrace, the last words he had spoken.

"I love you, Ariane."

Alone, her personal Guardsmen dismissed and carefully out of sight, Ariane walked slowly across the landing field. The *d'Artagnan* lay berthed in the restricted Marchand compound, gleaming and newly repaired. She let herself through the gate and passed among Marchand transports and yachts, her eyes locked ahead. The *d'Artagnan*'s ramp was already extended, everything in readiness for boarding.

She entered the hatch and sat before the console in silence. The engines remained quiet, the ready lights dark.

Stumbling up from the pilot's seat, Ariane abandoned the cockpit and stood in the common room. If she concentrated, she could hear the echo of Rook's voice, mocking her honor and her assumptions about the universe. His scent lingered in the air. Walking to the cargo hold where once they had dueled over her fate, she turned when she thought she heard the near-silent whisper of his bare feet on the deck.

And when she stood in the hatch of her cabin, her body quivered with the indelible memory of his touch.

Ariane sealed the cabin hatch behind her and lay down on the narrow bunk. Her Marchand advisers and assistants and guards knew not to expect her return this night; the next twelve hours were hers.

In twelve hours the *Kali* and *Shiva* would be gone—beyond the light of Espérance's sun, beyond her reach.

Ariane's hands moved unconsciously to her belly and rested there. A sudden, blinding vision came to her: an image of life, new life, hope given shape, cradled in a place of safety. A part of Rook, within her own body.

Staring blindly at the cabin walls, Ariane sat up. Her fingers cupped as if she held the child growing within her. With all her Healer's senses she felt Rook's final gift, the boy who would be born and grow to manhood stripped of his legacy, bereft of his true people, never entirely whole. As she had been. As she *would* be, as she had condemned Rook to suffer until the day of his death. . . .

No. Something wild blossomed in Ariane then, just as the child unfolded in her womb. The denial was so elemental, so profound that she could not give it voice.

No. All her life she had clung to duty and honor because there had been nothing else. Because her great-grandfather and House had expected it of her, because she had no other identity. No other ties to bind her.

Ariane leaped from the bunk and strode to the mirror. She asked herself a silent question, and before her eyes her face began to change. Brown eyes turned to copper; brown hair to black.

The child would be born full Kalian in every way. He would be proof of her own "tainted" blood. And Ariane knew she would die before she'd hide what he was from the Elite she had once called her equals.

She closed her eyes, heedless of the tears that traced her

cheeks. The price would be high; she would have to live with the guilt, knowing she had chosen for her child, for Rook—and for herself. Her decision would be irrevocable.

Changing back to the brown hair and eyes she'd known all her life, Ariane turned from the mirror and lay down on the bunk. When she arose twelve hours later, she left the yoke of Marchand honor behind.

The central garden of House Marchand was redolent with the scent of new blooms and ringing with birdsong. Ariane walked the winding stone pathways toward the pavilion where the Patriarch awaited her.

He looked up as she approached, a grim-faced figure nested among cushions like an old-Earth pasha. Ariane paused, glancing at Pascal, who stood close by his side.

"You're well?" she asked Bernard softly.

The Patriarch made an impatient gesture. Only his hand moved, but he still had the gift of command that always won him whatever he was determined to have. His mouth twisted in a wry smile.

"I have—permission to be here and out of that cursed bed," he said, voice rough with disuse. He looked her over critically. "I trust you aren't abandoning important business?"

Ariane met his gaze. "Not Marchand business," she said. "I think you'll find everything in order."

"Excellent." Bernard leaned back and closed his eyes. Ariane nodded to Pascal, whose hands tightened on the intricately carved balustrade of the pavilion. Pascal was prepared to take on what she'd offered him only an hour ago—prepared and far more suited to the job than she'd ever been. Passing the reins to Pascal would be easy after everything that had gone before.

Bernard was the sole obstacle, and he would have no choice but to accept in the end. Dr. Adler had said that the Patriarch had recovered beyond all expectations; the shock Bernard faced now would not be a fatal one.

Only painful. And necessary.

"I assume you've had a chance to look over the reports

and communiqués I transferred into your private files," she said. "Pascal was invaluable in implementing the most urgent operations. Agents are already working to undo the damage Wynn attempted to set in motion against House Marchand. I've scheduled a meeting with the League authorities regarding the investigation and forthcoming trial, and another with the Slayton heir, one of Wynn's cousins. The Slaytons are eager to cooperate."

The cry of a rainbird pierced the silence.

"And?" Suddenly Bernard was looking directly at her, his eyes as bright and hard as they'd been from her earliest memories. She drew in a deep breath, almost feeling Rook beside her.

"House Marchand is safe, Grand-père. From everything but the dishonor you tried for so many years to hide."

Gathering her innermost awareness, she Changed. She saw Bernard begin to understand, saw the alien Ariane—black haired, copper-eyed—reflected in his gaze. His face grew pale as he subsided back among the cushions.

"Stop it," he hissed. "I order—"

"No, Grand-père," she said softly. She walked to the couch and knelt by his side, willing him to see her as he had never seen her before. "This is what I truly am." She reached out to touch his hand, but he withdrew it, breathing harshly, condemning her with a thousand years of Marchand pride.

"Hide yourself," he said hoarsely. "Before someone sees—"

"Pascal knows—I told him this morning. I dismissed the servants. No one will witness Marchand's dishonor—this time."

She saw him begin to understand, and she continued in spite of the band of pain that tightened around her heart.

"You never told me why Wynn was so intent on revenge against our family. But I know all about it, Grand-père. How you rejected Ria Santini-Slayton because of her tainted blood, and then hid the impurity in Marchand's own lineage by disguising what I was. What my mother was. Kalian."

The muscles in Bernard's jaw trembled as he stared rigidly ahead, the only revelation of his shock.

"Necessary. It—was necessary—"

"Perhaps it was, once. But not anymore." She rose slowly, looking up into the blue sky overhead. "It's time to let the past go, Grand-père. You were the one who always fought for a future beyond this single world. You brought Espérance back into the League. Can you cling to the old chains that bind us to a dying way of life?"

He turned to her, eyes unseeing. "What are you saying?"

"I'm saying that I'm of no more use to you. That I can no longer deny what I am, *will* no longer deny it—not even at the cost of Marchand honor."

Bernard grasped the arms of his couch and struggled to his feet. Pascal moved in to support him. Within a moment all traces of vulnerability were gone from the Patriarch's face.

"I remember when the love of honor and duty I instilled in you was life itself," he said harshly. "I concealed what you were to protect our House, to see that what happened to my daughter and granddaughter would not be repeated. When the Kalians were pronounced lost aboard the *Bonaventure*, I thought it was over at last."

Ariane closed her eyes. "But it wasn't. It will never be over as long as I remain on Espérance. The League knows, Grand-père—they know what I am. Lumière, all Espérance will learn in time. Do you believe this"—she gestured at herself—"can be concealed forever? That the Elite will accept a Kalian as your heir now, as they would not have done so many years ago? That Marchand honor will remain untouched?"

Bernard pushed away Pascal's supporting hands. "You swore not to leave—"

"Then tell me, Grand-père—what is more important to you? The honor of House Marchand, untainted, still able to influence the future as you've always dreamed—or keeping me by your side as you see me now?" She swallowed back tears. "What will you choose?"

She knew the answer. She knew the unbending pride that

had guided the Patriarch's choices when he had set events in motion years ago—events that led to Wynn Slayton's tragic quest for revenge and all that had befallen the Kalians on Espérance.

Bernard looked away in silence.

"I know your answer, Grand-père. I have already given careful thought to the future of House Marchand. Pascal has proved his worth a hundred times over. He—"

The Patriarch's gaze fixed on Pascal. "Pascal. Were you a part of this—"

"No," Ariane said. "I spoke to him this morning about assuming my duties. It's become clear to me over the past weeks that he knows more of the workings of this House than I ever have." She smiled at Pascal, grateful for his quiet dignity. "I know that in the three years I was gone, you made an informal search of the cadet branches of our House. You found Pascal and gave him a chance to prove himself, and he's more than done so. I've come to realize, Grand-père, that Pascal is only one of many whose talent has been overlooked simply because of our Elite obsession with bloodlines and patrimony. If you, as Patriarch, should choose to make such a young man your heir—"

"My heir?" Bernard laughed harshly. "A thousand years' unbroken lineage to end with a cadet branch—"

"Look at me, Grand-père," Ariane demanded. "Pascal's Marchand blood is pure, unlike mine." She clenched her fists and met his gaze fiercely. "He is without dishonor of any kind, and dedicated to the House. As I will never be again."

Without the impetus of thought Ariane's hands came up to rest protectively on her belly. Bernard's eyes followed the motion.

"And my child—Rook's child—will never grow up denying what he is."

Bernard swayed, face drained of color. Pascal eased him back to the couch.

"Child—" he echoed.

"I already know he'll be born looking Kalian in every way," Ariane said. "I will bear this child, Grand-père, but I won't make my son a copy of a perfect Marchand." She smiled sadly. "You don't need me, because you know I'll never again be able to give my heart to this House, to the future of this world. I'll only be a liability to you as long as I live, reminding you of your own shame, your own dishonor."

"The shame was—never mine—"

"But the choices were yours, Grand-père. I made my choice—not yesterday, when I let Rook go, but the day I accepted my Kalian blood. It cannot be undone."

Slowly he looked up at her, his gaze moving from black hair to the toes of her half boots, coming at last to rest on her alien copper eyes.

Breathing harshly, Bernard gripped the curved edge of the couch until his tendons bulged beneath the paper-thin flesh. "Damn you." He swallowed heavily. "Go. Go back to him."

The first tears fell then, tears of grief and joy and release. She held out her hand. He stared at it bleakly.

"Once you brought the universe back to Espérance and sent our people to the stars again," Ariane whispered. "Now I'll carry Marchand blood beyond the limits of your dreams, Grand-père. That I promise you."

He did not take her hand, but for a moment there was acceptance in his eyes. "Go," he ordered hoarsely. "Go!"

Without her volition her muscles clenched, set her in motion at a run along the quiet garden paths. At the edge of the glade she stopped and turned. Her gaze met Pascal's across the distance and then fell, slowly, to her great-grandfather's pale and stubborn face. She touched her stomach gently.

"We'll return, Grand-père. No matter how far we go. One day, when Espérance is ready for my people, we'll be back."

And then her thoughts were far beyond the garden walls, beyond the mansion, beyond Espérance itself, bursting skyward on invisible wings.

"Mr. Galloway."

Rook turned from his vigil by the aft porthole on the bridge of the *Kali* to regard the young Marchand officer.

Capitaine Ravel-Marchand looked like Ariane, yet unlike her: brown of hair and eye, but ordinary. There was no Kalian blood in this one.

He had no sacrifices to make. By the time the *Shiva* and *Kali* rendezvoused with the Fahar colonists, the captain and his crew would return to Espérance. The Kalians and their alien brothers would be alone on this journey.

Rook realized how fiercely he had been staring when the young man dropped his eyes. "Mr. Galloway," the captain repeated, "we're sixteen hours behind schedule."

Rook pivoted on his heel to stare out the porthole again. "Are we, Captain?"

The man cleared his throat. "This delay—"

"This is a Kalian ship," Rook interrupted with dangerous softness. "Your command is nominal, Captain. We will leave the system when I give the order."

The distant murmur of voices and the constant hum of the ship's primary functions filled the silence. After a moment the Marchand walked away, accepting defeat.

Rook took no comfort in the victory. He looked down at the blurred ball of Espérance, knowing the captain was right in his concern. If Rook surrendered to his own personal madness, he could stand there while their stores were exhausted before they'd even left the system.

Three thousand Kalians depended on his leadership. They accepted him, trusted him, never questioned his decision to linger.

And he had stayed because of a half-grown Fahar's words. *"You are bound together—tied to the fate of your people. . . ."*

But Ariane had chosen.

Rook turned to survey the bridge. Efficient and detached, the Marchand crew went about their business and ignored him. Once, long ago, he had trained to take his place among them. In a few days all the old ties would be severed.

Striding across the deck, Rook joined the captain, who stood talking quietly to the first navigator. Both men looked up.

"You were correct, Captain. We've delayed too long."

Rook stared fixedly at the forward screens. "Please make preparations to jump."

He heard the two Espérancians consulting in a mumble of meaningless words, and then the captain touched his shoulder.

"Mr. Galloway—we're picking up an approaching ship."

Rook's heart stopped in his chest. "Identification?"

The captain frowned. "She's coming in silent. Shall I hail her?"

Impossible. But it wasn't impossible, this soul-deep awareness, this capacity for faith that Ariane Burke-Marchand had restored to him.

"Open the docking bay," he said hoarsely, "and guide her in."

The captain's mouth opened as if he would protest, but Rook had already started across the bridge at a run. He jumped into the lift and the closing doors cut off his last view of the Espérancian's startled face.

The deck rang hollowly beneath him—corridors that seemed endless, filled with curious Kalian eyes that tracked his flight. Rook refused to think at all, let instinct alone guide blood and bone and muscle as he flung himself toward the hope of salvation.

The doors to the docking-bay air lock hissed open. He stood in the air lock, heart in his throat, and stared through the clear window that looked out on the bay.

A ship was coming in, outlined by star-laced blackness.

For a time-lost moment Rook spun into a vacuum where sight and sound and touch ceased to exist. He whirled in a void that expanded inside him like a sun gone nova, until in a burst of brilliance the emptiness was filled with light.

Ariane.

The ship settled onto the deck as the outer bay hatches sealed against the coldness of space. Rook slammed his hand against the air lock's override and stepped into the thin air of the docking bay.

She was there.

Frozen, Rook watched her walk down the *d'Artagnan*'s

extended ramp, her hair loose about her shoulders, her stride long and free. She cradled a long case against her chest. As she reached the bottom of the ramp, she turned; her face was a pale blur across the distance between them.

Rook. He felt her speak to his very soul, a voiceless cry of joy. With nerveless fingers she dropped the case at her feet.

He had no memory of how they came together. One instant they were at opposite ends of the bay, and the next he had her in his arms. Her lips met his with the same savage hunger that coursed through his blood, a wild and reckless elation that sent them spinning so deep into the Sharing that not even the barriers of flesh stood between them.

When they broke apart, breathless, Rook caught her face in his hands and searched her eyes. Their brown depths blazed with copper fire. Her smile blinded him; he closed his eyes and drew her close again, afraid to let her sense the depths of his fear, afraid to let her go.

She shifted but made no protest against the ferocity of his hold. "Rook," she murmured against his chest.

"No," he groaned, his fear molded into a word of mindless denial. "Don't—"

Ariane pushed back, gripping his chin in one firm hand. "I'm not leaving you, Rook," she said softly.

He froze. Her gaze locked on his, hiding nothing, pouring her immeasurable love for him through the Sharing in wave upon wave.

"I'm coming with you," she said. Tears hung suspended at the ends of her lashes and slid along the high curves of her cheekbones. *"With you."*

Rook lifted her in his arms, crushing her mouth to his until every last doubt and fear was purged from his heart. Only then did he let her slide down the length of his body, his entire being singing at the touch of hers.

"How, Ariane?" he whispered, kissing her brows and eyelids and the tears on her lips.

With quiet, stammered words she told him all that had passed in that final conversation between herself and the Patriarch. Rook held her tightly, unwilling to add to her pain and sorrow, unable to hide his own fierce joy.

Ariane freed herself and entwined her fingers with Rook's. "Everything I told him was true, Rook. Soon enough all Lumière would have learned what I was. The Elite would never have accepted me. And my heart—" She smiled at him, that courageous, indomitable heart in her eyes. "My heart had already gone with you."

Rook buried his face in her hair. "That day in his room, he begged me—"

"Not to take me away. I know." She rested her forehead against his chest. "I believed I had to stay with him. You respected my decision—"

"And you didn't try to keep me with you, when you could have done it with a word."

Her gaze lifted to his. "We would both have done our duty. But I've learned there's something more powerful than honor, Rook—more powerful, and more enduring." She looped her arms around his waist. "I think even my great-grandfather finally understood. Perhaps, at last, the past can finally be laid to rest."

Laid to rest. All the pain, the hatred, the blind need for revenge. The devastating belief that you existed alone in all the universe. The emptiness only one woman could fill.

The world that had shattered around Rook that day in the Warren eight years ago could at last be made whole again. . . .

Suddenly Ariane grinned, smearing the wetness on her face with her palm. "I thought I'd have to chase you halfway across the universe, but you were still here. Waiting—"

Rook looked away. "I—hoped—"

Ariane silenced him with a kiss, lacing her fingers in his hair and dragging his head down to hers. After a small eternity had passed, she caught his hand and pulled him back toward the *d'Artagnan*. "I forgot something," she said. At the edge of the ramp she bent to gather up the case she'd dropped.

"A gift—from the Patriarch," she said, straightening.

"Pascal brought it to me just before I lifted from the spaceport." Almost reverently she undid the latch of the case and opened it to reveal a velvet-lined interior. Within lay two sheathed sabers with elegantly carved silver hilts.

Ariane blinked rapidly. "His. The ones his father gave him. He's treasured them all his life." She hugged the sabers to her chest and smiled up at Rook, an expression of unfettered joy.

"I never did teach you the proper rules of dueling," she said huskily.

Memory washed over Rook. His groin tightened, and he knew instantly that Ariane felt his desire. Her grin became sly.

"This search for a new world may take a very long time, Rook. We'll need something to keep us—occupied."

Suppressing a groan, Rook took the sabers from her arms, set them gently on the deck, and pulled her against him.

"Your Patriarch is a clever man," he murmured. "He saw to it that Marchand customs would go with us, no matter how far we travel."

Ariane's smile wavered. "Rook—"

Opening himself to her fully, Rook drowned her uncertainty in a wash of wordless, overwhelming emotion.

"I'll never ask you to forget your Marchand blood," he said, smoothing her hair back from her face. "It's part of you. Everything you are is—" He broke off, letting the Sharing speak for him. He kissed her, long and deep. "I love you, Ariane."

Ariane grabbed the front of his loose shirt and pressed her lips to the racing pulse at the base of his throat. "I'm glad you don't object to Marchand blood," she whispered. "Because it's going to be passed on to future Kalian generations."

Something in her voice made him push her back and stare into her eyes. Grinning, she took his hand and spread his fingers, settling them over her abdomen. "Do you feel him?"

He did. Suddenly there seemed to be no gravity at all in the docking bay. "Ariane—"

Her fingers brushed his mouth. "I know," she said. "I know. The past is gone, Rook. But tomorrow is ours."

With strong, loving arms Ariane drew him back to solid ground. Handing him the saber case, Ariane laced her fingers through the crook of his elbow.

"Don't you think it's time you took me on a tour of our ship?" she asked softly.

And so he did. On the bridge, side by side, they looked out the canopy and watched the stars light a silver pathway to the future.

About the Author

Susan Krinard graduated from the California College of Arts and Crafts with a BfA, and worked as an artist and freelance illustrator before turning to writing. An admirer of both Romance and Fantasy, Susan enjoys combining these elements in her books. She also loves to get out into nature as frequently as possible. A native Californian, Susan lives in the San Francisco Bay Area with her French-Canadian husband, Serge, a dog and a cat.

Susan loves to hear from her readers. She can be reached at:

P.O. Box 272545
Concord, CA 94527

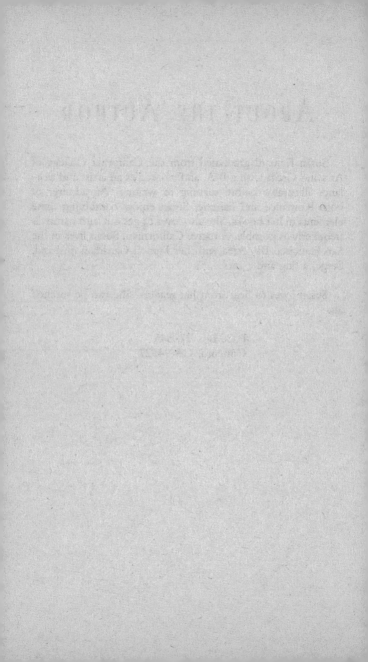

In Susan Krinard's next brilliant romance, she returns to the territory she made her very own with her national bestseller *Prince of Wolves*. Once again the hero has the legendary ability to transform into a wolf and from wolf into man.

In the following excerpt, wolf researcher Alexandra has taken in a gorgeous wolf from the wild to try to help him. But when the wolf vanishes, leaving something quite different in its place, neither Alexandra nor her new roommate has any idea what has transpired.

It was a long time before she slept. The sun was already streaming through her grandmother's worn lace curtains when she woke again. She lay very still, trying to hold the ephemeral happiness that always came to her at the very edge of waking. The bed was blissfully warm, lulling her away from any thought of the day ahead.

She freed one arm from beneath the blankets and stretched it out to the side with a groan. Her fingers brushed something firm and unfamiliar. She jerked her legs and found them trapped under an implacable weight. A deep, groaning sigh sounded in her ear.

Very slowly she turned her head.

A man lay beside her, sprawled across the bed with one leg pinning the blankets over hers—a perfectly naked, magnificently muscled man. His body was curled toward her, head resting on one arm, chest rising and falling with even, steady breaths. Straight, thick black hair shadowed his face.

Alex did no more than suck in her breath, but that was enough. The man moved; the muscles of torso and flat belly rippled as he stretched and lifted his head. Yellow-brown eyes met her gaze through the veil of his hair.

For an instant—one wayward, crazy instant—Alex recognized him. And then that bizarre sensation passed, to be replaced with far more pragmatic emotions. She yelled, a wordless cry summoned up from instinct, and shoved him with hands and body. His eyes widened as he rocked backward on the narrow bed, clawed at the sheets with clumsy fingers, and rolled over the edge.

Alex tore the covers away and leaped from the bed, remembering belatedly that she'd left the dart gun outside, and her granddad's old rifle was firmly locked away in the closet. She turned for the door just as the man scrambled to his feet, tossing the hair from his eyes. Her hand had barely closed on the doorknob when he lunged across the bed and grabbed her wrist in an iron grip.

Blind, treacherous terror surged in her. She struck out, and he caught her other hand. Then she remembered Shadow. She stared at the man's strange, piercing eyes and forced her throat to obey her will.

"Shadow." It came out as a croak, and she tried again. "Shadow!"

The man jerked as if she'd struck him. The muscles of his strong jaw stood out in sharp relief beneath tanned skin, and his throat worked. He closed his eyes, despair naked in his face, and his fingers loosened around her wrists.

Alex didn't think. She ripped her arms free free of his grasp, clasped her hands into a single fist, and struck him with all her strength.

"Can you hear me?"

He understood her question. Her voice, familiar and low, drew him back into his body.

The shock struck him again before he could open his eyes. The hair rose along the back of his neck, his muscles tensed, and he flattened his ears against his skull.

But everything was wrong. The dream had been real. His ears remained motionless, and a chill raced along his hairless spine. When he moved, his body responded without ease or grace, all overlong limbs and awkward shapes.

It had happened. He had felt the change coming over the past nights, the Other struggling to break free of the body that had held it imprisoned.

The Other was here. It was *himself*—himself, reborn, helpless as a newborn pup.

Human.

Terror clawed at the wolf within him, the beast that cringed at what it could not understand. He fought the emotion, as he had fought for survival a hundred times, and looked up at the only thing that was certain and familiar.

The woman gazed back at him with eyes the color of winter ice. Her hair was bright like trees before the snow, thick and tangled about her shoulders. Her scent filled his nostrils, made his heart pound in his chest, and summoned memories from the deepest part of his mind.

"What the hell are you doing in my cabin?" she demanded. "Who are you?"

He heard the way the words shook with emotion. *Words*.

He worked out the sense of them, tracking and catching them one by one like mice in a field. Sounds lodged in his throat, rough and unfamiliar.

Who am I? The thought formed in his head to match her words, but he could not voice them. He sat up, struggling to make his altered muscles obey his will. She scrambled back, her hands raised to hold him at bay, as if he were an enemy.

Hands. His own hands had reached for her, held her before she'd called his name and made him remember. She had tried to run, and he had thought only of keeping her close, regaining the warmth and comfort of the pack bond that had drawn him to her sleeping place.

No. There was a word for it—*bed.* And she had driven him from it, rejecting him as she rejected him now, with her body crouched and ready for battle. He looked into her eyes and read the set of her face.

She was afraid of him. Afraid. He closed his eyes, shaken. Her fear cut into him and squeezed his heart like the cruel steel jaws of a trap.

"I don't know how you got in here," she said, "or who you are, but I have a rifle, and I do know how to use it."

The warning in her voice was as explicit as a snarl, though her expression never changed. For the first time he saw the slim, bright tube of metal resting against the wall within her reach. More words, and a flood of memories.

Memories that came to him like dreams within dreams. Last night. Last night he had come here, drawn by his need to be with her. Deep in his bones he had felt the Other gaining strength, struggling to break free. He had come to the only place where he could be safe.

Safe—to return.

He struggled upward, finding his feet. The world spun, and the earth stretched away far beneath him. He took a step toward her, needing, his wolf instincts still strong within him. She was his pack; she had touched him with gentleness, accepted him into her den. He had found her.

"Stop," she commanded. His muscles clenched in automatic obedience. He took another step, ducking his head. She retreated. Frustration coiled tight in his belly. He reached within himself for a way to make her understand.

Shadow. She had called him Shadow, but now she didn't know him. He didn't know himself.

He touched his face. The smooth contours were strange and familiar at once. It was like hers. *Human*, he told himself. *Human*. He fought to remember, to find the bridge that would carry him across the abyss separating him from his only link to sanity.

The woman's gaze moved up and down his body. She wet her lips with her tongue, and her teeth came together with an audible click.

"You must be cold," she said evenly.

He went very still. The voice was different, but the words —they were the same. Images came back to him across uncounted years, like a waking nightmare.

He lay shivering between the cooling bodies of the wolves, alone as he had never been in all his life. But he was not alone; she was there, with her gentle voice and hands. "Please, let me help you," she said. But answers were locked away in his throat, sundered by terror and sorrow. He could only stare at her, memorizing her face as the only sure haven in the midst of insanity.

She had cried. He had seen the tears, smelled them, tasted them, absorbing her compassion into himself. She had become a part of him.

But her human pack came to take her back. He could not go with her. He had wanted to die, but her tears held him to life. He had looked at her one last time, and a word had come to him, a question wrung from the depths of his shattered heart: "Why"?

"Why?" he whispered hoarsely.

She started, a reaction she tried to hid from him. "So you can speak, after all," she said. "Who are you?"

She had asked that before—here, and in that dreamtime of long ago. It was vital that he remember.

Remember. *Remember.* . . .

He tried to build on the images of the girl she had been. Slim and gawky with adolescence, like a half-grown pup, but already beautiful. His understanding of human beauty came back to him in a rush; he recognized it when he looked at her now.

Changed and yet the same. Red hair and light blue eyes, long-legged and undeniably female. There was something different about her face, something other than age, but he could not isolate it.

So he remembered her as she had been, what she had tried to do for him, her offer of kinship that had kept him living. But his memories ended after he had fled into the woods from her human pack. The rest was a blur of emotion and sensation, changing landscapes, constant wandering— darkness, pain, and loneliness.

Always the loneliness.

He looked at her, wanting to touch her and hold her against him. His instincts warred among themselves, wolf and human. The wolf needed to reaffirm the pack-bond, but the man held him back. The man— He swayed under the assault of realization.

The man he was, the man whose name he could not remember, whose past remained so dark, knew she had a reason to fear him. Fear what he was, neither man nor beast. A creature never meant to exist.

You are an abomination, a voice told him. It was a voice he knew, faceless and ringing with authority.

"No," he rasped. He backed away from the woman until his legs hit the bed again. He shook his head violently, trying to rid himself of the voice that haunted him and rode on his returning memory.

Abomination.

Panic raced along his nerves. He twisted and leaped up onto the bed, circling to stare at the walls that imprisoned him.

Trapped. He was trapped, but there was a way out. The woman stood by the door, between him and escape from the voice. He had always run from the voice—he remembered that now. He had run, and run, and run. . . .

He jumped down, forgetting as he did the changes in his body. His miscalculation sent him crashing to his knees. He surged up again, flung himself at the door, and hit it with his full weight. It refused to give. He clawed at the wood with his bare, useless fingers until they were raw with pain.

Warm, strong hands caught and held them. He turned on his captor, a snarl tangled in his throat. The woman's eyes fixed on his. She challenged him, denying her own fear, with the implacable authority of a pack leader.

"Stop," she commanded. "Take it easy. You'll be all right." She tugged, pulling his hands away from the door. "Let me help you."

He shuddered and closed his eyes. He remembered those words. They had drawn him here. They drowned out the voice of judgment, worked a powerful magic on his soul.

He turned his fingers in her grasp and gripped her hands. Her body stiffened in resistance. His nostrils drank in the scent of her as his skin absorbed her warmth.

A name came to him. A name from the past—a gift the girl had given him so long ago. *Her* name.

Alexandra. He formed the word in his mind, worked his throat and shaped his lips to voice it.

"Alexandra," he said, lifting her hand to his mouth. He touched his tongue to her skin and raised his eyes to meet hers. "Alexandra."

His voice was deep, husky, and perfectly understandable, each syllable clear and precise.

He was at least half-crazy, and quite possibly dangerous. Rationally, logically, Alex knew she'd never seen him before.

But somehow he knew her name.

Alex shivered at the touch of his tongue on her hand. His gaze held hers with so powerful an appeal that she was helpless to look away or pull her hands from his grip. Only moments before she'd been trying to calm him, still his frantic attempts to tear down the door. Now, with a touch and a glance, he almost made her believe she had met his golden gaze a hundred times. His eyes spoke more eloquently than any words: *Don't be afraid.*

During the past few minutes her emotions had undergone a series of devastating transformations. First the shock of finding a naked man in her bed, then the fear when he'd come after her—and then the anger. Her counterattack had been instinctive, a primitive surge of violence at his trespassing, his attempts to hold her. For a moment this strange, wild man had been the focus of all her unarticulated rage.

But when she'd seen him lying there, hardly able to speak, with that desperate, haunted look in his eyes, her anger had died. And when he'd begun to claw at the door like an animal in a trap, she'd instantly responded as she'd have done with any panicked wild thing.

As she'd done with Shadow. Until the wild man had spoken her name and shattered that brief illusion.

He still looked wild, with his burning golden eyes and shaggy hair and unselfconscious nudity. She felt herself drifting into a strange, dreamlike state as his warm breath caressed her skin. It occurred to her what he most resembled: a prehistoric human from some old movie, hunting mammoths and saber-toothed tigers. Or a man raised by animals in the forest. . . .

His tongue stroked across the back of her hand again. The feel of it was incredibly erotic. Alex's eyes drifted closed. Another sensation, more fundamental than emotion, coiled in the pit of her stomach. She was suddenly, profoundly aware of his maleness, the clean and powerful and entirely unobscured lines of his body. *Like a preadator in its prime,* she thought distantly. *Like Shadow. . . .*

"Shadow," she murmured.

His eyes flickered and the spell they'd woven evaporated. Shocked at her lapse, Alex jerked her hands free and reached for the rifle propped against the wall. Her fingers stopped just short of the barrel. The wild man stepped back, regarding her with hooded wariness.

"You know my name," she accused. She hardly expected a response. His powers of speech seemed somewhat selective. "Why?" he'd said, and "no". He might be mentally disturbed, but he had passed up an obvious opportunity to attack her when she'd been asleep, and he didn't seem ready to retaliate for her defense. But she wasn't about to discount the impressive contours of his musculature and the way he looked at her. He was utterly focused on her face; she almost lifted her hand to touch her scar and stopped herself.

He was handsome in a stark, rawboned way, the kind of man plenty of women would fall for given half a chance. The only problem was that she wasn't "plenty of women," and he had broken into her cabin in the middle of the wilderness and turned up naked in her bed.

She looked behind him, at the floor and around the room. No sign whatsoever of clothes he might have abandoned. He must have left them outside the room. He'd stripped and lay down beside her, like a lover expecting a welcome.

He'd get no such welcome from her. But hostility wasn't going to solve her current problem. She'd have to get him at ease, off-guard.

Alex slid her fingers carefully around the rifle and grasped the doorknob in her other hand. Shadow hadn't come when she'd called before, and it was unbelievable that he'd let this man get past him last night, given his reaction to Julie. But if the wolf was waiting just beyond the door . . .

"It's cold in here," she said carefully. "I suggest we move into the living room. I'll need to get the fire going again."

He cocked his head. "Cold," he repeated, a look of intense concentration coming over his face. "Yes." He folded his arms across his chest. "Fire?"

Me Tarzan, you Jane, she thought absurdly. Could it be that he had a limited understanding of English? Had he suffered brain damage of some kind? He looked healthy—altogether too healthy.

It wasn't enough to treat this man like a potentially dangerous wild animal. Being male, he couldn't be trusted. Being human, he was by nature unpredictable and wouldn't play by nature's sensible rules. She pushed from her mind the fleeting thought that Shadow hadn't either.

The doorknob turned with a click. Alex meneuvered her body to pull the door inward, never taking her eyes from the wild man. She backed away down the short hall and into the living room.

"Shadow," she called.

The room was silent except for the muted pop of charred wood in the stove. She risked a glance at the old woven rug where Shadow had lain.

It was quite bare. Alex gripped the rifle in both hands. The doors to the other two small bedrooms were closed, and she could see the inside of the kitchen from where she stood. The front door was still firmly shut and showed no signs of having been forced. Neither did any of the windows.

Shadow was gone. He had vanished as mysteriously as the wild man had appeared.

But she had no time to spare for worry over the wolf. The man was emerging from the bedroom, nostrils flared. The quilted comforter from Alex's bed was draped around his shoulders like a cape, dragging along the floor behind him.

Alex choked on a harsh laugh. *Hysteria, Alex?* she asked herself, sobering instantly. There was nothing funny about this at all. She'd lost any hope of barricading him in the bedroom.

As if he'd heard her stifled snort, the man looked straight at her. His dark brows met over his narrowed eyes.

"Alexandra," he repeated solemnly. "Funny?"

His vocabulary is growing by leaps and bounds, Alex thought. "Not very," she muttered under her breath, and then louder, "Can you understand what I'm saying?"

He seemed to weigh her question with great care and then nodded. The movement was jerky and unsure, but it was recognizable. Dark hair tumbled over one eye; for the first time Alex noticed the single white streak amid the black, flowing out from one temple. "I—under-stand," he said. His voice still held a husky roughness, as if he hadn't used it in a very long time.

Maybe he hadn't, wherever he'd come from. She imagined a fantastic new scenario: he was a trapper from way up in the taiga across the Canadian border who'd spent so long alone that he'd forgotten how to talk; he'd wandered south and found a comfy cabin and a convenient woman. . . .

Alex shivered and backed closer to the front door. Crazy. This was the twentieth century, and he wasn't much older than she was.

"Are you thirsty? Hungry?" she said. Simple questions first, since he seemed cooperative.

His reaction was immediate. He wet his lips, making her stomach tighten with the memory of his tongue against her skin. Raking the room with his gaze, he fixed on the metal bowl she'd left for Shadow and went directly for it. Before she could stop him, he picked it up and drank the remaining water in one long swallow. The quilt fell from his shoulders.

"Not finicky, are you?" Alex said under her breath. She reached behind her to touch the front door, testing the knob. It was still locked, just as it had appeared to be. Solving that mystery was not a high priority. She could be out the door in a second.

The wild man made a sharp noise eerily like a growl. Alex snapped her attention back to him. He was looking at her hand on the doorknob, as if he knew exactly what she was thinking. As if he would stop her as he'd done before . . .

"No," she said sharply. "Take it easy." Slowly she raised her hand and flexed her fingers. "If you're hungry—"

In a few long strides he was before her, holding her gaze with his.

"How long?" he rasped. As she tried to make sense of the unexpected question, he reached out to touch her hand. Not to imprison it, but lightly, his fingers drifting across her own.

"I don't understand you," she said, keeping her voice very low. "How long—what?"

He flung back his head in a gesture of eloquent frustration. His long, dark lashes shielded his eyes. "How—long—wolf?" he said deliberately.

Wolf. Alex thought immediately of Shadow. The man must have seen the wolf after all. But what was he asking?

"Did you—see the wolf when you came here?" she asked. "Where did he go?"

He gave her a very strange look, as if she were the crazy one. And then he groaned deep in his throat, a sound that gradually changed. His shoulders tensed and began to shake, and the rough noise he made hovered between a sob and a snarl.

She realized after a moment of frozen fascination that he was laughing. Laughing with a strange helplessness, with more than a touch of madness.

Alex thought about the door again, and the rifle in her hand. She'd been bluffing about the rifle anyway; she'd got it out of the closet while he'd been unconscious, but the thought of shooting him made her feel the way she had when she'd tried to dart Shadow.

"Listen," she said. At once his laughter stopped; he focused on her again, and she almost wished she'd let him stay in whatever dark inner world he'd been visiting. "You need clothes. Where did you put yours?"

Again that strange look, and a flash of pain. "Don't—know," he muttered.

It was worse than she'd thought. "How did you get to the cabin?"

"Walked. Ran."

Alex took in a deep breath. "Why did you come here?"

He did something very odd then. With a shuddering sigh he backed away, moved directly to the rug in front of the stove, sat down cross-legged, and dropped his head into his hands.

"Don't remember," he grated, the words forced from behind clenched teeth. Suddenly he looked up. "Except—to find you. Alexandra."

The way he said her name was like a caress, as if it were something he could taste and savor. He might as well have licked her again.

He said he'd come to find *her*.

Alex swallowed. "You know me," she said. "Where have we met?"

An inward struggle passed visibly over the man's face. "Shadow," he said slowly. "*Me*. This—" He touched his chest, made a gesture that encompassed his entire body. "Don't remember—who."

She passed over the incomprehensible part about Shadow, though he clearly recognized the wolf's name. "You've lost your memory," she stated.

He nodded sharply. "Who, why, how long . . ."

Wonderful. Alex stared blindly over his head. Memory loss might explain a great deal, but it made him no less unpredictable. She considered the weather outside—there'd been sun, so it would be cold but relatively easy to travel in. One way or another this man needed help she couldn't give him, help she could only find in town. She wanted no more to do with him than was absolutely necessary.

With slow, cautious steps she left the door and circled around him toward the kitchen.

"I've got clothes you can wear," she said. "They might

not fit too well—they belonged to my grandfather—but they'll keep you warm. And there's food in the kitchen—"

She kept up a steady, soothing stream of one-sided conversation as she raided the closet for her grandfather's old sweats. *If only you were here to see this, Granddad,* she thought, holding the clothes to her face.

But Granddad had trusted everyone.

Alex realized she'd had her back to the wild man for a full two or three minutes. She turned around. He was on his feet, watching her, and she had another full frontal glimpse of his beautifully-formed body before she tossed the clothes at him in angry confusion.

He let the clothes fall at his feet and simply stared at them.

"Go ahead and get dressed," she snapped. Damn this crazy stranger for invading her sanctuary, forcing her to feel things she didn't want to feel. Shadow had been worth the risk—no *man* was.